Command

JULIAN STOCKWIN

Command

HODDER &
STOUGHTON

Copyright © 2006 by Julian Stockwin

First published in Great Britain in 2006 by Hodder & Stoughton
A division of Hodder Headline

Endpaper Maps: Front, *Chart of the Mediterranian Sea*, printed 1790.
Back, *Chart of Terra Australis*, printed 1814.
© National Maritime Museum, London.

A Hodder & Stoughton Book

1

A CIP catalogue record for this title
is available from the British Library

Hardback ISBN 0 340 89855 0
Trade Paperback ISBN 0 340 89856 9
Special Edition ISBN 0 340 92403 9

Typeset in Monotype Garamond by
Palimpsest Book Production Limited, Polmont, Stirlingshire

Printed and bound by
Clays Ltd, St Ives plc

Hodder Headline's policy is to use papers that are natural, renewable
and recyclable products and made from wood grown in sustainable forests.
The logging and manufacturing processes are expected to conform to the
environmental regulations of the country of origin.

Hodder & Stoughton Ltd
A division of Hodder Headline
338 Euston Road
London NW1 3BH

To do great things is difficult,
but to command great things is more difficult

Friedrich Nietzsche

Chapter 1

'Damn you, sir! You have set my standing orders to defiance and made *Tenacious* a spectacle before the Fleet. How dare you attempt an excuse for your conduct?' Captain Rowley's words could be heard right across the quarterdeck, even above the streaming rain and bluster of the filthy weather.

'Sir. M' respects, but I judged it t' be—'

'Judge? It's not your place to judge, Mr Kydd! No, sir! It is your sworn duty to ensure my orders are strictly obeyed. All of them – and most especially my written orders.' Rowley's nostrils flared. 'And this is not the first time I have had the disagreeable necessity of remonstrating with you concerning your conduct since I have come aboard.'

'Sir, this is—'

'Enough!' Rowley shouted. 'You, sir, have tried my patience too far.' Kydd's stomach tightened. 'You are now confined to your cabin until such time as the commander-in-chief is informed of your conduct and you have answered for it.'

At the words shocked faces turned: the place for a captain

to discipline an officer was the great cabin, not on deck within earshot of the entire watch.

'Aye aye, sir,' Kydd said thickly, and clapped on his sodden cocked hat. The die was now irrevocably cast: Captain Rowley was taking it further, to the august Admiral Keith, commander of the Mediterranean Fleet. Kydd turned stiffly and went below. This probably signalled the end of his naval career.

Rage washed over him. It was not so much the shame and futility, but the unfairness that of all the ghosts from his past it had been Rowley who had come back to haunt him. After the fearsome battle of the Nile two years ago Kydd had distinguished himself in Minorca and at the siege of Acre, then gone on to uneventful but steady service in *Tenacious* at the long blockade of Toulon, rising from fourth to second lieutenant under the cautious but fair Captain Faulkner. He had done well for himself, building experience and confidence, but now his hopes for substantial advancement in the fullness of time were crushed.

When Rowley had stepped aboard as the new captain of *Tenacious*, he seemed shocked to find Kydd among the officers. The last time he had seen him was on the night the famous frigate *Artemis* had struck rocks in the Azores; Kydd had been acting quartermaster at the conn and he the officer of the watch. At the subsequent court of inquiry Kydd had been prepared to testify against him but, with other seaman survivors, had been hastily shipped out to the Caribbean as an embarrassment.

Rowley, clearly troubled by Kydd's presence on this new ship, had reacted by making his life aboard *Tenacious* more and more difficult. It had been a hard time for Kydd and now it had come to a head.

Kydd bunched his fists as he relived the incident that had given Rowley the excuse to act. A squally spring north-westerly in the early hours of Kydd's morning watch had obliged him to shorten sail to topsails. He had duly sent notice of his action to the captain, in accordance with standing orders, then had employed the watch on deck to work mast by mast, leaving the watch below to their sleep.

A bell or two before the end of the watch, the squall had eased. East Indiamen and others had the comfortable habit of snugging down to topsails during night hours but Captain's Orders specified that *Tenacious*, in common with most vessels in the Navy, must press on under all plain sail. Kydd's duty, therefore, was to set courses again.

It would have been more practical, though, to leave it until the end of the watch, less than an hour away: after break-fast both watches would be on deck to make short work of it. In any case, a pressing need for speed was irrelevant in the endless beat of blockade.

Rowley was correct in the strictest sense, that Kydd was in dereliction of orders, and was bringing the matter – and all the other equally mindless 'offences' – to the attention of the admiral, who would be obliged to take the part of one of his captains.

An awkward shuffling and clinking outside Kydd's cabin signalled the posting of a marine sentry. There would no longer be any privacy and the officers would ignore him for fear of being tainted. Only the first lieutenant would take it calmly, logically. Renzi would know how to act in the matter, but Kydd had vowed that his friend would not be drawn into the insanity between Rowley and himself.

His anger ebbed but his thoughts raced. It was less than two years since he had stood, with bloody sword, at the ancient walls of Acre and watched as Buonaparte skulked away in defeat. How things had changed. With brazen daring, the man had abandoned his army to its fate and escaped to France, where he had risen to the top in a power struggle and declared himself First Consul of the Republic with dictatorial powers. He had then brought together the military resources of the entire French nation into one fearsome fighting machine.

For the British, their earlier return to the Mediterranean had been crowned with success: defeat and annihilation for Buonaparte's great invasion fleet at the Nile followed by domination of the sea. The last major French presence, the fortress of Malta, had recently capitulated after a desperate siege, and the fleet was free to concentrate on locking up the remaining enemy forces in Toulon, off which they lay in close blockade.

Why then was there a sense of unease, of foreboding in the wardrooms of the fleet? It had seemed to Kydd that the very pillars of existence had trembled and proved fragile. Then, too, his great hero Nelson had scandalised many by his open dalliance with the wife of the ambassador to Naples and his subsequent involvement with political intrigue in that city. Kydd had stoutly defended him, even when Nelson was relieved of his command and recalled.

More generally troubling was the resignation of Pitt, the prime minister who had been so successfully conducting the war against such great odds. On the face of it, this had been on a matter of principle but it was widely held that he was exhausted and in ill-health. His successor was Addington, whose administration, of colourless jobbery, had already drawn from Canning the cruel epigram: 'Pitt is to Addington as London is to Paddington.'

And everyone mourned at the news that the King had

suffered a relapse into madness on being informed of Pitt's departure from office. It was a depressing backdrop against which the war was being fought and bitterness surged back as Kydd contemplated his future . . .

His interview with the commander-in-chief had been mercifully brief. Keith, a forbidding figure whom Kydd had only seen before at formal occasions, had listened with an expression of distaste as Rowley had brought out his smooth litany of the younger man's shortcomings.

Before evening, orders had arrived that now saw him staring moodily out to sea as a passenger in HMS *Stag*, a light frigate escort to a convoy approaching Malta.

It might have been worse. He had received orders to report for duty in distant Malta and at least had not been summarily dismissed from his ship. No adverse entry would appear on his service record. His career, though, was now all but over. Malta had run down its naval presence since the surrender six months earlier and, as far as Kydd was aware, only minor vessels were attending to the usual dull tasks of a backwater. All of the real action was at the other end of the Mediterranean.

The officers of the frigate had taken to ignoring him and his moods, no doubt making up their own minds about the reasons for his removal. He didn't care: he was leaving their world and mentally preparing himself for the narrowing of professional and social horizons that would be his lot.

There was a scattering of familiar faces from *Tenacious* on the foredeck – Laffin, Poulden, others – part of an augmentation of hands from the fleet for the Malta Service. Away from the discipline and boredom of blockade, they appeared in good spirits. One of the midshipmen volunteers was Bowden; heaven only knew why such an intelligent and experienced youngster had turned his back on the opportunities of big-fleet service under the eye of an admiral.

An irregular blue-grey smudge became visible on the horizon, one of Malta's outer islands; the convoy would be safely delivered before night. His spirits rose a little with the familiar excitement of a new landfall, but the memory of Renzi's farewell intruded and bleakness lowered in Kydd over the loss of their friendship. Never again would they debate philosophy during night watches in the South Seas, or step ashore together in exotic foreign ports.

Kydd and Renzi had been able to stay together as foremast hands because volunteers could choose the ship they served in, but officers were appointed at the whim of the Admiralty. They had been lucky enough to remain serving in the ship into which they had been promoted, *Tenacious*, but it could not last and now they had finally parted.

He wondered if he would ever see Renzi again. It was more than possible that he would not, unless their respective ships were in the same port at the same time. As the war spread far across the globe, that was increasingly unlikely.

Renzi's farewell gift to Kydd had been his own first edition of Wordsworth, which Kydd knew he had treasured; he felt unhappy that he had had no gift of equal worth to press upon his friend. With few words spoken, they had parted quickly, each to his separate destiny.

Depressed, Kydd had no real interest in their arrival. The main town of Malta and their final destination, Valetta, was in the south-east, a series of great fortresses occupying the length of a peninsula, with indented harbours on either side and more fortifications on each opposite shore.

Kydd went below to find his dispatch case, given to him by Keith's aide. He had a duty to deliver the contents ashore at the earliest opportunity; the rest of his baggage could wait until he knew more of his fate. He returned on deck, waited for the boat, then climbed aboard with other officers for the short trip to the stone quayside.

More boats from other vessels of the convoy converged on the landing place in an unholy scrimmage as seniorities were demanded loudly and boats manoeuvred deftly to land their passengers ahead of others. The Barriera, a stockaded enclosure, held the new arrivals until they could prove a clean bill of health to the Pratique Office and were granted the right to land.

Kydd accepted an offer to share a small, horse-drawn carriage with a lieutenant of marines who had business with the government, and they ground their way up a long incline, past massive stone walls and through streets of tall, golden stone buildings.

His dispatches were for the Officer Commanding Troops, a General Pigot; a larger packet had the superimposition 'The Honourable Charles Cameron, Civil Commissioner for the Affairs of Malta and its Dependencies and Representative of His Britannick Majesty in Malta and Gozo'. Kydd had been instructed to deliver Cameron's in person.

At what seemed to be the top and centre of the peninsula, the carriage left the street and turned into the courtyard of an imposing building. Footmen conducted Kydd, dutifully carrying his dispatch case, along stately corridors to an anteroom.

'Mr Cameron begs you will wait on him presently,' murmured a clerk, showing him to a seat outside the office of the man Kydd understood to be the effective head of government.

The door flew open and a large, somewhat porcine individual appeared. 'L'tenant, dispatches, is it not?' Kydd allowed himself to be shepherded in. 'Cameron. Forgive the haste, sir. News! Boney made his move yet?'

'Not that I'm aware of, sir.' This was the first time Kydd had heard Buonaparte referred to as such, but he recalled having been told that the man himself had thought fit to trim his name of its Corsican origin to become 'Napoleon Bonaparte' because it was easier for his adopted countrymen to pronounce.

'Good. You'll excuse me if I take a quick peek at these first,' Cameron said, in a fruity voice. 'I've waited such a damnable long time . . .' He ripped open the sewn canvas with a small knife and shook out the packets on to the desktop.

'Ah, the corn trade and the Università. Just as I thought!' His forehead creased as he read further. Another paper brought from him a sharp frown before it was discarded in favour of a sheaf bound with a thin red ribbon, which Kydd recognised as an Admiralty pack.

Cameron grunted and looked up genially. 'At last. We're to have our sea force increased.'

Kydd smiled apologetically. 'I haven't m' orders yet, sir, and know little o' Malta.'

'Well, we're no great shakes in the Navy line, you know, just a few sloops an' such. Rely on the Eastern Med squadron to top it the heavyweight – when it's about!'

'The increase t' force, sir?' Kydd said awkwardly, as Cameron continued to riffle through the papers.

'Not as who should say a frightener for Boney. Just a brig o' sorts that was building in the dockyard when we took Malta, and only now completing.' He looked up, defensive. 'You should understand we account it welcome news, sir.'

'Of course, sir.' Kydd tried to put a level of animation into his voice. 'A brig-sloop indeed!' Even a small frigate would have near ten times the weight of metal in her broadside.

Cameron finished the Admiralty pack quickly, then extracted a paper with the ghost of a smile. 'And did you say, Mr Kydd, that you had no knowledge of your service here?'

'Not yet, sir,' Kydd said stiffly.

'Then I fancy this may be of interest to you . . .' He passed across the single sheet.

Kydd took it, frowning. It was under the hand of the commander-in-chief – but then he saw his name. Under Cameron's gaze he read on . . . and stopped. The words leaped up at him and, in a cold wash of shock, their meaning penetrated. From the hand of an unknown clerk came blazing, wondrous, thrilling phrases that left him breathless: '. . . you, the said Thomas Kydd . . . to take under your command His Britannick Majesty's Brig Sloop *Teazer* lying at Senglea dockyard, Malta . . . whereof you shall fail at your peril . . .'

Kydd raised his eyes slowly. Cameron chuckled and handed over a folded parchment. 'Your commission – Captain.'

Chapter 2

Kydd stumbled from Cameron's office in a haze, clutching his pack of orders. He went to put it into his dispatch case but his eyes strayed down to the superscription: *Captain, HM Sloop Teazer.* It was so improbable – but it was true!

The boat's crew would be waiting patiently for his return but the moment was too precious, too overwhelming, and he needed to regain his composure before he faced them. He took a deep breath and marched off down the main street as though on important business.

There was no denying that he had been lucky beyond imagining. His promotion would be subject to Admiralty confirmation, but the actions of a commander-in-chief of the stature of Keith would not be unduly questioned. He wondered why he had been elevated before the many young officers of the Fleet clamouring for recognition – and why his advancement had been notified in this unusual manner, carried as dispatches. But, then, why question it? He was now indisputably Commander Kydd, captain of His Majesty's brig-sloop *Teazer* and the luckiest man alive!

A tear pricked; it would not take much to set him to weeping with the joy of it all. Passers-by looked at him curiously but he didn't care. Warm thoughts of arriving home in Guildford to boundless admiration were followed by images of mounting his own ship's side to the piping of the boatswain's call. A surge of pure happiness threatened to unman him. He stopped and blinked into a shop window.

Pulling himself together, he turned and made his way down to the quayside. The fortress-like Grand Harbour had now taken on a dramatic splendour: a great port with vessels from all the countries of the Levant and further, it would be a glorious and challenging place to begin his first command.

The boat shoved off. Kydd's thoughts turned to Renzi: how would his friend take him now they were separated by a chasm as big as any they had crossed together? Renzi was not as seized with ambition as he, and took satisfaction in his own way from the ever-changing perspectives that a sea life provided – they would talk for a space of the metaphysics of being a child of fortune, perhaps, or . . . But Renzi was firmly of the past and Kydd had to accept that now he was on his own.

The thought took hold, and at his sudden bleak expression the midshipman gripped his tiller in apprehension. 'Sir?' he said anxiously. They came up with the anchored frigate that had been Kydd's recent home and the bowman looked aft questioningly.

'Going aboard,' Kydd called. There was his baggage to be roused out and landed and – above all – his new ship to be claimed, in proper style. His pulse beat with excitement as he stepped on deck. Should he proclaim his impossible elevation? He fought down the impulse and tried to reason coolly. But there was only one course that his hot spirits would allow. He would go to his ship that very hour.

That would not be so easy: to all the world he was still a lieutenant, and until he had the uniform and appearance of a commander it would be an impertinence to appear in his new vessel. Might there be a naval tailor and outfitter on the island after only six months in English hands?

The demand to take up the command before it faded into a dream was now impossible to deny. And in any case, he reasoned, he would need a place to lay his head that he could call his own. But what were the procedures for invading the territory of a hundred men and assuming a feudal lordship that demanded their unquestioning obedience? It all seemed so wildly incredible – except for the solid reality of the precious words of his commission now nestled against his chest.

Kydd brushed aside the idle questions of the frigate's officers taking their fill of the scene ashore and strode for the cabin spaces. The marine on duty outside the captain's cabin indicated it was occupied and Kydd rapped firmly on the door. 'Come.' The tone was even.

'Sir, please forgive m' gall in calling on ye at this time, an' you would infinitely oblige me should you . . .'

It was only after a firm promise to dinner in the very near future that Commander Kydd left the cabin, this time with a borrowed epaulette firmly in place on his left shoulder, denoting his new rank, and a gold-laced cocked hat athwart.

As he emerged on deck, conversations died away. There was a faint 'Good God!' Kydd turned to look coldly at the lieutenant, who hurriedly raised his hat, quickly followed by the others. It would give them something to talk about in the wardroom that night.

'If y' please, pass the word for Midshipman Bowden.' Kydd's head was brimming with plans, and he would need an accomplice in what followed.

Brushing aside the wide-eyed youngster's stammering recognition he snapped, 'So, you've volunteered for the Malta Service, Mr Bowden? Then I'm to inform ye that as of today y'r a young gentleman aboard *Teazer* sloop, fittin' out in the dockyard.' He would attend to the paperwork later.

'Y-yes, sir. And – and you're—'

'I am her captain, Mr Bowden.'

The frigate's barge threaded through the busy harbour. Although eager to make out which of the vessels would be his, Kydd held himself upright and unsmiling.

'Oars.' The midshipman coxswain brought the boat alongside the quay and Kydd disembarked. Seamen landed his baggage and the coxswain asked respectfully if they should lie off.

'No, thank ye,' Kydd replied. 'I shan't need you again. An' my compliments to y'r captain for the fine passage t' Malta.'

It was done, and no turning back. 'Mr Bowden, kindly watch over the baggage.' With a firm step, Kydd went into the offices next to a triple archway marking the entrance to a small boat-slip and yard. After service in a Caribbean dockyard he knew better than to bluster his way forward. 'Good morning, sir,' he offered, to the suspicious functionary who met him. 'An' I have an appointment with th' commissioner, if y' please.'

'Mr Burdock? I do not recall—'

'Thursday at ten?' Kydd took out his watch and peered at it. 'I do beg pardon if I'm wrong in th' details but—'

'At ten? Then if you'll step this way, sir.'

The commissioner looked up, distracted. 'Who's this?' he muttered at his clerk.

Before the man could open his mouth Kydd intervened

smoothly: 'Ah, Mr Burdock. It's so kind in ye to see me so soon – Admiral Keith did assure me of y'r good offices . . .'

'In . . . ?'

'In the matter of clearing a berth for y'r important inbound vessel expected directly for repair an' refit, o' course.'

'The master attendant hasn't seen fit to inform me of such a one.'

Kydd frowned. 'Damn quill-pushers! But then again, could be that, given her captain is . . . who he is, an' the ship so well known . . .'

'Who—'

'Admiral Keith needs t' ensure discretion, you understand,' Kydd said, looking around distrustfully. 'This is why he's sent me to ensure a clear berth before . . . Well, the brig *Teazer* was mentioned as being near complete.'

'Impossible – she's not fit for sea in any wise!'

'Oh, why so, sir?' said Kydd, innocently.

'*Teazer*? She's not even in commission.' It was becoming clearer: repair jobs on his books would bring in a far more satisfactory flow of cash if turned over quickly than long-drawn-out completion work; a vessel in commission had immediate recourse to the purse-strings of the fleet's commander-in-chief and therefore cash on the nail to disburse to demanding contractors.

'Why, sir, we can remedy this. I've been particularly asked by th' admiral to commission and man the brig – I had been expectin' to spend some time first in seeing th' sights but if it would oblige . . .'

'That's handsome enough said, sir,' said the commissioner, his manner easing. 'When do you . . . ?'

'If you should point out th' vessel concerned, I shall take it in hand immediately, sir.'

Outside, the midshipman rose to his feet. 'There she is, Mr Bowden,' Kydd said, with the slightest hint of a tremor in his voice. He gestured to a two-masted vessel at a buoy several hundred yards further up the harbour. 'Do ye go and warn the ship's company that I shall be boarding presently.'

'The brig, sir?'

'Never so, Mr Bowden,' Kydd said, with much satisfaction, 'A brig she may've been, but she has a commander, not a l'tenant, as her captain, and must be accounted a sloop – she is now a brig-sloop, sir, not your common brig-o'-war.'

Out of sight of *his* ship, Kydd paced along slowly, imagining the scurrying aboard as news spread of the imminent arrival of the new captain. Exaltation and excitement seized him: there would never be another moment like this.

It seemed an age before a punt arrived at the landing place. 'Couldn't find else,' mumbled a dockyard worker, inexpertly hanging on to a bollard. Another stood awkwardly at his sculls.

'Where's the ship's boat?' Kydd wanted to know. There had to be at the least a pinnace, cutter or gig in that class of ship.

'Ah, well, now, there's a bit o' trouble wi' that there—'

'And my boat's crew, damn it?'

The second threw his scull oar clattering into the bottom of the boat. 'D' ye want t' go to the barky or not, cock?'

Kydd swallowed his anger. 'I'll go,' he said. If he did not, then who knew when he might be able to later? He couldn't wait around so conspicuously on the waterfront – and he was damned if he'd be cheated out of his big moment. Trying to act in as dignified a manner as possible, he stepped into the flat-bottomed craft.

'Shovin' off, Mick,' the first said, and gave a mighty poke

at the stonework, hoping to topple Kydd, but Kydd had fore-seen the move and stood braced resolutely as the punt slid out towards the brig.

It would take more than the antics of these two dockyard mateys to affect Kydd's spirits. His eyes took in the vessel's lines hungrily as they neared her: a trim, bare-masted craft with an accentuated sheer and the sweetest miniature stern gallery. His heart went out to her – she was riding high in the water, her empty gun-ports and lack of any real rigging giving her a curiously expectant look. At the bow her white figurehead was a dainty maiden with streaming hair, and even before they had come up with her Kydd knew he was in love.

He straightened importantly. There were few crew visible on deck, but the punt was lower than *Teazer*'s modest free-board. His heart thudded, then steadied.

The punt spun about and approached. Bowden's anxious face appeared at the deck edge, then disappeared again; a pilot ladder slithered down just forward of the main-chains and dangled over the side. Normally a ship's boat would have the height to allow a simple transfer to the brig's deck but there was nothing for it. Cheated of his moment of grandly stepping aboard, Kydd grabbed the writhing ladder and heaved himself up with both hands.

A single boatswain's call trilled uncertainly as Kydd appeared, to find only a shame-faced Bowden plying the whistle, with three shuffling dockyard men he had obviously rounded up for the occasion. The salute pealed into silence and Kydd removed his hat, taken aback. 'No ship's company, sir,' Bowden whispered apologetically.

'We commission,' Kydd growled and strode to the centre of the quarterdeck, pulling out a parchment document and declaring in ringing tones to the empty deck that the latest addition to His Majesty's Navy was the brig-sloop *Teazer*, which was now officially under his own command.

He turned to Bowden and, glancing up at the bare, truncated masts, slipped him a roll of white silk. 'Be sure an' this gets aloft now.' It was a commissioning pennant and would fly at *Teazer*'s mainmasthead day and night from this time on.

Bowden did his best; without upper masts there was only the mortise of the main topmast cap but soon all ashore with eyes to see could behold a borrowed frigate's long pennant floating bravely from the stumpy mainmast of HMS *Teazer*. She was now in commission.

Kydd looked up for a long moment. Then, reluctantly, he dropped his gaze to the deck: he was about to face the biggest challenge of his life. 'Mr Bowden, return to th' frigate and present my duty t' the captain and it would be a convenience should he sign off on my hands into *Teazer*.'

'Y-your hands, sir?'

'O' course!' Kydd said sternly, 'Sent fr'm the commander-in-chief for duty in the Malta Service, by which he means ourselves and who other?' With reasonable luck, they could take their pick if they moved fast and have them entered before the proper authority came to claim them.

'Aye aye, sir. Er, how many shall I return with?'

A brig-sloop of this size would need somewhere between eighty and a hundred men. 'I'll take all the Tenaciouses, which are not so many, so say fifty more – as long as there's prime hands among 'em.'

Kydd knew he was being optimistic, but there had been genuine warmth in the frigate captain's congratulations that would probably translate to sympathy. And with men *Teazer* would come alive – boats could be manned, work parties mustered and the rhythm of sea life begun. His spirits rose. 'Oh, and be so good as t' give my compliments to th' commissioner's office and I should be pleased were they t' send word to m' standing officers that they're required aboard directly.' Every vessel had certain warrant officers standing by them, even out of commission, and no doubt they would be enjoying a peaceful time of it in some snug shoreside hideaway while the dockyard pressed on at its leisurely pace.

Bowden left in the punt and Kydd was on his own with just a pair of curious caulkers on the upper deck. Apart from the dismal thunks of a maul forward, the ship was an echoing cavern with little sign of life.

Now was the perfect time to make his acquaintance of the lovely creature. *Teazer* was a galley-built craft, one continuous deck running fore and aft, but then he noticed a singular thing – the even line of bulwarks ended in the after part all decked over. Closer to, he saw that in fact the top of a cabin was flush with the line of the bulwarks, which would make it only about chest-high inside. He pushed open the door gingerly – and nearly fell down the several steps that led to the cabin spaces, comfortably let into the deck a further few feet.

This was his home – despite the powerful smell of turpentine, paint and raw wood shavings. He saw that he was standing in a diminutive but perfectly formed lobby; the door on his right was to the coach, his bedplace and private quarters. The door ahead was to the great cabin – the whole twenty-foot width of the vessel. Illuminated by the decorous stern windows he had seen from outside, it was a princely space, vaster by far than any he had lived in before.

He went to the mullioned windows and opened one: the miniature stern gallery was a charming pretence but just as pretty for that. All in basic white, it would soon see some gold leaf, even if he had to pay for it himself. His steps echoed oddly on the wooden deck – he looked down and saw a snug-fitting trap-door, almost certainly his private store-room.

The coach was little longer than an officer's cot: washbasin and drawers would fill the width, but it was palatial compared with what he had been used to. He left the cabin spaces for the quarterdeck and marvelled at the cunning of the Maltese shipwrights, who had contrived the comfort of the airy cabin while keeping all along the flush deck clear for working sail.

He went forward to a hatchway and descended into an expanse of bare deck. This was the only true deck the brig possessed, above him the open air, below him the hold. It was empty, stretching from the galley and storerooms for-ward to what must be the wardroom and officers' cabins aft. Now it was gloomy and stank of linseed oil and paint: there was little ventilation – all cannon would be mounted on the upper deck and therefore there were no gun-ports to open. At sea, this would be home to eighty men or more and the contrast with his own appointments could not have been greater.

He stood for a moment, dealing with a surge of memory relating to his own time as a seaman. A stab of feeling for those faraway days of hard simplicity but warm friendships crowded into his mind. It would be the same here in *Teazer*'s mess deck but he would never know of it. He had come so far . . . Would fortune demand a pay-back?

Voices drifted down through the hatch gratings: this might be the first members of *Teazer*'s company. Kydd bounded up the fore hatchway to the upper deck. A short man in spectacles and a shabby blue coat abruptly ended his conversation with one of the caulkers. 'Do I see the captain of *Teazer*?' he said carefully.

'You do. I am Commander Kydd.'

The man removed his hat and bowed slightly. 'Ellicott, Samuel Ellicott. Your purser, sir.'

'Thank you, Mr Ellicott. We're only just in commission, as you see . . .' The man seemed nervous and Kydd added, 'I would wish ye well of y'r appointment aboard us, Mr Ellicott.'

'Mr Kydd – sir. I have to ask you a question. This is vital, sir, and could well rebound on both of us at a time now distant.'

'Very well, Mr Ellicott.'

'When I heard that you'd – taken it upon yourself to commission *Teazer* like you did, I knew I had to come post-haste. Sir, have you signed any papers?'

'I have not, Mr Ellicott.'

The man eased visibly. 'Fitting out a King's ship new commissioned is not the place for a tyro, if you understand me, sir.'

'Although this is my first command, Mr Ellicott, it is not m' first ship. However, it's kind of ye to offer y'r suggestions. I do believe we have a mort o' work to do – the people will be coming aboard tomorrow an' we should stand ready t' receive 'em. So we set up the paperwork first. Just f'r now, I shall use m' great cabin as our headquarters. Then we start setting out our requirements for the dockyard. No doubt they wants it on a form o' sorts.'

A thought struck him. 'Do ye know of any who'd be desirous of a berth as captain's clerk? Someone who knows Navy ways, c'n scratch away at a speed, discreet in his speech . . .'

'There may be ... but he is now retired,' Ellicott said. 'A few guineas by way of earnest-money should gain his interest. Was captain's clerk in *Meleaguer* thirty-two at Toulon in 'ninety-three, as I remember. Shall I ... ?'

'Desire him t' present himself this day or sooner and I shall look very favourably on his findin' a berth in *Teazer*.' There were a number of Admiralty placements by warrant to which a captain was obliged to accede: the boatswain, gunner, carpenter and others. For the rest, Kydd was free to appoint whom he chose. 'Shall we find a stick or two f'r a table and begin?'

The prospective captain's clerk, Mr Peck, arrived with commendable promptness, a dry, shrewd-eyed man of years who had clearly seen much. Together, he and the purser fussed away and came up with a list of essentials – which began with opening the muster book, in which the details for victualling and wages of every seaman of *Teazer*'s company would be entered.

Then it was the establishment of ship's documents, letter-books, vouchers, lists of allowances – it seemed impossible that any man could comprehend their number, let alone their purpose, and Kydd was happy to leave them to it.

Shortly, another of his standing officers puffed aboard. 'Purchet, boatswain, sir,' he said. The man had a lazy eye, which made it appear that he was squinting.

'I'd hoped t' see you aboard before now, Mr Purchet,' Kydd said mildly. 'We've much t' do afore we put to sea.'

'Aye, sir,' Purchet said heavily, glancing up at the bare masts. 'An' I hope you ain't thinkin' o' them false-hearted set o' rascals in the dockyard.'

'They'll bear a hand, I'm sure, but we'll be setting the ship up ourselves. It's a small dockyard I'll grant, but I'll have fifty prime seamen for ye directly.'

Purchet's eyebrows shot up.

The carpenter arrived and was soon complaining of his lack of stores. Time was slipping by: Kydd needed to prime the dockyard to begin releasing *Teazer*'s stores and equipment forthwith. If he failed, the men could not be accommodated on board or entered on the ship's books and he would quickly lose them to other ships. 'Mr Ellicott, be s' good as to accompany me to th' dockyard and advise.'

It transpired that the senior naval officer of the dockyard was neither a sea officer nor very senior. Owing allegiance directly to the Navy Board, Burdock's immediate superior was no closer than Gibraltar, which gave him a certain room for manoeuvre in his dealings. However, even with veiled threats, it still cost Kydd a dismaying pile of silver, all from his own pocket, to generate any sense of urgency in the case. That, and the promise to set the son of a 'good friend' on his quarterdeck as midshipman.

It had been a day of furious activity and Kydd found himself dog tired. They had made a good start, but in the absence of proper accommodation and with no ship's cook he could not in all conscience require anyone to remain on board for the night. Reluctantly he told them all to go ashore and return early the next morning.

The calm evening spread out its peace, the impressive stone ramparts speckled with light. Nearby vessels showed soft gold light in their stern windows; some had deck lights strung.

Teazer was in darkness and he was left alone on board – but, then, nothing could have been more congenial. Kydd paced slowly along the deserted decks, seeing, in his mind's eye, cannon run out through gun-ports where now there were empty spaces, a satisfying lacing of rigging against the bare spars standing black against the stars, men on the foredeck enjoying the dog-watches.

He stumbled in the gloom, his fatigue returning in waves, and, just as it had been for him on his very first night in a man-o'-war, there was no place to lay his head. A caulker's ground-cloth and his own unopened valise would be his bed – but it would be in the captain's cabin – *his* cabin! He grinned inanely in the darkness and a sudden thought struck.

Kydd found a lanthorn and carried it into the great cabin. The clerk had laid out the books of account, logs, journals and other necessary instruments in systematic piles, each new, some with slips of paper, scrawled notes, others with *Teazer's* name boldly inscribed. He began searching, and it was not long before he found what he was after. He lifted it reverently up to the carpenter's table that did duty for a desk.

Finding an ink-well and quill he opened the book, smoothed its pages and, in the dim lanthorn-light, he penned the first entry in the ship's log.

'Winds SSE, Clear Weather, at single anchor. Hoisted a Pennant on board His Majesty's Brig Sloop *Teazer* by Virtue of a Commission from Admiral Keith . . . on the Malta Service . . .' Duty done, he claimed his bed.

In the morning, the decks were wet following a light shower. Kydd called his standing officers to conference in the great cabin, the clerk at his notes. The cook finally arrived: a bushy-browed half-Italian, whose voluble explanations were cut short by Kydd: he wanted to feed fifty-odd hungry seamen whatever it took – he had just received a message that he should prepare to receive the body of men called for.

The seamen would come with their sea-bags but no hammocks or bedding; those must be supplied. And without doubt there would be some who had, by accident or carelessness, been left with no spare clothing; a slop chest would need to be opened. More largesse, it seemed, would secure an early release of stores.

The ship must aim towards self-sufficiency as soon as possible. Water, firewood for the galley, provisions, grog, its complement of ensigns, pennants, all proper devices. But this was only the first stage – mere existence. Then would come the main act: fitting out the ship for sea, using the skills of the seamen.

'They're alongside!' spluttered Purchet, as a confused bumping was felt through the ship's side, but it was not the hands, only the stores lighters from the yard being poled out as promised.

There was barely time for Kydd to apportion his best estimate of tasks by priority when the first launch was sighted. A small table was set up abaft the mainmast and Kydd took his place, his clerk to one side to note his decisions.

'Mr Purchet, any man desirous o' the rate of petty officer make himself known t' ye. Those I'll see first.'

The men came over the bulwark with their sea-bags and bundles, and were ushered forward indignantly by the boatswain. Kydd wondered whether he should make a rousing address but realised he would have to repeat himself when others came aboard.

The first prospective petty officers came to the table: hard, skilled men, but wary as they spoke to Kydd. He immediately accepted those who had served in the rate before – he would have the measure of them later.

Laffin, a boatswain's mate in *Tenacious*, showed no sign of recognition and stood four-square, gazing at a point above Kydd, even when spoken to. Purchet was entitled to one mate, he would do. Another, Poulden: Kydd recalled his fine seamanship and reliability, and rated him quartermaster. The man responded with a broad smile. One further was made quartermaster's mate.

The first wave of aspirants had no sooner been dealt with than a second boat arrived with more. Kydd attended to them, then stood up and hailed the boatswain: 'Mr Purchet!' he called loudly. 'I'll be dealing with th' rest later. But I'll have ye know that I want all these men t' have the chance to choose their own watch 'n' mess. As long as we has the same numbers in both watches they're free t' choose.'

There was an immediate stir: it was routine that men joining were assigned by ship's need and had little chance to stay with their friends. Wide grins spread and a happy babble arose. Kydd was pleased: it was a little enough thing, but it would mean much to those whose freedoms were normally so few.

Kydd returned to his cabin to take stock. Each class of vessel had its establishment – its allowance of guns, personnel, stores entitlement: he had prepared his scheme of complement against this and needed to see how the numbers were proceeding. He was only too aware that he was taking outrageous liberties in his manning but he was relying on the fact that without there being a proper naval presence – the dockyard did not count – bold and resourceful moves would pay handsomely now, with explanations saved for later.

The most conspicuous gap in his list was that of his only officer, a lieutenant. He knew only his name – Dacres, and a Peregrine Dacres no less. He was said to be in Malta but had not left word of his whereabouts.

There was also the lack of a sailing master, and he had heard of no one yet appointed. Kydd's allowance of two midshipmen was now filled with Bowden and the commissioner's nominee, and most of the key petty officers were in place, with a surgeon expected soon.

But where could a master's mate be found in so distant a post as Malta? It was a vital question because the master's mate in a brig would stand watch opposite the lieutenant and without one Kydd would have no alternative but to direct the master to take over or stand watches himself.

For the others he would make shift but *Teazer*'s final standing officer, the gunner, was still on his way from Gibraltar. Apparently a green, just-certificated warrant officer, he had probably been shuffled to out-of-the-way Malta where he could do little harm as he learned. Kydd bit his lip: skill at arms was the deciding factor in any combat and a strong figure at the head of the gunnery crew was an asset.

He had no lieutenant, no master or master's mate. They were all appointed by commission or warrant and therefore there was nothing he could do.

He returned on deck to hear raised voices from a boat coming alongside. 'To come aboard,' Kydd ordered, hiding a smile. It was the dignified black face of Tysoe, his servant, and by the appearance of things he had not wasted his time while he had been waiting in the frigate. He was jealously guarding two pieces of furniture, which looked much like an officer's cot and some kind of campaign-drawer set.

Tysoe was clearly determined to take charge below: the furniture was wrestled through and into the captain's bed-place to much clucking and keen glances, and a firm promise from Kydd to invest in the very near future in cabin appointments more in keeping with his position.

It did bring up the question of his other domestics. He would have to find a steward, not so much for serving at table but to be responsible for Kydd's own stores, which would be separate from the rest, and in this small vessel also to act as the purser's assistant in issuing provisions. And he would need a coxswain to take charge of his barge and stand by him when required.

Order was coming out of chaos: the boatswain was sending below the men who had sorted themselves into messes, and getting a semblance of balance of petty officers and seamen ready for assignment to watches.

Kydd tried not to look too hard at the men: these were the seamen who would work the ship and serve the guns for him. The success of his command – even the life of his ship – would be in their hands. He spotted Bowden talking with one of the *Tenacious* hands he had arranged to be sent from the frigate and crossed the deck. 'Thank ye, Mr Bowden, that was well done. Please to—'

His attention was diverted as a boat came alongside and an officer swung on to the main deck and made his way over. 'Commander Kydd, sir?' he said evenly, removing his hat.

'It is.'

'Then might I present myself, sir? Lieutenant Dacres, come to join.'

A peep of lace showed at his cuffs; Kydd saw that the uniform was faultlessly cut. 'Ye're expected, sir,' he said shortly. 'As y' can see, the ship is now in commission.'

'Ah – yes, sir, so I have heard. I was unavoidably detained by General Pigot. A social occasion, you'll understand.'

Kydd ignored the clumsy attempt to impress. 'Mr Dacres, I want this vessel at sea within the week. You'll stay aboard an' hold y'self in readiness for any task that I might require.'

He paused, then continued, 'I shall see you in my cabin in fifteen minutes.' A guilty thrill rushed through him at the sudden worried look this produced and he turned away quickly in case it betrayed him.

The interview was short: Dacres's experience, he had heard, was confined entirely to ships-of-the-line as both midshipman and lieutenant, but if his easy acquaintance with those in high places was to be believed then his time in *Teazer* was no more than necessary experience before his own command in due course.

'Start with the watch 'n' station bill, Mr Dacres. I've rated the petty officers – see to the rest if y' please. When we have th' outline of both watches, we'll shift to harbour routine. Tell the cook hard tack at noon, but I'd like t' see a square meal f'r all hands at supper.' He stood. 'Come, come, Mr Dacres, we've a lot t' do!'

By noon, stores were coming in at a handsome rate. Even while finishing touches were being applied, the boatswain's store was being stocked with pitch and resinous tar and hung about with cordage and blocks, and the carpenter fussed over all manner of copper nails, roves, augers and other arcane implements of his craft.

Countless fathoms of line were laid out on deck: they would be brought to the task of clothing *Teazer*'s masts with shrouds and stays to form, first, the taut standing rigging to brace her masts and, second, the operating machinery of the ship, the running rigging that controlled the yards and sails.

Kydd stood watching, pleased to see individual groups begin to apply themselves under their petty officers.

He turned and went below to his great cabin, now with a small sideboard and a twin-leafed table being vigorously polished. There would be other pieces he could probably cozen out of the dockyard but that could wait. What he wanted to do now required privacy and he shooed everyone out. He unlocked his valise, extracted his orders and sat down to read them properly – in all the activity he had barely had time to skim through the contents.

The preliminaries were mainly concerned with proper obedience to his various superiors. His duties would consist in the main of the conveyance of dispatches and important passengers, with the escorting of smaller convoys. The protection of trade was to be given the highest priority and he was to maintain his best endeavours to annoy the enemy by any means that lay in his power. And after these paragraphs was a direction that, as circumstances might arise from time to time, he was to render such services as requested to the civil government of Malta.

These orders, the first for a captain that he had seen, were broad but clear. His eyes went down the page, taking in the remainder. The concluding part, he noticed with satisfaction, dealt sternly with his duty to 'take, burn, sink and destroy' such of the King's enemies who had the temerity to cross his bows and the whole concluded with the forbidding 'Hereof you may not fail as you will answer to the contrary at your peril.' Keith's unmistakable sharp, angular signature followed the date.

Kydd sat back. It was all so general – but, then, these orders were not there to tell him how to be a captain or how to conduct his ship but only what was expected of him and his little bark. It was entirely his own responsibility how he carried it out, but so many regulations and orders hedged it about . . .

He laid down the papers. After the Articles of War, in the

hierarchy of orders and discipline, were the 'Fighting Instructions'. These were familiar enough to Kydd in detailing how the commander-in-chief desired his battles to be fought, specifically his signals, but were applicable only to the great fleets. Directly relevant were the weighty 'Regulations and Instructions Relating to His Majesty's Service at Sea, Established by His Majesty in Council'. These dictated the manner of the conduct of his command, covering details as diverse as how salt beef was to be cut up to the stowage of rum, many of which dated back to the hundred years after Sir Francis Drake.

Finally, one set of orders was considered so all-important that as an officer he had had recourse to them as to no other – in fact, they were considered so vital that in *Tenacious* they had been sewn into canvas and hung on a hook under the half-deck for urgent use by the quarterdeck. But it was no use trying to find them for they did not yet exist. These were the Captain's Orders: the final authority on how the ship was to be run – everything from liberty entitlements to the proper way to salute the quarterdeck. Usually they were inherited from the previous captain and adopted more or less unchanged: Kydd was faced with the task of creating them from scratch as the final arbiter of conduct for every man aboard *Teazer*.

Restless, he rose and went on deck. If *Teazer* was to be an effective warship of His Majesty, there was so much to do.

The next days saw satisfying progress. A milestone was passed when yards were crossed – now his ship had a lofty grace that was both fetching and purposeful. More standing rigging began to appear. Within her hull less spectacular matters were in hand: tables were fitted for messes, neat stowage for mess traps against the ship's side above each.

The cabins aft were varnished and outfitted: tiny, but snugly appointed, they were on each side of the main hatchway companion, while further forward the master and boatswain on one side, the surgeon and purser on the other completed the officers' accommodation.

The purser went ashore once more, this time with 'necessary money' provided by the Admiralty. Among his tasks was the purchase of lanthorn candles sufficient for the entire ship, the seamen making do with a 'purser's moon', a rush dip in an iron saucer.

Teazer received her allowance from the boat pond: a twenty-four-foot cutter, a twenty-two-foot pinnace and a jolly-boat. They were hoisted aboard on each quarter of the ship by davits, stout timbers that stood out over the sea and allowed the boats to be plucked directly from the water instead of the usual laborious arrangement with tackles from the yardarms.

The standing rigging went forward apace, taut and trim; the shrouds, stays and gammoning were stretched along and sailors then began to tar down with the rich, resinous, dark-brown Stockholm tar whose fragrance always spoke to Kydd of the sea and ships.

The end was not far off. Following Kydd's stated preference, the outside hull was 'bright-sided'. Above the waterline the side was scraped back and payed with rosin, the distillation of turpentine. When cured it would give a yacht-like brightness. It cost him dear from his own pocket but he was determined – and soon the gilders were at work with gold leaf about the pretty stern-quarters. Surveying their work from a boat, he longed to feel *Teazer*'s lively deck in the open sea and test her mettle against the winds, but he would have to contain himself a little longer.

31

Nearby, *Stag* was preparing to return to Gibraltar. The Blue Peter rose at her masthead; she would be gone from Malta within twenty-four hours. But her captain had not forgotten and a charmingly worded invitation arrived for Kydd to dine with him that evening.

'Give you joy of your command, sir!' It was a heady moment for Kydd. After he had been rowed out to the frigate, arrayed in his best uniform with its gold lace, then piped aboard in his own right as a full commander of a sloop of the Royal Navy, he had been greeted by the waiting Captain Winthrop, who took him below to his great cabin – just two captains for dinner.

'Thank ye, sir!' Kydd raised his glass. In his euphoria the twinkling gold from the lamps playing round its rim seemed a magical circlet of happiness. 'You're away t' sea tomorrow?'

'Gibraltar through the Adriatic. But then, I fear, more service off Toulon,' said Winthrop, with a smile.

The wide expanse of *Stag*'s mullioned windows opened on a view of the Maltese evening that was in turns mysterious and electric. In the future this would be *Teazer*'s home and Kydd's elation mounted. 'It could be interestin' service here, I'm thinking,' he said casually.

Winthrop uncovered the dish the steward had brought. 'Do try this baked lampuka. Local fare, but I dare to say it would be applauded in any company.' He helped Kydd to some succulent strips and continued, in the same tone, '*Interesting*. That's quite the word I would have chosen myself.'

Kydd was anxious not to appear naïve and kept silent. Winthrop moved on smoothly: 'Tell me, how is your fitting out progressing? Every morning I stand amazed at how your trim little brig is showing her plumage and stretching her wings. Quite your little peacock, I fancy.'

Glowing with pleasure, Kydd answered, 'Aye, sir, she's a fine enough craft. A little full in the run but long-floored and with a clean entrance. She'll do.'

'I'm sure she will,' said Winthrop, strongly. 'And her people? Are you satisfied?'

'I've some prime hands fr'm *Tenacious*, sir, an' others come from the fleet – I count m'self lucky they're sent for th' Malta Service at this time.'

Winthrop's smile widened. 'Should you ask Sir John you may receive a different opinion. Most would believe the men to have been destined for him.' Such a core of skilled seamen was almost certainly intended for the commander of the Eastern Mediterranean squadron of battleships continually at sea to thwart French moves east of Italy.

'I lack a sailing master,' Kydd said, changing the subject as quickly as he could. 'M' gunner's on his way, I'm told, but still there's no word on a master.'

Winthrop's expression turned grave. 'Then, in course, you are unable to sail. No doubt you are not relishing a month or so at a buoy waiting while the omission is rectified?'

Kydd gave a bleak smile.

Some years past, the rank of 'Master and Commander' had been discarded in recognition of the fact that navigation had become too specialised for fighting captains, and now, for all sloops and above, a professional master, certificated by Trinity House, was required.

Winthrop considered for a moment. 'There is a course you may wish to consider. In the customs house I met a gentleman who has been a master with us before. Stayed here when we evacuated the Mediterranean as something or other in the merchantry. The French seizing Malta must have put paid to that. He may be amenable at this time to an offer as acting master, the commander-in-chief to confirm. There can't be many masters at large in this end of the Med.'

'Thank you, sir, I'm indeed grateful for y'r suggestion.'

'He is Maltese, of course.'

'He c'n be a Chinaman for all I care if he gets me t' sea,' said Kydd, with relish. Impulsively, he went on, 'Sir – can I ask – what is it ye sees will make life *interesting* in these waters?'

Winthrop leaned back, delicately touching his lips with his napkin. 'As I remember it, for a brig-sloop your corsair will be an annoyance – Mahometans from the Barbary coast seeing it their holy duty to prey on the Christian, and you'll find privateers enough in the Sicily Channel to vex any convoy escort . . . but do believe that where you'll find it the hardest beat to wind'd is with our "allies".

'Did you know there is a strong Russian garrison in Corfu? You should – since Tsar Paul made common cause with the French they must certainly be accounted unfriendly, even though he is recently murdered and succeeded by Alexander. Yet we find that our most caressed friend, Turkey, is at sea this very hour in a combined fleet with the Russians under Kadir Bejja and Ushakov. If you come across them, do you clear away your saluting guns, or go to quarters?'

Kydd held his silence.

'And since the French hold Taranto, and Sicily is lost to us, what do you say to a Palermo merchantman bringing a lading of Marseille dried fish to Malta? To be safeguarded or – a prize?'

Kydd flushed and changed the subject. 'What of th' French at sea, do y' think? I dare t' say they have their cruisers out?'

In the excitement of taking possession and command of his ship, with all its unexpectedness, he had not given much consideration to other aspects of command. There was no question, in such a situation as mentioned, that the decision was his, and his alone. And he knew he was unprepared.

Winthrop gave an understanding smile. 'The French? There will be quantities of Marseille rovers about, but what are they to stand before a regular-going English man-o'-war?' He politely refilled Kydd's glass. 'You will be more concerned for the trade of Malta. These islands are poor and barren. The inhabitants must live by trade. Should their vessels be set upon by your corsair then it will be more than the merchant who must starve. You will hear from those in high places, I believe, were this to occur . . .'

'Yes, sir, this I can grasp,' Kydd said quickly. It was all very well for a post-captain to discourse lazily on what must seem simple enough affairs to him, but Kydd had been a captain only for a matter of days. There was a damn sight more to learn than he had first thought, and here in faraway Malta he would have no friends to ease the way for him.

At Kydd's grimace Winthrop picked up his glass. 'But I neglect my guest. Here, sir, I give you joy of your step – let us wet your swab in a bumper.'

There was so much fellow feeling in his expression that Kydd could not help but glance down at the gold of his single epaulette as he lifted his glass. 'I'd never have thought it, ever,' he said, pride overcoming his embarrassment.

Winthrop's smile stayed. 'You will never forget this moment. I remember when . . . But that was long ago. Your good health, Mr Kydd, and may the fortunes of war favour you always.'

Kydd glowed. After the toast he refilled their glasses and looked through the windows at a small, dark shape at rest within Dockyard Creek. 'To *Teazer* – taut, trim and true, the loveliest creature that ever swam.'

'His Britannic Majesty's Sloop-of-War *Teazer*,' agreed Winthrop, 'Tiger of the seas!'

The moment could not have held more for Kydd – but then, piercing through the haze of happiness, came a stab of grief: the recognition that he would probably never again know Renzi's friendship aboard a ship.

'Th-thank you, sir, that was nobly said,' he said, recovering.

'Then I shall not delay you. No doubt we shall meet again – this war seems destined to go on for ever.'

'Aye, sir. And the best o' fortune for y'rself, if I might say it.'

Winthrop moved to the door and gave orders for Kydd's boat. 'Oh, yes, there is one matter that would oblige me, should you see fit,' he said casually.

'Anything, sir,' Kydd replied, with warmth.

'Well, it does cross my mind that, at this time, I, having a superfluity of young gentlemen aboard *Stag*, conceivably one might profitably ship with you, if you understand me?'

There could only be one response: 'O' course, sir. Glad to be of service.' He was only too aware that he already had his permitted complement of two midshipmen and that he could not afford to offend the dockyard at this time. It would seem he would have to part with Bowden. A sad betrayal of the lad's loyalty.

'Splendid. Then I shall require our youngster to shift his berth to you without delay. Fare you well, Mr Kydd.'

Tysoe entered quietly with Kydd's breakfast of coffee and rolls. It was still a very strange thing to dine alone but at the least it gave time for thought.

He had no idea how he would explain to Bowden his sudden dismissal. No doubt in time he would find another ship, but the company would be strangers. And he would miss the young man's intelligence and trustworthiness: a midshipman was a rated petty officer and had duties elastic enough to prove more than useful in many situations. But he had no place for a third midshipman.

The irony was that he was nearly a third short of complement, most of them ordinary and able seamen, admittedly, but vital for all that. He could get to sea, possibly, with what he had, but he could not fight a battle nor provide a prize crew. And with an absent gunner and a problematic sailing master there were reasons aplenty for vexation.

And where would there be a master's mate in this part of the world? Unless there was, he would be obliged to stand watches which— It was obvious! Why hadn't he thought of it before? 'Mr Bowden!' he bellowed from his door – there were no marines to keep sentry-go outside his cabin. 'Pass the word f'r Mr Midshipman Bowden!'

'Do excuse my rig, sir,' the youngster said, in alarm, 'I thought I had better—'

'No matter, Mr Bowden. I have news for ye. As of this day you shall be acting master's mate. How do ye reckon on that?'

For a moment Bowden's eyes widened; then a boyish smile provided the answer.

Acting master's mate – Kydd didn't even know if he had the power to do this: a full master's mate required an Admiralty warrant. However, he was relying on the commander-in-chief to confirm his actions from his understanding of the situation facing Kydd.

'Y'r first duty, take the jolly-boat to th' customs house –
I've an important message for a gentleman there . . .'

Teazer was rapidly assuming her final appearance: yards black
against varnished masts, the very ends tipped in white to
show up to men working out on the yardarm at night. On
deck, the inside of the bulwarks was rousing scarlet against
the tar-black of the standing rigging and the natural hempen
pale of the working lines. The deck was not yet to a pristine salt-white finish but this would come, and with a lick
of blue and gold on their figurehead the ship was handsome indeed.

Within two hours Mr Bonnici came aboard. A short, well-
kept gentleman, he made heavy going of heaving himself
across the bulwarks before presenting himself, puffing with
exertion and supported by an ebony cane. In the plain black
of a sailing master and wearing a three-cornered hat of a
past age, he beamed at Kydd from a genially lined face.

'Sir, er, do I understand that you've served as master with
us before?' Kydd asked, somewhat dismayed by the man's
age. Could his old bones take service in a small but pugna-
cious man-o'-war?

Bonnici swept down in an elaborate bow, rising with an
even wider smile. 'In my time I had th' honour o' knowing
Adm'ral Howe, sir.'

'Admiral Howe, indeed!'

'As who should say – while I was master in *Romulus* I often
'mark this gentleman on his flagship quarterdeck a-pacing as
we close wi' the enemy before Genoa, stuns'l abroad an—'

'And since then?'

Bonnici drew himself up, dignified. 'An' since then, sir,
consequen' upon the Royal Navy quit of the Mediterranean,

I have been advisin' of the merchants abou' their shipping. You will know, sir, how difficult we have been wi' the French capture Malta, no one eat, our families—'

'Thank you, Mr Bonnici. Now, do ye have evidence o' this, Navy Board certificates of sea service possibly?' If the man could prove his service in a frigate Kydd would think about it, for without any master at all he was going nowhere.

'Sir.'

Kydd took the papers. 'These seem t' be in order, Mr Bonnici. Now, what do y' think o' *Teazer*? Do ye fancy a post as master in a brig after service in a frigate?'

Bonnici seemed to sense that the tide had turned and began to relax. However, Kydd still had doubts.

'Ah, well, sir, you names her *Teazer*, but she's Malta-built o' the Zammit yard, over yonder,' he said. 'For the sea service of the knights, o' course.' He swept a glance along the line of deck. 'Clean lines, some would say fuller in th' run but our shipwrights know our sea, which is short an' high. Sound timbers – Kyrenian, fr'm the Arsenale an' well seasoned these last two year—'

'That's as maybe,' Kydd said, with rising hope. 'An' I'd like your judgement on *Teazer*'s sailing qualities.'

'Fast. Faster than y'r ship-rigged sloop, handy in stays – say ten, ten 'n' a half knots on a bowline—'

Kydd made up his mind. 'I c'n offer you an acting appointment only, Mr Bonnici . . .'

Teazer's new master bowed once more, his manner reminding Kydd of his father's old-fashioned ways before a customer. He rose, and Kydd detected barely concealed relief. 'I'm at your service this hour, Captain.'

Their final suit of sails was due aboard shortly and Bonnici would need time to make professional acquaintance of his new ship. 'Then I'll let ye get t' know y'r new master's mate. Mr Bowden!'

Kydd took one last appreciative look at the busy scene on deck, then went below. His pulse quickened: the moment had come to plan sea trials – HMS *Teazer* putting to sea for the first time! The last major items in her fitting out were waiting at the ordnance wharf – her guns – and then the tons of gunpowder would be brought out in lighters under a red flag that would finally make her the lethal fighting machine she had to be, as long as she could find her gunner.

Ellicott and Peck scratched away at Kydd's desk in the great cabin: every last item of stores brought aboard had to be entered in the ship's books and accounted for. Kydd took a seat in the middle and began on the pile of papers awaiting signature.

Dacres appeared. 'Our gunner has arrived on board, sir,' he said neutrally. 'Baggage to follow.'

At last! 'Very well. Ask him t' present himself to me, if y' please.'

The purser and clerk left the cabin, leaving Kydd alone behind the desk. He assumed a suitably grave expression.

'Come!' he said importantly, to a knock at the door.

There was a shuffling outside and a small, wiry man of indeterminate age entered. 'Mr Duckitt, sir, Helby Duckitt,' he said apologetically, his hat held defensively in his hands.

'I had thought t' see you before now, Mr Duckitt,' Kydd said reprovingly.

'Aye, sir. We was delayed, see, the Gibraltar convoy havin' no escort and—'

'Can't be helped,' Kydd said, eyeing his worn, shabby coat. 'You've just got y'r warrant as gunner, I understand.'

'Yes, sir.'

'Then we'll get y'r gear aboard an' talk further at another time. Thank ye, Mr Duckitt, an' I mean to make y'r time in *Teazer* an active one,' he finished meaningfully.

'Sir, by y' leave.'

'Yes?'

'I thought it proper t' accept a share o' some hands in Gibraltar standin' idle. They was shipwrecked an' looking f'r a ship, as we might say. Three on 'em, good men all. Do ye want t' see 'em now?'

'Hmm.' Kydd was taken with the man's craftiness in reporting for duty with a sweetener. 'D' ye think there's a petty officer among 'em?'

'I'll tell 'em t' step inside, sir.' Duckitt touched his forehead respectfully before leaving.

The first of the shipwrecked men padded in. Taken utterly by surprise, Kydd saw standing before him a man he had admired even from his first few days as a pressed man in the old *Duke William*, a mariner he had fought beside as a common seaman in the wild single frigate action that had preceded his famous voyage round the world and who had been such a figure in his adventures in the Caribbean.

'Be damned t' it – Toby Stirk!' blurted Kydd in delight, rising. 'It's been s' long – let's see, *Seaflower*, th' Caribbean . . .' If anything, Stirk had hardened further: a leathery toughness now matched a ferocity that was almost visceral. 'How are ye, cully?' Kydd said, unconsciously slipping back into foremast lingo.

Stirk hesitated, delight vying with shock at the meeting. Then impulsively he grasped Kydd's outstretched hand. 'Right oragious t' see you, Tom.' The well-remembered rasp had deepened with time. 'Ah – that's t' say, sir.' His face crinkled with pleasure.

Kydd resumed his seat. 'I'm right glad t' see you, er, Mr Stirk. Y' have m' word on that,' he added firmly. If Stirk, a gun-captain of years and the hardest man Kydd knew, was to ship in *Teazer*, the temper of the whole gundeck would be transformed. 'An' very glad to have ye aboard *Teazer*,' he said carefully. 'Can I ask, what was y'r rate in your last ship?' It was said as kindly as he could.

'Quarter gunner, sir,' Stirk said easily, as though it was the most natural thing in the world for the young quartermaster's mate he had known to be a commander rating him for service in his own ship.

'I'd like ye to be gunner's mate – if I c'n square it with Mr Duckitt,' Kydd said warmly. This was by no means a given: it was the gunner's prerogative to choose his mates. It would, however, go with Kydd's most significant recommendation and would put Stirk as the most senior petty officer gunner and the only one carried in *Teazer*.

'That's very kind in ye, Mr Kydd, but as y' knows, I don't have m' letters—'

'That's as maybe,' Kydd interrupted. 'I doubt that'll trouble a gunner who's keen for his mates t' be as fine as you. You're rated gunner's mate fr'm this moment.'

After he had dealt with the two others, memories washed over Kydd. Hard ones, full of violence and terror – but also those of the wonder and beauty of a voyage around the world, the fires of experience that had formed him as a seaman – and a world within a world that he had now left behind for ever.

Stirk had been a part of it from the beginning, until an open-boat voyage in the Caribbean had seen Kydd raised to master's mate, his hammock no longer slung before the mast. But now there was the gold lace of an officer and the final majesty of command. How was he to face an old shipmate like Stirk? And how was Stirk going to regard *him*?

Chapter 3

'Well, sir? You've had two weeks – surely it don't take for ever to fettle your little barky for sea duty!' Major General Pigot rumbled, then dabbed his mouth with his napkin. 'Take 'em away,' he told the hovering footman testily, and the breakfast dishes were swiftly removed.

'She's not an English-built ship, sir,' Kydd tried to explain. 'We've had to make changes – an' it's not been so easy t' find hands t' man her this far from the fleet—'

'Tosh! Other Navy boats manage, why not you?' Before Kydd could reply he continued, 'Is it because you're a new-minted captain, b' chance?'

Kydd stiffened, but held himself in check. This was the Officer Commanding Troops and Military Representative of His Britannic Majesty in Malta. In the delicacies of line-of-command the Malta Service to which Kydd had been detached was a civil affair, including requirements for naval action, but when there were matters requiring a military presence, the general would be consulted. However, Kydd's authority as a commander was from Admiral Keith and the Mediterranean

44

Fleet – but his orders directed him to act under the advice of the Malta authority . . . 'I shall have *Teazer* ready f'r sea within the week, General.'

'Good.' He looked at Kydd keenly. 'Understand, Captain, we've got no standing naval forces. Since the frigate left, we've been pestered by vermin – small fry – that are taking the opportunity to make hay among our trade an' this is a serious matter, I'll have ye know! Sooner you can get your ship at sea, show o' force sort of thing, sooner they gets the message. End of the week?'

'Sir.'

Ready or not, they had to put to sea for trials. They had yet to ship guns and his ship's company, a third under complement, was an unknown quantity. Kydd had lost count of the number of vouchers, receipts and demands he had signed for Ellicott as stores had come aboard in a fitful stream – for all he knew he might have signed himself into perdition.

And when he was finally able to get away from the paperwork it was to find Dacres in argument with the boatswain concerning the best way to warp the vessel the mile over to the ordnance wharf while seamen lolled around idly and his new gunner stood defensively on the foredeck, arms folded.

How was he going to find the men to bring his ship to seaworthiness – and, even more importantly, to battleworthiness? Kydd's happiness was being drowned in a sea of worries.

'Sir.' Bowden touched his hat and waited.

'Er, yes?' Kydd answered, distracted.

'I've been talking with the master. He makes a suggestion that I think, sir, you should hear.'

'Oh?'

'We had a long talk about Malta. He is, er, rather open and told me about how things are ashore. They've suffered grievously in the two years the French were here, near to starving – and all because of them. Sir, what he is saying is that there are many hungry Maltese seamen who would seize any chance to get to sea – and pay back the French.'

'Ask him t' see me, Mr Bowden.' It was nothing less than a miracle. Foreigners could be found in every Royal Navy warship so this was no bar to the Maltese joining and being engaged directly in the defence of their islands. Trade would give point to their loyalty.

Bowden gave a discreet cough. 'Sir – a word?'

'What is it?' Kydd said impatiently.

'I'm not sure if you're aware that the Maltese, sir . . . They're reputed to be the Pope's staunchest sons.'

'Popish?' When promoted lieutenant, Kydd had sworn to abjure Stuart claims to the throne and the Catholic religion. 'If I don't see 'em at it, I'll never know,' he answered briskly. He hailed the master. 'Mr Bonnici. How many hands could ye scrape together – prime hands, mark you?'

'Perhaps one, possible two . . . t'ousand.'

Kydd grinned. 'Then I'll take thirty at once, d' ye hear? When can you get 'em aboard?'

'When ye needs them, sir. But . . .'

'Yes?'

'Sir, these men have not th' experience with the Navy I have. Sir, do not expec' them to . . . to spik English.'

A watch on deck who could not understand orders? Having to mime everything to be done? But nothing was going to stop him now: if they were intelligent, the common usages of the sea would draw them together. 'Then they'll have t' learn. Any who can't stand a watch on account o' not understanding orders in one month goes back ashore directly, an' we find someone who can.'

He rounded on the first lieutenant. 'So! Mr Dacres, why are we not yet at th' ordnance wharf?'

Beautiful! Kydd admired the deadly black six-pounders on their neat little carriages ranging down the deck edge – eight to a side, and two smaller, demurely crouched in his great cabin as chase guns. And all unused, originally from the arsenal of the knights of Malta. Gun parties were bringing the cannon to the right state of gleaming with canvas, brick-dust and the assiduous application of a sovereign mixture of blacking, Mr Duckitt's own recipe.

'Mr Purchet!' The boatswain looked aft warily. 'I'll see sails bent on th' fore – we'll start with the fore course, testing th' gear as we go.' The pace was quickening: Kydd wanted to see sail aloft, even if it was not in earnest. While still at anchor the fore yard would be braced round side on to the light morning breeze and the sail loosed. All the gear – bunt-lines and slablines, halliards and braces – could thus be proved without hazard.

And the men also. The two-masted brig would be handier in stays than any ship-rigged vessel and their resources of men were far greater than any merchant brig. But when fighting for their lives in action there could be no idle hands.

Evening light stealing in brought activity to a close, and Kydd felt he had some measure of his men. Purchet was too free with his rope's end and Laffin had followed his example with relish. He could not check the boatswain in front of the men but he would see him privately.

He was fortunate in his topmen – they seemed at home on *Teazer*'s yards and handled sail well; there was a pleasing rivalry developing between fore- and mainmast, which also implied an undeclared interest in the officers – Dacres at the main and Bowden at the fore. Kydd noted that Dacres went below for a speaking trumpet while Bowden urged on his men in a manly bawl.

The Maltese had come as promised, diverting to a degree for *Teazer*'s company. Bare-footed, each with a colourful sash and a long floppy cap from within which they found tobacco, papers and personal oddments, they were small but of a wiry build and had darting dark eyes.

Bonnici stood at Kydd's side as he inspected them. Their origins were the mercantile marine of Malta, now with their livelihood reduced to nothing. 'They may not wear a sash, Mr Bonnici, an' they vittle with our men,' Kydd ordered.

He turned to Dacres. 'Would you be s' good as to see me in my cabin with y'r workings, Mr Dacres? I mean to try *Teazer* at sea very soon.' Before they could, the ship's company would have to be detailed off to cover all the chief manoeuvres: unmooring ship, reefing sail, putting about – it was a complex job but essential if there were to be skilled hands in the right place to get it done. This was a task for a ship's first lieutenant; in *Teazer*, her only other officer.

Kydd saw that Dacres had made a fair start. Each man would have a place in either the larboard or starboard watch, which was further subdivided into the first and second part. With the men assigned to their part-of-ship it was possible to specify, for instance, that in the manoeuvre of setting sail it would be the main topmen of the first part of the starboard watch assisted by topmen of the second of larboard that would perform this particular action.

Every man had an entry in the muster book that specified

his rate and entitlements and there was a mess number that told at which of the snug tables of six friends he could be found at mealtimes. A hammock mark was the man's indication where his hammock should be slung and all was keyed together in a careful and consistent structure.

But it was only that – a structure: the quality and balance of the men comprising it would determine its success. Kydd inspected the paper lists: unknown names, numbers, duties. Would it hang together?

'Mr Peck will assist ye in drawing up y'r watch an' station bill. We leave the quarter bill for later.' The fighting stations in it would be relatively straightforward to bring to organisation.

'May I know when we shall have your orders, sir?'

Dacres was entitled to ask for written Captain's Orders, but they would have to wait. 'Later. How are th' people settling in?'

'In fine – fractious. They seem to have no idea of the difficulties we are under at this time, sir, and will persist in coming to me with their petty vexations. Daniel Hawkins had the effrontery to claim allowance against local victuals used in place of the scale of salted provisions, the rogue.'

A seaman's horizons were necessarily limited: if he saw that the safe, secure round of his daily routines was in disarray it was fundamentally unsettling. Sea routine would see to that, but Kydd knew that here an unwritten bargain was at risk: that of an officer's duty to provide for his men in return for their loyalty. Again, the comfort of settled routine at sea would take care of this. Hawkins was trying an old trick; there would be many more such.

Dacres was keeping his distance from the men, not understanding them, distrustful. Kydd did not let this dampen his spirits. 'But on th' whole a splendid day,' he said to his first lieutenant. 'Do ye care to join me f'r dinner, sir?'

It was the first time Kydd had entertained; his great cabin was not yet to his satisfaction because he had had no time ashore and diminishing means to pay for the necessary adornments that would give it individuality. As a result it now possessed a Spartan plainness.

He felt Tysoe's unspoken disapproval as he ladled the soup from a white china mess-kid acting as a tureen into plain wardroom dishes, and noticed his steward's raised eyebrows at the sailcloth table runner, but he did not care. Here he was king and owed excuses to no one.

Dacres sat opposite, his face a study in composure. He said nothing after the preliminary pleasantries; it was the custom of the service never to address the captain directly, politely waiting until spoken to.

'The ship all ahoo like this,' Kydd grunted, 'how we shall get t' sea this age I can't conceive.'

'Order and tranquillity will be pleasant enough when they come,' Dacres agreed carefully, and finished his soup.

It was quite a different experience from the warm conviviality of the wardroom that Kydd had been used to, the to and fro of opinions, prejudices, desires. 'Do ye come from a seafaring family, Mr Dacres?' he asked.

'That I do, sir,' he replied, loosening. 'You may have heard of my uncle, Admiral Peyton, now in the Downs, and perhaps Captain Edward Duncan who has hopes of the position of deputy controller at the Admiralty. We pride ourselves that we have provided sea officers for England since the first Charles and . . .' He tailed off stiffly at Kydd's polite boredom.

'Tell me of y'r sea service, Mr Dacres.'

'Well, sir, I entered *Pompee* as a youngster in 1793 – we took her at Toulon, if you recall – and served in the Channel Fleet until 'ninety-five.'

'So you were at th' Glorious First o' June?'

'To my great regret, no. We were in for a repair. I – I did suffer indignity at the mutiny of 'ninety-seven. Were you drawn into that evil affair at all, sir?'

Kydd had been under discipline before the mast, accused of treason after the Nore Mutiny. He had joined the insurrection in good faith, then been carried along by events that had overwhelmed them all. But for mysterious appeals at the highest level, he should have shared his comrades' fate. He drew a breath. 'It was a bad occasion f'r us all. Have ye service in the Mediterranean?'

'Not until my commission into *Minotaur*, Captain Louis, a year ago.' *Minotaur* was a 74, part of Admiral Keith's fleet and on blockade duty.

'So all big-ship service. How do you feel about *Teazer*?' It had probably been a shock to experience the tight confines of a small vessel: the closeness of the men, the lack of privacy and the sheer diminutiveness of everything aboard.

Dacres paused. 'Small, I grant you, but I look to keen service in her. I have heard your own service has been rather eventful?' he said, with a touch of defiance.

'I was fortunate enough t' be at both Camperdown and the Nile,' Kydd said, 'and a quiet time in th' North American station.' Dacres had never smelt gun-smoke in battle and would probably learn more in *Teazer* over a few months than from years in a ship-of-the-line. He changed the subject. 'How are our Maltese hands taking t' our ways, do ye think?

I have m' hopes of 'em – they look prime sailormen, seem to find 'emselves at home.'

'I have my concerns that they may not understand orders in stress of weather, sir. Do you not think—'

'Seamen that're well led will never let ye down, Mr Dacres. They'll catch on soon enough. We're to be working closely t'gether in the future an' you'll find—'

A knock on the door and a muffled 'Captain, sir,' from outside interrupted him. It was the midshipman of the watch. 'Mr Purchet's compliments and he'd like to see Mr Dacres on deck when convenient.'

Kydd rose. 'I won't keep ye, Mr Dacres. I've no doubt we'll have another opportunity to dine together presently.' He took his seat again: the man was so utterly different, in almost every way, so at variance with his own experiences. Nevertheless it was vital he got a measure of him. As with the rest of *Teazer*'s company, time would tell.

'God rot it, what're you *about*, Mr Bowden?' roared the boatswain, stumping his way forward. The fore yard lay at a grotesque angle, and before he could reach the scene there was a savage tearing and twanging as the fore topsail split from bottom to top. The big spar dropped jerkily to the caps of the foremast. Beneath, men scattered hastily. Purchet stood stock still, gobbling with rage. Dacres hurried up from the mainmast; he and Bowden looked back aft to Kydd, their faces pale.

Kydd had been watching the dry-exercises of the sail gear and stepped forward quickly. 'Set y'r clew-garnets taut – haul in on y'r topsail clewline. Get that larb'd fore course tack 'n' sheet right in!' he bawled. This would hold the yard up while a jury lift was rigged. For some reason the lower yard lift on one side, taking most of the weight of the heavy spar, had given way and the inevitable had happened. The only saving grace was that there were no men on the yardarm and they were still safely at anchor. Possibly the cordage had rotted in the storehouse. Incidents like this might happen again; the sooner faults were bowled out the better. 'Mr Purchet!' he ordered. 'See what it is an' report t' me.'

Kydd was afire with eagerness to see *Teazer* at sea, cutting a feather in that deep blue expanse and off to the glories that would assuredly be hers. But he could not risk it with an untried ship and crew. He jammed his hands into his pockets and paced up and down.

By early afternoon they had succeeded in loosing and furling sail on both masts without incident; each yard had been braced up sharp on each tack, halliards and slablines, martnets and leechlines, all had been hauled and veered, run through their various operating ranges.

Stations had been stepped through also, for wearing, tacking, setting and striking sail, and Kydd dared hope that the moment when *Teazer* was set free for her true purpose was drawing close.

'Noon tomorrow, I do believe, Mr Dacres!' he called, when it became clear at last that the ship's company was pulling together as one.

The following morning there was something in the air: an undercurrent of anticipation, tension, excitement. Exercises now had meaning and significance – the age-old exhilaration felt when a ship was making ready for sea, preparing for that final moment when the land and its distractions was cast aside and the ship and the souls she bore within her entered Neptune's realm.

Kydd felt in his heart that they were ready: men were familiar with their stations, drill at the sails was now acceptable, gear had been tested. He had some anxieties: the master was elderly and his navigational skill was still unknown, and the Maltese seamen appeared capable but would they remain steady under fire?

Yet more than any other worry he had one crucial concern. Would *he* measure up? Or was there to be this day a blunder that would set all Malta laughing? Or, worse, a casting of *Teazer* ashore in a helpless wreck . . . 'Mr Dacres, if th' hold is stowed, I believe we shall hazard a short cruise t' try the vessel. Pipe the hands to unmoor ship in one hour, if you will.'

The die was cast. Watching the preparations for sea, Kydd tried to appear impassive. He sniffed the wind: a playful southerly with a hint of east. They were going to be let off easily in their first venture to sea, just a matter of slipping from the mooring buoy and at the right moment loosing sail to take up on the wind on the larboard tack and shape course for the open sea.

It should be straightforward enough, but Grand Harbour was dotted with sail and no place to be aimlessly straying about. The sooner they opened deep sea the better.

Kydd heard the squealing of blocks as the boats were hoisted and saw the decks being readied fore and aft: braces, sheets, tacks, halliards – these were laid along clear for running; the helm was put right over on each side to prove the tiller lines, and all the other familiar tasks, large and small, that were essential before proceeding to sea, were completed.

Activity lessened. Then, finally, the shriek of Purchet's call, quickly followed by Laffin's, told *Teazer* that every man aboard should take station leaving harbour. There was the sound of a rush of feet, which gradually died away into silence. Dacres was in position at the foot of the mainmast, Bowden at the foremast, groups of men ready at the pin-rails looking warily aft. From right forward the knot of men on the foredeck at the moorings straightened and looked back expectantly.

Kydd's pulse raced. 'I have th' ship, Mr Bonnici,' he said, formally, to the master next to him. If there was to be any mistake it would be his alone. 'Lay aloft t' make sail, the topmen!' he roared. Men swarmed swiftly at his command.

He had already decided to move out under topsails alone, with staysails and jibs and the big mainsail – on *Teazer*, the large fore and aft sail abaft the mainmast. 'Lay out an' loose!' he bawled, and the topmen moved out along the yards, casting off the gaskets that held up the sails tightly. 'Stand by – let fall!'

It was a heart-stopping time: while sail cascaded down from fore and main they had to slip the mooring cable at just the right time to catch the wind and release the vessel for a surging start in the right direction. 'Man tops'l sheets 'n' halliards,' he bellowed to those on deck. 'An' clap on t' the braces!' A last glance aloft and alow, then: 'Let go!'

The crowning moment! The slip rope slithered free through the mooring buoy ring and *Teazer* was now legally at sea!

'Sheet home: brace up, y' sluggards!' Kydd roared, fighting to keep the exhilaration from his voice. *Teazer's* bow even as he watched was paying off to leeward, her bowsprit sliding past the long line of ramparts across the water. 'Haul taut!' There was a perceptible heel as her canvas caught and the headsails were hardened in. He snatched a glance over the side. They were making way: *Teazer* was outward bound!

A ponderous merchantman began a turn dead ahead and Kydd's heart skipped a beat. 'Two points t' starb'd,' he snapped at the helm. This was taking them perilously close to the castellated point under their lee but he guessed that the shore would be steep to there and a quick glance at Bonnici reassured him that this was so.

Teazer picked up speed as they passed to leeward of the ungainly merchantman and before he knew it they were clear of the point. The brig had a fine, uncluttered view forward and Kydd shaped course seaward with increasing confidence.

Excitement rose in him as the swell from the open sea caused the first regular heaving and the deck became alive under his feet. On either side grim fortresses guarding the entrance slipped past until the coast fell away and *Teazer* – his very own ship – felt the salt spray on her cheeks and knew for the first time the eternal freedom of the ocean.

She was a sea-witch! Her lines were perfect – her willing urge as she breasted the waves, and eagerness in tacking about, would have melted the heart of the most calloused old tar. Kydd's happiness overflowed as, reluctantly, they returned to moorings in the last of the light.

But there were things that must be done. He had learned much of *Teazer*'s ways – every ship was an individual, with character and appeal so different from another. As with a new-married couple, it was a time to explore and discover, to understand and take joy, and Kydd knew that impatience had no place in this.

There was not so much to do: the lead of a stay here, the turning of a deadeye there, redoubled work with holystone and paintbrush. His mind was busy: the ship's tasks included, among other things, the protection of trade and it would be expected that he begin showing the flag at some point, the ideal excuse for an undemanding cruise to shake down the ship's company.

Kydd found time to go in search of cabin stores: it was unthinkable for a captain to go 'bare navy' – ship's rations only – for there would be occasions when he must entertain visitors. It seemed, however, that 'table money' for the purpose of official entertainment was the prerogative of a flag officer alone, and therefore he must provide for himself. Fortunately he had been careful with his prize-money won previously, knowing that prospects of more were chancy at best.

He was no epicure and had no firm idea of the scale of purchases necessary, but he knew one who did. The jolly-boat was sent back for Tysoe, who had been previously in the employ of a distinguished post-captain. It was an expensive but illuminating afternoon, which left Kydd wondering whether the cherries in brandy and a keg of anchovies were absolutely necessary on top of the currant jelly and alarming amount of pickles; Kydd hoped fervently that the wine in caseloads would not turn in the increasing heat of early summer, but he trusted Tysoe.

Kydd took the opportunity as well to find some articles of decoration: the bare cabin was stiff and unfriendly – it needed something of himself. Diffidently he selected one or two miniatures and a rather handsome, only slightly foxed picture of an English rustic scene. These, with a few table ornaments and cloths, made a striking improvement – the silver would have to wait: his substance was reducing at a dismaying rate. Later, if he had time, he would do something about his tableware. If only his sister Cecilia were on hand . . .

*   *   *

There was no one of naval consequence to notice the little brig-of-war as she slipped her moorings and made for the open sea. No one to discern the bursting pride of her commander, who stood four-square on her quarterdeck in his finest uniform, her brand-new pennant snapping in the breeze, her men grave and silent at their stations as they sailed past the bastions of the last fortress of Malta, outward bound on her first war voyage.

Kydd remained standing, unwilling to break the spell: around him the ship moved to sea watches, the special sea-duty men standing down as those on regular watch closed up for their duty and others went below until the turn of the watch. The boatswain checked the tautness of rigging around the deck while the *ting-tinging* of the bell forward brought up the other watch, the shouts of a petty officer testily mustering his crew sounding above the swash and thump of their progress – it was all so familiar but, at this moment, so infinitely precious.

'Mr Bonnici,' Kydd called, to the figure in the old-fashioned three-cornered hat standing mute and still, staring forward.

The master turned slowly, the shrewd eyes unseeing. 'Sir?'

'I, er—' It was not important. They both had their remembrances and he left the man to his. 'No matter. Please – carry on.'

This was what it was to have succeeded! To have reached the impossible summit before which paled every other experience the world had to offer. He, Thomas Kydd of Guildford, of all men, was now captain of a ship-of-war and monarch of all he surveyed.

A deep, shuddering sigh came from his very depths. His eyes took in the sweet curve of the deck-line as it swept forward to the sturdy bow, the pretty bobbing of the fore spars in the following seas and the delicate tracery of rigging against the bright sky – and the moment burned itself into his soul.

In a trance of reverence his eyes roamed the deck – *his* deck. Within *Teazer*'s being were over eighty souls, whose lives were in his charge, to command as he desired. And each was bound to obey him, whatever he uttered and without question, for now all without exception were in subjection below him and none aboard could challenge his slightest order. It was a heady feeling: if he took it into his mind to carry *Teazer* to the North Pole every man must follow and endeavour to take the vessel there; in the very next moment, should he desire, he could bellow the orders that would clear the lower decks and muster every man aboard before him, awaiting his next words, and not one dare ask why.

The incredible thought built in his mind as his ship sailed deeper into the sea. Controlling his expression, he turned to Dacres and snapped, 'Two points t' starboard!'

'Two points – aye aye, sir,' Dacres said anxiously, and turned on the quartermaster. 'Ah, nor'-east b' north.'

The quartermaster came to an alert and growled at the man on the wheel, 'Helm up – steer nor'-east b' north.' While the helmsman spun the wheel and glanced warily up at the leech of the foresail the quartermaster snatched out the slate of course details from the binnacle and scrawled the new heading. Returning it he took out the traverse board and inspected it. At the next bell the line of pegs from its centre would duly reflect the change. He glanced down at the compass again, squinting at the card lazily swimming past the lubber's line until it slowed and stopped. 'Steady on course nor'-east b' north, sir.'

'Sir, on course nor'-east b' north,' Dacres reported

respectfully, nodding to the expectant mate-of-the-watch who hurried forward, bawling for the watch-on-deck. There would now be work at the braces, tacks and sheets to set the sails trimmed round to the new course before the watch could settle down.

'Very well,' Kydd said, in a bored tone but fighting desperately to control a fit of the giggles at the sight of the serious faces of the men around him under the eye of their new captain, who, no doubt, had a serious reason for his order. He had laid a course to raise Cape Passero and this indulgence would throw them off, but perhaps he should wait a decent interval before he resumed the old one.

They had made good time and landfall would be soon, an easy leg from Malta north-east to the tip of Sicily across the Malta Channel, with a second leg into the open Mediterranean to the east before completing the triangle back to port. But it was also a voyage in a state of war: at any time predatory sail could heave above the horizon.

The log was hove once more: their speed was gratifyingly constant and allowing for the prevailing current would give a precise time of landfall. In this straightforward exercise Kydd had no doubt of his own skills and now felt Bonnici was capable also. But the time arrived and there was no far-off misty grey smear of land dead ahead.

'We'll give it another hour on this course, Mr Bonnici,' Kydd said. He had gone over in his mind the simple calculations and could find no fault. Even his little dog-leg on a whim had been taken into account and—

'*Laaaand hoooo!* Land two – three points t' weather!' the lookout at the main royal masthead hailed excitedly, pointing over the larboard bow.

'Luff up an' touch her,' Kydd ordered. Although this land could not yet be seen from the deck, on the line of bearing reported, the cape would not be reached on this tack. Yet it *was* the cape. How was it possible?

Going about, *Teazer* laid her bowsprit toward the undistinguished promontory, which Kydd easily recognised. Already he had his suspicions. 'Lay me south o' the Portopaio roads,' he told Bonnici.

Obediently *Teazer* made her way to another headland a mile or two from Cape Passero, rounding to a mile distant from the scrubby, nondescript cliffs. It was a well-known point of navigation – Kydd had passed this way before as part of Nelson's fleet – and the exact bearing of the tip of the one on the other was known. However, the bearing by *Teazer*'s compass had strayed a considerable way easterly, much more than could be accounted for by local variation. The instrument could no longer be trusted, neither it nor the secondary one.

There were obvious culprits and men at the conn were searched for iron implements. Nothing. Kydd questioned whether he should have taken more care over the compasses before going to sea. Some held that not only the earth varied in its faithfulness in revealing magnetic north but that the ship's ironwork had a part to play in deceiving the mariner, but how this could be dealt with they did not say.

There were only two explanations for the delay in their landfall: that Sicily had changed its position, or that their measure of distance run was incorrect. And as the latter was more likely and was taken by one means alone, the log, it was this that had to be at fault.

'Mr Purchet, I'll have the log-line faked out an' measure the knots, if y' please.' Speed was arrived at by casting astern a weighted triangular piece of wood, the log-ship, that was carried astern as the ship sailed on. The line flew off from a reel held overhead and at the end of a thirty-second period it was 'nipped' to see how far it had gone out, indicated by the number of knots in the line that had been run off. As the ratio of thirty seconds was to an hour (really twenty-eight, to allow for reaction times) so the length of line was for one knot – at forty-seven feet and three inches.

The carpenter's folding rule was wielded industriously. And, without exception, the knots fell close enough to their appointed place.

Kydd stood back, trying to think it through.

'Sir – the glass?' suggested Bowden.

It was unlikely: the twenty-eight-second sand-glass was a common enough object and the grains were specially parched to prevent clogging. 'Go below an' check it against the chronometer,' Kydd ordered doubtfully.

While this was done he set *Teazer* about and they headed safely off shore in darkening seas; during the night he and Bonnici would take careful astronomical observations. Compasses were inaccurate at the best of times but it was possible that when they had adjusted theirs in Malta harbour they had been within range of the influence of iron on the seabed, perhaps an old cannon.

Bowden returned. 'No question about it, sir. This is a thirty-three-second glass,' he said, trying to hide the smugness in his voice.

Kydd looked accusingly at Bonnici, who reddened. 'Er, a Venetian hour-glass it mus' be, sir,' the master mumbled. 'We take fr'm the Arsenale when we store th' ship.'

But it was nothing that could not be put right, thought Kydd, with relief, thankful that the heavens had been restored to their rightful place and his ship sped on unharmed into the warm night.

Free from the routine of night watch-keeping, Kydd could take no advantage of the luxury of an all-night-in: excitement and anticipation coursed through him making sleep impossible. Then came memories: that lonely, exhausted night as a press-gang victim, new on board; the first time he had stood watch as a green and terrified officer-of-the-watch – and the bitter time following when he had felt he could never belong in the company of gentlemen. And now he was past it all and elevated above every one of them. Restless and unsleeping, he longed for morning.

At long last he heard the muffled thump of feet on deck and lay back, seeing in his mind's eye the activity of hands turned out and irritable petty officers urging them on to meet the break of day at quarters. He remained for a few minutes longer in his cot, aware that voices in the after end of the ship were respectfully subdued in deference to his august being.

As the early light strengthened he came on deck. Only *his* word of a clear horizon would be sufficient to allow the men to be stood down from quarters and go about their day. He acknowledged Dacres's salute and gave the word, savouring the instant activity it produced while he breathed deeply of the zest of a sea dawn.

Reluctantly he went for his breakfast, to be eaten in solitary splendour. He took his time, knowing that his presence would be unwelcome in the scurry of striking down hammocks, lashing them tightly and sending them up to the nettings, the domestics of the evening mess-deck now to assume a martial readiness.

A discreet knock: it was the carpenter, duly reporting inches only of water showing in the well. Then came Dacres, with a question about employment for the hands in the forenoon. The rhythms of the morning took hold without him and he was free to attend to his own concerns.

Later he ventured on deck; Dacres moved to leeward of the quarterdeck, as was the custom. Kydd, keyed up with feeling, acknowledged him politely, then began strolling down the deck.

The effect was instant: on either side men fell silent and stiffened, ceasing their work to straighten and touch their hats. He ducked under the main staysail and the men on the other side, tailing on to a jib sheet, lost their hauling cadence and came to an untidy stop. The petty officer in charge looked at Kydd warily, clearly at a loss.

It was no good. Kydd knew full well what was happening: there had to be some pressing reason why the captain, next down from God, should march the length of the vessel to see them – it could only mean trouble. He had to face the fact that, as captain, he was not at liberty to wander about his own ship as he pleased. Every movement, intentional or careless, had significance for the men, who would now be watching him as the creatures of the jungle regarded the pacing lion.

'Carry on,' he told the petty officer, and made his way back to the quarterdeck. The next time he wanted to stretch his legs and enjoy the sights forward on his pretty ship he would need to make some excuse to have the master or carpenter with him.

On impulse, Kydd crossed to the boatswain. 'Mr Purchet. I'm not comfortable with th' play we're seeing in the main topmast crosstree, th' t' gallant mast in the cap.'

'I'll take a look, sir,' Purchet said, glancing up.

'No, thank 'ee,' Kydd said quickly. 'I've a mind t' see myself.'

He handed his hat and coat to an astonished Dacres and swung easily into the rigging, mounting with the fluid agility of the topman he had been those years ago. He climbed around the futtock shrouds, ignoring the startled looks of two seamen working in the maintop, and on up to the cross-trees.

The lookout could not believe the evidence of his own eyes and stared at Kydd as he heaved himself up and on to the trestle-tree. Kydd hung on in the lively movement, muscles aglow, and took his fill of the lovely symmetry of *Teazer*'s foreshortened length far below, hissing through the seas in a sinuous line of foam-flecks. After making a pretence of inspecting the topgallant mast as it passed through the cap he then shaded his eyes and looked away to the horizon.

An immensity of sparkling sea stretched before them as *Teazer* sped eastwards into emptiness, mainland Greece more than a hundred leagues distant and nothing ahead but the unchanging even line where sea met sky. It was a breathtaking sight from this height, one that in times past he had always thrilled to.

Reluctantly, he started to descend, then became aware that the clean line of horizon was broken. Eyes honed from a hundred watches scanning into nothing soon picked it up: a speck of paleness occasionally flashing brilliant white as the sun caught it.

'*Sail hoooo!*' he roared to the deck below. '*Fine on th' weather bow.*' His hail to the deck caused the lookout beside him to jerk with surprise. Kydd then saw, in place of the sharp angularity of the usual Mediterranean lateener, the more blocky indication of square sail. '*Square sail, an' studding athwart!*'

This was not a trading felucca or any other of the myriad small craft native to this part of the great inland sea: it was of significant size and European built; perhaps a transport for Napoleon's lost army – or a hunting frigate . . .

Realising he had an urgent need to be back on deck, he reached out for a topmast backstay and swung into space. In seconds he had slid hand-over-hand down the backstay, arriving with a light jump on his own quarterdeck.

He was conscious of eyes on him: this was now the classic dilemma faced by every smaller ship, to sail towards a poten-tial prize or retreat from what could be a more powerful enemy. To play safe would be to put up the helm and slink away, but that would be to throw away any chance of securing their first prize. Yet if he pressed on to investigate and it turned out to be one of the French admiral Ganteaume's fast frigates then *Teazer* stood little chance.

'Course t' intercept, Mr Bonnici,' he snapped. He had a bounden duty to stop and investigate every sail. If things turned out against them, it couldn't be helped.

'Clear for action, sir?' Awkwardly Dacres held out Kydd's cocked hat and coat, which Kydd accepted but did not put on, mindful of his ruined cotton stockings and tar streaks on his hands.

From the main deck, the top-hamper of the chase was not yet visible. 'No. We'll have time enough later. Report when he's topsails clear, I'll be below.'

It seemed an age before the report finally arrived, but Kydd had already guessed the chase must be a smaller vessel or a merchantman that had decided to make a run for it – and they were slowly overhauling it. There was always the chance that it was leading him on into a trap, and with a new ship and untried crew the consequences could be serious – but it was unlikely.

When he went up on deck he deliberately left his sword on its hook below as a sign that he did not expect to fight. 'Chase bears ahead nine miles, sir,' Dacres said importantly. Hull-up, the ship was clawing to windward in a losing battle with the brisk breeze; *Teazer* had bowlines in their bridles drawing out the leading edge of her courses and topsails and was slashing along in exhilarating fashion. The end could not be in doubt.

At long cannon-shot Kydd ordered a gun to windward. It took another before the vessel set topsails a-fly in surrender and came up into the wind. With the greatest satisfaction he set *Teazer* hove to a little to windward.

The ship resembled the Marseille traders that Kydd knew so well from blockade duty off Toulon, and if this was so it was almost certainly a French supply transport. A flutter of white and gold jerked up her mizzen halliards.

'Naples,' muttered Purchet. 'Won't save 'em,' he added happily. Kydd was not so sure: Naples had been occupied by the French, as had Sicily, but as far as he knew the Bourbon Kingdom of the Two Sicilies still existed in exile and was an ally. As well, of course, a vessel could hoist any colours it chose.

'Call away the cutter, an' I'll take a dozen men.'

'You'll—?'

'Yes, Mr Dacres. You're in command. I don't have t' tell you, any sign o' trouble you're to run out our guns, show 'em our force.' It was not at all usual for a captain to perform a boarding himself, but this was not a job for the inexperienced.

'Aye aye, sir.'

The cutter pulled strongly towards the merchant ship. Stirk, forward with bared cutlass, would be the first to board. Bowden sat set-faced next to him, other seamen ready close by.

The ship was larger than *Teazer*, four hundred tons at least and well laden, wallowing weightily in beam seas. There was something strange, almost menacing, about the drab, dark-stained timbered vessel. Kydd gave an involuntary shudder and was guiltily glad that Stirk was going over the bulwark first. They neared and prepared to hook on: now would be the most likely time for a line of vengeful French soldiers to stand up suddenly at the deck-line with muskets trained, but only a row of bored, dark-featured Mediterranean sailors looked down on them.

Stirk seized the flimsy rope-ladder and with a snarl swarmed up and on to the vessel's deck. The others followed quickly and Kydd found himself confronting a short and red-faced individual. The master, he guessed.

'*Le capitaine?*' Kydd growled, pleased that his hours with Renzi at French lessons in the dog-watches were now paying off. But French was virtually unknown in the eastern Mediterranean and the master shook his head angrily. Kydd mimed the riffling of papers and waited patiently for him to return with them.

The man's hands trembled as he handed them over and his face showed as much anxiety as bluster. Kydd inspected the papers, looking for a bill of lading, but all the papers he held were in an impenetrable foreign language.

'*Sbrigati, abbiamo una fretta del diavolo,*' the man burst out angrily.

Kydd looked at him in surprise, then handed the papers to Bowden, who studied them in puzzlement. 'Er, sorry, sir, I've no idea – I think it's a form of Italian.'

'Where – you – go?' Kydd asked slowly. Suspicions were forming: the unusually wide cargo-hatch covers, the heavy stay tackles still triced in place along the yards . . . 'Stand to, you there,' he growled at his party, some of whom clearly shared his unease. He snapped, 'What – is – your – cargo?'

The man's eyes flickered once then he drew himself up and shouted venomously at Kydd, '*Una fregata da ghiaccio! Capisci? Ghi-acc-io!*'

There was a definite air of anxiety now and Kydd's suspicions hardened. 'We're going t' take a look at his cargo,' he called to his men. The course of the vessel was fair for the deserts of north Africa – and Alexandria: the desperate French would seize on any means to deliver cannon to their beleaguered army.

Thrusting past, Kydd strode across. The hatches were well secured: battens nailed down firmly over canvas sealed the contents of the hold and the little hutch that normally allowed entrance to the hold was nowhere to be seen.

'Get a fire axe!' Kydd told Stirk, who found one at the ship's side. The master's eyes widened in horror as he saw what was happening and he threw himself at the hatch, shouting hoarsely. The axe splintered the first batten as he tried to wrestle it away. 'Carry on,' Kydd barked. Two seamen forcibly held back the frantic master.

Using the pointed end of the axe Stirk levered aside the battens on one side, then dealt with the opposite side. The master's struggles ceased and he now moaned loudly. Kydd looked warily at the rest of the crew, but they stood stolidly as if the events were none of their business.

'Quickly now,' Kydd urged. The top of the hatch was merely planks that were smartly lifted away but under – there was straw. Nothing but straw to the very top of the hatch.

Kydd told Stirk to stab down with his cutlass point. Such a heavy cargo – it could not be straw. Stirk's thrust brought the unmistakable sharp clash of metal. He tried in another place – the same betraying clang.

The master now fell to his knees, imploring, sobbing. '*Ghiaccio! Per amor di Dio – ghi-acc-io!*'

'Clear th' straw!' Kydd knew his voice sounded weak, nervous. The straw was quickly pulled away to reveal an expanse of shiny metal sheeting. 'Open it,' he said thickly.

Seeing no easy way Stirk brought the axe to bear on it, and began to hack a hole through to see into the interior. The smash of the axe in the stillness sounded against the moaning of the master. Then Stirk fell back abruptly and pointed to the hole. Glistening through the rent torn in the metal was tons and tons of ice and snow.

Kydd stared at the sight as the hot sun began to melt the top layer. He was completely at a loss. Then he heard Bowden mumble, 'I did hear once, sir, as how there are ships that bring ice from Mount Etna to the tables of the Barbary princes . . .'

'Then why th' devil did you not tell me, y' bloody villain?' Kydd snarled.

In the seclusion of his great cabin Kydd smiled wryly. The aggrieved master had been mollified with silver and a hastily scrawled pass, but it had been a less than glorious first encounter for *Teazer*.

Still, as they beat further to the east the ship was pulling together well; his insistence on daily practice at the guns was paying off and small tokens of homely sea life were making an appearance. A dog-vane cunningly crafted of cork and feathers on each shroud to indicate the wind direction for the benefit of the quartermaster, an elaborate turk's head knot worked on the centre spoke of the wheel so the helmsman could find the midships position by feel – all reflected an increasing pride and respect in the little ship.

Kydd quickly retrieved his equilibrium and when *Teazer* had reached far enough into the eastern Mediterranean and needed to put about for the remaining leg of returning to Malta he was sincerely regretful. The watch-on-deck was now, without being told, taking the trouble to flemish down lines neatly after sail trimming and he had seen several sailors pointing rope, an unnecessary but most seamanlike ornamenting of a rope's end in place of the usual twine whipping.

'Mr Dacres!' he called.

The officer came up, touching his hat. 'Sir?'

'I have it in mind t' grant a make 'n' mend for all hands this afternoon – make today a rope-yarn Sunday, as it were. Did y' have anything planned for 'em?'

Dacres frowned, but could not object. A make and mend was given to allow seamen time to make repairs to their working rig and draw slops from the purser to fashion clothes. It also meant that they could sit on the foredeck in the sun gossiping amiably while they sewed, out of reach of an irascible boatswain or others wanting men for duty about ship. But Kydd knew the value of allowing the men time to add individuality to their rig and their ship: later it would translate to ownership, pride in themselves and their sea home.

Thus it was that after the grog issue and noon meal *Teazer*'s men set out their gear for an agreeable afternoon.

'Mr Dacres, a turn about the decks?' Kydd removed his hat ostentatiously and placed it firmly under his arm, a sign that he was off duty; Dacres reluctantly followed suit and they paced forward slowly. The decks were crowded and Kydd was careful to step round the industrious; others drew back respectfully.

There were some with the gift of the needle and they were turning their talents to account for their messmates, a favour that no doubt would be returned in grog. To Kydd, it was not odd to see hardened seamen deftly turn a seam in a smart jacket complete with white piping, or crafting exquisite buttons from bone, but it might just extend Dacres's education.

Some sailors told salty yarns or closed their eyes in the simple luxury of the sun, others busied themselves at whalebone scrimshaw: fine pieces would fetch a good price ashore. At the bow, pairs of seamen plaited each other's pigtails – Kydd's own tie-mate had been Nicholas Renzi.

Teazer was a small ship with tight living conditions and it was essential her company quickly settled into amicable sea routines: the process, Kydd was pleased to see, seemed already well under way.

Chapter 4

'Damme, but you took your time, Captain,' General Pigot grumbled but Kydd detected a certain satisfaction. 'So, we can account the good ship *Teazer* one of our company, hey?'

'We are ready f'r operations now, sir,' Kydd said carefully.

It was a delicate matter: his direct allegiance was to his commanding admiral, yet he was on detached service from the fleet and in the service of Malta, now governed by a civil power. In turn the civil commissioner would rely for military matters on the garrison general, Pigot. Thus, in elliptical fashion, Kydd would in effect report to Pigot – but he had no wish to become a creature of the Army with its ignorance of the sea and its perils.

The general looked at Kydd speculatively. 'T' be quite honest with ye, Captain, I didn't think you had it in you to get your ship up to scratch in time. What is it? A brig?'

'Aye, sir – a brig-sloop.' Then Kydd added warmly, 'She mounts eight six-pounders a side, an' more besides for close-in work.'

Pigot nodded slowly. 'Well, as long as ye don't come up against a bigger,' he said, as if to himself. He raised his eyes to meet Kydd's. 'I'd be obliged if you'd wait on me in the morning. I may have a service for you.'

'Now, I'd like you to get a sense o' how important these dispatches are, Mr Kydd,' Pigot said, leaning forward seriously. 'Our landings in Egypt are bein' hotly disputed – if Johnny Crapaud gets resupply it'll turn the situation right round.'

He looked at Kydd shrewdly. 'This is news of the French admiral, Ganteaume. A powerful crowd o' battleships an' such sailed from Leghorn to God knows where. Be a good chap an' let your Admiral Warren know about him just as quick as y' can.'

There had been a landing in Egypt by the British under Abercrombie with the objective of dealing with the still-potent French Army stranded there by Nelson's dazzling victory at the Nile. Any threat to its lines of support would be serious indeed. Kydd stuffed the dispatches crisply into the satchel. 'Aye aye, sir. I sail afore sunset.'

The rest of the day was needed to stow last-minute stores and water. This was going to be no simple exercise: *Teazer* would shortly be embarking on a deep-sea voyage to face all weathers and whatever enemy lay outside. What was not aboard when they sailed could not be obtained until they returned after their mission.

With the men below at their midday meal, Kydd called his officers to his cabin. 'I'll not have you in ignorance of th' ship's movements,' he said, trying not to sound pompous. 'It's straightforward enough, gentlemen. Dispatches – th' French under Ganteaume are out an' tryin' t' supply their army in Egypt. If they find they c'n beat us, I don't have to tell ye, it's as if the Nile never happened an' they have a royal road to India. We have t' rendezvous with Admiral Sir John Borlase Warren an' advise him in time.

'Mr Bonnici, show us y'r charts.' There was a new chart of the Alexandria coast by the Admiralty Hydrographic Office, the first Kydd had seen, but the others were of questionable reliability.

'Th' reigning wind's fair fr'm the north-west, o' course, and we'll make good time – I expect t' be at the rendezvous in five or six days at most. I shall be pressing *Teazer* hard, an' I want you all to be watching f'r strains aloft.'

He thought for a space, then added, 'Were we to fall in with an enemy, m' first duty is to the dispatches an' I will not offer battle. But we might have t' fight our way clear, so . . .' He tailed off at the blank faces. Then he understood – all this was so much a waste of words: the men knew full well what was to be expected of them and their ship without his needing to spell it out, but were too polite to say so.

He dismissed them, and remained alone in his cabin. It was the first proper mission of his first command and failure or mistakes were unthinkable. It was coming home to him just what being a captain meant: there was not a soul he could talk to, seek advice from or even reveal his feelings to about the momentousness of this occasion.

Other thoughts jostled. Now he had all of the responsibility but at the same time all of the power. He could give orders for anything within reason but unless it was the right order . . . Where before things had just happened, which his responsibility was to conform to and support, now it would be his role to think about and *make* those things happen or nothing would. In the past if he failed in a duty it would be a matter of reproof. Now it would be the ship and her company who suffered calamitous consequences.

Anxieties flooded in: supposing he had overlooked a vital task and *Teazer* suddenly found herself helpless before the guns of an enemy? What if a strange man-o'-war loomed up and he had forgotten to give out the secret recognition signal to the signals crew in time? And had he taken aboard sufficient of the right sort of stores, enough water, powder, charts – were they wise to trust in Kydd, the raw new captain of *Teazer*, to get the crucial dispatches into the right hands?

He tried to throw off the demons. Rationally there was no future in worry, in formless anxiety, and it was vital to keep a strong, calm manner in front of the men. He reached for composure. Then he found Renzi's reassuring image materialise before him. What would be his closest friend's advice, his calm and ordered appreciation of his position?

He saw Renzi's expression assume a saintly sorrow, as it always did when there was a hard truth. And he knew what it was before the vision faded. He was the captain: there was no other alternative than that he must find the strength, courage and intelligence from within himself.

'Let go!' HMS *Teazer*'s last bond with the land was cast off; her jack forward was struck and her largest ensign, the blue of the Mediterranean Fleet, soared up her main halliards just as the crack of her salute to General Pigot sent gun-smoke wreathing agreeably across Kydd's nostrils.

In the brisk southerly, *Teazer* leaned to the wind, eased cautiously to the north-east in the busy harbour and made for the open water. The following seas, with their swelling rhythm from astern, seemed to urge the ship on to adventures ahead.

'Mr Dacres!' Kydd called across the quarterdeck. 'Set sea watches, starbowlines to muster.' From now on there would always be at least half of *Teazer*'s complement closed up on watch, ready to meet any challenge at every hour of day and night until they made port again.

He stood looking on as the watch mustered. The petty officers were consulting their lists and jollying the tardy to their stations. It was satisfying to feel the familiar routines establish themselves and Kydd found it difficult to keep a stern appearance.

He saw Stirk approaching. With a grin that could best be described as huge, he said, 'Ready t' scale the guns, sir.'

Kydd smothered an answering smile. 'Carry on, Mr Stirk.' The six-pounders had been in store at the arsenal long enough for rust to form in the bores and scaling by dry firing would scour them clear. Soon the flat *blang* of the reduced charges sounded along the deck.

He looked across at Dacres. 'You have th' ship. Course east b' south, all plain sail.'

As simple as that! He brightened at the thought of never having to stand a watch again, instead taking charge or handing over whenever he felt inclined. 'Aye aye, sir,' Dacres murmured, and went to the conn.

Kydd knew he should go below and start on the work that was waiting in neat piles on his desk but it was too exhilarating on deck with the regular heave of the waves under the keel and their stately move forward, the boundless blue expanse of sea, flecked with white under a perfect Mediterranean sun.

The log was cast and the result pegged on the traverse board: nine and a half knots. Given the lateness in the day, he would leave until tomorrow the agreeable task of exploring

Teazer's sailing qualities and quirks to bring out the best in her. The southerly was veering more to the west but holding steady – they should have a soldier's wind in the morning.

Eight bells, the first dog-watch. The decks cleared as men went below for grog and their supper. It would be a cheerful conclusion to the day for them and Kydd could picture the jollity as they settled in with new chums, shipmates who would share with them the dangers aloft and in the fighting for their lives. The talk would be of their new ship, the calibre of their officers, their prospects for their voyaging and, the most important topic of all, their new captain.

Alone on deck but for the lookouts and the small group at the helm, Kydd felt even more the peculiar isolation of his position, the utter absence of any he could relax with in the same way. This was the hidden price for the fulfilment of his ambitions. In the gathering dusk he became aware of the flash of eyes in the cluster by the helm: they were affronted by the captain's continued presence on deck, his implied lack of trust in them. Kydd turned and went below.

'Oh, sir,' said Tysoe reprovingly, 'you never sent word. Your supper is no longer hot. Shall I tell the steward—'

His cabin table was spread. 'No, thank 'ee,' Kydd said: the galley fire was probably out by now. He had forgotten the behind-the-scenes activity that accompanied even the smallest domestic want of the captain. 'Open a claret an' I'll take a glass. The rest t' go to the midshipmen's berth.' The small gesture might help to allay the anxieties of the two new faces going to sea for the first time, perhaps even hinting that their captain was of the human species.

He sat alone by the light of a candle, chewing tepid cutlets and sad greens, feeling by turns dispirited and exalted. Hammocks were piped down – he had ordered that for tonight going to quarters could be overlooked – and the watch below turned in. After Tysoe had cleared away, Kydd pulled over the pile of papers and set to. A knock on the door an hour or so later interrupted his concentration. It was Laffin, with the thick-set figure of another seaman in the shadows behind carrying a dim lanthorn.

'Sir. Galley fire doused, lights are out fore 'n' aft, two inches in th' well, no men in bilboes,' Laffin said impassively. As a boatswain's mate in a sloop he took the duties of a master-at-arms, which included ship's security.

'Thank ye, Laffin,' Kydd said. These reports, made to him as captain, allowed the silent hours officially to begin.

'Er, do you . . .' For some reason he was reluctant to let Laffin go. '. . . go an' prove the lookouts,' he finished lamely.

'Aye aye, sir,' the seaman said stolidly.

Kydd put aside the paperwork and retired for the night, but he lay awake in his cot, mind racing as he reviewed the day, senses jerked to full alert by every unknown noise in the new ship, then lulled as his seaman's ear resolved them into patterns falling in with the regular motions of the invisible ocean.

The wind had freshened in the night and the morning dawned bright and boisterous, white horses on a following deep blue sea. *Teazer*'s sturdy bowsprit rose and fell. Kydd was concerned to notice the foredeck flood several times, even in these moderate conditions, the water sluicing aft before it was shed to the scuppers – with the working of the vessel's seams this would translate into wet hammocks for those below.

He heard a tinny sound above the sea noises: a young sailor at the main hatchway was enthusiastically beating away at an odd-looking small drum, breaking into the ordered calm of the early morning.

'Wha—'

'Quarters, sir,' said Bowden, hiding a smile. As master's mate, he was taking watches opposite Dacres and had the deck. Kydd wondered at his confidence: he remembered his own first watch on deck as an officer and the nervous apprehension he had felt.

But that drum would have to go: the martial thunder of *Tenacious*'s marine drums left no doubt about their purpose – the men to close up at their guns to meet the dawn prepared for what the new day would reveal.

With no enemy sail sighted, quarters were stood down, hammocks piped up and the men went to breakfast. There was no need for Kydd to remain on deck but he found it hard to stand aside from the routine working of the ship. He had been an intimate part of it since he had first gone to sea, and particularly since he had become an officer.

He turned abruptly and went below to his cabin. If he chose, there was nothing to stop him remaining in the comforts of his great cabin for the entire day – but then he would not *know* what was going on on deck. 'Thank ye, Tysoe,' he said, as the man brought in coffee. As routines became evident Kydd's needs were being intelligently anticipated: Kydd blessed his choice those years ago of Tysoe as servant.

An unexpected surge of contentment surfaced as he gazed through his stern windows at the swelling seas. *Teazer* had a pleasing motion, predictable and rarely hesitating – that was the sign of sea-kindliness: neither crank nor tender, she would lean before the buffets of wind and sea and smoothly return to a stable uprightness.

Today he would discover more of his men and his ship. Dacres was the most imperative task: he was the entire officer corps of *Teazer* and, in practical terms, a deputy-captain. Kydd needed a right-hand man – but, more than that, someone he could confide in, trust, one with whom he could not only mull over ideas and plans but whom he could place in hazardous situations and discover how far he could rely on him. The trouble was that Dacres's studiously polite but reserved manner made him difficult to approach.

As he finished his coffee, the thumping of bare feet sounded loud on the deckhead above. It would be the after-guard racing across the top of his cabin to the cro'jack braces, which, as in all Navy ships, were crossed and led aft. He longed to know why they were being tended but forced himself to stay seated. Then the ship heeled to larboard for a space before returning. It was too much. He left his cabin, just remembering his hat, and bounded on deck. A quick glance at the binnacle and out over the exuberant seas told him, however, that all was well. He saw Dacres steadying himself by the weather main-shrouds and looking fixedly forward.

At Kydd's appearance, Dacres moved to leeward, as was the custom. Kydd asked him, 'How does she go for ye, Mr Dacres?'

Dacres glanced at him briefly, his pale face taut, then hastily looked away without speaking.

Kydd frowned. 'I said, how is she, Mr Dacres?'

The officer remained silent, obstinately turned away. If there was going to be bad blood between them due to some imagined slight the situation would become impossible. 'Mr Dacres. I desire you should wait on me in my cabin – directly, if y' please!' he snapped, and strode below.

'Now, sir!' he said, rounding on Dacres as he entered. 'You'll tell me what it is ails ye, d'ye hear me?'

Holding to one side of the desk with *Teazer*'s lively motion Dacres stared at Kydd. His eyes were dark pits and he seemed to have difficulty forming the words. Kydd felt a stab of apprehension.

Dacres tensed, his eyes beseeching. Then he swung away in misery, scrambling to get out. Kydd heard the sound of helpless retching from beyond the door.

The south-westerly hauled round steadily, now with more than a little of the north in it until *Teazer* was stretching out on the larboard tack in a fine board deep into the eastern Mediterranean. More close-hauled, the motion was steadier but the angle of the waves marching in on the quarter imparted a spirited twist to the top of each heave.

This rendered Dacres helpless with seasickness. Kydd left him to claw back his sea legs, trusting in his sense of duty to return to his responsibilities as soon as he was able. For a sailor it was different: seasickness was not recognised as a malady and any man found leaning over the side was considered to be shirking and failing his shipmates. A rope's end was hard medicine, but who was to say that it was not a better way to force attention away from self-misery?

The morning wore on: it was approaching noon. 'Mr Bowden! Where are y'r young gentlemen? The heavens wait f'r no man. I will see them on th' quarterdeck one bell before noon or know the reason why, sir!' Kydd growled.

The two new midshipmen could not have been more different. Attard, the nominee of the dockyard, was slightly older at fifteen. Wary but self-possessed, he clearly knew his way about ships. The other, Martyn, was diffident and delicately built, with the features of an artist.

'Carry on, Mr Bowden,' Kydd said, but stayed to observe their instruction in the noon sight ceremony.

Martyn struggled with his brand new sextant. It was a challenge to any to wield an instrument in the lively motion of the brig and Kydd sympathised. Attard had a well-used piece that seemed too heavy but Bowden's easy flourishes encouraged them both.

Kydd adopted a small-ship straddle, standing with legs well apart, feet planted firmly on the deck with a spring in the knee, then lifted his octant. He noticed Bowden's imitation – he was learning quickly.

Local apparent noon came and went; Bowden and the young lads importantly noted their readings and retired for the calculations. Kydd delayed going below: the prospect from the quarterdeck was grand – taut new pale sails and freshly blacked rigging against the spotless deep-blue and white horses of the sea. With the brisk westerly tasting of salt, *Teazer* was showing every sign of being an outstanding sailer.

The four days to the rendezvous saw Dacres recover and *Teazer* become ever more shipshape. The boatswain twice had the brig hove to while the lee shrouds were taken up at the lanyards where the new cordage had stretched, and the marks tied to the braces to indicate the sharp-up position were moved in. And, as Kydd had surmised, a light forefoot made for a drier fo'c'sle but livelier motion. He was getting to know his tight-found little ship – and loving her the more.

At fifty miles north of Alexandria the fleet rendezvous was an easy enough navigational target, a line rather than a point, the latitude of thirty-one degrees forty-five minutes.

Kydd felt anxious at the thought of meeting an admiral for the first time as a commander. Sir John was known to be a stickler for the proprieties and probably had his powerful force arrayed in line ahead with all the panoply of a crack squadron at sea — gun salutes of the right number, frigate scouts to whom a humble brig-sloop would tug the forelock and all manner of other touchy observances.

Yet *Teazer* was the bearer of dispatches — news — and for a short time she would be the centre of attention. As the rendezvous approached Kydd saw to it that her decks were scrubbed and holystoned to a pristine paleness, her brightwork gleaming and guns readied for salutes.

Before sailing from Malta, the dispatches had been placed into padlocked canvas bags weighted with grape-shot. Kydd looked them out and placed them on his desk in anticipation of the instant summons he expected; his dress uniform and sword were ready in his cabin and his coxswain went off to prepare his boat's crew.

They reached the western end of the rendezvous line: all that was necessary now was to run down the line of latitude until the squadron was sighted. At the foretop there was now a pair of lookouts and Bowden had two seamen at the main as signals party. They were leaving nothing to chance. 'Th' foretop lookouts, ahoy!' bellowed Kydd, 'T' keep y' eyes open or I'll . . . I'll have ye!'

They shaped course eastwards along the line. With a height-of-eye of eighty feet at the main they would be able to spy the royals of a ship-of-the-line from a fifty-mile broad front in clear weather. In the quartering winds *Teazer* was at her best point of sailing and foamed along at speed.

By noon, however, they had nearly reached the mid-point of the thirty-mile line with Warren's squadron not yet in sight.

Kydd was aware of the momentous events taking place not so far to the south, the landings near Alexandria intended to wrest the whole of Egypt and the Levant from the French. But if the dispatches did not reach their intended recipient in time it left the whole seaward approaches wide open to Ganteaume.

Towards evening they finally reached the other end of the line with still no sighting. In the privacy of his cabin Kydd checked his orders yet again: the rendezvous was specified in two distinct places and could not be in error. Might there be in fact two locations as there were off Toulon, for close in and more distant? If so, it was never mentioned in orders. Had the squadron sailed on further beyond the end of the line due to navigational error? With the figuring of half a dozen ships to rely on, this was unlikely. Was their own navigation at fault? Had he missed the delivery of his charges through some ridiculous oversight?

Kydd chose to sail beyond the end of the line until dark before going about and returning. The night-recognition signals he had on hand only applied to Keith's main fleet; he had none for Warren's detached squadron. Tension increased as *Teazer* wore round and snugged down to double-reefed topsails, waiting for dawn.

Daybreak brought with it no welcome sight of sail, only the empty vastness of the sea. The westerly now headed them and Kydd could make progress only in long, uneven tacks each side of the line, a wearying sequence that had the brig going about twice in every watch with no assurance that they would intercept the squadron.

They reached the mid-point of the line: still no sign. They approached the western end of the line – ominously there was not a sail in sight anywhere. For Kydd, the elation and excitement of command had slowly ebbed into a stomach-churning morass of worry as he reviewed for the twentieth time what might have gone wrong.

He could heave to and wait for the squadron to return but if it was on station at some other place he would never meet up with it. But could he thrash backwards and forwards along the rendezvous line for ever? Time was running out.

At three in the morning, in the dimness of yet another sleepless night, Kydd resolved on action. He would leave the line and look for the squadron – the details would wait until morning. He fell sound asleep.

At first light he appeared on deck and sniffed the wind. 'Put up y'r helm an' steer sou'-sou'-east,' he told Dacres. They would head towards Egypt and the fighting: if the squadron was anywhere, the probability was that it would be there.

Full and bye, *Teazer* stretched south nobly. In three hours they were sighting sail, small fry and a possible frigate who did not seem inclined to make their acquaintance. In a few more hours, as the coast firmed ahead in a lazy blue-grey, more vessels showed against it – but no ship-of-the-line. When Kydd recognised an untidy straggle of buildings and a distinctive tower as Alexandria, he knew that the gamble had failed: the squadron was not there.

He ordered *Teazer* to put about, knowing that he could now be judged guilty of quitting his station without leave, a grave offence. Kydd went to his cabin with a heavy heart and had barely sat down when there was a knock. 'Captain, sir!' Martyn shrilled. 'Compliments from Mr Dacres and a vessel is sighted!'

Kydd hastened on deck: a small topsail cutter flying a blue ensign was leaning into the wind trying to close with them.

'Heave to, Mr Dacres,' Kydd called, and waited while the sleek craft came up and exchanged private signals.

'You've missed 'em!' shouted the young lieutenant-in-command as the vessel rounded to under their lee. 'That is, the East Med squadron, if that's who you're after,' he added, shading his eyes against the sun. 'What's the news?'

Kydd bridled at the familiarity and answered shortly, 'No news, L'tenant. What course did Sir John take when he left?'

'Why, to the rendezvous, I should think, sir,' said the lieutenant, remembering himself.

'North,' Kydd ordered.

Teazer's signal of dispatches aboard ensured her swift passage past officious scouting frigates within sight of the squadron, which was in tight formation and precisely on the line of the rendezvous.

'To place us t' loo'ard o' the flagship, Mr Bonnici,' Kydd told the master and went below to prepare, in obedience to the summons to place himself and his dispatches before the admiral immediately.

Teazer's cutter smacked into the water and the boat's crew swarmed aboard. Kydd's coxswain, Yates, sat at the tiller importantly, a beribboned hat with *Teazer* picked out in gold paint incongruously smart against his thick-set, hairy body.

'Stretch out, yer buggers!' he bawled. Kydd winced. This was not the coxswain he would have wished but the man was a veteran of both St Vincent and a blazing frigate action.

The whole squadron lay hove to, the flagship *Renown* at the centre. The boat rounded the noble stern of the battle-ship, all gilt and windows and with her name boldly emblaz-oned. Mildly curious faces looked down from her deck-line above.

Renown's boatswain himself set his silver call to piercing squeals to announce the arrival on board of the captain of a vessel of the Royal Navy, an honour that would have sent a delicious thrill through Kydd if it had come at any other time.

In the admiral's quarters the flag-lieutenant murmured an introduction and left Kydd with the admiral, who stared at him stonily, waiting.

'Ah, Commander Thomas Kydd, sloop *Teazer* with dispatches, sir.' Warren had a powerful air of intimidation and Kydd found his own back stiffening.

'From the commander-in-chief?' The admiral's hard tone did nothing for Kydd's composure.

'Er, no, sir, from Malta.'

'Malta! Who the devil thinks to worry me with dispatches from *there*, sir?'

'Gen'ral Pigot, sir – he says they're urgent,' Kydd said, and handed over the satchel, which the admiral took quickly.

'These are dated more than a week ago,' said Warren sharply, looking up.

Kydd added in a small voice, 'We thought t' find you at the rendezvous, sir. We beat up 'n' down the line for several days an' then – an' then, sir, I thought it best to – to leave station an' look for you t' the s'uth'ard, sir . . .' He tailed off.

Warren's frosty stare hardened. 'It took you that long to find I wasn't there and go looking? Good God above!' He snorted. He still held the dispatches and riffled through them. 'So what do we have here that's so damned urgent it needs one of the King's ships to tell me?'

'The French, Sir John – they're out!' said Kydd, his voice strengthening, 'Sailed fr'm Leghorn just this—'

'From Leghorn – yes, yes, I know that. Why do you think

I've been away from the rendezvous? No other than chasing your Ganteaume.' His face tightened. 'And this must mean, sir, you have sailed right through them on their way back! What do you have to say to that?'

Kydd gulped, he had ignored all sail sighted in his haste to reach the rendezvous. And with his precious dispatches shown to be not much more than gossip, he felt anything but a taut sea-captain with a vital mission. He flushed, but stubbornly held Warren's eye.

Something in his manner made Warren pause. 'Do I see a new-made commander before me, Mr Kydd?'

'Aye, sir.'

'Your first errand, I venture to say?'

'Sir.'

A tiny smile appeared. 'Is all as you expected it to be?'

Kydd's tensions eased a fraction. 'It's – different t' what I expected, yes, sir.' It was difficult to know whether the admiral was making conversation or had an object in mind.

'Expect the worst, Mr Kydd, and then you'll never be disappointed.' He looked pleased at his aphorism, adding, 'And give the men not an inch. They'll never thank you for it.'

'Have you any dispatches for Malta, sir?' Kydd asked.

'Malta? What conceivable interest would I have there? No, sir, carry on about your business and be thankful I'm not taking you under command.'

Teazer put about and made off to the west, her commander standing alone on the quarterdeck. As soon as the ship was settled on her new course he went to his cabin.

Kydd realised that he was still a very new captain but a future of being a lap-dog at the beck and call of any senior to him was not how he saw a fighting ship should spend her time. He had broadsides and fighting seamen ready for his country's service. He had achieved the peak of his ambition: his own ship.

For a captain loneliness was inevitable, but he hadn't realised how much he would feel it. It was something that came with the job, though, and he would have to get used to it. The only 'friend' he was in a position to contemplate was the single other officer, Dacres, but he could find little in common with the man.

The seas coming on the bow produced an energetic dip and rise and an eagerness in the motion that Kydd could sense even this far aft. The willingness in his ship reached out to him and his moodiness eased. Looking around his cabin he felt a quickening of the spirit: he was captain of the ship, damn it, and he was a sad looby if he failed to make the most of it.

'Tysoe!' he bellowed – he must find a bell or something: without a marine sentry outside ready to pass the word this was the only way he could send for his servant.

Tysoe appeared quickly, only slightly aggrieved at the manner of the summons. 'Sir?' he said quietly, now carrying himself nobly as befitted the manservant of the captain.

'I shall have some veal for m' dinner – an' open one of the pino biancos to go with it.'

'Certainly, sir. Could I be so bold as to remind you that your cabin stores include some pickled berberries that would accompany admirably?' The flecks of silver in the man's bushy hair added maturity to his appearance and Kydd knew that he could expect Tysoe to function with distinction on any ship's occasion.

'Yes, rouse 'em out, if y' will.' Tysoe inclined his head and left, Kydd smiling at the way he kept his dignity while bracing against *Teazer*'s playful movements.

The papers on the desk, weighted with a half musket-ball, recalled him to duty. Captain's Orders: now, just how did he want his ship run? For *Teazer* there were no precedents from a previous commander, no existing orders to copy and adopt, and Kydd had the chance to set out his own ideas.

'Instructions and Standing Orders for the General Government and Discipline of His Majesty's Sloop *Teazer*'. The well-remembered heading now preceded his own orders: he must start with due obeisance to His Majesty in Council, the Lords Commissioners of the Admiralty and so on – Peck could be relied on to chase up the wording.

And the meat. Conduct of the watch-on-deck with particular attention to the logs; the rough log of the mate-of-the-watch with entries by others listing provisions and stores expended, returned or condemned and so on, to be later taken to the appropriate officer for signature. And only then would the master deign to gather up the threads and transcribe this officially into the ship's log for Kydd's approval.

The signal log: this would most certainly be used in evidence in any court-of-inquiry as would officers' journals detailing the day's events and any reckoning of their position; he would, of course, require that Dacres regularly submit his journal to him.

The bulk of the rest would be as much advice as regulation: if the officer-of-the-watch sighted a strange sail at night, water shoaling – all the hundred and one things that could suddenly slam in on the unwary. If there was no provision for guidance in a Captain's Orders the negligent could plead ignorance. Kydd's rich experiences gave him an advantage in foreseeing these situations.

There were whole sections on the duties of the first lieutenant, master, boatswain, even the petty officers. They would all be left in no doubt about their responsibilities, as far as Kydd was concerned.

And on to working the ship: silence fore and aft when major manoeuvres were being performed; the precise line of demarcation between the captain, master and officer-of-the-watch, and other general matters. He debated whether to include instructions for topmen aloft for their varying situations but decided against it, not least because it was turning into a wearisome task indeed.

Kydd was thankful for midday and his necessary appearance on deck at the noon sight, with its welcome vision of sun and sea. He left the others comparing their readings and returned to his cabin to find Tysoe standing solicitously with a cloth-encircled bottle and a steaming dish neatly set.

While the men congregated noisily at their mess-tables and the officers gathered in their tiny gunroom Kydd sat down to his solitary dinner – and, be damned, he was going to enjoy it.

A timid midshipman knocked later at the door with their workings, the position of the ship at noon by their own estimation. He had asked to see these but the two sheets had identical handwriting. To succeed in their profession the young gentlemen must know their navigation faultlessly – and individually. He would speak to Bowden.

A passing shower pitter-pattered on the cabin deckhead above, then strengthened to a drumming and at the same time *Teazer*'s leaning lessened as the wind dropped. With a surge of sympathy Kydd realised they must be having a wet time of it on the upper decks working at their gun practice.

When he picked up his own work again he focused on the

people, the men and officers, aboard. His orders would see them properly clothed, the sanctity of their mealtimes preserved and hammocks maintained clean, lashed and stowed clear of seas flooding aboard. There was so much to think about – scrubbing decks: how often and by whom? Sea-chests or sea-bags allowed on the main-deck? Slinging hammocks next to hatchways in bad weather? When to rig windsails for ventilation? It went on and on for as many things as Kydd could remember to include.

Yet was this what it was to create a taut, happy ship? He well knew the answer: it all depended on the goodwill and intelligent practicality of his subordinates, and their success, inspired by himself, in drawing out a spirit of excellence, of unity and pride in themselves and their ship.

The noise of the rain squall fell away and there was a sudden cry from a lookout. '*Sail hoooo!* Two sail three points t' loo'ard!'

Kydd dropped his work and scrambled to his feet, hastening on deck. 'Sir!' Dacres pointed with his telescope. There were two vessels lying stopped together just ahead and to leeward, clearly surprised by *Teazer*'s sudden emergence from the shower.

Heads turned to Kydd in expectation. 'Y'r glass, Mr Dacres,' he snapped, and steadied the telescope on the pair.

There was not much doubt: they were witnessing the predation of one vessel upon the other. No flag on either, but one had the unmistakable low, rakish lines of a corsair. Kydd's eyes gleamed: he could not go far wrong if he took action. If the victim was friendly he would earn undying gratitude, and if enemy, *Teazer* would be taking her first prize.

'Down y'r helm – set us alongside, Mr Bonnici!' he roared, thrusting back the telescope at Dacres. The last image he had seen was of an ants' nest of activity on both decks as, no doubt, the corsair prepared to flee. A mile or so downwind and both vessels dead in the water; the circumstances could not have been better.

'Brace round, y' lubbers,' he bawled as, close-hauled, *Teazer* loosed bowlines and came round to lie before the wind, picking up speed now she was not in confrontation with the waves.

'Hands t' quarters!' he snapped. Wincing at the ridiculous drum, he was pleased nevertheless at the enthusiasm the guncrews showed: with wet clothing still clinging they readied their weapons for what must come. On both sides of the deck – eight six-pounders a side – gun-captains checked gunlocks, vents and tackle falls with ferocious concentration.

The corsair was now poling off from the victim, on its three masts huge lateen yards showing signs of movement: it had to be a xebec and, judging from the polacre rig of its prey, this was a merchantman.

In his excitement Kydd could not hold back a wolfish smile as they bore down on the two vessels and he could see that the others aboard *Teazer* were as exultant. Stirk's head popped up at the fore hatchway and its owner stared forward. His quarters were at the magazine but he obviously wanted to see what was going on.

This was what *Teazer* had been built for – destined for! One by one reports were made to him of readiness for battle. Dacres's quarters bill would be shortly tested. Kydd could see him forward, scribbling in a notebook. But it would be an easy baptism of fire for the ship: they would get no fierce broadside-to-broadside hammering from the undisciplined rabble in a corsair.

The xebec had its sails abroad now: the two larger forward

94

ones a-goosewing, spread on opposite sides to catch the following wind and the smaller mizzen taken in. Its low, wasp-like hull would give it speed but *Teazer* was no plodder.

They were coming up fast on the merchant ship, which was untidily at sixes and sevens and with no clue as to its flag. Its side timbers were bleached and drab, the sails grey with service. However, Kydd had eyes only for the chase, which was making off with ever-increasing speed.

'Cap'n, sir,' said the master, quietly. Kydd spared him a glance. 'Sir, you're not a-chasin' this pirate?' Kydd frowned. Of course he was – the merchant ship would still be there after they had dealt with the corsair.

'You c'n wager guineas on it, Mr Bonnici,' he said testily, and resumed his eager stare forward. The master subsided meekly.

They plunged past the merchantman under every stitch of canvas they possessed. 'Give 'em a gun, there,' he threw forward. 'Let 'em know we're not forgetting 'em,' he growled, in an aside to a solemn Dacres.

Kydd snatched a glance at the master, who was watching events blank-faced. The chase was just what was wanted to sort out the real warriors among them, and if Bonnici was not up to it his days in *Teazer* were numbered.

'Stretch out aloft, there, y' old women!' he bellowed, to the foremast topmen who were sending up stuns'ls but making a sad mess of it. Kydd stared ahead through his pocket glass until his eyes watered, willing *Teazer* on. As far as he could judge they had a chance. The xebec seemed over-pressed with sail, with much white around its bows but not making the speeds he had seen in similar craft. One thing was certain: with the large number of men crowding its deck he would be very sure never to come close enough to allow them to board.

95

A popping and a puff of smoke from its high, narrow stern was met with contemptuous laughter by the seamen in *Teazer* – they had no bow-chasers worth the name but all they needed was to come up with the vessel and settle the matter with a couple of broadsides. A xebec, like all corsairs, was intended to board and overwhelm, never to try conclusions with a warship.

It began angling away, trying for a better slant, and Kydd was certain they were slowly overhauling it, now no more than a mile ahead. His excitement increased and he recognised a rising bloodlust.

'The merchantman is falling astern, sir.'

'Thank ye, Mr Dacres,' Kydd snapped. The ship was now at quite a distance, but it was still apparently immobile and could wait. Should he try a yaw? That involved suddenly throwing over the helm briefly to bring *Teazer*'s broadside to bear, but it would be at the cost of losing way in the chase and he could not allow that.

It was fast and exhilarating, this hot-blooded flying after the corsair, knowing that there was little doubt about how the battle would end, and then a triumphant return to the grateful merchant ship.

Kydd turned to his midshipman messenger. 'Go an' get my sword, if y' will, Mr Martyn.' The heft of his fine fighting sword was satisfying and he saw that they were decidedly nearer. It would not be long now – neither darkness nor a friendly port would save their prey.

Every eye forward was on the xebec. It seemed to hesitate, the big lateens shivering, the speed falling off. Surely not – it couldn't be so easy. *Teazer* came on in fine style, Kydd giving away nothing to chance. The corsair's aspect changed slightly to larboard. He would take it ranging up on his starboard side for the first broadside and then—

As quick as a warhorse wheeling for the charge, the xebec's sheets flew in and it slewed round. Was it trying to fall upon *Teazer* before it was ready in order to board her? 'Stand by y'r guns!' Kydd roared.

Heading back towards them at speed, its lofty lateens drawing hard, it seemed intent on a suicidal last charge. 'Hands t' shorten sail!' If the madman wanted a yardarm to yardarm smashing match, he would oblige.

The sharp drawn bow of the corsair was aimed like a lance at *Teazer* and Kydd felt the first nagging doubt. What was going on? Had he missed something? His ship slowed ready for the struggle but the xebec still hurtled down on them. The cheers and pungnacious mockery faded away on *Teazer* at the bewildering sight.

It was a successful manoeuvre for the xebec as its head-on charge prevented any of *Teazer*'s guns being brought to bear, but it could not last. Sheering suddenly to starboard it would pass down the brig's larboard side. Then the action would begin, Kydd thought savagely.

At the last possible moment the xebec sheered aside – now it must brave *Teazer*'s broadside. It angled nimbly away to increase the range before daring its passage. Kydd saw the evil craft under his guns and did not hesitate: 'A broadside, on m' word – fire!'

Teazer's guns spoke in anger for the first time. Her broadside, however, was more a ragged series of *cracks* than the full-throated blast that would have come from *Tenacious*. Kydd waited eagerly for the smoke to clear – but there were only some ragged holes low in the sails and no other significant damage he could see. The xebec slashed past in a flurry of white, largely untouched.

But on one side *Teazer* was defenceless until the guns were reloaded. The corsair could now strike like a snake to lay itself alongside and board. 'Load wi' canister!' Kydd shouted urgently. He wheeled on the helm. 'Hard t' larboard!' This would bring their opposite broadside to bear if they were quick enough but *Teazer* seemed to be in thrall to the menace off to one side and turned so *slowly*.

'Stand by t' repel boarders!' Men not at the guns raced to the masts and to the stands of boarding pikes. Others went to the arms chests in the centre of the deck, casting anxious looks at the crowded deck of the xebec. Kydd drew his sword. They would shortly be fighting for their lives.

Where would the strike come from? The corsair had passed *Teazer* but could now turn and fall away downwind to pass her again, or place itself across *Teazer*'s stern and grapple.

'What the devil—?' The corsair was showing no interest in closing with *Teazer*. In fact, it continued on its course, steadily making off into the distance without so much as a backward glance.

Teazer wallowed about on her turn, which was taking her away from the diminishing sight of the xebec. 'Belay that – come up t' the wind,' Kydd snapped. *Teazer* obediently stopped her turn and rotated back to face the way they had come – as far as she could.

And then he understood. The chase had been long and downwind, the corsair had deliberately drawn *Teazer* after it and then at the right time had put about and, with its fore and aft rig superior in lying close to the wind, was now heading back upwind to the helpless merchantman to finish the job.

Kydd's face burned. To be gulled so easily! To let his fighting spirit heat his blood to the point where it had taken the place of cool reasoning! This was not how it was to be a successful captain. The corsair had made a cunning show of desperate flight, staying just out of reach, luring Kydd on and on before casting loose a hidden drag-sail and flying back to secure its prize. *Teazer* was left clawing back in slow tacks.

Kydd stole a quick look at Bonnici, still standing impassive. He had known all along, and said nothing. Kydd's embarrassment deepened. He glanced forward: there he saw Stirk at the fore hatchway, looking down the deck at him. While he watched, Stirk turned away and went below again. His humiliation was complete.

Alone in the great cabin, Kydd balled his fists with frustration and bitterly went over the day's events. The first lesson was burned into his soul for ever – never again would he allow the ardour of battle to cloud his reasoning; it needed more than dash and courage to be a leader of men. The feeling of shame, of every eye on him as he slunk below, would live with him for a very long time.

From now on, it would be an icy calm, an automaton-like analysis of the situation and a ruthless focus on bringing about a victory. Nothing else would serve.

There were other things, practical matters he had discovered. *Teazer*'s broadside was insufficient in weight of metal, although in accord with her establishment. Before he next sailed he would add carronades to his armament, by whatever means.

And sail: he could see no real reason why he could not ship a main-yard in place of the cro'jack on the mainmast. At the moment it acted solely to spread the foot of the main topsail, which left the fore as the only course. More substantial sail area there would surely add speed, especially sailing by the wind and he had seen several Navy brig-sloops so fitted.

But the chief objective for Kydd at the moment was to win back the trust and confidence of his ship's company. When he met the corsair again on the open sea it would not hesitate to take on *Teazer*, knowing she had a raw and impetuous captain, ripe for the taking. Kydd was determined that next time things would be different.

Chapter 5

Set-faced, in full-dress and sword, Kydd boarded his cutter for the pull across the busy stretch of Grand Harbour to Porta della Marina gate. His report for Pigot had cost him hours of word-grinding and now would be put to the test.

'Toss y'r oars, God rot it!' his coxswain grated at the boat's crew. Kydd noticed signs of resentment at Yates's manner but all his focus was on the imminent meeting. He sat rigidly in the sternsheets rehearsing his words as the boat stroked across to the stone steps below the ramparts of Valletta.

'Oars – I'll split yore ear, y' bugger, you feather like that agen!' Yates swore at the stroke oar. As bidden, the man ceased rowing but sat sullenly at his oar.

'I'll thank ye t' be more civil, Yates, while I'm in th' boat,' Kydd muttered, then addressed himself to the task of stepping out with his cocked hat, sword and frock coat unmarked.

He was met by General Pigot's aide. 'Good voyage, Captain?' he asked smoothly. 'His Excellency will see you shortly.' Was Pigot now taking the airs of a governor? Kydd wondered wryly.

He did not have to wait long but the man seemed pre-occupied. 'An' good morning to you, Captain,' he said, rummaging on his desk. 'Blast it,' he muttered. 'Was here before, dammit.' He glanced up. 'An' what can I do for you, Mr Kydd?'

'Ah, here is my report on th' voyage just concluded, sir.'

'Oh? What kind o' passage was it, then?' he said politely, as he put it down in front of him and went back to his rummaging.

'Er, we found Admiral Warren, sir, but he already had word o' Ganteaume sailing.'

'Good. Our soldiers are very exposed at the landing, need 'em to be well protected. Anythin' else?'

Kydd gulped. 'We fell in with a merchantman being set upon by a pirate. I went in chase but – but he got away.'

'Tut tut – can't be helped. Did you see Ganteaume at all? Blasted man seems to be everywhere these days.'

'I didn't. No, sir.'

'Well, that's that. You'll be on your way, then?'

This was like no other naval operational discussion he knew of: what about the strategics of tasking his ship, an appraisal of intelligence, some kind of indication of future planning? What should he do now? 'Er, sir, I'm a little hazy about what m' duties are, an' those of m' ship. We have no senior officers until th' fleet is here – er, do y' have orders concerning me at all, sir?'

'Orders?' Pigot frowned. 'From me? Does seem you have an odd notion of what we're doin' here.' He pursed his lips. 'We – that is, the British – freed Malta from the Frenchies but this doesn't mean t' say that Malta is now ours.'

'Er, then whose—'

'In course, we have t' give it back. To your knights – the

Knights of St John who've been here since afore King Henry's day. Meantimes we keep Malta in trust for 'em.'

'Are they returning to claim, sir?' Kydd asked.

'Ah – there we have a problem.'

'Sir?'

'The last Grand Master died in exile when he an' the other knights were driven out by the French and the others elected a new – then asked the Tsar of Russia for a home an' protection. He gave it – and now the Grand Master who wants t' claim Malta is a Russian. So do you fancy a sovereign Russian territory astride the centre of the Mediterranean? Strongest fortress outside Gibraltar? Hostile t' England? Neither do I, sir!'

'And so—'

'And so we stay until we're told t' hand 'em over an' do nothing precipitate like.'

Kydd was beginning to see why there was such a lack of order in this place and no formal naval presence. Money would not be wasted on works that would have to be given up at any point. 'Then you have no instructions for me, sir?' he persisted.

Pigot said gruffly, 'Sir, I'm not one of your admirals as knows the sea. I recommend you find someone who does and take your orders from him.'

Kydd rose. 'Thank you for y'r time, sir.'

It was all most irregular, Kydd pondered, in the boat on the way back to his ship. If Pigot did not want him, who did? If he reported to the distant commander-in-chief off Toulon for clarification that would take weeks. By the letter of his orders he should attach himself to the 'Malta Service' – if anyone could be termed senior officer of such an operational force he was obliged to accept that it was none other than himself.

No King's ship was at liberty to do as she pleased: if he took to the high seas on his own account it was piracy – even the act of going to sea required orders of some kind, if only to cover the routine expenditure of stores accountable against the object of the voyage. By rights he should remain at moorings until he received specific orders for the employment of his ship.

Could he endure swinging about a buoy for long weeks – months? Was it even morally right to do so while others fought? No, that was intolerable.

He could think of one solution: he would issue orders to himself. Orders for the prosecution of the war in these waters: chasing down pirates, spying out for the French, other warlike moves – and, where unavoidable, carrying dispatches. It would, of course, be prudent to have them counter-signed. He brightened at the thought of his own war without a senior to interfere. A satisfied smile spread as he ordered his coxswain to turn about and return. This time he would go to the Grand Palace and see the civil commissioner on quite a different matter.

Cameron seemed mildly curious to see him. 'Anything I can do, Cap'n?' he said cheerfully.

'Indeed, sir, there is,' began Kydd, importantly. 'I have been placed in command o' the Malta Naval Service, an' I beg you will acquaint me with your chief concerns that they might be taken into account in our planning.'

'Malta Naval Service?' Cameron murmured absently.

'Aye, sir. The man-o'-war *Teazer* is returned from sea trials, as ye know . . .'

'Well, now, an' I do have my worries as well you c'n understand.' He leaned back and regarded Kydd curiously. 'An' the chief one, o' course, is trade protection, destroying th' pests that infest these seas. We're particularly vexed by privateers in the Sicily Channel – that's your passage between Sicily and the Barbary coast. Quite upset the trade from the west. And then there's always troubles around the Greek islands, Ligurians and similar.'

'A serious matter, sir.' That would be an aggressive war patrol to the west, then, showing the flag and spreading the dismaying news among the vermin of the sea that a Royal Navy warship was now to be reckoned with in their hunting grounds.

'But of most importance at the moment is the need to support our trade in the Adriatic.' Cameron rubbed his jaw speculatively. 'What with the Italian ports in French hands directly across the water, it leaves only the Balkans in the whole eastern Mediterranean open to our cotton exports. You'd be doing us a great service should you be able t' offer us any protection in that area.'

'O' course, sir.' A fast strike north into the unsuspecting Ionians – he would have as much action as he could wish for in the near future.

'Excellent. Splendid.' Cameron leaned back in his chair. 'I shall immediately issue a public notice to that effect.'

He got up from his chair and came round to Kydd. 'This is fine news, and ye must know will give much heart to the people, sir.' Kydd mumbled an embarrassed acknowledgement. 'It only needs us to agree the date when the convoy sails, then, Captain.'

'Convoy?' Kydd blurted.

'Yes, of course. And let me tell you, when they hear that it will be escorted b' one of Nelson's victorious sea officers, why, they'll be fighting each other to be part o' such a one!'

*   *   *

Outside Grand Harbour a tight cloud of sails massed. Of every conceivable shape and size, exotic and homely, all were united in the common objective of making it safely to Ragusa in the republic of Dubrovnik on the Balkan coast.

Any sight more different from the stern discipline of an Atlantic convoy would be difficult to conjure – no divisional pennants, masthead wefts, numbered columns or even identity vanes. Instead, in the five days left to him, a harassed Kydd had everyone he could find scribbling away at Convoy Instructions for the mass of ships.

All that could be expected was the bare minimum: private recognition signals and one or two for manoeuvring. The formation of the convoy was to be simply a giant advancing square with the escort to windward. It was the best he could do.

A single gun from *Teazer*'s fo'c'sle set the whole mass in motion, an enthusiastic scrambling of sail to fit within the square defined by the four marker ships Kydd had chosen and which bore the distinctive Republic of Dubrovnik flag above the British. Kydd's strict orders were that any vessel that strayed from this square for any reason, impatience or laggardliness, would no longer be considered under protection.

It was crazy – by count about twenty-seven merchant ships and a single escort – but Kydd was determined to see it through. 'Take us t' wind'ard, Mr Bonnici,' he said hoarsely. 'I'll have th' ship ready t' drop down on any who make a false move against us.'

Teazer eased into position on the weather side of the square and trimmed canvas to stay with the slow-moving crowd of sail. Kydd remained on deck until he was sure the convoy was on its way, then turned to the officer-of-the-watch and said, 'I'm going below, Mr Dacres. Call me if ye think there's anything amiss.'

He climbed into his cot without undressing.

There was no incident for three days: the convoy was getting used to sailing together, a singular thing for merchantmen who had no real conception of using the set of the sails to spill wind in order to match speed to that of others.

The square was still more or less together, but now they were approaching the choke point of the Strait of Otranto where it was almost possible to see the coasts of Italy and Albania at the same time, and where any predators could be expected.

As the morning light displaced the darkness of night on the fourth day, at the narrowest part of the strait with a rugged blue coast distantly to starboard, company was spotted. A pair of small but speedy vessels paced together some way off to leeward of the convoy. Their lazy progress, just out of gun range, was that of sharks cruising round a school of frightened fish.

Kydd lowered his telescope and turned to Bonnici. 'It's a xebec I recognise, but what's th' other?' It was more substantially built than the low, fine-lined xebec, and on the very much smaller lateen mizzen a tiny but complete square sail topped the mast.

'They both Algerines,' Bonnici said quietly, as though they could be overheard.

For Barbary pirates ranging far from their desert lair this larger vessel would hold their stores and booty while the smaller xebec could swarm aboard their selected victim. At eight guns a side, though, it would not do to dismiss the larger too lightly.

'The large, he a *barca* – do not confuse wi' the Spanish one,' Bonnici added, carefully studying it with the glass.

Those of the convoy nearest shied away from the threat, huddling closer. If any of the deep-laden merchantmen ran a-foul of another they would be instant prey – Kydd could not risk leaving the others and they would be on their own. He tried not to think of the fate in store for any small merchant crew overwhelmed by Barbary pirates.

The evil pair, however, did not appear in any hurry as they glided along with the convoy, no doubt picking out victims.

Kydd was confident *Teazer* could win against either of them and probably both, but this was not in question. The safety of his convoy was. He could not leave his precious windward position for the sake of a few weak sailers and race down on the pirates through the convoy to rout them, then be faced with a long beat back against the wind to save the rest.

The raiders would probably take one or two hapless ships on the fringes and then fall back, knowing Kydd could not pursue.

'Mr Dacres – Mr Bowden, I have a service for ye. Now, mark m' words, an' let there be no mistake . . .'

The two Algerines made their move not much more than an hour later straight at the heart of the convoy. Wheeling about, the two vessels leaned into the wind. Unknown pennons streamed from the tip of their lateen yards as they readied for the onslaught.

Instantly a complex hoist soared up from *Teazer*'s signal halliards, then another. The pirates slashed onwards, but from one of the convoy's front marker ships then from a rear one answering signals streamed out. Large battle ensigns broke out bravely on both ships and they threw over their helm to lay a course directly for the Algerines.

The 'trap' was well sprung and it did not take the attackers long to realise their danger. With a brig-of-war bearing down on them directly and several obviously disguised warships closing in fast on both flanks they were not going to stay and dispute. They turned about abruptly and fled.

Teazer recovered her signal teams from the marker ships and resumed her vigil. Climbing back aboard, Lieutenant Dacres smiled uncharacteristically. 'Such a to-do, you'd never have believed it – I had to draw my sword on the craven villains to get them to conform!'

The rector of the Republic of Dubrovnik himself came aboard with the thanks of the merchant community when the convoy was delivered safely, but Kydd needed to press on. After an uneventful return passage, the massive crenellations of Malta were a welcome sight. He wished that Renzi was there to admire the ancient town with its long city wall and stonework mellowed by the centuries. He was probably still in *Tenacious*, first lieutenant of an old and weary ship with a vindictive captain. And on endless blockade.

Teazer found her berth again in Dockyard Creek and Kydd gave leave to all the Maltese hands. With certain employment in difficult times they could be relied on to return and their absence released space for the rest.

The muster book had to be sent to Gibraltar and proved before pay could be authorised, and even then it might be months in arrears. The British sailors would have only what they had kept from their previous ship but Jack Tar would never be renowned for frugal habits. Not for nothing was it said, 'They earn money like horses and spend it like asses.'

Kydd resolved to try for an advance from the clerk of the cheque in the dockyard.

The shipwrights and riggers tut-tutted over the amount of extra rigging, blocks, pendants, clew garnets and the rest involved in spreading a main-yard but it was the appearance of young Attard, brimming over with self-confidence and full of salty yarns about his experiences, that most eased the process, and *Teazer* prepared for her new sail, the langard mainsail.

It was more difficult in the matter of carronades. It was not a weapon much seen in Mediterranean arsenals and in the peculiar circumstances of Malta the Board of Ordnance did not figure at all.

No carronades but still, Kydd accepted, six-pounders were not to be despised; *Teazer*'s sixteen long sixes were normally more than enough to settle an argument with a privateer, and even if they were to find carronades it would mean re-equipping with special slides in place of the usual wheeled gun-carriage.

Kydd returned to his ship; there would be some delay while these improvements were put in train and he had time on his hands. 'Mr Dacres.'

His lieutenant came across the quarterdeck from where he had been watching the movements of the exotic little craft about the great harbour.

Kydd removed his cocked hat and smiled. 'I have a mind t' step ashore and see a little o' Malta. I thought to hire a carriage, save m' legs a hard beat t' windward. I wonder if ye'd care t' join me f'r the day?'

'I would like that, sir,' he replied, but then added, 'But without we have a pilot with Italian or the Maltese lingo, I fear we would be at a stand.'

'O' course. Then as this is a problem o' navigation, who better than our master t' plot the course?'

The sun was warm to the skin and had a benign cast that set the mood for Kydd. For the first time in weeks he could let tranquillity take hold. In the sternsheets of the cutter he relaxed against the backboard and grinned at Dacres in the sheer escapism of the moment, but Dacres only smiled back politely.

'Mr Bonnici,' Kydd asked, 'I'm intrigued t' know – who was it built this mighty place? Seems t' me that it's the strongest citadel in all Europe.'

'Well, sir,' Bonnici said, 'ye have to understan' that in the time of your Queen Elizabet' we were attack by the Turk, an' suffer a long and cruel siege. We win, but the knights say they never suffer such again, an' build Valletta – only fifteen year and finished!' he said proudly.

Kydd picked up the 'your' and wondered at Bonnici's loyalty, but remembered his years of service to the Royal Navy. 'They did a fine job, right enough. An' since then, Mr Bonnici, has any dared t' invade Malta?' In the magnificence of Grand Harbour the island seemed one extended fortress and quite impregnable.

'None, sir,' said Bonnici, simply. 'The French were let here b' treachery, no fight.' He stopped and added, 'Ah, none saving th' English – only one time Malta taken, an' that was you, last year against the French.'

'I rather fancy you're glad to see the back of them,' Dacres murmured.

'Yes!' Bonnici spat with the first emotion Kydd had seen him display. 'They come as robber, bandit – take fr'm our church an' the people. We hunger, starve, our trade finish.

They say they come as *liberatore*, to throw out th' knights, but really they wan' to take, seize.'

Kydd let him subside then asked, 'Where are th' knights now, then?'

'The Gran' Master and most o' the knights go to Russia an' wait to return,' he finished abruptly.

'You don't want 'em back?'

'For me – no, sir, they are no good f'r Malta.'

'But if they are Maltese – y' knows, of th' noble orders—'

'They are not, sir. They come in th' year 1530. Ver' old, but they given Malta by others.'

'So *you* were before . . . ?'

'No, sir. The Normans were here before, the Count Roger.'

'And before then, you?'

'No, sir. Before them the Arab, an' before them the Greeks.'

'I see.'

'Before them th' east Roman, an' the empire, they call it Melita.'

'And—'

'The Carthaginian before, stay seven hundred years. An' before them . . .'

'Er, yes?'

'Before them many say we are giants – at Tarxien, in the country, are strange an' magic dwelling of stones, even th' wisest cannot tell of them . . .'

The boat approached the landing place on the flanks of the fortress city and Yates stood for the final approach. 'Hold water larb'd, give way starb'd – Jones, y' fawney bastard, ye're nothing but a mumpin' packet rat. Do I 'ave ter show y' how?'

The trio climbed a short way up some broad steps before

a water fountain with a statue of Neptune. 'We call this th' Nix Mangiare Stairs, on account of the beggars have nothing t' eat. This is their cry,' Bonnici said, then went ahead for a carriage.

'The *cales*,' he said. In the four-seater Kydd and Dacres sat facing forward with Bonnici opposite. They set off, with the driver walking, bridle in hand, and wound up into the city proper. People streamed past, most ignoring them; the women, many in hooded black silk capes, were all prettily adorned with rings, bracelets and silver shoe-buckles and stepped out proudly, while the men affected either dress that would go unremarked in Oxford Street or colourful country garb of trousers and a long sash.

As he took in the sights Kydd realised he had been more than a little distracted before. They began with the five-hundred-year-old Grand Master's Palace, now occupied by Cameron and his administration. The interior of the Cathedral of St John took Kydd's breath away. A riot of gilded tracery, with a blue-stone altar before a life-size religious group in marble, it reeked of a past age of splendour and devotion.

'Th' Manoel theatre – it's lower down, an' some say th' oldest in Europe.' It was not large but well appointed.

Then followed sightseeing of the mighty walls, and the public gardens in Floriana outside the massive gates offering views without end of surrounding bays and inlets with their fortifications.

Over a simple meal Bonnici finished their education: the ancient capital, Mdina, was apparently a perfect medieval walled city, complete with drawbridge and castle. At nearby Rabat there were catacombs and noble buildings, while on the coast the alluring Blue Grotto waited to bewitch unwary seafarers. And if it were at all possible the little port of

Marsaxlokk and the enchanting Dingli cliffs should not be missed, to say nothing of Zurrieq and Kirkop, Qrendi and Mqabba. Proudly he described in detail the bravery of the Maltese sailors when the apostle Paul was wrecked in a bay up this very coast after meeting with a *gregale*, a fierce local storm, on his way to Rome.

Kydd was sorry when the day ended and they made their way down to the Marina and their boat.

'Sir – for you.' Bowden was waiting at the gangway and passed across a note. It was sealed inside expensive card and addressed impeccably to himself as 'The Captain, His Britannick Majesty's Ship *Teazer*'. Kydd took it down quickly to his cabin away from curious gazes.

'Well, damme!' he muttered. It was an invitation: but this was no ordinary social occasion. Phrases like '. . . sensible of the obligation owing to Commander Kydd upon his late meeting with the Barbary pirates . . .' and '. . . we, merchants of Malta in the Adriatic trade, do wish to render plain our deepest appreciation . . .' left no doubt of its drift.

There was to be a presentation of silver to the brave captain who had defied the sea-robbers so cunningly, and this was to be made by the distinguished English merchant Mr Roderick Mason in the presence of Chevalier Antonio Mancini, fifth Baron Baldassare.

'Tysoe!' Kydd roared. 'D' ye think m' best red 'n' green with th' lace will serve for a baron?' He held out the invitation with the merest trace of smugness.

'Oh, sir, my opinion is . . .'

'Spit it out, man!'

'Then sir, if you'll permit me . . .'

'Yes or no, y' villain!'

Tysoe's eye held a glimmer of complacency as he con-

tinued suavely, 'Sir must be aware that he cuts a fine figure
– in uniform blues, and most especially in full-dress. The
guests will be expecting you to appear in the character of a
sea officer and we don't wish to disappoint, do we, sir?'

He was met by torchlight and conveyed in a carriage to a
well-proportioned building with an impressive entrance.
Standing waiting were several elderly gentlemen of apparent
wealth – silk stockings and lace, ostrich-fringed hats, gold-
tipped canes, and jewels on their shoe-buckles.

Kydd felt his relative youth but took assurance from the
splendour of his full-dress uniform with the substantial gold
of the epaulette, cuffs and lapels against the discreet dark-
blue and white of the rest. He took off his gold-laced hat
and waited politely.

'Captain, so happy you were able to come.' A dignified
man greeted him with a quick bow. 'Mason, Roderick Mason,
at your service.' His shrewd grey eyes appraised Kydd.

They went in together to an enclosed inner courtyard
crowded with people. The murmur of voices stopped as they
appeared. 'Gentlemen, might I present HMS *Teazer*'s gallant
commander? Captain Thomas Kydd!'

There was a spatter of genteel applause, and he bowed
civilly to right and left. A footman appeared at his side with
wine in a tall crystal glass. He accepted it and turned to
Mason. 'S' good of ye t' invite me, sir.'

'Our honour entirely, Captain. Shall we proceed?'

The room was not large and was warm with the glitter of
candles on a long table. Mason ushered Kydd to its head
where a jovial man in scarlet stood up to meet them. 'Sir,
may I present Captain Thomas Kydd?' He turned slightly.
'Chevalier the Baron Baldassare.'

'Y'r servant, sir,' Kydd replied, with a workmanlike bow, and allowed himself to be seated between the two, trying to remember the graces taught so patiently by his noble-born friend Renzi. Turning to the chevalier he opened, 'Rousin' weather we're having, this time o' the year, or do ye prefer it the cooler?'

The dinner passed most pleasantly. Lingering looks were cast his way by the ladies, and valiant attempts made to engage him in conversation over the energetic sawing of a string trio. Mason leaned closer. 'I must allow, sir, it was a fine service you performed for us. Have you any conception of the value, for instance, of a single Ragusa-bound brigantine in currants?'

Kydd shook his head.

'It would probably amaze you to learn that the ship – if tolerably new – would be of the order of some *migliaia* of *scudi*. If we then add in the desideratum for insurance and other expenditures on the vessel, the capital outlay on the cargo and loss of expected profit, then the depredations of these vermin stand as an *impossible* burden on any merchant and therefore deleterious to the trade of Malta as a whole.'

Kydd nodded and added quietly, 'An' not t' mention y'r sailors slaughtered by the Moor, Mr Mason.'

Finally the cloth was drawn and the chevalier stood up; fine words were said, then Mason took the chair. 'My lord, the distinguished ladies and the gentlemen of Malta here gathered, we are come this night to do honour to the Royal Navy – and in particular the brave Commander Kydd who . . .'

Pink with embarrassment Kydd sat through it, only relieved that he had not let down his ship or her company.

'And so I give you Captain Thomas Kydd!'

He stood and a footman entered bearing a tray. On it were

two articles of handsome silver, which Mason lifted up and presented to him. He accepted them graciously.

When he turned to address the guests, he was ill-prepared for the storm of applause and cries of support that echoed about the room. It was all he could do to stutter something about stern duty, the trade of Great Britain and the new prosperity of Malta, but it seemed to suffice and he sat down.

'Well spoken, sir,' said Mason, and the rest of the evening passed in an agreeable blur of sociability.

'Mr Bonnici, if ye has the time, I'd like t' speak with you in m' cabin.' The master followed and sat, politely attending. 'I've promised Commissioner Cameron a war cruise, let the Frenchy know we're about, an' I'm exercised to know as t' where we should go to annoy them the most.'

Bonnici's brow furrowed. 'Sir, wi' respect, this is not a thing for I, a sailing master,' he replied slowly.

Operational matters were for the commissioned officers and Kydd knew that, strictly, it was improper to approach him. 'I understand, Mr Bonnici,' he said, 'yet you'll hold better acquaintance than we with th' waters in the eastern Mediterranean, I fancy. It is y'r opinion only that I'm seeking – the decisions are mine.'

'Er, it is my difficulty, sir. If some – gentlemen in Malta hear I tell you where t' go for taking the private ships . . . it may be they think I do this for other reason.' Bonnici's family were all in Malta and in their closed community would bear any suspicion if it seemed questionably coincidental that they had appeared suddenly on the scene. Kydd would have to make his own guesses.

'I see. On another matter entirely, may I have y'r opinion?

Should *Teazer* go south-about to th' Sicily Channel this time o' the year? Do you think this a . . . wise course?'

Back on deck, Kydd checked again the progress with the new main course. Purchet seemed to have it all in hand. The main-hatch was off and stores were coming aboard; *Teazer* could keep the seas for several months, if necessary, but water was the limiting factor. He watched the seamen hoist the big barrels aboard – the Maltese were doing well, laying into their tasks with a will, their clothing now far more in keeping with a British man-o'-war. It was all deeply satisfying: it would be *Teazer*'s first true independent cruise, something that every captain of a man-o'-war yearned for.

But what was particularly pleasing to Kydd was the new mainsail. It had cost some keen thinking to figure how to spread a sail, complete with all its gear, on the biggest yard in the ship where none was before. Even a stout chess-tree needed to be fashioned and bolted on the ship's side forward to take the tack of the new sail out to windward when close-hauled, exactly the same as could be seen in a ship-of-the-line.

Teazer was settling into her routine and, to Kydd's critical eye, was showing every evidence of contentment. He knew the signs: easy laughter from seamen as they worked together, good-natured rivalries out on the yardarm, the willing acceptance of orders where surly looks would be the first sign of discontents.

He knew that he himself was on trial: he was expecting the men to follow him into peril of their lives but they would not do this unless he had first won their trust, their respect. He had reached the first stage, a wary deference, which he could tell from their direct gaze but ready responses. There were ways sailors had of conveying their feelings – he would instantly recognise silent contempt, but he had seen nothing of it.

There was a tentative knock at his open cabin door; Kydd could see Bowden and some others.

'My apologies at the intrusion, sir, but these men have something on their mind and they'd be obliged if you'd hear them.'

Kydd looked sharply at him. 'What's this, Mr Bowden? Do ye not know—'

'Sir, I think you should hear them.'

There was something in his tone that made Kydd pause. He looked at the foretopman standing next to Bowden. 'What is it, Hansen?'

He was a reliable hand, not given to trivialities. 'Sir, if y' pleases, we got a worry we think ye should know of,' he said quietly.

His eyes slid away to the others for support as he talked and Kydd felt the first stirring of unease. Deputations as such were punishable under the Articles of War and they were taking a big risk in bringing it before him like this. 'Well?' he growled.

'Sir. Could be we'll be voyagin' quite a ways soon,' Hansen mumbled.

Behind him another, older, hand said, more forcefully, 'Aye, an' this means we have t' be ready.'

'F'r rats!' added a third.

'What th' devil is this all about, Mr Bowden?'

'Er, I think they mean to say that *Teazer* being a new-built ship, she doesn't have yet a full crew on board. They tell me they're very concerned that our stores and provisions are as yet still unprotected . . .'

Kydd was beginning to see where it was all leading and eased into a smile.

'. . . therefore, sir, they're requesting you take aboard a – a ship's cat.'

'Ah. Well, that is, I may have omitted t' bring the complement completely up to strength in this particular. I see I must send a hand ashore to press a suitable cat –' There was a shuffling, eyes were cast down. Kydd saw and went on, '– that is unless a volunteer c'n be found, o' course,' and waited.

Glances were exchanged and then the seamed old sailmaker, Clegg, was pushed forward. Nearly hidden in his horny hands was a scrap of fur from which two beady black eyes fixed themselves solemnly on Kydd.

Kydd's eyebrows rose. 'Seems a hard thing t' put such a morsel up against a prime ship's rat, I believe.' At the sullen silence this brought he hastened to add, 'But, o' course, he being new t' the sea he'll have a chance to show something of himself later.' After the ripple of relieved murmurs faded, he snapped, 'Volunteer, this day rated ordinary seaman.' Grins appeared and Kydd continued, 'Er, what name goes in th' muster list?'

Clegg gave a slow smile and, in his whispery voice, said softly, 'It's t' be Sprits'l, sir, on account we being a brig we don't have such a one, an' now we does.'

Kydd spread out the best chart they had of the area, a copy of a French one, and pondered. The Sicily Channel was the only pass between the east and west of the Mediterranean, discounting the tiny Strait of Messina. Through this hundred-mile-wide passage streamed the tide of vessels heading for the rich trading ports of the Levant, among them neutrals with contraband, and French trying to slip past to supply their hard-pressed army in Egypt. But with a hundred miles width of open sea, what would be their likely track?

It was important to make the right choice. How long would it be before a senior officer arrived to put a stop to his independence? He emerged restlessly on deck and caught the flash of sails as a cutter rounded the point into the inlet.

'She's our'n!' Work on deck ceased as every man gazed out at the new arrival come prettily to her mooring.

'Mr Purchet, get th' men back to work this instant!' Kydd snapped. A few minutes later an officer got into a boat, which stroked across to *Teazer*.

The visitor was of a certain age, with shrewd eyes and a strong manner. Removing his hat he said, 'L'tenant Fernly, in command *Mayfly* cutter.' It was naval courtesy for an arriving junior to call upon the ranking officer and this was due Kydd as a full commander.

'Shall we step below, L'tenant?' Kydd said. In his great cabin glasses were brought and respects exchanged. *Mayfly* was with Army dispatches and material from Gibraltar for General Pigot, with a side voyage to Alexandria in prospect later.

'An' you, sir?' Fernly asked politely.

'I shall be puttin' t' sea shortly on a cruise, but not before I have time to beg y' will take dinner with me,' Kydd said.

'That's right kind in you, sir,' Fernly answered, easing into a smile. 'I don't often find m'self able t' sit at table with a new face, as you'd understand, sir.'

Kydd certainly did understand. He warmed to the prospect of a convivial evening and, with a light heart, he set Tysoe to his preparations. The gunroom decided to hold an evening of their own, and as the sun dipped in the west the first seamen from *Mayfly* arrived to claim their age-old right to ship-visiting while in port.

'You're right welcome,' Kydd said warmly, holding out his hand as Fernly came aboard again. Forward, lanthorns were being triced up in the fore shrouds and groups of men below were gathering in noisy groups until the first hornpipes began. Later it would be sentimental songs at the foremast and well-tried yarns to capture and enthrall.

It was a good sign, and with the length of the ship separating them it would not be a trial for them in the great cabin. The table was laid; Tysoe had contrived another easy chair to complement Kydd's own and the two naval officers sat at the stern windows, taking their fill of the fine evening view of Malta.

The candles cast a mellow gold about the cabin and set Kydd's new pieces of silver a-glitter. The local Maltese wine, *chirghentina*, was cool and delicious, and Kydd felt a spreading benevolence to the world take hold. 'Ye would oblige me extremely, sir, if we might talk free, as it were,' he said, hoping the officer's courtesy would give way to the forthright character he suspected lay beneath.

'By all means,' Fernly replied, perhaps picking up on Kydd's mood. 'It's a damnably lonely profession, in all.' He set down his empty glass, which Tysoe noiselessly refilled. 'May I ask ye a question?'

Kydd looked up, surprised.

'Forgive me if I'm adrift in m' reckoning, but y' have the look o' the fo'c'sle about ye.'

'Aye, this is true,' Kydd admitted. He saw no reason to hide it.

'Then c'n we raise a glass together – we're both come aft th' hard way.' There was brittle defiance in his tone.

Cautiously, Kydd raised his glass in agreement. 'T' us.' It was rare for a King's officer to have crossed the great divide from the fo'c'sle to the quarterdeck and Kydd had come across few of the breed. 'Do ye not find it an advantage in command?' To Kydd, it was of considerable benefit to be able to know the mind of the seamen in his charge, to understand the motivations and simple but direct elements of respect that so often differed from those of the quarterdeck.

'Of course. I flatter m'self that I'm at least two steps ahead of the lazy buggers. Let 'em dare t' try any o' their slivey tricks in my watch, is what I say.' Fernly grinned mirthlessly and pushed out his glass to Tysoe.

Kydd did not reply. He knew of hard-horse tarpaulin captains who used their familiarity with the seamen to make life difficult for them. He was also aware that there was an ocean of difference for the foremast hand between obedience and respect, which the older man seemed to have forgotten.

Fernly seemed to sense Kydd's feeling and changed the topic. 'Can't say I've seen *Teazer* in Malta before. A trim craft, very handsome . . .'

Kydd thawed. 'Goes like a witch in anythin' like a quarterin' blow, an' I'm going after more b' crossing a main-yard in place of the cro'jick. Rattlin' fine work b' y'r Maltese shipwrights.'

'You mount fours or sixes?'

'Six-pounders, an' hoping t' find carronades. Couldn't help but notice – *Mayfly*'s clencher-built, not s' common as who would say. I was in a cutter in the Caribbean, *Seaflower* b' name, an' she was lap-straked as well.'

'Caribbean? I was there in *Wessex* frigate in 'ninety-four.'

'Were ye really? I remember . . .'

The talk livened agreeably at the subject of old ships. Fernly had been an able seaman with the good fortune to have impressed a captain sufficiently that he had been plucked from the fo'c'sle and placed on the quarterdeck as a mature midshipman. This had led to promotion in due course, but the later demise of the captain had left him without interest at high level and he had not been noticed.

Dinner was served, the conversation turning now to land-falls and seaports across the seven seas; between them they had seen so much of a world unknown and unexplored to the generation just past.

As justice was being done to a cunning Buttered Meringue La Pompadour, Fernly cocked his head and listened, holding up his hand. The strains of a violin and sounds of merriment from the main deck had stopped and there was a sudden quiet.

Then, faintly on the night breeze, from forward came a familiar air:

We'll rant and we'll roar like true British sailors;
We'll rant and we'll roar across the salt seas
Until we strike soundings in the Channel of old Eng-a-land
From Ushant to Scilly 'tis thirty-five leagues . . .

'That's m' quartermaster,' Fernly said softly, 'an' a right songster indeed.'

Kydd looked at Fernly. '"Spanish Ladies",' he blurted happily.

Fernly returned the look with impish glee, mouthing the words while waving a glass in the air and Kydd responded in a creditable baritone, his own glass spilling as he beat time. Soon Fernly came in with a fair tenor.

The old sea-song finished and, faces flushed, they moved

back to the easy chairs. 'Rare time,' Kydd said, easing his waistband.

'It's a sad profession, without it has compensations,' Fernly agreed, helping himself to Madeira. Tysoe had cleared decks without either man noticing and a baize cloth now bore a neat cluster of decanters.

Kydd sighed deeply. His gaze slipped down to the glittering gold of the epaulette on his coat, which was now draped over the back of his chair. He looked up and his expression became wistful. 'I own that I've been a copper-bottomed, thorough-going lucky wight. Here am I, a Guildford wigmaker, topping it th' mandarin as commander, writing m'self orders f'r a cruise. Who would've smoked it?'

He stopped. 'Ah – that is not t' say . . .' In the fuddle of wine, words failed him. His guest was still only a lieutenant and a silver-haired one at that, with only a tiny cutter to show for his years at sea. And a lieutenant-in-command could not possibly compare with a commander of a sloop.

Fernly lifted his glass and, closing one eye, squinted at the table candle through it. 'Y' told me before as I was t' talk free. Should I?' He spoke as though to himself.

'Fill an' stand on, I beg,' Kydd said warmly.

Still staring at his glass Fernly continued in the same tone: 'You're senior in rank, an' I in years. Gives you a different slant on things, y' must believe.' His voice strengthened. 'Only f'r the friendship I bear ye for the night's company do I speak out, you understand.'

'Just so,' Kydd said neutrally.

'You're new made t' commander, this is plain.'

'Why Keith gave me th' step I still don't understand.'

'Nor will you ever. My guess is, he had others waitin' that by movin' the one into a sloop the other would protest. You were to hand and got th' berth – but if half th' reason was fortune, the other half must be y'r shinin' past. That must still the tongues o' those who would object.'

Kydd leaned forward and refilled his glass. 'But you—'

'Do I hear a dash o' pity on my account? Pray don't trouble y'self, sir. I'm content with m' lot because I'm a philosophical. I'm a tarpaulin an' know it – I never hoisted aboard y'r polite ways, I had no one t' teach me. My pride is in good deepwater seamanship an' prime sailing.'

Looking steadily at Kydd he continued, 'I'll be straight – I've been in the sea service long enough t' take inboard some hard facts, which I'll share with ye.

'The first: y' speaks of a cruise you means to take. That's a brave thing t' do when y'r Articles of War – I mean th' thirteenth – says much about any who, an' if I remember th' words aright, hangs back fr'm "pursuing the chase of any enemy, pirate or rebel", which chasin' prizes instead must surely be.'

He sipped his wine, regarding Kydd calmly. 'An' the seventeenth – pain o' death or other, should ye fail in protecting trade, which is goin' after the privateers and similar and not lookin' after th' merchant jacks.' He paused, then added, 'Y'r flag officer likes prize-money shares but likes better zeal agin the enemy – just ask His Nibs, Adm'ral Nelson!'

Kydd coloured. 'I know the Articles well enough,' he muttered.

Fernly went on remorselessly: 'Still an' all, I've knowledge that the eastern Med squadron will be returning here shortly f'r their regular repair 'n' store, which will be fatal to your enterprise in any case.' So much for his independence, Kydd thought resentfully, but waited for the older man to say his piece.

'Then shall we speak o' your situation.' Fernly glanced mean-ingfully about the cabin and added, 'You must feel content with y'r lot.'

Kydd nodded.

'Then consider this: it's not th' best but the worst thing f'r an officer, being away on y'r own like you are. In the sea service you'll agree the only way t' get promotion is to be noticed. Some fine action, with a butcher's bill to follow, sort o' thing you're well acquainted with, I believe. Now, what chance have ye got t' be noticed in a small ship that you're frightened of the smallest frigate? You're out o' sight, no one knows y' exist. You do well, an' you're accounted a reliable, safe pair o' hands, which will suit their lordships fine t' keep you so for ever.'

It was galling but there was no arguing with it. Fernly leaned over and made a show of smoothing the hang of Kydd's coat with its lustrous gold lace, continuing mildly, 'I give ye joy on y'r promotion – I hope it brings satisfaction.'

Kydd kept mute. Clearly Fernly was about to make some point.

'A commander? I once saw service in a flagship. A real caution, some of th' things you'd see.' He twirled his glass by the stem as he considered Kydd, a lop-sided smile in place.

'The Commander-in-Chief – a lot o' things he has t' worry over. Enemy fleet, state o' the ships, spies 'n' such, but y' know what troubles him most? How t' satisfy those he owes an obligation by way of a place. Relatives o' his, of others, even th' highest in the land, all clamouring f'r preferment.

'So, he removes a favoured l'tenant into a brig as com-mander. He's now out o' sight an' mind at the other end o' the Med for, say, a year, two. Then someone's nephew gets uppity, has t' be quieted with a ship. What then? It's sad enough, but th' first has had his chance for distinction and must give way to another. As simple as that, m' friend.'

Fernly's expression held sorrow and Kydd felt the warmth of the wine and fellowship fall away.

'It gets worse. Our first commander, what is he t' do without he has a ship? If he was a lieutenant – like m'self – we can see him entered back into a ship-of-the-line, second l'tenant or some such. But a commander . . . There's above a hundred commanders more'n there are King's ships I've been told, so what's his fate? A commander may not undo his promotion; and so we see that while th' country fights f'r its life, our brave officer cannot be found employment – an' must retire fr'm the sea.

'Mr Kydd,' Fernly said softly, 'I do believe you're under notice. T' make yourself remarked upon – or perhaps learn how to grow turnips . . .'

Chapter 6

Kydd glowered at the paperwork on his desk, his dark mood sinking fast into depression. It had been a cruel let-down, the intrusion of hard reality into the euphoria of first command. It was not as if he was unaware of the things Fernly had said – every naval officer knew something of the situation – it was more the cold realisation that, like the diagnosis of a disease, it now applied inescapably to him.

He picked up a scrawled sheet, trying to fix his thoughts on stations for fire-fighting, but his eyes glazed. There was no way he could concentrate. The cruise would have to be cancelled: he could not risk being away without real orders when the squadron arrived back in port. His so-brief days of roving free were over. *Teazer*'s fate would revert again to fetch and carry, convoy escort, dispatches – he would be the menial of any who cared to make use of his little ship, with never a chance at true battle and glory.

Yet the worst part was that he could see now that if he failed to distinguish himself in *Teazer* his longed-for elevation would ironically ensure that he must abruptly leave the sea, and without appeal.

One thing was certain, though: a report to the admiral had to be rendered. He had been putting it off as long as he could but there would be no time to spare after he had arrived. Kydd sighed and took a fresh sheet of paper – and a dozen sharp needles clamped themselves to his stockinged leg. As he shot to his feet, banging his head on an overhead deck beam, his eyes flicked down.

There was a terrified squeak and a pair of imploring black eyes looked up into his. Kydd opened his mouth to roar for Tysoe but stopped; he bent and picked up the warm little body, which lay trustingly in his cupped hands. 'Ye're nothing but a tiger, young Sprits'l,' he found himself cooing. A tiny pink tongue gave a tentative lick at one finger and Kydd's heart was lost to the little creature. It had been years before, but he had not forgotten the ship's cat of the old *Duke William* that had shared his first night in the Navy.

The kitten let go and scampered across the deck, then disappeared under a side table, its face reappearing mischievously. Kydd smiled: if this little creature could not only brave the unknown world but turn it into a place of fun and play, who was he to complain at his lot? His depression began to lift and he turned back to his report.

Attard, midshipman of the watch, knocked timidly at the door. 'S-sorry to disturb, sir, but, er, have you—'

'Under the table yonder – an' I'll thank ye t' keep it forward,' Kydd growled, hiding a grin.

It was amazing how such a tiny life had brought proportion to his own. Now he could turn his mind to a more constructive course. His independence was about to be checked

– but then was not this at heart a falsity anyway? An admiral had seniors; even the great Nelson must take orders from above. Nelson – now there was his example: to do his duty to the utmost and when the big chance came to seize it full-heartedly and without hesitation. And, meanwhile, he would try to be like little Sprits'l, taking joyously all that life had to offer of the moment . . .

'Never mind that,' Admiral Warren said, slapping Kydd's report down on the desk, 'I haven't the time. Tell me what you've been doing with yourself.'

'Well, sir,' Kydd began carefully, 'in th' absence of direction fr'm a senior officer I conceived it m' duty to fit out th' ship immediately by any means. Being ready in all respects I proceeded to sea.'

He paused – this was the delicate part. 'I came up with a corsair plunderin' a merchant ship an' tried to catch him but as a xebec he went about close to th' wind and – and I lost him.'

The admiral's granite expression did not change. 'It happens. Go on,' he rasped.

'Er, at the suggestion of Mr Cameron I took a convoy t' Ragusa and fell in with two Algerines. They left without joining action on seein' my hostile motions.'

Warren's eyebrows rose, but he didn't pursue it further. 'Well, then – you have your senior now and it is to be admitted that your presence here is not unwelcome.' Kydd smothered a sigh of relief and tried to look eager. 'While my fleet repairs and stores, it would be of service to me should you look into the south for word of Ganteaume. Even as I've been searching for him in the north, he may have been at large in the Gulf, refitting.

131

'You shall have orders for a reconnaissance along the coast east of Tripoli. I don't have to tell you, if Ganteaume is sighted you will spare nothing and nobody to bring me the news. If at the end of ten days there is no word, then your voyage will not be wasted as you shall be able to render me your appreciation of the situation in those parts.'

'Aye aye, sir!' Kydd said crisply.

Warren glowered. 'And if you're under the impression this scouting voyage is an excuse for prize-taking, let me disabuse you, sir. You're performing this vital task because I can't spare the frigates. Understand?'

'Mr Purchet! Those forrard backstays are a disgrace,' Kydd said savagely, as he stepped back aboard. 'And why is not th' rattlin' complete on the main shrouds?' He didn't wait for an answer and plunged below.

He had no charts of the Barbary coast. No car-ronades. There had been only a brief discussion with the flag-lieutenant concerning intelligence, which seemed contra-dictory and nothing much beyond conjecture: the British were newcomers to the Levant, which had been mainly a French trading preserve before, and it showed. Any charts that might be available were copies of captured enemy ones, of varying age and quality, and provisioning was only to be had at either Malta or by barter with the Moors of north Africa.

There was no word of Ganteaume or his fleet – they might be at large anywhere except in the north where Warren had just been with his squadron. His orders called for a search to the south-east from Tripoli deep into the Gulf of Sirte, pre-sumably returning along the north-trending coast. Any one of the indentations in the lonely desert coast might harbour the powerful enemy squadron; when he came upon them it was in the lap of the gods if the wind was fair for a rapid retirement or whether he would find himself set upon by fast frigates intent on his destruction to preserve the secret of their presence.

There was no possibility of action and glory in this kind of work, no credit for fleeing a superior enemy and simply returning with the news – but every chance of oblivion if he came back with nothing.

Kydd screwed up his attempt at orders in the case of fire on board and flung it into the corner. He snatched up another paper and tried to concentrate on planning the voyage: stores, of course, charts. Where could they water? Their sea endurance would probably not extend to the near thousand-mile round trip. What were the inshore wind and current conditions? He had been in a frigate that had touched ground at the other end of the Mediterranean and it had been a terrifying experience. Was Bonnici up to the hair-raising coast-hugging of this voyage? Was *he*?

They slipped and put to sea early in the morning, shaping course directly south the several hundred miles to Tripoli, the winds fair for a fast passage. *Teazer* leaned into it with a will, but her commander stood unmoving on his quarterdeck, staring ahead in a black mood. Dacres reported sea watches set and Kydd grunted an ill-humoured acknowledgement.

He noticed that several men were the worse for wear after a final run ashore before they sailed: if they fumbled a manoeuvre he would see there was a reckoning.

A line of men on their knees with holystones were working their way aft across the deck, kept well supplied with water from a bucket-man and sand from the petty officer in charge. As they approached, Kydd caught furtive glances – was he going to yield the deck to the lowly seamen or stand his ground? A stubbornness born of his mood kept him rooted to the spot. The men came near. Then, without looking up, awkwardly tried to work round his unmoving shoes. He kept his position, staring forward fixedly as the line passed by. Close to Kydd and well within his hearing, Daniel Hawkins said, in a raised voice to the man on his left, 'Be gob, an' does we have t' top it the heathen slave an' all?'

Kydd stiffened in surprise.

'Silence, damn y'r hide!' Purchet's outraged bellow came from behind him. 'I heard that, y' villain! Y'r own captain you'd chouse, y' rascal!' The boatswain came up to Kydd. 'I'll see him afore Mr Dacres for ye, sir.'

'Thank you, Mr Purchet, but—' Kydd said, then stopped. Any interference would be seen as weakness, an allowing of disrespect to his person and situation. His authority would begin to unravel as of that moment.

With grim inevitability the little drama expanded. The sullen sailor was hauled off and, within minutes, Dacres had solemnly reported that he had confined a member of *Teazer*'s crew to irons, to appear before Kydd at his pleasure.

There was no point in delaying the inevitable: half an hour before the noon grog issue the ship's company was mustered. For appearance's sake, Kydd required his warrant officers and midshipmen to fall in behind where he would stand, facing the mass of seamen. An improvised lectern was set up and when officers and men were all present Dacres went below to report.

Composing his expression to one of solemn judgement Kydd emerged on to the upper deck. The seamen were mustered in a mass forward with the small number of minor officers aft.

Kydd strode purposefully to the lectern. 'Carry on, Mr Dacres,' he intoned, with as much gravity as he could muster.

'Sir. At two bells this forenoon Daniel Hawkins, ordinary seaman, was heard to utter words of calumny and disrespect to the person of you, sir, his lawful commander, in contravention of Article the Twenty-third of the Articles of War.'

'Witnesses?' Kydd said sharply. 'Mr Purchet?'

'Sir,' began the boatswain, with ill-concealed relish, and repeated the accusation.

'Thank you. Is there any t' speak for him?'

'Sir.' Bowden stepped forward manfully. 'Hawkins is in my division, sir, and I have never found reason to remonstrate with him.' It was carefully phrased, the absence of positive qualities revealing.

Kydd turned to Hawkins. 'Have ye anything t' say?' Hawkins stood loosely, with an expression of boredom. He lifted his eyes to Kydd's. There was nothing in them that could be read. Then he shrugged.

'Articles o' War, if y' please.'

'Orf hats!' Purchet roared. Heads were bared with a single rustle of movement.

Peck came forward and read from the frayed leatherbound booklet. 'If any person in the fleet . . .' his voice was flat and reedy and almost certainly not heard at the back '. . . uses reproachful or provoking speeches . . .' Kydd watched the men carefully for any sign of unrest behind the glazed expressions and shuffling feet '. . . upon being convicted thereof shall suffer such punishment . . . and a court-martial shall impose.'

'On hats!' bawled Purchet. The rustle of movement stopped quickly: it was of deep interest to all to hear how their captain would punish.

'Ye can have a court-martial if y' desires it.' This would mean remaining in irons until they returned to Malta.

'No, sir,' Hawkins said evenly.

'Very well. I find ye in contempt of good order an' naval discipline an' you shall take your punishment this very day.' It was a good opportunity to address the assembled ship's company sternly but Kydd could not find it in himself. He waited for a heartbeat then drew himself up. 'Six lashes!'

There was a wave of murmuring but it could have been worse. Kydd stood back from the lectern and thrust his hands behind his back. 'Strip!'

'Carpenter's mate,' growled Purchet, looking about. A grating was removed and, in the absence of a half-deck, it was triced up to the main shrouds. The boatswain's mate took up his ready position with a cat-o'-nine-tails.

In a deathly silence, broken only by the low hissing of the ship's wake, Hawkins's thumbs were secured above his head with spun yarn. His head flat on the gratings, he fixed Kydd's eye, then deliberately looked the other way and tensed.

Feeling a sick emptiness inside Kydd croaked, 'Do y'r duty, boatswain's mate.'

There was no mercy in Laffin's low, sweeping strokes: aboard *Teazer* there were no marine drummers to heighten the tension with furious volleying, only the swish and harsh smack of the lash, as powerful as the kick of a horse. Apart from a first muffled grunt, Hawkins made no sound, and when sentence was complete and he was cut down, he made play of picking up his shirt and jauntily throwing it on his shoulder, over livid purple and red-seeping weals.

Kydd nodded at Purchet's enquiring glance and the boatswain pealed out his call. 'Carry on, the hands.' The assembly turned forward and dissolved into a babble of talk as they streamed below for the grog issue. Not wishing to meet anyone's eye, Kydd left the deck to take refuge in his cabin.

The whole affair had been his fault. The black depression riding on his back was no excuse; childish petulance, unworthy of a real captain, had precipitated the incident.

Kydd's table was spread for the midday meal, a ragoo of kidneys gently steaming and a cold collation tempting, but he was in no mood to enjoy it. Tysoe entered noiselessly and began pouring a sea-cooled white wine. 'Thank 'ee, Tysoe, but ye can carry on, if y' please – leave the wine.'

He drank deeply in the silence of the great cabin, the gentle sway of the little ship sending bright dapples of sunlight from the stern windows prettily back and forth. This usually brought a welling of contentment, but not now.

More wine. He told himself that his mood was probably the consequence of being too euphoric at his sudden life change, that he had been due a dose of reality, but that was no remedy. He splashed the last of the wine into his glass.

Hawkins was forward, separated only by a few dozen feet, and while he himself sat with his wine, the sailor, probably surrounded by his shipmates offering rough consolation and a gulp of grog, was in great pain – all of Kydd's doing.

There was no getting away from it: he had failed. 'Tysoe!'

he called loudly. His servant appeared suspiciously promptly. 'An' I'll have another – open me a red for th' kidneys.'

What was happening to the new-born spirit of comradeship and pride in the ship that he was trying to cultivate? If he was not careful, it would fly apart.

The red wine had the coolness of the wine-store about it; a tiny smile twisted his lip. He had caught out Tysoe for once that he had not a carefully nurtured room-temperature bottle ready to serve. This steadied him: being a captain involved far more than the exercise of absolute power. Insight into human nature, the wise foreseeing of threat and neglect, the assiduous assimilation and control of the mass of detail that was the smooth running of a ship-of-war – these were the skills that had to be acquired, not the indulgence of personal vexations.

But he had no one to talk to, to reflect things back into a measure of proportion. He slammed the glass down and got to his feet. Renzi was no more. He had to find his own salvation – and he would, damn it!

The coast of Barbary was much the same as he had seen it before: low, desolate, mile after mile of scrubby sand and little else. The untidy jumble of Tripoli lay to starboard as *Teazer*'s helm went over and she began her quest for the enemy.

As every headland approached it had to be assumed that on the other side was the dread sight of ships-of-the-line at anchor, ranging frigates cruising in pairs suddenly sighting *Teazer*. What then?

The winds were briskly from the north-west, as expected, and could not have been fairer for their run along the coast but would be in their teeth in the case of a desperate flight back to Malta. And with offshore sandbanks and unknown currents it would need fine seamanship indeed to get through.

Bonnici had a general knowledge of the coast and a number of well-thumbed charts, but was withdrawn and apprehensive: for him this was the lair of the Barbary corsair, who had plagued his people for centuries.

Headland after point, cape after promontory, gulfs, bays, coves – for days, the never-ending low, anonymous line of sandy coast. It was tense, wearying work, which tried the nerves and endurance of men in the confines of the little ship. They stopped several of the ever-present coastal feluccas, not much larger than ship's boats, but there was never a word of any French ships.

Each night *Teazer* stood out to sea and at first light closed with the coast, scrupulously taking up the search where she had left off. Provisions began to fail; one of the three remaining water casks proved foul. If they replenished at any one of the straggling settlements they would find victuals and water well enough, but at the cost of both revealing their presence and later bringing down on themselves a full quarantine in Malta for touching at a Barbary port.

Kydd's spirit hardened. He knew his manner had stiffened at the worry and care that had entered his soul. He was now unsmiling and abrupt; few dared open conversation with him and talk died when he approached. If this was the price to be paid to be a captain, then so be it.

A garrulous Sicilian trader had no word of any French fleet in the vicinity but had heard rumours of a lone cruiser to the north. Discounting this, it seemed increasingly obvious to Kydd that there was no substantial French presence: if they were to fall on the British reinforcements they would be best advised to conceal themselves more to the far north until they were ready, then make a sally in force. Either that or lurk to the west of Sicily and attack the transport at source.

Obedient to his orders Kydd kept *Teazer* ever eastward until they reached the deepest extent of the Gulf of Sirte, still with no sign of Ganteaume. And then it was time to return.

With a worsening state of provisions and water now three upon four, *Teazer* lay over on the larboard tack as close on the wind as she could and left the desolate desert land astern. She made good time to thirty-five degrees north, then went about for the second leg to Malta.

In the empty expanse of the eastern Mediterranean it was odd for the masthead lookout to hail the deck and stranger still for him to be in some confusion about what had been sighted.

'Get up there an' report what you see,' Kydd told Bowden, who swung himself smartly into the shrouds clutching a telescope and joined the lookout.

'A boat, sir,' his report came down. 'I think in distress.'

This far from land the constant south-easterly current in these parts would be sweeping it further and further into the lonely vastness. *Teazer*'s bow turned towards it and they drew nearer. There was a small mast but no sail spread and the five aboard lay in postures of exhaustion.

One in the bow had sufficient strength to take a line and they drew the boat alongside. Sailors from *Teazer* dropped into it to bring up the pathetic creatures waving feebly with thin cries. From the quarterdeck Kydd watched them helped aboard, guessing from the rising jabber of his Maltese sailors that they were probably survivors from a local craft caught in a storm.

It was odd, however, that there had been no undue movement in the barometer lately that Kydd had noticed and also puzzling that the boat was of western European style. He glanced up at the sails flogging in their brails – the wind was backing more to the west and he was anxious to be on his way before he was headed for Malta.

'Get a move on, Mr Dacres!' he bawled.

'Go forward an' tell 'em to take th' rest inboard,' he snapped to Martyn, standing meekly at his side. 'And make the boat fast under our stern – an' main quick, dammit!' he threw after the youngster.

Kydd stood motionless. More mouths to feed, water to guzzle when they themselves were so short . . . Was his heart hardening so much that he was begrudging this of shipwrecked sailors? He did not want to answer the question.

Sail was loosed and braced round, and *Teazer* resumed her course homewards. Kydd knew he could leave the details of caring for the passengers to the good-hearted seamen, who in all probability would give them the shirts from their own backs.

'Sir, I talked wi' them an' I think you mus' know.'

'Yes, Mr Bonnici.' Kydd's interest quickened. They had seen Ganteaume afar off, perhaps? Or even . . .

'Th' French, sir. It was the French did this t' them!' Bonnici's eyes glittered.

'And?'

'Not ships-o'-the-line. A ship – corvette. To save prize crew they cast adrift all th' prisoner!'

'They were taken by a National ship? When? What was his name?' This was very different: a unit of the French Navy loose on the sea lanes. He would not be going back with nothing. Warren could not afford any interference with shipping in the approaches to Alexandria and would quickly dispatch a frigate to deal with it.

'Sir, his name *La Fouine*, ship-rig wi' eight-pounders, an' fast.' He added, 'They were took three day ago.'

Kydd gave a wry smile. The corvette would be well clear of the area and could be anywhere. But he had something to tell.

'T' twenty degrees east, sir, conformable to y'r orders.'

'And nothing – not even a whisper?' Warren said testily, his gouty foot was supported discreetly by a cushion under the table.

'Nothing, sir.'

'You spoke with merchantmen, of course.'

'Yes, sir. No word of Ganteaume anywhere in this part o' the Mediterranean.'

Warren glowered at Kydd.

'Sir, we picked up a boatload o' survivors on returning. They say they were taken by a French National ship – a corvette, sir,' Kydd added hastily, seeing Warren's sudden jerk of interest. 'And this two or three days ago.'

'So he's on the high seas somewhere to the east at last report,' Warren mused. 'Nothing for a battle squadron to concern themselves with. But if he gets among our transports ...'

The usual corvette was bigger than an English ship-sloop but smaller than a frigate; with extended quarterdeck and bulwarks well built up, they had been called by some 'petty-frigates'.

'Do ye know his name?' he rumbled, leaning forward.

'Sir – it's *La Fouine*.'

'Ha!'

'You know him, sir?'

'Never heard of him in my life. Your French not up to it, I see?' Warren's grim face eased into a thin smile.

'Er, it means some sort o' bird?' Kydd hazarded. His lessons with Renzi had been workmanlike and to the point, but it sounded a bit like—

'It does. What we might call a stone marten.' His look of amusement increased. 'And were ye not a gentleman in France and were addressed so, it might be comprehended as "weasel-face",' he added, with a sudden fruity cackle.

Kydd tried to crack his face into a comradely chuckle but the proximity of a rear admiral of the Mediterranean Fleet was too much for him and the smile sagged weakly.

Warren looked speculatively at Kydd. 'Can I take it, sir, that you're at leisure as of your return to Malta?'

'Sir,' Kydd stuttered.

'Then you shall have orders that I believe will keep you tolerably employed. I desire that you will seek out and destroy this corvette, should he have the temerity to sail east or south of Sicily.' Warren peered at Kydd to see the effect of his words. 'I will not have frigates absented from my squadron before Ganteaume, yet I cannot tolerate such a one astride the approaches to Egypt. Can ye do it?'

'Thank you, Mr Bonnici – spread 'em out, if y' please.' Kydd's great cabin seemed small with three in it; himself one side of his table, Dacres and now Bonnici on the other, scrutinising the charts.

'Now I want y' best thinking. If *La Fouine* is here,' Kydd indicated the broad area to the south and east of Sicily, 'then where should we start?' Focus on a single war-like object had done wonders for his spirits. If anything was going to bring him to notice it would be a successful action against a true French man-o'-war.

'It would be of great assistance were we to discover his mission, sir,' Dacres said diffidently. 'Is he a common prize-taker, or does he seek to distress the lines of supply to our army? The one, he will desire to place himself at the point of most shipping, the Sicily Channel to the west; the other, he will keep well to the east at the seat of the fighting. Which is it to be?'

'Well said, Mr Dacres,' Kydd replied. 'And we must assume that as Admiral Warren is fresh come from th' north, we will not find *La Fouine* thereabouts.' He rubbed his chin and pondered. 'There is besides one thing other t' consider – how does he keep the seas for long without he has a friendly port at his back t' keep him victualled an' in powder an' such?'

'They have a treaty with Sicily but I doubt they would operate from there – I have heard Taranto has been visited by them,' Dacres offered.

'Aye, could be, but this is a mort distant fr'm both the Sicily Channel and the fighting. If it were me, I'd like t' find somewhere between the both – but there's none I can see. Mr Bonnici?'

'Not f'r me saying, sir, but has he sail back to France?'

Kydd bristled. 'No, he hasn't – we'll find him sure enough!' If he could not, this chance of distinction was gone for ever. He looked from one to the other but each avoided his gaze, and stared down at the chart. This was hardly Nelson's band of brothers before a battle, he brooded; but was he not the captain with the full power, and responsibility, to make decisions?

'Very well, this is what we'll do.' He collected his thoughts.

'Er, th' most important is our landings. We start there, say, thirty degrees east, an' then track west. Because we've a head wind we'll have t' proceed take b' tack – but this is no matter, for it obliges us to crisscross the shipping lanes, which in course we must do until we've raised Sicily again.

'A hard flog, gentlemen, but it's the only way I can see we'll lay him by th' tail.'

Empty seas. Seas with every kind of vessel imaginable. The dreary north African coast yet again. Once, a British convoy straggling in a cloud of sail. It went on for long days, then weeks of hard sea-time with never a whisper of a rumour of their quarry.

Kydd was tormented with thoughts that his decision was a failure, that the corvette had turned back after seizing its prize and was now in Marseille. But surely there would be no point in the Frenchman turning out its prisoners to save on prize crew unless it intended further predation?

And was he correct to insist on flogging back against the weather, instead of making a judgement on where the corvette must pass and wait comfortably until it did?

They turned south, deep into the lee shores of the Gulf of Sirte and the hunting grounds of the pirate corsairs of Tripoli and Tunis. They beat against the north-westerlies and suffered the withering heat and blinding dust of the sirocco. Still there was no sign.

Scoured by sea salt and dust storm *Teazer* was no longer new. Her bright sides had faded and her lovely white figurehead had lost its gold, now defiantly weather-beaten. There were also signs of hard usage – ropes turned end for end when they became too hairy at the nip, smart canvas now a bleached grey and everywhere a subtle rounding of sharp corners, a shading of colours about a shape.

However, Kydd saw only a growing maturity, a sea-tried ship to which he could trust his life. But this was war and there would come a time when she must be pitted in merciless battle against another, bigger and stronger than she was. Kydd steeled himself against the thought of what an enemy broadside would do. But if *Teazer* could not find and then overcome her opponent it would mean the end for him.

Kydd kept the Barbary city of Tripoli well under his lee as they passed: the British were in amity with the rapacious pasha, but within the distant stone ramparts of the city there were reputed to be Christian slaves in miserable squalor.

They rode out a storm from the north-west, the seas punching their bows with short, savage blows, the spindrift in whipping, horizontal sheets that left the eyes salt-sore and swollen.

When they closed the coast again, the boatswain and Dacres approached Kydd. 'Sir, I'm truly sorry to have to tell you that Mr Purchet advises that the last water cask in the hold is foul,' Dacres reported.

'Aye, sir, beggin' y'r pardon, but this'n means we shall have t' return . . .'

Now he would have to head back with nothing to show for his voyage; it was unlikely that he would be given another chance, which, of course, probably meant that it was a return to dispatches and convoys, then a quiet relieving of command and forced retirement from the sea.

'Sir,' the master began.

'Mr Bonnici?' Kydd replied, aware of the irony that this

man whom he himself had taken on would continue to remain at sea professionally while he—

'We c'n get water,' the master continued softly.

'Where?' To call at any port on the Barbary coast would be to condemn *Teazer* and her company to the insupportable tedium of a Malta quarantine.

'Sir, all they who sail th' Mediterranean know where is water. Not at the port – no, on th' shore, in the rock.' His shrewd eyes crinkled with amusement.

'Go on!'

'Near Zuwarah. Another five leagues, no more.'

Cautiously, *Teazer* shortened sail as the little bay opened up. Miles from any settlement that Kydd had noticed, there was a ragged point of land with a small beach, ending in an untidy jumble of rocks and a tight cluster of tall date palms. Not far beyond was another point, which provided the opposite enfolding arm of a calm haven.

'What's the depth o' water?'

'Good holding in seven fathom, jus' four cable off.'

While watering they would be vulnerable, but the bay was set back and out of the way of casual coastal transits. The prize of perhaps another week at sea was too good to pass up.

'We'll do it!'

With a leadsman chanting the depths they ghosted in and anchored – with chancy desert winds inshore, Kydd took the precaution of laying out a kedge first and *Teazer* came slowly to rest.

The hold was opened. As quickly as possible, the planking of the mess-deck was taken up and the hatchways thrown back to allow tackles between the two masts to be rigged to sway the big casks up and into the cutter for the pull to shore.

Dacres returned from a quick exploration. 'Water indeed, sir! Comes out from between the rocks in that cliff.' Heaven only knew how water was present in such quantities in rocks of the desert, but Kydd was not in the mood to question; the sooner they were under way again the better. He paced impatiently up and down, then retreated to his cabin.

He stared out of the stern windows at the watering party ashore: with an exotic earth beneath the feet they might be difficult to control. Perhaps he should have sent Dacres instead of midshipman, but he knew he could not grudge them a light-hearted seizing of the moment.

A sudden shout of alarm pierced his thoughts. Confused thumping of feet sounded and, as he stood up, the door burst open. Attard was wide-eyed. 'Mr Dacres's compliments – sir, there's a frigate! A thumper! He says—'

Kydd knocked him aside in his rush on deck. It was the nightmare he had feared – Ganteaume! They were neatly trapped in the little bay as if by special arrangement. And there it was, frighteningly close in, and manoeuvring to close off their escape.

'That's not Ganteaume – that's one of ours!' Dacres exclaimed, with relief.

'One o' Warren's frigates?'

'No, it ain't, sir,' Purchet said heavily. 'Can't say as I know 'oo he is – but one thing's f'r sure, he's not ours.'

Kydd ignored Dacres's anxious look and snatched his telescope. He did not recognise the vessel either. Big, very big. In a sudden rush of hope he searched the mizzen rigging, the image dancing with the thump of his heart, until he found what he was looking for. 'Thank God,' he breathed. 'Stars 'n' stripes,' he said, in a louder tone, snapping the glass shut decisively.

'Stars and what, sir?' Dacres asked hesitantly.

'They're Americans,' Kydd said happily. 'The United States Navy!'

'The United States?'

'Yes, Mr Dacres. They have a regular-goin' navy now, I'll have ye know.' It was not the time to explain that two years or so before he had been aboard the first war cruise of the newly created United States Navy.

What was puzzling was that their concern, as far as he knew, was in the defence of the seaboard of the United States and their interests no further distant than the Caribbean. Why were they in the eastern Mediterranean?

Then another thought struck: he had not heard that the quasi-war was over, the undeclared war that had broken out between the United States and an over-confident France over the latter's arrogant interpretation of the rights of neutrals and the subsequent taking of American prizes. Could they be here as a consequence of quasi-war operations?

'Clear away th' pinnace and muster a boat's crew. I'm t' call on the Americans, I believe, Mr Dacres.'

It soon seemed clear that their manoeuvring was an evolution to allow them to remain, probably for watering, and while he watched, sail was struck smartly while their anchor dropped. Kydd made sure that *Teazer*'s ensign flew high and free and put off for the American. She had a no-nonsense, purposeful air, spoiled for Kydd's English eye by the bold figurehead of a Red Indian chief and a rounded fo'c'sle instead of the squared-off one to be seen in a King's ship.

As they approached, he saw activity on her decks. At first

he feared his gesture of respect had been misconstrued: in his experience the young navy could be prickly and defensive, but then again there could be no mistaking his own purpose, with boat ensign a-flutter and his own figure aft. Then he saw they were assembling a side party to pipe him aboard.

The boatswain's call sounded, clear and piercing, as Kydd came up the steps, his best cocked hat with its single dash of gold clapped firmly on as he mounted. At the top he stopped and deliberately removed his hat to the flag in the mizzen, then turned to the waiting officer. 'Commander Kydd, Royal Navy,' he said gravely, 'of His Britannic Majesty's ship *Teazer.*'

The officer, young and intense with a high forehead and dark eyes, straightened. 'Lootenant Decatur, United States Navy frigate *Essex.*' He did not offer to shake hands, instead bowed stiffly and stepped aside to make way for his captain coming out on deck.

Kydd bowed and allowed himself to be introduced. 'Cap'n Bainbridge. Welcome aboard, Commander. Might I offer you some refreshment?'

The pinnace lay off; Bowden could be trusted to keep his boat's crew in order and be ready for the signal to return. 'That's kind in ye, Captain,' Kydd said politely.

The great cabin was plainly furnished but clean, with a sense of newness and the scent of North American pine. 'Ye have me at a disadvantage, sir,' Kydd said carefully, over some wine. 'We were at our watering, as you can see.' If there was going to be any friction then it would be this: access to the single water source.

'Our intention also, Commander.' Bainbridge was an impressive figure, over six feet tall and with a striking fore-knot in his plentiful hair. 'I've a ready respect for your service, Mr Kydd, and that's no secret. Why don't you take your fill of the water and we'll stand by until you're done?'

'That's handsome in ye, sir, but I know th' spring an' there's enough f'r us all. We'll take it together, cask b' cask.'

'A good notion. We'll do that,' Bainbridge said genially, and got to his feet.

'Sir,' Kydd said earnestly, 'I was in th' United States when y'r quasi-war with France started. It strikes me there's grounds here f'r – who should say? – mutual assistance against th' aggressor?'

Bainbridge's eyes went opaque. 'Commander, the quasi-war is now concluded.'

'Ah. So—'

'The treaty of 1778 is no more. We are neutrals, sir, and will faithfully abide by our obligations. I will wish you good-day, sir.'

It had been worth the try, but it did not furnish the real reason for an American presence so deep into the Mediterranean. 'Sir – may I know of y'r interest in these parts, if y' do not think it impertinent t' ask?'

'I do. Good day to you, sir.' He conducted Kydd back on deck.

Out in the sunlight Kydd blinked, aware of every eye on him. 'Thank ye, sir, f'r your hospitality – it's a very fine ship y' commands.'

He passed a silent Decatur, sensed the burning eyes following him and was making to step over the side when someone grabbed his shoulder. He swung round and saw a grinning officer holding out his hand. 'Be darned – and this must be Tom Kydd as was. A commander, no less!'

'Aye. An' don't I see Ned Gindler afore me?' It was half

a world away from Connecticut but the same friendliness that had so cheered him as a new lieutenant again reached out to him. 'Well met, Ned!' Kydd grinned. The deck remained silent and still about them. Kydd turned and crossed to Bainbridge again. 'Sir, it's not in m' power t' return y'r kindness to all of ye in my little ship, but it would give me particular pleasure t' welcome L'tenant Gindler aboard.'

'Thank you, Commander. Mr Gindler would be pleased to accept. Until sundown, Lootenant?'

Gindler lifted his glass to Kydd. 'Well, I have to declare, she's one trim lady – I guess she's handy in stays?'

'She is that,' said Kydd, smugly, 'A real flyer on the wind. Not as you'd say spankin' new, but she'll get a lick o' paint when we have time,' he added defensively.

'You must be very proud, Tom,' Gindler said softly, looking at Kydd with an enigmatic expression. 'Captain of your own ship, and all.'

It brought Kydd up with a start: what were his present worries compared to what he had won for himself? 'A noble thing it is indeed, Ned. Do ye know, I have more power than the King of England?' At Gindler's quizzical look he added, 'I may hale a man before me an' have him flogged on the spot – by the law of the land this is somethin' even His Majesty may not do.'

It brought laughter from the American but all Kydd found he could manage was a lop-sided smile. Gindler's amusement receded. 'My dear fellow – if you'll pardon my remarking it, your demeanour is not to be expected of a grand panjandrum. No, sir! Too much bowed by care and woe in all . . .'

Kydd's smile turned to a grimace. 'Aye, I will admit t' it.'

He stared through the pretty stern windows at the bright, sunlit sea outside. 'I have m' ship, this is true, but unless I can shine in its command I'll have t' yield to another. And there's no glory t' be found in small-ship work, all convoys 'n' dispatches, so how am I to find it?' Gindler started to come in but Kydd went on bitterly, 'We got word of a French corvette in these waters an' I was sent to bring it t' battle. My one chance – but the cruise is finished without so much of a smell o' one.'

He looked up half hopefully. 'Ye haven't word of it at all, Ned?'

Gindler murmured noncommittally.

Kydd's eyes fell. 'Then, o' course, you havin' made y'r peace with the French you'll be honour bound not t' tell me even if ye knew.' Gindler continued to look at him wordlessly.

Tossing off his wine, Kydd changed his mood. 'But here I sit, neglectin' m' guest! Tell me, Ned, have you hopes y'self for an advancement at all?'

Gindler's face shadowed. 'You may recall, friend, that our war is finished. We're now neutrals not just in name. No war, we don't need ships – or officers is the cry.'

'Did m' eyes deceive? Is not *Essex* as fine a frigate as ever I saw?'

Looking uncomfortable Gindler replied, 'Yes, but I have to say there are few more.' He hesitated, then went on, 'We have a new president, m' friend, a Thomas Jefferson. Now, in the past we've been handing over bags of gold to the Barbary pashas to keep 'em from raiding our trading ships. Jefferson loathes this craven knuckling to pirates and hates even more what it's costing us. We are here to do something about it.'

Kydd made to refill his glass, but he shook his head. 'Have ye?'

'Not – yet.'

'You—'

'Some would say that Dale, our commodore, is a mite lacking in spirit. We surely put their noses out of joint at first, but all we've achieved is threats of war from all four pashas, who are put out by not getting their due tribute.'

'So you'll have y'r war.'

'Not so, I'm grieved to say it, for Congress has not declared war back. In the main, we're to leave their ships in peace to go about their "lawful" occasions of plundering our trade.' His face tightened.

'It has t' come to war,' Kydd said warmly, 'and then you'll get y'r ship, Ned!'

Gindler said nothing, and at his dark look Kydd changed the subject. 'The *Essex* – a stout enough frigate. Must be a fine thing t' be an officer aboard.'

Gindler threw him a look of resigned exasperation. 'Dear Tom, we're a small young navy and everyone in it knows everyone else. Therefore preferment and seniority are a matter of characters, origins and hearsay.

'I speak only between we two – but under the strict and unbending Cap'n Bainbridge, whose treatment of the enlisted hands is, well, shall we say less than enlightened?, I share the wardroom with our absurdly young first l'tenant, Stephen Decatur. Who is of burning zeal but given to duelling, a vice much indulged in by us, I fear. Therefore I'll leave it to your imagining what it is to be one of such a company who do suffer our frustrations to such a degree . . .'

Kydd had never been in such a situation, but he could see

what it meant to his friend and felt for him. 'Ned, y'r New England trees in spring should be a famous sight, I believe. Do tell me, I c'n remember 'em now . . .'

'You're in the right of it, friend. All along the—'

There was a hesitant knock at the door: it was Dacres. 'Sir, I'm sorry to say, there's some kind of – of altercation at the watering place. Midshipman Martyn seems unable to keep order in his men. Shall I—'

'No. Call away the jolly-boat, an' I'm going ashore m'self.'

'And if you have room . . .' said Gindler, smoothly. At Kydd's look he added, 'In the instance that I may be of service in the article of translations, as it were.'

The source of the altercation was easy enough to detect: the slippery runway for the casks up to the rock fissure from where the water sprang could take only one, either coming or going. Boatswain's mate Laffin stood astride it with fists at the ready, a sailor opposite him, a bull-sized black man, grinned savagely, and other Americans were bunching behind him.

'Moses! Step back now, d' you hear?' Gindler shouted, from the boat. 'You want to start another war?'

A harsh bass laugh came from the huge frame. 'They wants 'un, I c'n oblige 'em, Mr Gindler.'

Kydd quickly crossed to Laffin. 'What's this, then?' he snapped.

'Cousin Jonathan – can't take a joke, sir. Thinks mebbe they're better'n us—'

There was a roar from the Americans and Kydd stepped between them, holding up his hands. If he could not pacify both sides, and quickly, there was every likelihood of a confrontation and repercussions at an international level.

'I'm surprised at ye, Laffin,' he began. The man looked at

him sullenly. 'Do ye not remember how we settle these matters in the fleet?' Laffin blinked without reply.

He turned to Gindler, whose eyes were warily on his men, now spreading out as if taking positions for a fight. 'Sir.' He took off his cocked hat and flung it on the sand in front of Gindler. 'I do challenge th' United States Navy!' There was an audible gasp and he saw Gindler tense. 'T' find which is th' better ship – fair 'n' square – we challenge *Essex* to a contest o' skill an' strength. A race o' one mile, under oars.'

After a dumbfounded silence there were roars of agreement. Gindler stepped forward, picked up Kydd's hat and returned it to him with a bow, saying, in ringing tones, 'On behalf of my fellow Americans, I accept your challenge, Mr Kydd.'

He turned to his men and said, 'We can't let 'em think that as a nation we do not know how to play fair. We'll have the same number of men, of course, but – we exchange boats before we start.'

Kydd grinned. Clearly Gindler was no stranger to the stratagems common in fleet regattas. This would put paid to anything underhand.

The watering was completed at breakneck speed and a course laid out from under the bowsprit of *Essex* to a buoy half a mile along the coast.

The two boats were readied. In deference to the smaller craft that *Teazer* carried, her pinnace was run against *Essex*'s yawl, both pulling four oars. Much was made of the transfer of oarsmen from one to the other, particularly the remarkable sight of the sovereign flag of each nation proudly at the transom of another. Wry comments were passed concerning the workmanship of their boats of the occasion, Teazers scorning the carvel build of the yawl while the Essexes sighed theatrically at the clencher-build of the pinnace, but the four oarsmen took their places readily enough, adjusting foot-stretchers and hefting the fifteen-foot sweeps.

Every boat that could swim lined the course, filled with hoarsely yelling spectators; the rest crowded the decks of their respective ships. On the fo'c'sle of *Essex* Kydd slowly raised a pistol. The shouting died away as the oarsmen spat on their hands: the crack of the pistol was lost in a sudden storm of cheering and they bent to their sweeps in a mighty, straining effort.

The boats leaped ahead, nothing between them. Bainbridge and his officers grouped together on the foredeck, solemnly observing progress – the first to return and pass under the bowsprit would be declared winner.

It was a tight race; the shorter but quicker strokes of the Americans contrasted with the longer but deeper pulls of their opponents and they were round the buoy first – but on the run back the gap narrowed by inches until it became too close to call.

'America by a nose!' Decatur yelled, punching the air as the two craft shot under the line of bowsprit.

'Not so fast, Lootenant,' Bainbridge said, in a hard voice, among the deafening noise of cheering and argument.

'Sir, I know what I saw,' Decatur protested, moving to confront Bainbridge, 'and it was not an English victory.'

With his eyes still on the lieutenant, Bainbridge said quietly, 'Mr Kydd, what do you say?'

Kydd stepped forward and spoke loudly: 'Captain, it was a near-run thing. I'll have ye know I'm proud of my ship, sir!' He paused for just a moment. 'But I own, it was the Americans who beat us this day.'

The frigate broke into a riot of cheering and noise.

Bainbridge held out his hand. 'I hope we meet again soon, Commander.'

Gindler saw Kydd to the side. 'It did me a power of good to see you, my friend,' he said quietly.

'Aye – and we'll be sure t' meet again . . . an' in better times f'r us both.' Kydd signalled to the pinnace and donned his hat.

'And that was handsomely done of you, if I may say,' Gindler said, his glance as fond as a brother.

Kydd murmured something, but Gindler cut him short. Leaning forward he said, in an odd manner, 'If you're returning to Malta, you will be passing by Lampedusa. You might wish to admire the scenery. It's remarkable – especially in the sou'-sou'-west . . .'

Chapter 7

'Run out!' The eight larboard six-pounders rumbled and fetched up against the solidity of the bulwark at the gun-port with a crash, the sailors at the side-tackles heaving like madmen at the cold iron. The gun-captain threw up his hand to indicate that the exercise was finished – but three aimed rounds in four minutes was not good enough.

'Mr Stirk, y'r men would not stand against a Caribbee mud-lark,' Kydd called irritably down the deck. 'Shall we see some heavy in it this time?'

It was now sure: thanks to Gindler, there would be a meeting shortly. And not with a despised privateer – this was a fully fitted out man-o'-war, an eight-pounder corvette of the French Navy, bigger, heavier and possibly faster than *Teazer*.

Now that the reality was upon him the looming fight was awaking all kinds of feelings in Kydd; before, he could always glance back and see the captain standing nobly on his quarterdeck, a symbol of strength and authority to look to in a time of trial, the one who would see them safely through.

But did he, Thomas Kydd, former perruquier of Guildford, have it in *him*? The simple act of taking command had become complicated by so many elements that were not amenable to plain thinking and common logic: men's character, the probability of the enemy taking this course or that, and now the requirement that he should show himself as a strong commander, contemptuous of danger and sure of himself – a leader others would follow.

His back straightened as he watched the men at their gunnery exercise. It was not simple duty and obeying orders that was making them sweat: an alchemy of character and leadership was turning their mechanical actions into a willing, purposeful working together. But was it for him or their ship? Or both?

He was still in his twenties, but Kydd's face was hardening. Lines of responsibility and authority had deepened and changed his aspect from the carefree young man he had been. The simple ambition that had driven his thirst for laurels had become multi-faceted; his need for personal triumphs was now tempered by the knowledge that men were following him, trusting him, and he had a bounden duty to care for them. His quest for professional distinction must now be subordinate to so much else.

The gun crews stood down, drinking thirstily at the scuttled butt after the strenuous exercise, but Kydd's thoughts rushed on. They would be meeting the enemy shortly and much depended on him. The combat, when it came, would be far from the country he had sworn to defend, far out of sight of the Admiralty and the statesmen who had decreed that he and his men should be there to fight for them. He would strive to his utmost for a victory – but would he be able to forge that precious spirit of steadfast devotion in their cause that would bring *Teazer*'s company with him?

When Stirk roared at a gun captain, Kydd threw off the mood and focused his thoughts. Lampedusa: a wretched little island to the south of the Sicily Channel, hardly inhabited. A temporary base for their quarry? Possibly, provided there was a suitable haven. Bonnici had surmised it could be Capo Ponente and a cove beyond of the sort apparently common there – rocky cave formations and small beaches well protected with ugly shoals.

This left the question of the plan of attack. In the absence of any charts of scale worth the name it was a waste of time to attempt anything detailed. The only course he could see was simply to appear at where his best guess was for the corvette's lair and be prepared for anything – assuming it *was* there and not on its trail of devastation on the high seas.

The immediate future of *Teazer* and her entire ship's company were now in his hands: in the morning men were going to live or die depending on the cunning and effectiveness of the course of action that he alone must come up with.

He remembered Nelson's tactics at the Nile. Expecting a classic fleet action at sea he had instead been confronted by the enemy securely at anchor, a wall of guns. Immediately he had conceived a brilliant and original plan. He sailed before the wind but had stern anchors ready to swing them to a stop alongside the enemy and his fleet had gone straight on to achieve a legendary victory. What was his own strategy compared to this?

Kydd did not spend a good night: they would be off Capo Ponente at daybreak, ready at battle quarters.

He was on deck well before the first light stole in to bring form and life to the dark waves. Then, the black mass of the island resolved into a featureless low tumbling coastline of bleached grey, and the masthead lookout screamed, '*Deck hooo!* Ship at anchor close in wi' the land!'

Kydd snapped from his muzzy fatigue. There was no doubt that this was Lampedusa, and there, in a cove between two small headlands about four miles away, was a ship-rigged vessel at anchor.

Excited chatter broke out. 'Still!' he roared. All eyes were upon him. This was the moment – the point at which he must justify his captaincy of a man-o'-war, and he needed to think.

His senses brought the picture to him immediately: a coast-line trending to the north-west from where the steady morning breeze was coming – winds would be parallel with the shore. If the ship was going to strike for the open sea then at best it could beat out at an angle from no better than seventy degrees off the wind close-hauled, to sail down the coast running free.

With rising hope he knew what he must do. If he closed quickly with the entrance of the cove he would be in a posi-tion to force the enemy to battle as he emerged. The clear image of the ship through his telescope showed no sail bent on and therefore no capability to flee. Realisation dawned: he had trapped his quarry!

A new respect showed in Dacres's eyes as he approached for orders. 'Remain at quarters,' Kydd said crisply, 'We take him as he comes out – loose courses.'

Teazer sped towards the distant ship. The enemy was at bay! Excitement took hold of Kydd as he went over in his mind what had been done to prepare.

He noticed that he had increased the speed of his pacing

about the decks and forced himself back to a confident stroll. 'Pass th' word for my sword,' he ordered. Fighting would start in hours.

Then doubt rushed in like a returning tide. What proof had he that this was the ship he was pursuing? There were no colours, no one knew its distinguishing features. Was this all to be in vain? But, on the other hand, what was an innocent ship-rigged European-built vessel doing in such a place? Somehow he knew that this was *La Fouine*.

If it was, they were in for a sharp fight. By eye he appeared about a quarter as big again as *Teazer*, and there were nine ports along that graceful side, an eighteen against their sixteen. If the report of eight-pounders was correct, *Teazer* was appreciably out-gunned as well as out-manned. A twisted smile acknowledged the irony that he, the smaller, was assuming the role of aggressor.

There was a chance, but he was raw and untried in the art of captaincy at war, while a significant unit of the French Navy on an independent cruise far from home would surely have an experienced and formidable commander.

In all probability, within hours, the lovely *Teazer* would be a shattered ruin and . . . He fought to keep himself expressionless while he crushed the betraying thoughts. His ship would need every ounce of his strength and will in the near future and he would give it.

'A cool one, sir,' Dacres said, beside him. 'No sign of a fluster aboard even as we close.'

Kydd said nothing, gazing through his glass at the vessel. Indeed, there were figures just visible on deck but, puzzlingly, none in the rigging as they bore down. 'They know we're here. That is sufficient,' he said.

'Sir!' Bonnici was wearing a small-sword for the first time.

Kydd wondered if the older man expected to be in a boarding party but assumed that it was probably more as a gesture for personal protection if they themselves were boarded.

'Yes?'

'I cannot advise but you mus' not keep in wi' the land. There are rock offshore, so many an' not to be seen!' In the breakdown of his English there was no mistaking the man's urgency. It brought a complication: if they remained off-shore for their prey, the ship, with superior local knowledge, could slip through the shoals and away.

'We take th' risk,' Kydd snapped. But advancing with a leadsman in the chains forward was no way to go into battle and he had reluctantly to concede that there was a seaward limit to his approach. He lifted the telescope again. This time there was movement about his mizzen peak halliards and a flash of colour jerked aloft. The ensign of a French man-o'-war.

There was now no doubt, and scattered cheers about the decks of *Teazer* showed that it had not been lost on the men. At this point it would be usual for the captain to step for-ward and deliver a stirring call to arms, to excite and inspire – but it was the last thing Kydd felt capable of doing. He was only too aware of the nervous excitement building and the challenge to his confidence, and was afraid that anything he said would come out too weakly.

'We'll shorten sail, I believe,' he ordered instead. They were close enough now that whatever *La Fouine* did they would be up with him quickly. They would be fighting in topsails. There was no point in racing past their target: the more sail-trimmers aloft the fewer on the guns.

Kydd had decided how far in he was prepared to risk *Teazer*. They were rapidly approaching that point and still there was no move from the French to put to sea. He lifted the telescope and braced it, steadying the image, staring long and hard.

He had been mistaken: there *was* sail bent to the yards, but it was in such a fine stow along the yardarms that he had not noticed it: *La Fouine*'s captain was a seaman. He was anchored side towards but then Kydd noticed the line dropping away from the stern-quarters. So it was at no chance angle that he lay – the captain had laid out a mooring by the bow and stern both, which kept his broadside trained resolutely on any who would dare enter the little cove.

'They're anchored by th' stern as well,' he grunted, keeping the glass up.

'Sir,' said Dacres.

But it was not his problem, Kydd thought sourly; it was the captain's. 'Heave her to,' he growled, still searching with his telescope. Not a single move to ready for sea – they might as well have been alongside in their home port. 'While he's there we can't touch him.'

To approach the vessel they would have to present their unprotected bow for an unendurable pounding before they reached him – and, with unknown rocks lurking, tricky manoeuvring would be impossible. *La Fouine* was quite safe where she lay.

'Sir, that point—'

'God rot it f'r a poxy—!' Kydd exploded in useless anger. Although they were hove to and stopped in the water, an insistent current was slowly but surely urging them towards the low, rocky southerly point of the cove. And stretching well out from it were the tell-tale hurry and slop of dark irregularities in the wave pattern that betrayed the threat of unknown rocks below the surface. 'Get sail on an' take her out.'

He bit his lip in frustration: this was not how it should be. Keyed up for a desperate clash of gunpowder and blades he had not expected a long wait until the Frenchman decided he was ready.

'Boats, sir – a cutting out?'

'No.' Dacres was a fool or worse to suggest that. Boats pulling madly towards a prepared warship would be blown out of the water even at night – and this captain would certainly have lookouts to detect an approach in any direction.

'Er, land a gun an' drive 'im out?' Purchet countered.

Kydd ground his teeth. 'No, damn y'r eyes – he'd be a prize simkin should he neglect t' land sentries on both points, an' that's not the kind o' man I think he is.' His sister's patient tuition in polite discourse on his promotion to King's officer was wilting fast under the strain.

The quarterdeck fell into silence, *Teazer* obediently stretching out away from the shore – and Kydd's only chance of making his name. 'Wear about an' keep us with th' land,' he threw at Bonnici, whose expression remained blank.

And still no sign of movement in the anchored vessel. Was it ever going to make a break for the open sea?

Teazer closed rapidly with the coast again. 'Pass th' word for the purser.'

'The – the purser, sir?' Dacres said in astonishment.

'Yes, you heard. The purser.'

Kydd kept his silence while Ellicott scrambled up the hatchway. 'How many days' vittles do we have at hand?' he asked the man.

Ellicott shot a shrewd glance at the motionless French vessel. 'Sir, as you remember, you gave directions—'

'How – many – days?'

'Er, no more'n three, five if we're three upon four.'

All *La Fouine* had to do was sit tight until *Teazer* had sailed away and then he could depart into the unknown. Kydd clenched his fists. No glorious fight, no conclusions, just a hungry and miserable return to Malta to report that he had seen the corvette, but had done nothing but leave him in peace.

There had to be something. A rammer clattered to the deck at a nearby gun and the seaman shamefacedly retrieved it. Kydd swung round at the distraction, then realised the gun crews had been at quarters since dawn. 'Stand down at y'r weapons,' he ordered loudly. There was no question about dismissing them in the face of the enemy but at least they could take a measure of relaxation at the guns. 'And they shall have their grog. Mr Dacres?'

The gun crews accepted their three-water rum on the upper deck from the grog-monkeys with hushed voices and stifled laughter. They would usually be in a roar of jollity below on the mess-decks at this time. By the long custom of the service they were entitled to a double tot before battle and Kydd had ensured they got it. Besides, it gave him precious time to think.

He paced up and down, oblivious of the glances that followed him. His passion had cooled and he now directed all his resources into cunning. *La Fouine* was bigger in all respects – by definition that probably meant defeat if they attempted a land battle even if he sent every last soul ashore to storm him. And a sea battle? He was more than willing to stand against this foe but how the devil was he going to drive him out?

Then it came to him. 'Mr Dacres, find me a trumpet, an' someone who knows how to play one! This minute, d'ye

167

hear?' Without waiting for a reply from the dumbfounded lieutenant he turned on his heels and went below. 'Mr Peck! Rouse out y'r writing tackle an' please to wait on me in ten minutes.' It would give him time to jot down a few ideas.

He settled at the table. Now just how was it done? He knew what he wanted, but was hazy in the details. Was it not a *chamade* he was contemplating? A formal parlay? No, that was just the flourish of a trumpet necessary to get attention and a cease-fire. What was it called? Did it matter? He scrawled away.

'Sir?'

He motioned Peck to the other side of the table. 'You c'n write Frenchy?' he said severely.

'I do, sir, yes.'

'Then write this – in y'r best round hand.' Peck busied himself with his quill and Kydd focused his thoughts. His mind produced an image of the French captain in his own cabin, frowning over a paper handed to him by a shadowy petty officer. He began composing.

'*Au capitaine de vaisseau—*' No, this was an unrated vessel, so, '*Au capitaine de frégate* La Fouine, *au mouillage à Lampedusa . . .*' He presumed it was spelled the same way in French, if not then they could guess. Then the meat. That he was disappointed with the dull spirit of the famed French Revolution that they felt unable to try the fortune of their flag against such an insignificant and lone brig-sloop of His Majesty's Navy. That for their convenience he was shortening sail and holding fire until they were both fairly on the open sea and would salute their flag with the utmost politeness before any act of hostility. In effect this was no less than a personal challenge.

He waited for Peck to finish, then snatched the paper and

scanned it quickly. The painful hours of learning with Renzi had yielded a workmanlike competence in the language but by no means a familiarity with the high-flown courtliness that seemed to be the style required in high diplomacy. But with a savage smile he decided that if he had erred on the side of plain speaking then so much the better. 'Ask Mr Dacres t' attend me,' he said to Peck. Dacres was fluent but Kydd did not want to be told what to say: they had to be his words – but with no misunderstandings.

Dacres took the paper as if it would catch fire but manfully worked his way through it. 'Sir, if I could suggest . . .' To Kydd they were footling changes but he allowed them in the final draft.

'Did you find a trumpet?' he asked, when they had regained the deck.

'Er, Able Seaman Ridoli – it would seem he has tolerable skill at the flügelhorn, which he assures me is a species of trumpet. As he will never be parted from his instrument, he therefore has it on board—'

'Get him in the boat. Mr Bowden, ye know what to do? When you reach th' rock, set Ridoli t' play for a space, then return.'

'May I know what he should play, sir?'

'Damn it, I don't know!' Kydd said irritably. 'Some kind o' *tan-tara* as the lobsterbacks like playing – use y'r initiative.'

The boat left *Teazer* under a huge white flag of truce and headed shorewards. There was no response from the French, and through his telescope Kydd saw Bowden head purposefully for a prominent flat rock. There was a wild leap from the bowman and then Bowden and Ridoli clambered uncertainly through the seaweed to stand atop the craggy outcrop. Ridoli took up his instrument, glittering brassily in the sunlight and the mellow, haunting strains of some Italian air floated back across the wavetops. Bowden waved him to silence and they boarded the boat again for the pull back.

But there, in plain view, resting on top of the rock, was the white dot of the letter that Bowden had left. 'Stay in th' boat, if y' please,' Kydd ordered. He stared at the French vessel until his eyes watered. This was his last throw of the dice.

'Sir!' Attard's eyes had caught sight of something around the bow of the corvette; then a boat pulled smartly into view. It also had a flag of truce and it headed for the rock. The letter was snatched up and handed down into the boat, which lost no time in returning.

It had worked! So far. By now word of Kydd's action would have spread the length and breadth of *Teazer* and the deck was crowded with excited men who had no business being away from their quarters for battle but Kydd could not deny them.

Time dragged. *Teazer* wore round for another stretch out to sea – but the boat reappeared and again headed for the rock. A figure mounted the highest point and sounded off a meticulous and elaborate call on his trumpet, so much more martial than their offering. And when the boat headed back there was a letter waiting in the precise centre of the rock.

'Go!' Bowden and his crew needed no urging, pulling directly for the rock and claiming the letter. In a fever of anticipation Kydd took it below, in passing snapping at Dacres to send the men properly to quarters.

It was exquisitely written, the wordy introductory paragraphs ornate with unnecessary curlicues. Kydd's eyes went to the closing salutation; it seemed the commander of *La*

Fouine had the honour to be Capitaine de Frégate Jean Reynaud. There was no other clue about the man he had the duty to kill or vanquish – or who would do the same to him.

Kydd began the laborious task of penetrating the thicket of verbiage then, too impatient to continue, he summoned Dacres. 'There – what do ye think o' this?' he said.

Skimming the text with a frown Dacres looked up. 'Er, it seems plain enough, sir,' he said, with a degree of wary puzzlement.

'I asked ye what you make of it, Mr Dacres.'

'Well, sir, he, er—'

'Read it out, man – in English, th' main heads.'

'Aye aye, sir. Starts with compliments on our fine vessel—'

'Th' *main* heads.'

'Yes, sir. Er, he accepts that we are in a state of war and therefore we have a certain duty to assault his ship . . . but notes that while he is tranquil in a secure anchorage, well supplied, we are obliged to ply the sea until he decides to quit it. And, er, as this is not convenient to him at the present time he is desolated to be obliged to decline your gracious invitation . . .'

Kydd's spirits sank. The French captain knew that *Teazer* could not wait indefinitely and had made exactly the decision he himself would have made in like circumstances. For the French captain it was a hostile sea with no friendly harbours or dockyards for repair; there was no compelling reason for him to risk damage that would cut short his cruise of depredation, and therefore he would lie at anchor until *Teazer* left. Quite the logical thing to do, in fact.

But Kydd had had to try. Before they left, could he think of any other card to play? What would Renzi have said? Perhaps this was not the kind of problem he would have

been best placed to resolve, he being such a martyr to logic . . .
Of course. 'Mr Dacres! Time is short an' I'd take it kindly
if you would assist me!' With Dacres sitting at the desk writing
French in a flying hand at Kydd's dictation and Mr Peck
hovering by, the task was quickly completed.

It was nothing elaborate, no cunning scheme of deception, it merely pointed out that as the clandestine anchorage
was now known, *Teazer* would have no alternative but to
lie off waiting for a period of time before quitting to secure
provisions – *or* she would leave immediately and soon return;
La Fouine would never know which, and the chances were
that he would be set upon almost immediately he departed.
The logical course therefore would be to stop wasting time,
deal with his tormentor at once, and so be sure of the situation.

The letter was sealed and taken out to the rock with all
due ceremony and *Teazer* waited once again. The answer was
prompt and unequivocal. One by one, at every masthead, the
ensign of France floated free. At the same time the yards
were manned and activity at bow and stern revealed work at
the anchor cables.

Nervous exaltation seized Kydd. He had what he wanted:
this was now to be no less than a duel between two ships-
of-war, and more than pride was at stake. 'Shorten t' tops'ls,'
he ordered, conforming to his promise.

Under easy sail, *Teazer* slipped along in a feather of water,
all aboard at a knife-edge of tension. There was one final
thing Kydd wanted to do. 'With me, Mr Attard,' he said, to
the solemn-faced youngster. 'I'm taking a turn about the
decks, Mr Dacres. If anything—'

'Aye aye, sir,' said Dacres, who crossed to the helm, his
expression grave and resolute.

The gun crews turned to watch Kydd pass, some with studied nonchalance, others with a smile or an air of bravado. 'Where's y'r stations f'r boarding?' he challenged the most cocksure.

'Why, sir, th' foremast wi' Mr Bowden,' he said easily.

'And?'

'Oh, well, barkers an' slashers in course – jus' follows Mr Bowden, sir.'

'Aye, that's well said,' Kydd said gruffly, and moved on.

It was the way of it. Nelson always had said that if in doubt no captain could go wrong if he placed his ship alongside that of an enemy, and in this he was only taking to a higher plane the lion-hearted spirit of the seamen that was so much the reason for the invincibility of the Royal Navy.

Forward, Bowden touched his hat; his gaze was direct and untroubled. 'All forrard ready and waiting, sir,' he said gravely.

'Thank 'ee, Mr Bowden. I hope . . .' But Kydd could not finish and turned away abruptly.

The gunner was imperturbable in his tiny, claustrophobic magazine; the carpenter and his mates waited patiently at the forward end of the mess deck for the first smashing cannon strike through *Teazer*'s side.

Acknowledging the boatswain's sketchy salute as he handed out from his store the tackles and stoppers for emergency repair to the rigging Kydd mounted the fore hatchway, nearly tripping over the sailmaker who was mustering his gear. 'Ye're going t' be busy in a short while, Mr Clegg,' he said.

'Sir,' he acknowledged, in his dry, whispery voice. The man had probably seen more service than that of any other two aboard put together.

Kydd moved to go, then paused. 'Ah, I'd like t' be very

certain *Teazer* is properly at quarters in every part. Er, can ye tell me – slipped m' mind – what's the quarters f'r battle of, er, Able Seaman Sprits'l?'

Clegg's face creased into a pleased smile. 'Why, sir, you'll find him in y'r cabin safe 'n' snug,' he said, without embarrassment, 'Mr Tysoe standin' by.'

La Fouine took the wind to starboard and gathered way, his bowsprit as unwavering as an arrow, fixed on *Teazer*, who lay quietly under topsails two miles offshore.

'He's comin' out!' The yell went up from all parts of the ship, dissolving into high-spirited cheers. If there was to be any doubt about the outcome it would not be from before the mast.

Kydd stared forward resolutely, trying to penetrate the mind of the man who opposed him but receiving no hint from the cloud of canvas the ship carried as he pressed on through the entrance. What would be his next move? A flying pass, bow to bow, followed by a sudden turn to rake across *Teazer*'s stern? A stand-off bombardment, given his greater range guns? Close-in carnage? He must foresee every possible move and be ready to parry. And have his own counter-moves.

La Fouine came on fast with all plain sail set, no topsails for him. Kydd grew uneasy: what did it imply? He was just about to send topmen aloft when, clearing the mouth of the cove, *La Fouine* put up his helm and plunged downwind through the unknown coastal shoals, making for the open sea at the south end of the island.

'Be buggered! He's runnin', the shy cock!'

It was totally unexpected and Kydd had no option but to throw *Teazer* round and follow at a safe distance offshore, losing ground until his own courses were set and drawing. The straggling headland at the last of the land came and went; there was nothing now but a vast and empty sea, the ultimate battlefield.

Was *La Fouine* enticing *Teazer* towards a more powerful consort? Or simply making a break? At least his duty was plain: to use all possible means to close with the enemy and bring him to battle. But *La Fouine* was making fine speed away to the south-east and *Teazer* had yet to get into her stride.

There was one niggling fact, however: if *La Fouine* was trying to get away, why had he not set stuns'ls and all other possible aids to speed in running before the wind? Whatever the reason Kydd would not set them either; if *La Fouine* saw them laboriously rig stuns'l booms and bend on such sail he need only wait until all was in place, then go hard up into the wind, leaving *Teazer* to thrash along for the time she needed to take them in again.

The two ships stretched out over the sea until it became evident by sextant that the angle from waterline to *La Fouine*'s masthead was increasing. *Teazer* was gaining! For all *La Fouine*'s fancy ship-rig and smart seamanship *Teazer* was the faster vessel before the wind.

Thumping the rail Kydd urged his little ship on. *La Fouine* was now visibly nearer and a plan for close action would be needed. Through his glass Kydd thought he could pick out the blue and white figure of the captain on his quarterdeck: what was he thinking of *Teazer* now?

Then, not more than a quarter of a mile ahead, *La Fouine* spun at right angles to take the wind hard on his starboard cheek, angling away to the right. At the same time as his side lengthened his whole broadside bore on *Teazer* – he did not waste his chance and up and down his length hammered the flash and smoke of his guns, the breeze gaily sending the smoke rolling away over him to leeward.

Teazer's guns could not bear, but she made a narrow target, bows on; as far as Kydd could detect there was no damage.

Quickly he bellowed orders that had her pirouetting round as fast as the braces could be won, but *La Fouine* had gained vital points by reducing *Teazer*'s advantage to weather.

In the contest of ships' speeds it did not take the sextant to tell that close-hauled *Teazer* was even faster. Kydd guessed that *La Fouine* was overdue a careening, and a brig-sloop had the edge over the less handy ship-rigged species, but even so he felt a jet of pride.

A conclusion was now inevitable, and Kydd's mind raced. In the chase to windward he had the same kind of quandary: close-hauled, the best advantage to be gained was to toggle bowlines to their bridles and stretch forward the weather edge of the sails. This took time and, in just the same way as with the stuns'ls, if *La Fouine* were to revert back before the wind they would need removing. Again, he took his cue from the Frenchy: no bowlines, therefore none for him.

Kydd stepped over to the quartermaster at the wheel. 'Luff 'n' touch her,' he ordered. Tentatively Poulden eased the helm, watching for the slightest flutter at the taut, windward edge of the sail, at which point they were straining as close to the north-westerly as it was possible to be. Kydd was bargaining that *Teazer* had the speed to overcome the disadvantage of being so tight to the wind compared to one slightly fuller, and thus claw back some distance into the breeze. It would take longer to overhaul their quarry but the advantage would be priceless.

By two in the afternoon the end was in sight. After miles of a sea chase *Teazer* was comfortably to windward of her opponent and was about to establish an overlap – the guns would be speaking soon.

Kydd had done all he could to prepare his ship and her company. Now it was time.

'Firing to larb'd,' Kydd warned. There was no doubt of their target, slashing along just ahead of them and to leeward, but by this he was indicating that he would not be putting his wheel over suddenly and crossing the enemy stern for a savage raking broadside from his starboard side – that would offer one chance only and, with six-pounders, it was not a battle-winning tactic. Instead he would continue coming up, then pound away broadside to broadside until there was a result – one way or another.

And because of *Teazer's* hard-won weather position his foe could not turn away from the onslaught as that would present his vulnerable stern-quarters to a double broadside. The French commander must have come to the same conclusion for he could see aboard *La Fouine* that they were shortening sail: it could only be in readiness for combat.

At last: no more tactics, manoeuvring, hard racing. This was the moment.

Kydd allowed *Teazer* to move ahead before he ordered sail shortened and their frantic speed faded to a purposeful trot as they squared away to their opponent. As he had seen his captain do at the Nile, he started pacing slowly up and down to throw off the aim of muskets in the fighting tops of the enemy picking him out as an officer.

Along the exposed decks the gun crews tensed, held to a hair-trigger, seeing their enemy so brutally clear. Kydd saw no reason to delay: as soon as the last gun had slewed round and could bear it was time to begin. 'Mr Dacres, fire when ready.'

All along the larboard side the six-pounders woke to violent life, eight ringing cracks joining in one ear-splitting discharge, which, Kydd noted again, was quite unlike the deep smash of *Tenacious*'s twenty-four pounders. Still, when the smoke cleared there were several tell-tale dark blotches on *La Fouine*'s sides.

But there would be pay-back. The gun crews worked like maniacs; Kydd remembered from his past at the lower-deck guns that the best cure for cannon-fever was furious work at the guns. Then *La Fouine*'s eight-pounders replied in a vicious stabbing of gunflash and smoke. A musical twang sounded as a stay parted, and a single scream came from forward, cut off almost as soon as it began. *Teazer* seemed to have escaped serious injury.

Firing became general, guns spoke as soon as they were loaded in a harsh cycle of labour and pain, which was now the lot of the gun crews. Kydd's glance went down to the facings on his coat, smeared with the soft grey of gun-smoke. This was now a smashing duel and it was only just beginning.

He turned at the mainmast and began his pace back to the wheel. He knew only too well that the helmsman had the hardest task: the target of so many sharp-shooters, he could neither move nor retaliate, but at the same time he had the vital responsibility of keeping the ship from veering wildly off course, a fatal matter in the heat of battle.

He glanced across – it was still Poulden at the wheel, calm and measured, a fine example to all who saw him.

From far forward there was a distinct strike of shot, the shock transmitted down the ship through her frames, even to where Kydd stood. Then followed a slow, rending crack as of a tree falling – which could have only one meaning.

'Hold her!' he bawled at Poulden. *Teazer* was sheering up out of control into the wind, her sails banging and flapping as they were taken full aback and her speed dropped away to nothing.

A seaman pelted up, wild-eyed. 'Sir, we took a shot in th' bowsprit at th' gammoning an' it carried away.' Chest heaving, the man seemed to be looking to Kydd for some sort of miracle, but with the bowsprit and therefore all the headsails gone there was nothing his captain could think of that would salvage the moment. One thing was imperative: to stop the wild flogging of the sails – even as he glanced over the side they were slowly gathering sternway under their impetus.

Mercifully, *La Fouine* had shot ahead, leaving them flailing astern, his guns falling silent as they ceased to bear. Kydd hurried to the bows. *Teazer*'s dainty bowsprit had taken an eight-pounder shot squarely at its base and now lay in the sea under her forefoot, shattered and tangled in an appalling snarl of ropes and blocks. With the ruin so complete, *Teazer* was now dead in the water.

A single lucky shot: it was unfair so early in the fight – and in the worst possible place. Completely out of balance *Teazer* could neither turn away nor keep a straight course and was now terribly vulnerable.

Over the fast-opening stretch of sea *La Fouine* continued on, the smoke around him dissipating quickly. Now was his chance to make his escape to continue unimpeded on his voyage of destruction.

But he did not. He wore round in a lazy circle that would end with the methodical annihilation of his helpless opponent.

A cold pit of fear opened in Kydd's stomach, not so much for himself but for the men who had trusted him, for his lovely ship that had minutes of life left – and he knew for a certainty there was nothing he could do about it.

The circle was closing. As a carnivore stalks its kill, *La Fouine* was going to make sure of his prey. Out of range of *Teazer*'s little six-pounders he was coming round to cross her stern – a true deciding blow, for with perfect impunity he could slowly pass by, sending every shot in his broadside in deadly aim smashing through her pretty stern windows and on into her vitals, unstoppably down the length of the ship. It would be an onslaught of death and devastation that would be unimaginably violent.

It was the end. The only question left was, at what point did Kydd stop the carnage by yielding to the enemy?

La Fouine came round and steered straight for *Teazer*'s forlorn stern. If war was logical, thought Kydd, dully, now would be the time to give up and strike his colours. But war was not logical; if he hauled down his flag, after mere minutes of fighting, he and the Navy would be damned for ever as cowardly. Therefore there was no alternative: *Teazer* and her people must endure what came until – until *Teazer*'s commander put a stop to it . . .

As he straightened for the final run, *La Fouine*'s cannon showed in a sinister line along his side. Kydd imagined he could see the slight movements at their black muzzles as gun captains triumphantly trained their weapons for maximum damage. He closed silently, aiming to pass no more than ten yards away.

Just before he reached *Teazer* Kydd roared, with all the passion of his frustration and sorrow, 'On th' deck! Everyone – get down!'

The gun crews, seamen with pikes waiting to repel boarders, the boatswain and his party, all lay prone, cringing in anticipation at the hideous storm about to break over them. Kydd was about to follow suit when some scrap of foolish pride – perhaps a death wish – kept him standing tall and glaring contemptuously at the nemesis gliding in for the kill. Then he became aware of others: Dacres, standing with him, Bowden, the little midshipmen coming up, Poulden, more.

He tried to order them down but the lump in his throat was too great. *La Fouine* slowed; they were going to take all the time they needed. His bowsprit reached them not thirty feet off, sliding past, men on the deck in every detail, watching them, waiting for the single shout of the order to fire. At any second . . .

The shout came – but there was no sudden eruption of violence. The shout was repeated but Kydd's mind refused to accept what was going on until he realised that the guns were still silent. *La Fouine* slid past slowly while the shouting grew strident. They were calling on him to surrender! A figure in blue and white on the quarterdeck was shouting angrily through a speaking trumpet.

Now was the sensible time to admit to his helplessness and to save lives, finish *Teazer*'s plucky resistance. Inside he was in a maelstrom of emotion, his first command, the pinnacle of his life, all to end so bleakly. It just could not—

'*Non!*' he thundered back. '*Je ne capitule pas!*'

The corvette glided silently past and began circling again. On his return there would be no mercy shown and there would be death and blood in the afternoon. Defiantly, Kydd and his ship waited.

Chapter 8

'Dear fellow, it was nothing! We were signalled to investigate the firing and there you were, helpless as a sucking shrimp under the guns of the Frenchy.' Winthrop, the frigate *Stag*'s captain, looked amiably over his glass and chuckled. 'Never does to vex those who are bigger than you.'

'Aye, sir, but I must thank ye on behalf o' the ship,' Kydd said stiffly. It had been a hard time for him during the lengthy tow to Malta coming to terms with *Teazer*'s hair's-breadth escape and its implications for his future.

Winthrop sighed. 'Do forgive me if I appear . . . unfeeling, Mr Kydd, yet I am obliged to remark that my providential appearance on the scene seems as much a fortune of war as the cannon strike on your bowsprit – do you not agree?'

It was nothing but the truth, Kydd had to admit. 'The fortune o' war, yes, sir – but where is m' reputation, my prospects with th' admiral? Sadly out o' countenance, I'd wager.'

'Not necessarily,' Winthrop replied, topping up Kydd's glass. 'Consider, while you are not distinguished in any measure, you have disgraced neither yourself nor your flag.

If I catch your meaning aright, then unless Lord Keith at this moment has a particularly shining young officer he is desirous of advancing in the service then your position is secure . . . for the time being, of course.'

Kydd felt his spirits rising, but he could not help adding, 'T'would be a fine thing if y'r same fortune c'n throw me a chance of a bold stroke as would set th' world t' talking – and me t' notice.'

Winthrop regarded him soberly. 'You may discover your chance earlier than you think. We are all placed in the way of opportunity. You will not have heard yet, but it seems the late and much lamented Abercrombie is to be replaced by the grand General Hely-Hutchinson. And I have it from a valued source that the Egypt campaign will therefore take a decidedly active turn. Do try to get yourself to sea as soon as you may, Kydd. I feel this is not to be missed.'

'Then, sir, you'll see *Teazer* there right enough!'

There was a vehemence in Kydd's voice that evoked a frown. 'Sir, all the world applauds an officer of audacity and character – but, if you'll forgive me remarking it, where is the line that marks off for him the aspiration to laurels from vainglory and rash imprudence?'

Receiving no answer, he let it hang, then said gently, 'Distinction will attend a virtuous endeavour, never doubt it, but the pursuit of peril and hazard in the expectation of glory will damn for ever the officer who sets his course thus.'

The loss of a bowsprit was catastrophic in the heat of battle, yet was an easy enough repair for a dockyard: the stump was withdrawn, the new spar stepped and the original jibboom heeled to it. There was little other damage and therefore *Teazer* could look forward to getting back to sea soon.

A ship from England had arrived with precious dock-yard stores – among them *Teazer*'s carronades and a stern instruction from the Board of Ordnance to ship them in place of her entire current fit of carriage guns in accordance with latest practice in England for the smaller classes of warship.

Teazer's present six-pounders were to a carronade as a cutlass to a rapier. They were short, brutish weapons with a vicious recoil – but they multiplied by four times the weight of metal of her broadside. At short range to any opponent the twenty-four-pounder carronade would be indistinguishable from the guns of a ship-of-the-line – but it had to be close in fighting for the lighter-charged weapons to reach out and do their work.

Kydd was not so sure: the entire armament, bar a pair he would replace the small chase guns with? His whole experience in the Navy had been with ships whose main weapon was the long cannon. With refinements such as a ringed cascabel for angled fire and dispart sights, action could be opened at a remarkable range and only at the climax would any carronades carried come into play. Now he was being asked to retire all but two of his six-pounders in favour of an all-carronade armament. Would he come to regret this?

Stirk was in no doubt. 'Remember th' *Glatton*, Mr Kydd.' She was an old Indiaman that had been outfitted entirely with carronades. A few years previously she had been set upon by no less than four frigates and two corvettes and had destroyed two of the frigates and set the remainder to flight.

'That's true enough,' Kydd said, allowing himself to be mollified.

Orders for the attention of the commander of HMS *Teazer* soon arrived. From Admiral Keith himself, they were terse and to the point. Being in all respects ready for sea, she should forthwith attach herself to the forces before Alexandria commanded by Captain Sir Sidney Smith.

Kydd laid down the orders with satisfaction. Smith – now there was a fighting seaman! There was sure to be a chance for bold deeds with his old leader at the great siege of Acre in command.

Teazer sailed within the week. It was an easy passage and four days later they were in sight of Pompey's Pillar, the distant white sprawl of Alexandria and, ahead, the disciplined and purposeful progress of a small squadron of the Royal Navy under easy sail.

'Well met, Mr Kydd.' Sir Sidney Smith held out his hand. The sensitive features, the odd, almost preoccupied air brought back a floodtide of memories from when Kydd had been truly blooded in personal combat. 'It seems I must offer my felicitations,' he continued, eyeing Kydd's epaulette.

'Aye, sir – a mort unexpected, I have t' allow,' Kydd said modestly, his broad smile betraying the satisfaction beneath.

'And ready to try your worthy craft in an early meeting with the enemy?' Smith spoke drily, apparently ignorant of Kydd's recent encounter, or perhaps he had chosen to ignore it. Kydd knew that Smith was still in his original ship *Tigre*, unaccountably with little to show for his epic defence of Acre, Napoleon's first personal defeat on land.

'Sir, would ye be so good as t' lay out for me the situation ashore?' Before, he had been merely a lieutenant on secondment; now he was commander of a not insignificant unit of the fleet, with a valid interest in the larger picture.

Smith got to his feet, went to the broad sweep of windows and stared out pensively. 'Very well. Since the glorious

Nile the French have been cut off, some might say stranded, in this land of vast antiquity and endless desert. And following our late success in Acre, Napoleon has cravenly fled, leaving his great army to its fate.'

He folded his arms and continued to gaze out wordlessly; Kydd thought he had been forgotten. 'Nevertheless,' he resumed suddenly, 'they have not been idle. Under Kleber, their second before his assassination, they brazenly faced the Turks – who are still the nominal rulers of Egypt – and bested them at every turn.

'It is vital to our interests to eject the French Army from Egypt, for it is folly in the extreme to leave a still potent force in being, ready to do untold mischief if loosed. And, besides, it costs Lord Keith a sizeable portion of his ships of force to stand before Alexandria and many lesser vessels to enforce a blockade of the French forces.'

'And our army, sir?' Kydd knew it had made a successful and courageous amphibious landing some months before but at the cost of its general, Abercrombie, and had heard nothing since.

'Yes, yes, I was coming to that. In essence, our army is heavily outnumbered and has been in a state of stalemate since. With the French in strong possession of Cairo, the capital, and Alexandria, the chief port, there is little they can do.'

'An' therefore nothing we can do,' Kydd said, seeing his chance of action ebb away.

'I didn't say that,' Smith said sharply. 'I have laid out a plan before General Hely-Hutchison that I am sanguine has sufficient merit to interest him. For its accomplishment it will require participation by the Navy.'

Kydd brightened. 'May I know y'r plan, sir?'

'No, you may not. You will, of course, as a commander of one of His Majesty's ships be required to attend the general's councils at which, if the general is in agreement, the plan will be divulged to the meeting. Until then, I would be gratified at your attentions to squadron orders – your immediate tasks will become apparent at the council.'

'And Commander Kydd, sir, of HMS *Teazer*, brig-sloop.'

Kydd bowed studiously to the splendid vision of the Army officer before him. 'Delighted t' be part o' your force, sir,' he said.

'Quite so, Commander. We shall find work for ye soon enough.' The eyes moved on and Kydd yielded obediently to the next in line.

'The sea officers will sit by me,' Smith announced, when the ceremonies were complete and they had moved into the stuffy operations room with its vast table. Half a dozen naval officers clustered defensively round him, opposite the imposing chair at the head.

Kydd nodded to them; to his gratification a good half of Smith's squadron were luggers, gunboats and other small craft, which merited no more than a lieutenant-in-command, and therefore over all of them he was nominally senior.

Further introductions concluded and Hely-Hutchinson opened proceedings. 'Gentlemen, I have been accorded the privilege of the overall command of this endeavour, and I do not propose to waste time. The French are undefeated and lie before us in superior numbers. I intend to strike fast and thrust deep into Egypt, thereby separating the two main concentrations of French.' He paused and looked round the table before continuing.

'I shall first reduce Rosetta. This will secure the Canopic

mouth of the Nile for us, of course. Then I shall follow the river as my path of advance inland through the desert and set Cairo to the sword before the French in Alexandria can achieve a junction with them.'

It was a bold and imaginative stroke.

'Sir, if I may – how will we—'

'The Navy will be told to precede the attacking columns up the river to sweep the banks clear with cannon fire. Is that clear?'

Kydd saw Smith's blank expression, his fixed staring at the table and knew immediately where such audacity had originated.

'Splendid! Now we shall get to the details . . .'

An Ottoman squadron of Turks and Albanians joined the English soldiers landing opposite Rosetta. The town duly surrendered and the way was now clear for their daring thrust into the heart of Egypt.

But that did not include Kydd. 'No, sir! Do you not see that upriver your otherwise charming sloop would be sadly discommoded by her draught? This work is for others.' There was no shifting Smith, and *Teazer* was left to watch the dust of the troops disappearing round a bend in the river, leaving nothing but date palms and dunes behind them.

It was galling to be beating up and down guarding the seaward approaches to the Nile delta while Smith had taken personal command of the flotilla of gunboats clearing the way for the Army's advance. There was now every prospect of a titanic struggle in the trackless sands before the immeasurably ancient pyramids; 4,500 untried British soldiers against 10,000 men and 300 guns of the most experienced army in the world, safe behind the walls of the capital of Egypt. Only the surprise and daring of the approach was in their favour.

Days stretched to weeks: the endless sailing along past the low, ochre sands and straggling palms bore down on the spirit. There was no glory to be had in this – no French vessel worth the name was going to risk the ships-of-the-line of the blockade force, while the smaller feluccas, djerms and the rest were no prey for a man-o'-war.

Kydd could feel time slipping – with nothing in view that would give any kind of opportunity to win recognition and secure him in his command. He forced himself to patience.

News from the interior was slow and confused: there was talk of a general rising among the population against the French, but that transmuted into a petty insurrection against the Mamelukes. Word then came that Hely-Hutchinson had reached Cairo and had had the gall to demand the instant surrender of General Belliard and his army. With double the English numbers it was hardly surprising that the French had refused. The stage seemed set for either catastrophe or head-long retreat.

Returning gunboats appeared and made straight for the little harbour at Rosetta with the news that, by an astonishing mix of diplomacy and bluff, Hely-Hutchinson had persuaded the French general to capitulate. The price? That his troops would be shipped safely back to France. Shortly thereafter, a flood of vessels of all sizes converged on Rosetta from upriver, each packed with unarmed French soldiers.

It was a brilliant stroke: in one move the British had driven a wedge between the French, eliminated one side and forced the other to draw in their defensive lines around the city and port of Alexandria. At last it appeared that, after a miserable start to the war, the Army could now feel pride in themselves.

With the return of the victorious Hely-Hutchinson, plans could be made for the investment of this last stronghold. A council-of-war was ordered, Commander Kydd in attendance with Sir Sidney Smith and the other naval captains.

Smith made a late entrance: in a room dominated by the gold frogging and scarlet of army field officers, he appeared dressed in Turkish robes and a blue turban, with side-whiskers and moustache in an Oriental style. In scandalised silence, he took his place, remarking offhandedly as he sat, 'The Grand Vizier calls me "Smit Bey".'

With a brother the ambassador in Constantinople, and his consuming interest in the Levant, Smith was known as an authority on the region and Kydd had heard him speak easily with the Arabs and Ottomans in their own languages. Perhaps, Kydd concluded, his outlandish appearance was Smith's notion of a gesture of solidarity with them, the lawful rulers of Egypt.

An ill-tempered 'Harrumph!' came from Hely-Hutchinson. 'Why, Sir Sidney, I had no notion that you meant to be a character,' he added, and without waiting for reply took up his papers. 'The reduction of Alexandria. We have been attempting that very object since the first. Some say "impregnable" but I say "vulnerable". And this is the reason: Lord Keith tells me that the twin harbours are not to be assailed in a frontal manner from the sea – but offers us a landing place on the shores of Aboukir. This I reject out of hand because we would be constrained to fight our way on a narrow front all the way to the city. Nonsense.

'So here is what I shall do. It has come to my attention that the low region to the inland side of Alexandria was known to the ancients as a lake – Mareotis, if I recall correctly.'

Kydd stole a sideways glance at Smith, who caught the look and rolled his eyes furtively. Not knowing how to respond, Kydd gave a weak smile and returned his attention to the general.

'I am going to cut every waterway, every canal and every rivulet and send their waters cascading against the French – Lake Mareotis will live again! And by this means I will be empowered to trap Menou and his troops in an impassable enclave. They may neither be supplied nor can they run away. By my reckoning, with the timely assistance of the Navy, it can only be a short period before we entirely extirpate the French from this land.' A stir of interest rippled about the stuffy room: this was more bold thinking, the kind that won wars – or cost men their lives.

Smith leaned back in his chair. 'Sir, you may be assured that the Navy is ready to play its part,' he said languidly. 'In fact, such is the urgency of the matter that I have this day placed Commander Kydd in a position of absolute authority over the plicatiles.'

Cold grey eyes bored into Kydd, who quailed. What, in heaven's name, were the plicatiles?

'I have always placed the utmost reliance on Mr Kydd's technical understanding and take the liberty of reminding the general that this is the same man who fought by my side so valiantly in Acre.'

The meeting moved to details – troop movements, lines of advance, field-sign colours for the order of battle – but Kydd was in a ferment of anxiety concerning his role with the plicatiles. The developing plan gave no further clue: the Army would advance on Alexandria but at the same time there would be a determined and noisy diversion from the sea, the squadron commanded in person by Sir Sidney. Yet another element would be the clandestine transfer of troops around the rear of the French made possible by the flooding of Lake Mareotis.

At least the Navy's role was clear enough – and who knew? There might well be chances in the deadly scrimmages likely at the entrance of the port – a great deal of shipping lay at anchor inside, including frigates, and *Teazer* would not hang back.

The meeting broke up. A worried young lieutenant tried to ask Kydd about his role in a gunboat but Kydd brushed him off: he had other things on his mind. Smith was deep in conversation with a Turkish field officer and he waited impatiently for it to end, then the two began to move off together.

'S-sir! If y' please—'

Smith broke off and turned to Kydd.

'Sir, about y'r plicatiles . . .'

'And do I hear an objection? Let me remind you, Mr Kydd, that I've gone out of my way to accede to your evident desire for the opportunity of distinguished conduct by an independent command – are you now about to renounce it?'

'B-by no means, sir!' Kydd stuttered. 'I shall bend m' utmost endeavours. It's – it's just that . . .'

'You find the service too challenging?' Smith's eyebrows rose.

'No, sir!'

'Then I can safely leave the matter with you.' He turned his back and resumed his animated conversation with the Turk.

*   *   *

'Be damned t' you, sir!' the elderly colonel spluttered, his fist waving comically in the night air. 'I'm not about to risk m' men in that contraption! What kind o' loobies d' ye think we are?'

A seaman patiently held the blunt prow of a boat for the milling and distrustful soldiers to board. But this was no stout and seaworthy naval launch – it was a flat, awkward beast built in sections joined with leather seams, a portable boat that had been carried across the desert on the backs of soldiers: a plicatile. It was now ready to take to the waters of the rejuvenated Lake Mareotis to catch the unsuspecting French in the rear. And it leaked like a colander.

Kydd took a ragged breath. It had been a nightmare, ensuring that there were enough reliable seamen to con the hundreds of craft and that each had a boat compass and dark-lantern, repair kits, balers and so on as well as the right fit of army stores. The tedious and bitingly cold night march through the anonymous sand had been preceded by days of Kydd's organisation and planning that had taken its toll on his stamina and he was in no mood to debate the wisdom of embarking the troops in the transport provided.

'Then, sir, I'm t' tell Gen'ral Hely-Hutchinson that his regiments refuse t' move forward?' he retorted. 'Th' colonel says he might get his feet wet?'

'Have a care, sir!' the officer spat dangerously. 'I'll remember your name, sir!'

'Aye, Kydd it is – meanwhile . . . ?'

All along the reedy 'shore' of the new lake more and more of the plicatiles took to the water. It was vital that a credible force was assembled ready at the appointed point on the opposite shore at dawn. This implied a departure time of not later than two in the morning if they were to avoid being revealed by a rising moon. They had to board now.

Stumping along the shoreline, shouting himself hoarse, goading, wheedling, ordering, it was a nightmare for Kydd. If the night succeeded, there would be not much more than an avuncular pat on the back: if he failed, the whole world would hear of it.

He had also come to realise bitterly that Smith had probably engineered his removal ashore during this phase to remove a hungry rival for glory in the only true naval enterprise on offer. Dacres had been at first surprised, then transparently avaricious at the prospect of temporary command of *Teazer* and was now somewhere out to sea in her while Kydd stormed about in the marshes ashore.

It was time: ready or not, they had to start. He fumbled for his silver boatswain's call, set it to his lips and blasted the high and falling low of 'carry on'. It was yet another thing to worry about, setting some thousands of men into an advance without the use of trumpets or other give-away signals. From up and down the line of shore came the echoing peal of other pipes sounding in a caterwaul of conflicting notes. They died away but then the first plicatiles tentatively began their long paddle across the invisible dark of the lake.

In a fever of impatience Kydd watched their slow progress, but then more and more ventured out until the dark waters seemed full of a cloud of awkward shapes disappearing onwards into the night. Energised to desperate hope, he scrambled aboard the nearest and they pushed off. Water instantly began to collect in the flat bottom and sloshed about; Kydd growled at one of the nervous redcoats and threw him the baler.

The boat felt unstable and Kydd was grateful for the

absolute calm of the waters. He snapped at the four pad-
dlers for greater efforts; he wanted to close with the main
body ahead before they reached the other side. To his right
despairing cries turned to shrieks. Why the devil could they
not drown quietly? he mused blackly.

Ahead, from what must be over the dunes to seaward, a
rocket soared. Several others answered and distant gun flashes
lit the sky, with continuous dull crumps and thuds. The sea
diversion was beginning: if the French thought it was the
main assault it would draw them there and the rear assault
would have a chance – but if not . . . Kydd knew that if their
own attack attracted the majority of defenders, the enterprise of the Navy would attempt a landing of their own:
marines and seamen would be establishing a vital bridgehead
while his lightly armed force was cut to pieces.

'Stretch out, ye haymakin' shabs!' he ground out fiercely,
at the hapless soldiers plying the paddles. He had to be up
with the others when they made their surprise move – but
when they did, exactly what orders would he give?

A soft edge to the darkness was turning into the first delicate flush of dawn. He could see ahead much further and
the reed-fringed bank of the opposite shore materialised.
Mercifully it seemed they had not yet been seen, and under
cover of a low ridge the boats were touching ashore and
being pulled up.

An impossible mass of men was assembling at the water's
edge; he had not realised the minimum area of ground a
thousand men or more must occupy. His feverish imagination rushed stark images into his mind of the muzzles of
cannon suddenly appearing at the skyline to blast a storm of
grape-shot and canister into the helpless crowds – what could
he do? What orders should he give the moment he landed?

The boat nudged into sandy mud and he splashed into the shore, urgently looking about and swallowing his concern. Then from random parts of the mass came stentorian bellows – he recognised the colonel's – and up and down the milling mass other military shouts. Here and there pennons were raised high with regimental colours, attracting men to them. Order coalesced out of chaos and, with a sudden emptiness, Kydd knew his job was done. The Army was taking charge of its own.

Columns formed, scouts and pickets trotted forward and the force prepared to move out in disciplined silence. The fireworks display was still playing out to sea but now the deeper thuds of heavier guns could be heard in the distance; closer to, the light tap of muskets became more insistent, then a marked flurry before dying away. The men moved forward into battle.

'That was clean done, Mr Kydd,' Smith said equably, seated in a tent in an encampment overlooking the city. He had resumed his Turkish raiment and, with the pasha of Egypt, was bubbling away on a hookah with every indication of enjoyment. 'Achieved its object. With our fearsome motions from seaward and the sudden appearance of an unknown number of men in their rear, where before they felt safe they now have no other option than to retreat into the city. Well done, sir!'

It was all very well for Smith to feel so complacent, Kydd thought sourly. He was the one mentioned in the general's account.

'I rather think it is now a matter for the French of treating for the most honourable capitulation they can get – they cannot continue, of course.' Polite words were exchanged with the pasha, who beamed at Kydd, accepting his best bow with an airy gesture.

'It only remains to make a show of strength sufficient to allow Menou to yield honourably,' Smith continued. 'Probably the squadron forcing the harbour entrance with guns run out should suffice.' He took another puff and finished smugly, 'Then the whole of the Levant, north and south, east and west, will be ours. Makes you a mite proud at this time, don't you think?'

'Aye, sir,' Kydd said heavily. 'Should I square away *Teazer* for th' entering?' At least he would be one of the triumphant ships entering the ancient port.

Sir Sidney came back smoothly, 'Sadly, that will not be possible. I require that you will take my dispatches to Malta. Their secure arrival is of importance.'

Dispatches. While the last grand scenes of a great army of conquest capitulating to one of lesser number were played out, brought about by the unanswerable exercise of sea power of which HMS *Teazer* was a proud representative, she would not be present.

Tysoe came in to set the table for dinner but saw Kydd staring through the stern-lights at the ship's wake stretching away on a rapidly darkening sea. He left as quietly as he had entered.

The situation was complex and not at all as Kydd had expected. With the final ejection of the French from the eastern Mediterranean it was probable that this part of the world would revert to a backwater, as far as naval occasions were concerned, but in the hours since they had left Alexandria for Malta he had made a reappraisal of his situation.

It was not *Teazer*'s fault. Neither was it his. It was, as Renzi would strongly concur, in the nature of her being, that as a brig-sloop she had been designed for humble roles on a larger stage. It was therefore inappropriate and foolish to dream of glory and daring while his ship was faithfully doing the job for which she had been created.

Now that the war had subsided there was never going to be a chance of real distinction. The wise course would be to take comfort and pleasure from her willing performance of these tasks and, while he could, taste to the full the sensations of command. There was only a short time left to him, perhaps a few months, before the commander-in-chief needed to satisfy a situation and he was replaced. His eyes pricked, but only for a moment: he would make the most of the days left to him before it was time to coil and belay his seagoing life.

Tysoe appeared with wine, the glass glittering in the candlelight. Kydd did not make a habit of drinking alone, fearing it might take hold in the solitude of his great cabin, but this night was different.

If it had to finish now there was much he could be proud of: there were precious few in the Navy who had made the awesome step from fo'c'sle to quarterdeck, and even fewer who had gone on to command their own ship. When he settled back in Guildford he would be a gentleman of consequence, one whom the townsfolk would point out to each other. When he settled . . .

The cabin was now as he wished it; his eyes roamed wistfully over the miniature sideboard for his silver and the polished panelling with his pictures and a small framed old sea-chart of Anson's day. He could sit six at the table at a pinch, although no occasion for such entertaining had presented itself, and he had been able to secure a neat little

Argand lamp in its own gimbals for reading at night. There were other ornaments, keepsakes and a handsome mercury barometer, but without a woman's touch it retained a pleasing masculine order.

A swell lifted *Teazer*'s bows; as prettily as a maid at a dance she acknowledged with a lissome dip and unhurried rise as it passed down her length. Kydd warmed to the grace and charm that was so natural in these, her native seas. With such a lovely ship it would be brutish not to take pleasure in her embrace.

Suddenly restless, he got to his feet, opened the door and pushed past a surprised Tysoe out on deck. The night had a velvety soft darkness that allowed the stars to blaze in unusual splendour in a celestial vastness so low it seemed possible to touch, while the light north African night breezes brought dry, pungent scents to blend with the comfortable smells of shipboard life.

He became aware that the quiet drone of voices from the dark shapes around the wheel had ceased: the captain had come out on deck.

Kydd moved across to them. 'Good evening, Mr Dacres,' he said agreeably, and sensed the other relax – the captain was not on the prowl. 'All's well?'

'Yes, sir,' Dacres answered cautiously.

As captain, Kydd could expect no light conversation in the night watches; this was one of the crosses he must bear.

Kydd turned to the midshipman. 'Tell me, Mr Attard, where do I look t' find the Pleiades?'

The lad swivelled and pointed. 'There, sir, the head o' the bull – Taurus, I mean.'

'Just so. Not as we'd use 'em f'r our navigating. And—'

'The Arabs say El Nath, that's "the one who butts", sir

– and it's the first of their zodiac, which they calls Al Thuraya, "the crowd", by which they mean a crowd of camels, and—'

'Thank 'ee, Mr Attard. Ye knows the tongue o' the Moors, then?'

'Sir. Most who are born in Malta know it.' Now abashed before his captain he retreated into silence.

Kydd looked up at the dark splash of sails against the star-field, moving gently, never still. He stood for a precious moment, then returned below.

The next day was bright and clear and Kydd had no doubt of what he wanted. 'A right good scrubbing, Mr Dacres. Brightwork a-gleam an' get some hands aft to point every fall the ends on th' quarterdeck.' He had no idea who his guests would be, but Commander Kydd would be entertaining in *Teazer* when they arrived in Malta.

He was insistent, nonetheless, that there would be a live firing of the carronades; a round from three guns after loading practice. It was odd not to hear the squeal of gun-carriage trucks or men straining at the training tackle to simulate recoil. The sound of their firing was different as well: deeper-throated, perhaps, even though the powder charge was less. What was most satisfying was the massive plume sent up by the twenty-four-pound ball, but the scant range was still of some concern.

By evening *Teazer* was trim and neat; they would be at moorings under the guns of the fortress of Malta by this time the following day and Kydd's thoughts turned to those whom he felt he could invite to his little entertainment. It would be gratifying to a degree to have ladies attend; for some reason their presence always seemed to bring out the best in conversations and politeness. What his sister Cecilia would not give to host the evening, he thought wistfully.

The final day of the voyage dawned with a light drizzle and murky skies, but later in the morning a fresh wind from the north-west cleared it away and the watch on deck was set to swabbing the wet decks dry.

Over on the south-east horizon to leeward the lightening sea contrasted pleasingly with the uniform dark grey of the retreating cloud masses in a precise line, lighter sea to darker sky, the inverse of the normal order. The new wave of Romantic artists should take a sea voyage, thought Kydd, and capture striking scenes such as this, particularly when the white sails of a distant ship showed so dramatically against the dark grey, like the one now lifting above the horizon— 'Be damned! *Th' lookouts, ahoy!* Are you asleep? Why did y' not sight that ship t' loo'ard, ye rogues?'

There was a lookout at the fore-topmast head, another at the main, but their attention was forward, each vying with the other to raise the cry of 'Land ho!' when Malta came into view ahead.

'Hold y' course, Mr Dacres,' Kydd ordered. Carrying dispatches took precedence over all and therefore there was no need to stand towards and go through the motions of intercepting possible contraband. In the unlikely event of an enemy of force the security of the dispatches was paramount but *Teazer* was well on her way to Malta some dozen hours ahead.

The brig plunged on close-hauled in the freshening breeze, the other vessel on the hard line of the horizon stood at a slight angle away, crossing her stern. 'Sir, I do believe he's signalling.' Dacres handed over his telescope: there was indeed a distinct dash of colour at the mizzen halliards but directly to leeward it was impossible to make out the flags.

'Is she not *Stag*, sir?' Dacres asked. The vessel was now visible as ship-rigged and had come round to the wind and bore towards them. If it was *Stag* she must have good reason to wish to speak them and it would be prudent to await her.

'We'll heave to, I think,' Kydd ordered, still watching the vessel. Bows toward, it was difficult to make an identification. 'Mr Bowden, hang out the private signal, if y' please.'

An answering hoist appeared at the main. 'Er, still can't make it out, sir,' Bowden reported. Kydd waited for the ship to come up with them.

Then he stiffened. There was something about . . . He jerked up the glass and screwed his eyes in concentration. That fore topgallant, the dark patching that looked like stripes – it had to be! If that vessel was not *La Fouine* he was a Dutchman!

Instantly his mind snapped to a steely focus: this was now much more than a simple incident at sea. The need for instant decision forced itself to the front of his consciousness – all matters such as the corvette's reason to be so close to Malta would wait. Fight or flee? That was the question now.

Arguments raced through his mind: dispatches were the priority, therefore strictly he should fly for the safety of Malta. Yet there had been occasions in the past when vessels carrying dispatches had offered battle, even tiny cutters, but they had generally been in a threatening situation and had had to fight for their lives. Could he justify it before a later court of inquiry if he decided to close with *La Fouine* and lost the day?

On the other hand *La Fouine* was most certainly a grave

danger to the trade of the islands as well as lying athwart the lines of supply to Egypt. Did he not have a duty to deal with such a threat?

But all internal debate was a waste of time. In his heart he knew that he would fight. As simple as that: no explanations, no analysis – in the next few hours *Teazer* would face her enemy again and force a conclusion.

Once this was decided Kydd's mind raced over the alternatives. The overriding necessity was for *Teazer* to get her carronades close – *La Fouine*'s eight-pounders far out-ranged them and she could end lying off and being bombarded at leisure.

What did Kydd have on his side? There was the element of surprise – but that only counted if he could manoeuvre *Teazer* to a killing range. What else? Yes! There was still surprise! At that very moment *La Fouine* was crowding on sail, thinking *Teazer* had been deceived by his false signals. Furthermore, he knew *Teazer* as a six-pounder brig and would have no hesitation in moving in for the kill. Finally, he had had the better of Kydd before, and would not be inclined to think it might be different this time. They had a chance.

'Hold her at this,' he ordered the conn, and roared, 'Clear f'r action!' Seeing Bowden about to bend on the two huge battle ensigns he intervened and instead a puzzled 'please repeat your last signal' rose slowly up while they wallowed in the brisk seas. To any spectator *Teazer*'s raw captain had clearly been taken in by *La Fouine*'s stratagem: he believed the other ship to be British and her signals unclear.

It would take nerve, and precise judgement: they had to be under way and manoeuvring before *La Fouine* reached them, but too early would not achieve their object of luring him near. There was apprehension on the quarterdeck – what was Kydd thinking, to lie helpless before the onrush of their enemy?

La Fouine knifed towards them; at the right distance Kydd hoisted an ensign and loosed his men in a panic-stricken effort to get away. A desperate last-minute attempt at tacking had them fall away helplessly in stays and, with savage delight, Kydd saw *La Fouine* shape course to come down and fall upon them.

Kydd sent for Stirk and told him what he was planning to do; the man grinned and went to each gun captain in turn. Dacres looked grave when he received his orders; Poulden's reaction was a gratified salute. Now nothing more could be done.

La Fouine drew closer, coming in from astern as *Teazer* tried to make way after the 'failure' of her tacking, her guns run out along her length, men standing forward to catch sight of their victim. There was an unmistakable air of triumph aboard: his bowsprit drew level with *Teazer*'s quarterdeck. Kydd was relying on the corvette's cupidity: that they would not wish to damage their future prize unduly.

The first guns spoke: balls whistled overhead from *La Fouine*'s eight-pounders aimed high, and *Teazer* continued to claw into the wind, apparent panic on her decks. The corvette sheered confidently across, men massed on the fo'c'sle. Their purpose was all too plain – boarders!

Kydd watched the distance narrow and held his order until the moment was right – there would be only the one chance. He roared the command: *Teazer*'s helm went down and as she slewed across towards *La Fouine* the carronades blasted out together. Shot three times bigger still than *La Fouine*'s smashed into his vitals – but every other gun was loaded with canister on grape-shot and these turned his decks into a bloody charnel-house.

The shock and surprise were complete and the two ships came together in a splintering crash. Acrid gun-smoke hid Kydd's final throw. Drawing his sword he leaped for the bulwarks and on to the enemy deck. Impelled by both dizzying nervous excitement and desperation he battered down a cutlass-wielding seaman's defence then mercilessly impaled him. A pistol banged off next to him, catching another in the belly as a wild-eyed Frenchman lunged at Kydd with a pike, then dropped screaming. An officer with a rapier flicked it venomously at him but at that moment the two ships ground together again and they both staggered. Kydd regained his footing first and his blade took the man in the neck; the victim's weapon clattered down as he clutched at the blood spurting over his white uniform facings.

'Teazers t' me!' Kydd bellowed, seeing a gap in the milling mass and pounding aft towards the wheel. He heard others behind him and hoped they were his men; the two Frenchmen at the helm fled, leaving the area clear about the wheel. They were in a position to turn the tables on their attacker – but, to Kydd's dismay, the smoke cleared to reveal the worst. The two ships had drifted apart and he was left stranded on the enemy deck with only the men who had been able to scramble across before it happened.

He looked round rapidly; none were behind him on the after end of the ship but, forward, the French had recognised the situation and were beginning to regroup. *Teazer*'s hull slid further away – there could be no help from her. Then the French charged and once again there was frantic hacking and slashing: Kydd had learned in a hard school and fought savagely.

They were being driven to their last stand – the after-deck with the mizzen mast in the centre, then nothing further but the taffrail and the sea. Still the widening gap of sea between the two ships. Should he cry, 'Enough', then surrender and save lives?

In a split-second glance about the decks he noted a sky-light in the centre of the deck and did not hesitate. 'Here!' he bawled, and leaped feet first, smashing through the glass into the cabin below. Others tumbled after him in disarray. Staggering to his feet he saw that, as he had guessed, this was the great cabin. A flash and bang of a pistol from a side cabin made him wince, the bullet's wind passing close to his face, but the man paid for his temerity at the point of Poulden's cutlass.

Kydd reached the ornate door to the cabin spaces and barred it crudely, only just in time. There came the unmistakable sounds of men clattering down the main hatchway forward and battering at the door as the French seamen realised where they had gone. Soon there were ominous thumps and the wicked point of a pike pierced the door with a ringing thud. It was only a matter of time before the maddened men broke through.

The eyes of the men trapped below showed the whites – but then came the most beautiful sound in the world: the heavy smash of *Teazer*'s carronades. Those aboard had seen Kydd disappear below, leaving the deck clear and had obliged with grape-shot and canister once more.

The buffeting at the door faltered and stopped: the French were hastily returning to man the upper-deck guns but were being cut down by the murderous carronades. On the edge of reason with blood-lust, Kydd forced himself to cold control but when the crunch and grind of the ships' coming together again sounded he threw back the door and, cheering frantically, he and his men burst on to the deck to take the defenders from behind just as they were overwhelmed by waves of Teazers swarming over the bulwarks.

They had won.

The great cabin of HMS *Teazer* was alive with laughter, feminine faces and excitement, the candlelight glinting on the ladies' adornments and Captain Winthrop's gold lace, and it was hard to concentrate in the hearty bedlam. Kydd, flushed and happy, sat at the head of the table and beamed at the world.

'Wine with ye, Mr Dacres!' he called across the table. It had been difficult to know whom to invite to his victory dinner and he had settled on *Teazer*'s other officer, with the frigate captain and an envious lieutenant-in-command of the only other man-o'-war in harbour. The two ladies were of Winthrop's acquaintance and had been nearly overcome to be chosen to attend the most famous event in Malta.

Miss Peacock's tinkling laugh at a sally by Dacres brought a smile to Winthrop's weathered features. 'My dear Kydd, I do wish you joy of your evening – it does one's heart good to see audacity and courage at the cannon's mouth rewarded in such measure!'

'I thank ye, sir, but do y' not think—'

'No, I do not, Mr Kydd! You are fortune's darling, for you have seized what she's offered and turned it to best account. Go forth in trust to take your portion of glory and never again repine. Your health, sir!'

Red with embarrassment Kydd raised his glass and mumbled something.

'Of course things have changed for you now,' Winthrop said archly.

'Sir?'

'Why, it's not every officer who may claim a gazette,' he said significantly.

'You think . . . ?'

'I do.'

With a sense of unreality, the implications of what Winthrop was saying dawned on Kydd. A famous action at sea was a matter of the deepest interest to the whole nation and it was now the established tradition that the personal dispatches of the senior officer concerned would be published in full in the *London Gazette*, the government's publication of record, for all to peruse. His actual dispatch – his words – would appear along with the Court Circular, the highest legal notices and the weightiest of news and would, of course, be read by every noble and statesman in the land. Even the King himself would read it! The *Naval Chronicle*, of course, would want a fuller account and his few hours of madness would later be taken in thoughtfully by every ambitious naval officer . . .

'And it hardly needs remarking, no flag officer would dare to contemplate the removal from command of an established hero. Sir, you have your distinction – you may nevermore fear that your ship be taken from you.'

When it had penetrated, a profound happiness suffused Kydd's being to the very core. No more to fear the brusque letter of dismissal, the dread of being cast up on an uncaring land, the—

A scream of terror pierced the merriment and the cabin fell rapidly into a shocked silence. Everyone turned to Miss Peacock, who was staring into a corner, struck dumb with fright. Kydd hurried over to her and followed her pointing finger. Chuckling, he bent down and retrieved a petrified scrap of fur. 'Sprits'l, bless y' heart!' he said, turning to the throng, 'Doesn't care f'r cannon fire – we've searched the whole barky, fore 'n' aft, looking for the little rascal!'

Miss Peacock came to see for herself. 'Why, it's a wee-bitty kitten!' she cooed, offering her finger to be licked. 'It's so thin, the poor bairn – to be kept in this awful ship to be fired at with guns! Whoever could do such a thing?'

'Miss Peacock,' said Kydd, 'this is Able Seaman Sprits'l, a member of *Teazer*'s ship's company, an' he has his duties.' The button eyes moved about in sudden interest and the tiny nose twitched. 'I've an idea he'll need t' be used to the sound o' gunfire if he's going to be a Teazer!'

Chapter 9

Teazer was heading north to the trading routes around the heel of Italy. She had been sent on a cruise of her own with the barely concealed purpose of acquiring a prize or two to line the pockets of her brave commander and crew.

They had been fortunate indeed: there had been remarkably little damage and only a small number with wounds, such was the speed with which it had all happened. The French captain, Reynaud, had been mortified at his misreading of *Teazer* and the result of his overweening confidence, and had sulked below during the short but triumphant journey back to Malta at *Teazer*'s tail.

It had done wonders for the Teazers' morale, and as Kydd strolled about the decks that fine morning he was met with grins and respect; even Tysoe assumed a regal bearing.

For Kydd only one thing mattered: he had achieved distinction and his command was secure. He and *Teazer* would be together from now on.

And that meant he could make plans for both *Teazer* and her company. In Malta he had seen a new ship fitted with patent windsails for ventilation that would be perfect for keeping a flow of fresh air through the length of the mess deck. There were other things he had in mind: Yates, his coxswain, had been among the wounded left at the hospital and he would take the opportunity to rate up the cool-thinking Poulden to the position. Perhaps tonight he would invite the two midshipmen to dinner – they had grown considerably in both stature and confidence and were a lively pair . . .

His pleasant musings were interrupted by the lookout's call of *'Sail hoooo!'* There had been sightings aplenty since their departure but only feluccas and other small vessels, not worth the wear and tear of a chase.

'Deck, ahoy! Ship-rigged, an' holding f'r the north!'

A sizeable vessel. Was it predator or prey? That they had overhauled it under full sail suggested a fat-bellied merchant ship. This would be confirmed by a sudden sighting and hopeless bid for escape, but it would take a racehorse of a ship to outrun *Teazer*.

Kydd waited for the expected outcome – but, to his puzzlement, there was neither the instant reaching for the weather position of a man-o'-war nor the consternation and fleeing of a merchant vessel, simply a steady northward course.

Why such confidence? It might be a guiltless neutral or, even more unlikely in these waters, a friend, but its actions were not natural to either. Unknown sail was a threat until proved otherwise and this one seemed to have not a care in the world – or was it leading them into a trap?

'T' quarters, Mr Dacres. I don't trust th' villain.' There were no colours evident but that was not significant: owners of merchant packets were not inclined to waste money on flags that would blow to tatters in weeks at sea.

By early afternoon they had come within gunshot of the

vessel, which still held to its course. Doubled lookouts at the masthead could spy no skulking sail, no gathering jaws of a trap – it was deeply unsettling.

'It's a plague ship, sir,' Dacres suggested unhappily.

It fitted the facts: the lack of activity in the rigging, the monotonous and unvarying course, the lack of fear. Kydd took his pocket telescope and trained it on the vessel's decks. There were the usual small number of merchant-ship crew, just a couple about the wheel and a few others around the forebitts.

'Mr Dacres, there's something amiss. Give 'em a gun.' A two-pounder ball sent up a plume ahead of the vessel. It had no effect. The ship stood on regardless, curious gazes on *Teazer* as she hauled up on them. Another gun brought a sudden burst of angry shouting that was incomprehensible, but no action.

'Half pistol shot t' wind'd, Mr Bonnici,' Kydd grunted, at a loss to comprehend the situation. They closed and Kydd added, 'This time I'll have ye sight close enough t' scratch his varnish.'

The threat brought a grudging heaving to, a sullen wallowing with backed sails. 'Board him, Mr Dacres, an' find out what he's up to,' Kydd ordered. He had considered leading the party himself but he did not want to leave *Teazer* in this unknown situation.

'If it has plague—' Dacres protested feebly.

'He has nothing o' the sort. He's under our guns an' you'll take no nonsense. Two shots fr'm us to return directly, a wave of y'r hat should ye want assistance. We're looking to a possible prize. Do y' have the latest interrogatories?' he asked, referring to the questions issued by the Admiralty to assist boarding officers in their assessments.

'Aye aye, sir,' Dacres muttered.

The cutter pulled away smartly and disappeared round the leeward side of the ship while Kydd went below to his paperwork. It generally took an hour or so for the preliminaries of a prize boarding to be concluded.

After just ten minutes there was a knock on his door, and the message, 'Sir, our boat is returning.' This made no sense and Kydd hurried on deck.

Dacres climbed over the bulwarks with an acutely worried expression. 'Sir, may I see you privately?' he said urgently.

In Kydd's cabin he looked about carefully, then closed the door firmly. 'Sir, I have to inform you . . . If you'd please to read this.' It was a French commercial newspaper, not the government *Le Moniteur*, notorious for its lies and sweeping claims, but a sober publication from Marseille, intended for merchants and others in trade. A phrase blazed out in the headlines: '*La Paix*' – peace!

Kydd stumbled through the rest, and the impossible became real. Apparently for more than a week it had been known that negotiations for peace from the English government had been accepted and an armistice declared, pending full ratification.

Peace? It was not possible! Had not the French been thrown so recently out of their Oriental empire at great cost? And with brilliant victories this was not a time to be treating for *peace*! He held up the newspaper. It seemed ordinary enough, a little grubby, with a pencilled column of trading figures. There was nothing to suggest it was a forgery.

Now he understood the reason for the confidence, the steady course probably to a port on the other side of the Adriatic. Peace! The implications were endless – the treaty that must follow had to decide the fate of empires, colonies, whole peoples. Peace! In a world at war for nearly ten years it was hard to think in any other terms.

'Er, sir?' Dacres looked anxiously at his captain. 'The people – when shall I . . .'

The men: how would they take the news? Kydd's mind spun. He knew he could not keep it from them long. 'Get back to th' ship with our apologies an' let 'em go. We return to t' Malta.'

The news had arrived in Malta the day after *Teazer* had sailed. Addington's government had seen fit to accept humbling terms to secure any kind of peace in a war that was reaching titanic proportions, spreading over the globe and waged now by Britain on her own at an appalling cost.

It seemed that, for Downing Street, the limits had been reached, the price finally too great. From now on England would have to learn to live side by side in a world dominated by the colossus of France and First Consul Bonaparte.

Kydd landed in Malta amid a ferment of rumour and anxiety; there was widespread fear on the small island, which had done well under the umbrella of British protection. The population now faced a return to the rule of the ancient knights who had allowed in the French.

Cameron had no information and Pigot was less than helpful. Kydd's only option was to report himself and his ship to the Commander-in-Chief, Keith, in person. Kydd realized the admiral would no longer be on blockade off Toulon: he would be falling back on Minorca and its capacious fleet anchorage.

The three-day voyage passed in a haze of unreality; the sea seemed full of ships going about their lawful occasions. Neither friend nor foe, all were now simply fellow seafarers.

Dawn was not met at quarters, the guns' charges were drawn and *Teazer* proceeded with only a signal swivel gun loaded. It was unnatural.

What did the future hold? Increased trade in the Mediterranean would require the guarantee of a naval presence but what would peacetime life be like? With a wry smile Kydd acknowledged that he had no idea: his entire time at sea, from pressed man to commander, had been spent at war.

There was one bright prospect, however: with all the fleet in harbour he would at last see his great friend Renzi, first lieutenant of *Tenacious*. There would be so much to tell and, for the first time since he had assumed the mantle of command, Kydd would know the company of one to whom he could at last unburden his soul.

Teazer raised the distant blue of the conical peak of Mount Toro, then shaped course for the south-east of the island and the grand cliff-sided harbour of Port Mahon. Passing the ruined fortress of San Felipe at the entrance to larboard, they entered the port.

The entire Mediterranean fleet was at anchor in the three-mile-long stretch of water. These ships, their sombre lines marked by ceaseless sea-keeping, the gloss and varnish long since gone from their sturdy sides but their appearance still neat and Spartan, had kept faithful watch on Toulon over the long months to make it impossible for Bonaparte to impose his will on the world. And now they were withdrawn, idle and without purpose. It was as if the world had gone mad.

As they passed by the massive ships-of-the-line, Kydd tried to make out *Tenacious* but could not find her: there were just too many vessels. *Teazer*'s anchor fell from her bows and

Kydd reappeared on deck in full-dress uniform with white gloves and sword to call on the Commander-in-Chief.

He mounted the side-steps of *Foudroyant* with mixed feelings: as a victorious captain he could be certain of a warm welcome, but in these circumstances who knew what lay ahead? After he was piped aboard he was ushered respectfully into the admiral's presence. In the vast great cabin there were three other officers who, to Kydd's surprise, did not make their excuses.

Keith looked up, his face drawn and tired. 'Ah, Mr Kydd. Joy of your encounter with *La Fouine*, of course. Your actions were in the best traditions of the service and do you much credit.' He shook Kydd's hand vigorously but was clearly distracted. 'In more tranquil times you should most certainly be my guest at dinner, but I do beg forgiveness in this instance and hope to receive you at another time.' His legendary chilliness melted into something akin to melancholy as he added, 'But, then, these are not normal times and I can promise nothing.'

He paused, staring into space for long moments, then seemed to focus again. 'I have this hour received Admiralty instructions. Your orders are being prepared, Commander, and will be delivered by hand to your vessel by evening gun.'

Kydd murmured something, but Keith cut him short. 'You will be desirous of returning to your ship. Pray do not delay on my account.' As he turned to go, Kydd felt Keith's hand on his arm. The flinty eyes bored straight into his. 'Please believe, Mr Kydd, I would wish you well for your future.'

Kydd went down the side to the strident squeal of the boatswain's pipe and into his boat. What did this mean? Was

Keith conveying more than approval of his recent triumph? Perhaps he was to be accounted as an admiral's favourite.

As they made their way back to *Teazer* a chance veering of the wind direction had the great ships swinging to their anchors, and past two 74s he saw at last the familiar shape of the ship he had spent so much of his sea life aboard, HMS *Tenacious*.

'Stretch out f'r that sixty-four,' he ordered Poulden.

'Aye aye, sir,' his new coxswain replied.

As they approached *Tenacious* she seemed dowdy and down-cast; she was well ordered, but in small things she wasn't the fine old warhorse he remembered. In places the gingerbread – the gilded carved adornments round her stern and beakhead – no longer gleamed with the lustre of gold leaf and had been economically painted over in yellow. The rosin finish between the wales of her side was now a dull black and her ensign seemed limp and drab.

But for Kydd this was a moment long coming. The first satisfaction – to be well savoured – would be in encountering Rowley once more. How would he find it in him to utter the words of civility due to a fellow captain?

Poulden answered the hail from *Tenacious* with a bellowed '*Teazer!*' indicating that not only was a naval officer to board but that this one was a captain of a King's ship. They approached slowly to give the ceremonial side party time to assemble and to warn *Tenacious*'s captain to stand by to receive.

Mounting the side steps Kydd saw with a jet of warmth all the familiar marks left by countless encounters with the sea and malice of the enemy still there.

The blast of the boatswain's call pealed out the instant his head appeared above the level of the bulwark and Kydd gravely removed his hat and acknowledged the quarterdeck, then the small group who awaited him.

A young lieutenant stepped forward anxiously. 'Sir, L'tenant McCallum, second o' *Tenacious*.'

'Commander Kydd, *Teazer*,' Kydd said crisply. 'To visit th' first lieutenant.'

Hesitantly McCallum replied, 'Captain is ashore, sir, and the first lieutenant at the dockyard, but he'll be back aboard presently. Er, we'd be honoured if you'd accept the hospitality of the wardroom in the meantime.'

One satisfaction deferred, then, but another pleasurably delayed. Renzi could be relied on to manage the niceties of a captain come to visit a lieutenant instead of the more usual summoning in the reverse direction.

'First l'tenant's sairvant, sir, an' would ye desire a wee drop?' It was not like Renzi to have a youngster with a Scottish brogue as manservant – he normally favoured a knowing and dour marine.

'No, thank ye,' Kydd answered, and settled automatically into his old second lieutenant's chair, looking around the well-remembered intimacies of the first ship in which he had served as an officer. So many memories ... When the servant had left he tiptoed self-consciously to the end cabin, larboard side, the most junior officer's. He guiltily pulled aside the curtain and peered in at the ludicrously tiny space that he had once considered the snug centre of his domestic world. The cunningly crafted writing desk was still there, a small gilded portrait of someone's young lady peering shyly at him from the bulkhead above it.

He let the curtain fall and feeling washed over him. From the anguish of those long-ago times to now, captain of his own ship. Could fortune bring more?

'Ahem. Sir?' A tall, stooped officer stood at the door looking mystified.

'Yes, L'tenant?' Kydd answered pleasantly.

'Well, er, sir,' he said in embarrassment, 'Edward Robbins, first lieutenant.'

It took Kydd aback. 'Oh, er, Mr Renzi is not y'r first – he's been moved on?'

'Oh, no, sir,' said the officer. 'I've only been in post these three weeks since Mr Renzi was landed with the fever. It's been a busy time keeping in with things.'

'Fever?' Kydd said blankly, a cold presentiment creeping into him.

'Why, yes, sir – did you know Mr Renzi at all?'

'I did – do.'

'Oh, I've sad news for you then, sir. Mr Renzi was taken of an ague, let me see, this month past off Toulon. The doctor exhausted his quinine and having only a few leeches remaining there was little that could be done.'

'He is . . .' began Kydd, but could not finish.

'We sent him in a lugger – to here, sir, the Lazaretto, but our doctor told us then that he was not responding and we should be prepared.' Seeing Kydd's stricken face, he finished lamely, 'I'm sorry to be the one to tell you this, sir.'

Icy cold with the fear of what he would shortly know, Kydd headed down the harbour past Bloody Island and to the landing place on the bleak-walled Lazaretto island. The nervous boat's crew insisted on lying off while Kydd went in to enquire. It took him moments only to discover that Renzi was no longer there; apparently he should have gone to Isla del Rey, the round island up the harbour where the hospital and its records were.

'L'tenant Renzi of *Tenacious*,' he insisted yet again, to the man at the door. This time it brought results: an intense, dark-featured Iberian appeared. 'Yes?' he asked brusquely, wiping his hands on a towel. Kydd explained himself. 'He lives still,' the man grunted. Hope flooded back. 'But not for long. If you wan' say goodbyes, come now.'

The cloying, sickly smell of suffering humanity hit him like a wall, bringing back unbearable memories of his time in a yellow-fever hospital in the Caribbean. 'Here,' the Iberian said, with a gesture, and stood back cynically.

Kydd bent over the pitiable grey form. It was Renzi. 'M' friend—' he said huskily, but a lump in his throat prevented him continuing.

'He c'n not hear you.'

'May I know – the fever, is it—'

'Is not infecting. Th' fools on your ships know nothing.'

'How – how long?'

'It is th' undulant fever – do you know this?'

'No,' said Kydd, in a low voice.

'He has a week – a month. Who know? Then . . .'

'Is there any cure, at all?'

'No.' The finality in his voice sounded like the slam of a door. Then he added, 'Some believe th' change of air, but I cannot say.'

The boat trip back to *Teazer* in the bright sunshine was a hard trial; all he wanted now was the solitude of his cabin to grapple with what he had seen. His dearest friend on his deathbed, a motionless grey form. So different from the man who had roped himself to Kydd when they cast themselves into the sea at the wreck of *Artemis*, who had been by his side at Acre with bloody sword as they defied Napoleon himself. More images came and Kydd bit his lip and endured until the boat finally reached *Teazer*.

After he had come aboard Dacres handed him a packet. The promised orders had arrived. But Kydd needed time to face what had happened. His particular friend, who had shared so many of the adventures that had formed him, and given him the chances that had led to this, the culmination of his life, was dying – and he could do nothing.

His fists balled while helplessness coursed through him. Then he took a deep breath to steady himself.

He took up his orders, now his only link with normality, the real world, and his duty. Life – naval life – had to go on, and if there was anything to which Renzi had scrupulously held, it was his duty.

The packet of orders was thin. Normally containing signals in profusion and pages of ancillary matters, this appeared to consist only of a single folded paper. He slit the seal and opened it out: it was curt, precise and to the point. *Teazer* was to sail for England with immediate effect. She was to proceed thence to Plymouth, the nearest big port. There, her commission would come to an end and she would be placed in ordinary, laid up, her masts, riggings, sails and guns removed. Her ship's company to disperse, her officers' commissions to terminate and her commander to become unemployed.

It was the end of everything.

Chapter 10

It was not as it should have been, his return to the land of his birth. Still numb with shock at the way his fortunes had changed so precipitously, the sight of the sprawling promontory of the Lizard, bleak against the desolate cold grey autumn seas, left him sad and empty.

The disintegration of the life he had come to love so much had started almost immediately when the Maltese had refused to continue to England and had left the ship. He had let Bonnici go with them and the few others who preferred a Mediterranean sea life to the uncertainties of peacetime Britain, and sailed short-handed.

Some of *Teazer*'s company were eager to return, those with families, loved ones, a future. Others were subdued, caught by the sudden alteration in their lives and the uncertainty of what lay ahead.

The Eddystone lighthouse lay to starboard as they headed for Plymouth Sound and shaped course for the naval dock-yard. There seemed to be so many more craft plying the coasts than Kydd remembered and each seemed bent on throwing herself across *Teazer*'s track.

The desolation Kydd felt had only one small glimmer of light: Renzi still clung to life. Kydd had seized on the one thing that he had heard might benefit his friend: a change of air. He had cleared out his great cabin, then stretchered Renzi aboard and set Tysoe to caring for him. The fever was still in full spate, coming in spiteful waves, and while Kydd sat with him there was no sign that Renzi understood what was going on.

Time passed in a series of final scenes: the growing defin-ition of land to greens and blacks and the occasional scatter of village dwellings, passing Drake Island and the grandeur of Plymouth Hoe, then the concluding passage to larboard and around Devil's Point to the wider stretch of the Hamoaze.

The vast Admiralty dockyard was located along the east side of the Tamar river; for the best part of a mile the shore was pierced with graving docks and lined with ordnance wharves, quays and jetties without counting. And inland, as far as the eye could see, there were long stone buildings and chimneys, storehouses and smith's shops, sail lofts and mast houses in endless industrial display.

But Kydd had no eyes for these wonders. Even the impres-sive sight of ships-of-the-line in stately rows and the heart-catching sadness of the long file of little ships secured head to tail in mid-channel in ordinary did not divert him. There was one last service he could do for Renzi: his poor racked body, tightly wrapped against the late autumn misery, was landed and taken to the naval hospital at Stonehouse.

In the days that followed Kydd himself suffered: HMS *Teazer* had reached the end of her sea service and, by degrees, was rendered a shell fit to join the melancholy line of others at the trots. As they were de-stored, the ship's company was paid off and departed until, in an unnatural, echoing solitude, there was left only the purser, his clerk and the standing officers, who would remain until the ship was sold or disposed of – the boatswain, carpenter, gunner and cook.

Kydd tried to spend as much time as he could with Renzi; the prognosis was not good and he was visibly weakening, still in a febrile delirium. Then the day came when Ellicott laid out the last papers for his attention, and he signed away for ever his life at sea.

With an hour until the dockyard boat made its round Kydd had nothing to do but wander the forlorn husk of his ship. Empty space where once victorious carronades had roared out their defiance, over there a beautifully worked patch in the deck where once an iron-bound block had fallen from aloft. And on her bow the laughing maiden in white . . . Not trusting himself to keep a countenance, Kydd turned abruptly and went below.

The mess deck, now a deserted hollow space, still carried the same wafting odours of humanity and cooking it had always had and, leaving the boatswain to his rummaging, he passed for the last time into his cabin. The panels were bare but he had left the table and other furniture, for what use were they to him on land? His bedplace no longer contained his few possessions: they were on deck, ready to be taken ashore.

A lump came to his throat.

A soft knock and a low murmur interrupted his thoughts. 'Sir.' It was the boatswain, cradling something. 'Sprits'l, sir. Thought ye'd like t' know he's going to be looked after, like, no need t' worry y'self on his account.'

'Th-thank ye, Mr Purchet. I know he's in th' best o' hands . . .'

The boatswain left just in time: for the first time since his youth Kydd knew the hot gush of tears that would not end.

The solid, hard and hateful land was finally under his feet for good. Kydd knew what his first move would be, but little after that. He had no alternative than to return home to Guildford – but under very different circumstances from those he had dreamed of out in the bright Mediterranean. Now there was nothing of that life but memories.

His uniform was stowed with his baggage and his fighting sword. He needed to get used to the soft clinging of civilian garb – and even more quickly to the mysteries of shore ways.

Thinking of this final removal from the sea world now upon him brought a catch to his throat. And what would happen to Renzi? He might have only days, or perhaps the fever would break long enough for them to talk together for the last time.

There was only one thing possible: he would take Renzi with him and his mother would care for him. For one so ill there was only one way and that was to go by coach, which would probably mean the hire of the entire vehicle. Having lavished so much attention on *Teazer* Kydd's means were now severely stretched, but he could not desert his friend.

The long and tedious journey tried Kydd sorely. The eternal grinding of wheels and soul-destroying inactivity was not best suited to his mood. Renzi was as comfortable as he could make him, suspended in a naval cot across the seats, but the swaying and jolting were remorseless. If he did not survive the journey, Kydd had argued to himself, then it would be the same as if he had remained in a hospital bed to die. At least there were no wounds to hurt his friend and work open.

It took two days even with the turnpikes to reach Surrey and Guildford. The wartime years had been kind to the quiet township and little had changed. It seemed so small, tidy, placid. But *he* had changed: the places and scenes that had seemed so significant in his memories had receded into the picturesque tranquility of a pretty market town.

They reached the river Wey, clattered over the old bridge and began the steep climb up the high street, past the little shops and taverns. It was as he remembered, but overlying it all was a detachment that put him over and above these scenes. Since last he had been here in these untroubled old lanes he had been at the grand and horrifying scenes of the Nile with Nelson, had stood with bloody sword at the gates of Acre – and been captain of a man-o'-war. What kind of person did that make him in the context of this gentle existence?

Under the splendid clock at the Guild Hall, then up towards School Lane. His heart beat faster for he was returning home – the only one he had now. The horses made the level, then continued the last hundred yards to the schoolhouse. Kydd was touched to see that the flag hoisted proudly over all was the blue ensign of Admiral Keith's Mediterranean squadron, no doubt strictly observed by Boatswain Perrott. It was quiet in the schoolrooms and he guessed that it was holidays.

'Here an' wait, if y' please,' Kydd instructed the coachman, when they reached the small gate to the school. He descended, stretched his cramped limbs and made his way to the school cottage. He hesitated for a moment before he knocked: in the time he had been away on the high seas almost anything could have happened to the family. His father had not been so spry then and . . . He braced himself and knocked firmly. Holding his breath, he waited.

The door opened. 'Th' Kydd residence. An' what's y' business, sir?' A young maid whom Kydd did not recognise was looking at him suspiciously.

'Mr Kydd t' see Mr Kydd,' he could not help replying.

The maid's expression tightened. 'I'll tell th' mistress, sir.'

The door closed in Kydd's face. He heard light footsteps then the door opened.

'Thomas!' Cecilia shrieked, throwing her arms round him. 'Darling Thomas! Do come in – where have you been? You're so dusty! Sit down, sit down! I'll get Mother.'

In seconds Kydd learned that his father was well but frail, the school was doing splendidly, that Boatswain Perrott had taken the pledge – could it be believed? – and that Cecilia herself was now resting, following her release from the employ of Lady Stanhope after Lord Stanhope's resignation.

'It's so marvellous to see you!' Cecilia sparkled, holding Kydd at arm's length to see him. 'I vow I can't wait until you tell us all about your wonderful ship.' She linked his arm and drew him to the mantelpiece, her vivacity eliciting a reluctant smile from Kydd. 'And Nicholas, do you ever see him at all?' she added gaily.

'Cec, I've been tryin' to say . . .'

Her hand flew to her mouth.

'He – he's very ill. Not as you'd say certain of a recovery.'

Cecilia went white, all traces of gaiety gone. 'Wh-where is he now, Thomas?'

'Well, er, he's in th' coach outside. I wanted to—'

She tore herself away and ran outside. Kydd hurried after

her, disturbed by his sister's distraught reaction. 'We'll take him inside, Cec – Mother will know what t' do.'

Kydd sat at the old-fashioned writing desk, absentmindedly nibbling the end of his quill; the words of the letter were not coming easily. From the next room he could hear the steady murmur of Cecilia reading aloud to her patient. With that and the distracting sounds of animals being driven past to the North Street market, the cries of pedlars and street urchins, it was difficult to concentrate.

After the flurry of his arrival, arrangements had been put in hand: Kydd was to take lodgings in the town with Renzi, Cecilia insisting that she be trusted to supervise his care and treatment. Luckily the family doctor knew of undulant fever from another case – he snorted at the talk of leeches and quinine, and pronounced confidently that the febrile spasms would diminish in their own good time on Renzi's return to a cooler clime. With his sea constitution, there was every prospect of a good recovery. They listened gravely, however, as he had gone on to warn of the danger to be apprehended from a marked tendency to depression in those suffering from the illness, leading in some cases even to suicide.

While the weakened Renzi began slowly to take an interest in the world, Kydd's fears for his own future were confirmed. His first letter to the Admiralty indicating his availability for appointment was acknowledged curtly with not the slightest indication of interest and he was working now on some excuse to broach the subject again. He was on half-pay – enough to exist in genteel carefulness but no more. With Renzi's half-pay they could stay in their rooms indefinitely, but on full recovery Renzi would be on his way back to his own family, leaving Kydd to half a living and a hole in his pocket from the fifty pounds he had paid for the coach.

Cecilia was in no doubt where his best course lay. 'This is your chance to settle down, take a wife – raise a family! You're a hero. The war is over and you've played your part. You're a retired sea-captain, dear brother, free to do anything you want!'

His mother had as strong feelings on the matter as Cecilia but was wise enough not to press the issue. Kydd did, however, notice that the sword yielded to him by the French captain, which he had proudly presented as a trophy to her and which had been accepted and reluctantly displayed over the mantelpiece, was now put away safely, as were the other keepsakes and stout sea ornaments that had been so much a part of his life but now appeared out of place and quaint.

Weeks succeeded days and Kydd's waking hours were a comfortable nothingness; there had been no further word from the Admiralty and despondency settled in. It was now most unlikely that there would be a ship.

Renzi improved slowly until he reached the point at which he could hold a conversation. Guarded by a jealous Cecilia, he was weak but his mind seemed focused. However, there was a change from the urbane, light-textured conversation of the past to a darker, introspective vein. And when Cecilia read to him he would sometimes turn obstinately to face the wall.

With Renzi so out of character Kydd could not bring his own situation to him. Yet something must be decided: he could not go on as he was. A pitiable eking out of his means in an attempt to be seen as a gentleman was a bitter prospect.

The weeks became a month, then two, his sea life a memory too poignant to bear. He knew in his heart he was not intended for the land, with its complexities and odd obsessions, and made up his mind to travel to London. There, he would go personally to the Admiralty and, exerting every ounce of influence and interest he could muster, he would lay siege until he found employment at sea; he would accept any position, any vessel that floated, as long as it took him back to the bosom of the ocean.

The faded wallpaper and damp corner of the little room did not dismay Kydd unduly – he had endured far worse. What had taken him aback was the way London had grown and changed. It was now generally acknowledged the biggest city in the world with the unthinkable population of one million souls. A stinking, strident and energetic city, it nevertheless had an animation, a vitality that at first reached out to Kydd and did much to temper the universal dank smell of sea-coal smoke, crowded streets and concentrations of squalor.

His first day in the capital had been spent in finding accommodation; near to the Admiralty in White Hall was his goal but he soon found the rents there ruinous. Weary hours later, it was plain that he could not afford any of the more fashionable residences to the west, and having passed through the commercial heart of the city to the east, he could see there was nothing that could be termed fit for a gentleman officer.

The south bank of the Thames opposite, although it was connected by the imposing Westminster Bridge, was nothing but roads away to the timber-yards and open fields where wooden tenter-frames spread gaily coloured textiles; further to the east, it transformed into the stews of Southwark.

But the sheer size of the city became intimidating and depressing, endless miles of jostling humanity, which set

Kydd's nerves a-jangle. In Charing Cross near the public pillory he had spied a tap-house and soon found himself a pot of dark, foaming beer. He drank thirstily and it calmed him.

A stout gentleman next to him, jovial and in an old-fashioned periwig, was quite taken with making the acquaintance of a naval officer and loudly insisted on shaking his hand. Kydd took advantage of the situation and made enquiry about lodgings, touching lightly on the fact of his temporary inconvenience in the matter of means. He learned that as a rule naval gentlemen found Greenwich answered, being half-way between the Royal Dockyard at Woolwich and the Admiralty and served by the river wherries.

Kydd now reviewed his plans for an early call at the Admiralty Office in White Hall. He had to present a petition for the attention of the First Lord of the Admiralty that would set out why he was so deserving of a ship, a hard thing indeed when this was no less than Sir John Jervis, Earl St Vincent and a national hero, recently in post and said to be beginning a massive reform of the Navy's administration and support.

In this it would be vital to bring to bear every scrap of 'interest' that he could; he concentrated on recalling who could possibly put in a word for him. First, there was Lord Stanhope, highly placed in diplomatic circles and with whom he had shared an open-boat voyage in the Caribbean. But he had resigned from his post in protest at the terms of the peace. Captain Eddington? His nephew Bowden had shaped up well for Kydd – but, if rumours were to be believed, Eddington was in the country on his estates awaiting any call. The Commander-in-Chief Mediterranean, Admiral Keith, had given every indication of his approbation of

Kydd's conduct but that very morning's newspaper detailed how he had returned to Scotland for a well-merited retreat. Was there no one?

The next morning he had not been able to think of more, but set off for the Admiralty Office with hopes high. His gazette had been duly published and the *Naval Chronicle* was talking about a small biography piece. He was not unknown, therefore, and his request for a ship of any kind would surely be looked upon with sympathy if it were made in person.

The fast-skimming wherry revealed quite a different London. Around the Isle of Dogs and its docks was a dense forest of masts from vast amounts of shipping, rafted up together and in continual commotion of lighters and barges. The wherry darted through the vessels, the hard-jawed waterman with his distinctive round cap leaning into his oars with the lithe ease of long practice. Then past the cargo wharves with their pungent fragrances of cinnabar and ginger, and on to shipbuilders' slips and the last green fields before the Port of London proper.

With the ancient walls of the Tower of London on the right, the craft approached London Bridge, the first crossing possible across the powerful river. Kydd heard the booming rush of water past the stout piers of the bridge. It did not seem to daunt the waterman who lined up the light boat and brought it under the bridge with short, fast strokes. Beyond it was a much more capacious river, free of sea-going vessels and with the sights grander. The dome of St Paul's on the right was followed first by Fleet Ditch and the nearby Puddle Dock, then graceful Somerset House, and ahead, as the river straightened the great heart of London, Westminster Abbey, Parliament in its ancient palace where, no doubt, the last details of the peace were being debated at that very moment. Then there was the distant line of the noble Westminster Bridge.

At White Hall stairs the wherry lay off while Kydd fumbled for silver. Then he went quickly through to the broad avenue that was White Hall, opposite Horse Guards, a right turn and then the colonnaded façade of the Admiralty offices with their imposing buildings beyond offset by the curious structure of a shutter telegraph on the roof.

Kydd's pulse quickened at the sight. Within those grey stone walls had been enacted all the sea dramas of the century: great battles had been planned; the shocking news of mutiny in the British fleet had been received there. And following the victory of Camperdown off the Dutch coast the decision to approve the field-of-battle promotion of a master's mate, one Thomas Paine Kydd, had been taken.

Clutching his small case with the precious petition inside it, Kydd passed into a cobbled courtyard; before him was a portico and the main door, massive and oaken. The Admiralty. He went up to the doorman and slipped him his 'fee'. The man took the money with a bored expression and showed Kydd through the buff-coloured entrance hall with its gleaming brass lamps to the second door on the left. 'Cap'n's room,' he said laconically.

He entered the high, beautifully arched room. It was full of people, talking, playing cards, pacing about, dozing. Few looked up at Kydd's entrance, and from their conversations he realised they were there for much the same purpose, seeking promotion or ships – and had been there for a long time.

Kydd kept to himself while he awaited a summons. One came, but that was to part with guineas to the First Lord's keeper to ensure delivery of his petition. There was apparently no indication to be had as to the timing of a possible audience and Kydd went back to the waiting room. First minutes, then hours passed. He struck up a desultory conversation with others, but the talk was despairing and bitter, touching mostly on the fearful reduction of the Navy to peace-time numbers and the consequences for employment.

The hours dragged unbearably in a tense yet mind-numbing tedium but nothing eventuated. He would have to return the next day. And the next. On the third day, well into the morning, word finally came: the First Lord would see him at four precisely.

Excitement flooded in – at long last! As a commissioned officer Kydd had every right to call on the Admiralty and be heard. And by a sea officer, not a civil appointee, as the previous incumbent. This had to be where his fortune changed.

Time passed even more slowly; his nervous pacing and rehearsal of his words was watched cynically by the others but Kydd knew this was his only chance. At five minutes to four he presented himself and was ushered upstairs to a large room.

'Commander Kydd, m'lord,' the functionary said, and withdrew, closing the doors.

Kydd stood before the great desk and tried to meet the hard grey eyes of Earl St Vincent, whose splendid uniform and decorations filled his vision. 'S-sir, it is kind in ye to see me at this time.'

The eyes were level and uncompromising – and red with tiredness. 'You wish a ship.' The words were bitten off as though regretted.

'Sir. As ye can see fr'm my—'

'I can read as well as the next man, sir.' He had Kydd's painfully written petition in his hands and glanced once at it, then resumed his impaling stare. 'If this were a time o' war you should have one, Mr Kydd. Since we are not in that state, I cannot give you one – as simple as that, sir.'

'Then, sir, any sea appointment would be more than acceptable . . .'

'If you were a l'tenant, that might have been possible, but you are not. As a commander you must command, and I have no ships.'

'Sir, not even—'

'Sir – do tell me, which vessel do you propose I should turn out her captain that you should take his place? Hey? Hey?'

At Kydd's silence he went on in a kinder tone: 'Your situation is known. Your services to His Majesty's Navy are well noted, but I can give you no hope of a ship – no hope, do you understand me, sir?'

Kydd stared unseeingly at the damp walls of his rooms, his mind full of bitter thoughts. St Vincent was upright and honourable and he had had a fair hearing. Probably no amount of interest or influence could overturn the odds against him. The very situation he had feared since that fateful talk with the cutter lieutenant had now come about, ironically so soon after he had secured the distinction he had sought.

His means were fast dissipating and there were few alternatives. He had gone over these in his mind many times – there was the Impress Service that ran the press-gangs, the Sea Fencibles that were in effect a naval militia, the Transport Board with its storeships and craft for the Army, and finally hospital and prison ships. Even supposing he could find a berth, there was the undeniable fact that any would be poison to his future career as a first-rank sea officer: it was generally expected that a gentleman officer should retire to his country estates to await a call if there was another war.

A knock at the door brought a quickly scribbled letter from Cecilia. Kydd bit his lip as he read that Renzi had disappeared – had simply vanished from his sick-bed without hint or warning and was presumably wandering the streets, disturbed in his intellects and not responsible. Remembering the doctor's strictures about depression and suicide Kydd's first thought was to rush back to look for Renzi. Then cold reason came and told him that Cecilia would ensure that measures were taken to find him and he could add little by returning to Guildford. He set the letter down.

The cheap candle guttered like his hopes. Things had gone now from disappointment to real worry. Living in London was ruinously expensive and at some point he would find that he must let go his hopes of any more sea employment – and return home. To what?

A sudden thought struck. There was little difference between a merchant ship and a warship if ship-rigged. He was a known quantity in the matter of leading men and, as for the seamanship, he was sure he could make a better fist of it than many he had seen in his convoy days. He would do as the common sailor always did – slip easily between man-o'-war and merchant jack.

The cream was the East India Company, vessels run on naval lines of discipline and efficiency and with ample prospect of profitable ventures for the captain. But John Company was known for its closed structure and there was probably no opening for an outsider. The élite Falmouth Packet Service? Greyhounds of the sea, these little ships would race across the Atlantic with mails and even chests of gold to the New World, again with rich pickings for the captains. Was it worthwhile to make the long trip to Falmouth on the off-chance that he, among so many in like circumstances, would be able to break into such a sea community and secure a command? Probably not. London was, however, the premier maritime centre of the kingdom and if he could not achieve something here, then . . . The heart of this activity was just downstream of the Tower of London, at the final resting place of the ceaseless stream of vessels from all parts of the world. The factors, agents, owners and others all had their offices nearby. He tried to remember company names, any who would favour a naval officer as captain. That was it – Burns, Throsby and Russell; they had been the prickly owners, he remembered, of the brig once chartered for a cartel voyage to the Mediterranean. He set to work to prepare an approach that would persuade them to take on a new captain.

The Burns, Throsby and Russell building was set back from the noise and stench of the Ratcliffe Highway, a haughty paean to the empire of trade. It seemed that Mr Burns was unavailable but Mr Russell would be in a position to accept Kydd's calling in half an hour.

Kydd sat in a high-backed chair and tried not to appear too obvious as he looked about the great hall. The entire floor was populated with scores of identical raised desks, each with its clerk and scratching quill. An overpowering musty odour of old paper and ink pervaded the air in much the same way as the fug of a frigate's berth deck but here there was no sound other than an echoing susurrus of half a hundred pens.

'Cap'n Kydd?' A kindly old clerk hovered in front of him. 'Mr Russell can see you now.'

Russell was old-fashioned in appearance, punctilious, his small pince-nez glittering as he peered at Kydd. 'Well, Captain, it is certainly not every day we are able to receive such a distinguished sea officer as your own good self, sir.'

'You know of my action with *La Fouine*?' Kydd said, in surprise.

'*La Fouine*? I'm not sure I follow you, sir. I was simply referring to your remarkable sagacity in devising a stratagem to preserve a convoy off Sicily from depredation. Our agent in Malta speaks highly of you, Mr Kydd.'

Kydd looked down modestly. Was he right to hope . . . ?

'And now, sir, of what service may we be to you?' Russell said mildly, taking off his spectacles to polish them.

'Mr Russell, as ye will be aware, with th' late peace, the King's service is less a place f'r an enterprising officer. As a mariner of ambition I see that th' merchant service may provide me more of a future, an' I ask if ye will consider me as suitable f'r your ocean-going trade –' he took a deep breath '– as a master.'

The polishing stopped. At first Kydd thought that Russell had not heard, but then he answered, with no change in his expression: 'You'll be sound in your nauticals, I will believe,' he said, 'Pray tell me, sir, your notion of the monetary risks the master of a merchant vessel incurs on behalf of the owner under a charter party voyage.'

Kydd shifted uncomfortably.

'Or the rule for calculating *per diem* demurrage should a particular freight require re-stowage by cause of the consignee? The bottomry premium if calculated on . . .'

At Kydd's embarrassed silence he stopped, then resumed gently, 'You will see, Commander, our ways are different, we have other concerns. You will understand if I say that

I do wish you well for your future, but at the moment there does not appear to be a marine post now open with us that would be suitable for a gentleman of your undoubted quality.'

'I do understand,' said Kydd, meekly, 'an' I thank ye for your time, sir.'

He had come full circle: now there was nothing more. With a polite bow he turned and left, joining the streaming bustle of the street. He felt light-headed and detached; in a way he was relieved that it was all over, no more pretence, no more futile hoping.

Stepping round a pair of drunken, brawling sailors he made for the river but became aware of someone distant calling his name. He looked back and saw the old clerk hurrying after him. 'Sir, Cap'n, Mr Russell begs you will grant him a further minute of your time, should you be at liberty to do so.'

Russell sat Kydd down and did not waste time. 'Mr Kydd, my junior partner has just informed me that, indeed, we may well have a position vacant such as you describe. Due to an illness, one of our senior masters is unable to take post and we stand embarrassed in the matter of our obligations. Is it at all possible that you may consider taking the situation, bearing in mind that this will be an ocean voyage of some months and at short notice to sail?'

Kydd fought to appear calm. 'Er, could ye tell me more of th' ship, Mr Russell?'

'The *Totnes Castle*. A fine barque of four hundred and twenty tons, fully rigged and lying now at Deptford. I should think you will find yourself well satisfied with her.'

Trying to hide his soaring hopes, Kydd asked, 'Th' cargo? As y' know, I have no experience in cargo handling.' He was dimly aware that cargoes such as textiles and rice were stowed differently from exotics like joggaree and Prussian blue.

Russell leaned back expansively. 'She's under government contract for the far colonies, so you will have nothing to worry about there – in any case you will have the first mate, Cuzens, to assit you,' he added smoothly.

On a long voyage Kydd knew he would have plenty of time to learn the ropes before they made port to discharge. And, glory be, he would be back at sea – as the captain of a ship once again. Elation flooded him. 'I'll take her!' he blurted.

'Splendid!' Russell purred. 'Then there's just the matter of the formalities, Captain. We are a business, you know.'

Papers were sorted, presented and signed. Kydd sighed deeply. He was now master of a ship in the employ of Burns, Throsby and Russell, expected to step aboard and take command directly.

'Er, what will be m' first voyage?' he asked tentatively.

'The *Totnes Castle* will probably call at Tenerife before sailing south. You're familiar with the Atlantic? Then it would be usual to touch at the Cape before dropping to forty south until you feel able to bear up for New South Wales.'

'New Holland!' The other side of the earth – four, five months at sea. And then, at the end of it, what in heaven's name could be there to justify a trading voyage? Sudden suspicion dawned.

'My cargo—'

'Will be stores, grain, tools and so on, the usual supplies for our colonies in Port Jackson.'

'And . . . ?'

'A small number of convicted felons, of course, but naturally you will have guards.'

A convict ship. His mind froze in horror. He was to command one of those hell-ships that transported unfortunates beyond the seas to Botany Bay? It was . . .

'Mr Kydd,' Russell continued earnestly, 'we have the utmost faith in your abilities at this very short notice and recognise that the post may not meet with your entire satisfaction. Therefore, subject to a successful conclusion to this voyage, we shall look to offering you a more permanent berth on your return.

'Now, sir, shall we look more closely at the details?'

Chapter 11

Kydd gripped the paper fiercely. 'This Charter Party of Affreightment made and Concluded upon . . . to Port Jackson in New South Wales, on the Terms and Conditions following, Viz . . . and shall be fitted and furnished with Masts, Sails, Yards, Anchors, Cables, Ropes, Cords, Apparel and other . . . the said Burns, Throsby & Russell, do Covenant that . . . the said Convicts, their Births, Sickness, Behaviour, or Deaths . . . at the rate of Seventeen Pounds Seven Shillings and Sixpence per head for each Convict . . .'

It was a bewildering and disturbing sea world he was entering. The familiar sturdy dimensions of conduct of the Navy were replaced by a different imperative: success in his profession was now to be measured in cost and profit, his acumen in dealing with traders and authorities to the best advantage of the owners, and the securing of an uneventful and minimally expensed voyage. However, it was the life he had chosen: if he was to move up to a better class of vessel on his return then he had to make a good fist of this, whatever it took — and so little time to learn!

The master's cabin of *Totnes Castle* was small and utilitarian, gloomy with dark, oiled wood and a smell of close living. The ship herself was of a size, nearly double that of the lovely *Teazer*, but her interior was undoubtedly for one over-riding purpose: the carrying of cargo.

As ship's master he had a dual role, as captain, and as representative to the world of the merchant company Burns, Throsby and Russell. In token of this, his signature was sufficient in itself to incur debt and expenditure without apparent limit in the company's name. To Kydd's disquiet, he had discovered that *Totnes Castle* did not rate a purser and he was expected to function as one, with the assistance of the steward, whose other duties were to wait at table.

Then there were the officers. The mate Cuzens, a fat, blustering man, did not inspire Kydd; neither did the second mate, a sharp-featured Dane. The third was not yet appointed. In deep-sea three watches, if he sailed without one he would end up himself taking the deck. And the others: a sly boatswain, elderly carpenter and witless sail-maker, whose senseless muttering as he worked had got on Kydd's nerves when he had first come aboard. That left only the eighteen seamen and four boys – apprentices they were termed but they had the knowing look of the London dockside.

Kydd had so little time left. He had worked into the night, trying to get on top of the terrifyingly large number of matters needing his attention. Even the most familiar were subtly different; he was beginning to feel punch-drunk at the onslaught.

With a casual knock at his door Cuzens entered before Kydd could reply. 'Y' papers, Mr Kydd,' he said, slapping down a thick envelope on his table. He had the odd habit of seldom looking directly at people – his eyes roved about restlessly. 'Hear tell they're comin' aboard when y' tips the wink,' he grunted.

Totnes Castle was moored out in Galleon's Reach, within sight of both the Woolwich Royal Dockyard and Deptford, making ready to take aboard her cargo of criminals. The banging and screeching Kydd could hear was the carpenter and his crew preparing the 'tween decks for use as a prison.

'Thank ye, Mr Cuzens,' Kydd said heavily. 'That'll be all.' With ill-natured muttering, the man left and Kydd spread out the contents.

One document of thicker quality than the others caught his eye: 'The Transportation Register'. He smoothed it open: columns of neatly inscribed names – and sentences. This was the reality of what was about to happen: the meaningless names were under sentence of law to be Transported to Parts Beyond the Seas for terms ranging from seven years to the heart-catching 'term of his natural life' – and Kydd was under the duty of ensuring that this took place.

He pushed the papers away in a fit of misery. That he had been brought so low! To be master of a prison-ship and personal gaoler to these wretches. Their crimes were dispassionately listed: the theft of lodging-house furniture, probably sold for drink; a soft-witted footman pawning a master's plate that no doubt bore an incriminating crest; a cow-keeper thinking to add to his income by taking game in the woods at night. A pickpocket, a failed arsonist. It went on and on in a monotonous round of idiocy and venality. These, of course, were the lucky ones: there were others at this very moment in Newgate prison whose next dawn would be their last.

At another knock on the door, Kydd called wearily, 'Come!'

He looked up dully as a stranger entered. 'Mowlett,' the man said quietly, and helped himself to Kydd's only arm-chair.

'Oh?' said Kydd, noting the deeply lined yet sensitive face.

'Dr Mowlett – your surgeon,' he said, in a tone that was half casual, half defiant.

'Ah. I was told—'

'I would think it imprudent to be too credulous about what one is told in this business, Mr, er, Kydd,' Mowlett said. 'Do you object?' he added, taking out a slim case and selecting a cheroot.

'If ye must, sir,' he said.

Mowlett considered for a space, then replaced the small cigar. 'Are you in any wise ready to show me your prepar-ations, sir?'

'My preparations?'

'Of course.' Mowlett smiled. 'In that as surgeon I am also, as of this voyage, your government superintendent. You are responsible for landing the prisoners in a good state of health – in accordance with your government contract, I hasten to add. Shall we inspect their quarters?'

Kydd had quickly made his acquaintance with *Totnes Castle* before. Her capacious hold was still being readied; the car-penter had done the job before and seemed to know what was needed. Kydd had simply let him get on with it.

He and Mowlett stepped gingerly through the half-constructed bulkhead, studded with heavy nails and with loop-holes. Their entry was a small door, but it was more like a slit, requiring them to squeeze through sideways. At sea if the ship was holed this would be a hopeless death-trap.

With hatches off, the entire drab length of the space was

illuminated pitilessly, a reeking grey-timbered cavity with iron bars fitted as a barrier at midships, another further forward. As soon as the convicts were aboard the hatches would be battened down securely with gratings and this would change to a dank hole. The carpenter straightened and offered, 'Men 'ere, females the next, an' the nippers right forrard.'

Kydd had forgotten that he was to carry women and children as well; with a lurch of unreality he realised that nothing in his previous sea experience had prepared him for it. Mowlett moved over to the side of the ship where most of the work was going on. Two levels of berths were being fitted along the sides with a narrow central walkway. They were like shelves: four or more would be expected to sleep together. It was all a hideous travesty of sea-going and Kydd's gorge rose.

He glanced at Mowlett and saw his lips moving as he counted. The surgeon swivelled round to count on the other side, then turned to Kydd and drawled, 'Upwards of two hundred human beings confined in here, for four, five months. All weathers, half the world over and in chains.'

What was he expected to do? Kydd wanted to retort. The contract was for 214 convicts and the ship was being stored and victualled accordingly. Kydd stepped forward doggedly and checked the fore hatchway; the compartment led up the ladder to the foredeck, where pens for cattle and poultry were ready. Barricades had been erected at each end of the open deck with firing slits facing inwards, and everywhere bore evidence of the real purpose of the ship.

Four or five *months* at sea in this! It was inconceivable, and with not a soul aboard who could in any sense be called a friend to share with him the grievous assaults on his soul. He turned and tramped back to his cabin.

Glowering out through the salt-misted stern windows at the busy Thames, Kydd was startled by a light laugh behind him. It was Mowlett, who must have followed him in, now sitting at his ease in the armchair. 'So you're Kydd, a victor of the Nile and now prison-ship master! What possessed you to take the post I can't possibly conceive.'

Something in Kydd's look made him add, 'Easy enough. An unusual name and I do read the *Gazette* sometimes.' He went on offhandedly, 'So we can take it that it's in your interest to land the convicts in Port Jackson fit and healthy at more than seventeen pounds a head, then.'

'Aye,' said Kydd, cautiously.

'No, it's not,' retorted Mowlett, half smiling, 'It's much more in your interest to have a sickly voyage with half the convicts shaking hands with Davy Jones. Claim their rations and sell it on in New South Wales – on that alone you'll make twice your figure for landing 'em healthy.'

Kydd was speechless.

'But, then, of course you'll be venturing privately? A decent freight of baubles and trinkets will have all Sydney a-twittering. It's expected, you know, and if you come all that way without you have something, well, consider the disappointment.' As captain, Kydd was free to arrange cargo stowage for any such speculation and it did not take much imagination to conjure the effect in the desperately isolated colony of the arrival of the latest London items of fashion. It would be a captive market.

'You are a man of the world, Mr Kydd, and you will know that this is not where the greatest profit lies – oh, no . . .'

'So then, what is—'

'Why, I'm astonished you confess ignorance! All the world knows the one cargo perfectly sure of a welcome, that will be snatched from your hands by free and bound alike, and that is – rum! Rivers of the stuff are thrown down throats daily to dull the pains of exile, to make brave the weak, to blind the eyes to squalor. I should think the whole colony will be safely comatose in a sodden, drunken stupor for at least three weeks after our arrival . . .'

The bitterness he could detect under the banter eased Kydd's misgivings and he replied gravely, 'Then they'll be disappointed, Mr Mowlett, for there'll be no rum cargo f'r *Totnes Castle.*'

Mowlett seemed taken aback, then added, in a milder tone, 'We shall hope that our squalid cargo of humanity does not bring the usual gaol-fever or worse – you have the easier task. I ask you to conceive of my dilemma in the selecting of physic to meet all and any scourges of the flesh brought aboard by the poor wretches and which invariably will become apparent only in the midst of the ocean.'

He got to his feet. 'Good luck, Doctor,' Kydd said quietly.

'It's you who will need the luck, Captain.'

Kydd watched the lighters approach with bleak resignation. The vessel was as prepared for the convicts as it was ever likely to be: the 'tween decks were now one long prison-cell. He and the officers would inhabit the raised after cabins, what the Navy would call a poop, while the seamen had a corresponding raised fo'c'sle forward. Apart from store-rooms and hideaways for the boatswain and carpenter, the rest was so much prison lumber. There was, however, a state-room on either forward wing of the officers' cabins. These were prepared for two free settler families apparently booked for the passage; they would board at the last possible moment before they sailed to minimise any distasteful exposure to the prisoners.

The lighters had put off from the dark hulks moored further along; foetid, rotten and stinking, they were worse even than the disease-ridden bridewells ashore. Later there would be carts with unfortunates from Newgate and other London gaols to crowd aboard.

In his pocket was a letter just received from Cecilia. She had understood Kydd's need to be away to sea again and had avoided reference to his ship, only stating a forlorn request for a souvenir of the far land they would reach after so much voyaging. Renzi was still missing but Cecilia stoutly believed they would find him soon. Kydd felt there was little hope if he had not been found by now, and he could not shake off an image of his friend lying dead in a ditch somewhere like any common pauper.

Totnes Castle had been warped alongside the wharf. A scruffy troop of redcoats arrived, took station at either extreme and, with musket and bayonet, stood easy, taking no notice of the fast-growing numbers of spectators. Kydd was determined to get away on the afternoon tide; once the hundreds had come aboard they would be consuming ship's stores and precious water.

More worries nagged at him: he had sent for the usual charts from Falconer's in the Strand but all they had of New Holland were the meticulous but single-track charts of Cook and hopeful productions from the small number of those who had passed that way in the score and a half years since, and whose accuracy could not be guaranteed. For his own cabin stores he had relied heavily on the placid steward, Cahn, who had made a previous voyage. Was he trustworthy? Should he have taken on a speculative freight? It had been tempting but he had no idea of how to go about it and, in any case, he had neither the time nor the capital.

The lighters neared. Kydd's gaze strayed to the plain, blocky deck-line of his ship. Within the compass of its small length more than two hundred souls would spend the next four or five months under his care and command. Had he taken enough aboard to see them safely through the months ahead?

A surge of interest rippled through the throng as a lighter bumped alongside the small landing place ahead. The crowd pressed forward with a buzz of excited comment and were met by the redcoats who held them at bay to form a clear path behind them. Then there was an expectant quiet and rustle of anticipation.

Suddenly a loud sigh went up: the head of a pathetic caterpillar of ragged individuals appeared, shuffling and clinking along, a line of humanity that went on and on. Sharp orders from the black-coated guards brought them listlessly to a halt at the end of the gangway.

Two officials went up to Kydd. 'Cap'n?' The moment he had dreaded was upon him. He looked once more at the column of human misery. Some were apathetic, their fetters hanging loosely, others gazed defiantly at the ship that would tear them from the land of their birth; all had the deathly pallor of the cell. He took the book and meekly signed for 203 convicted felons, the rest to be picked up at another port.

Nodding to the guards he retreated to the afterdeck; it seemed indecent to peer into the faces of the pale wretches as they shuffled up the gangway. The gawping onlookers, however, appeared to feel no shame, revelling in the delicious sensation of being in the presence of those condemned to a fate that, after a dozen years, was still a byword for horror: transportation to Botany Bay.

More shambled aboard; it did not seem possible that there was room for the unending stream. The unspeaking Dane and brash new third mate were below with the seamen and the stiffening of soldiers who oversaw the embarkation and berth assignments. Kydd was glad that it was they who had to bear the brunt. He could hear the wails of dismay and sharp rejoinders as the unwilling cargo of humanity saw their home for the next half a year, and tried to harden his heart.

The female convicts began to come up the gangway: hard-faced shrews, terrified maids, worn-out slatterns, some in rags, others in the drab brown serge of prison garb. As they filed below there was an immediate commotion, squeals of protest mingling with lewd roars and anonymous screams.

'Mr Cuzens, I'm going to m' cabin,' Kydd said thickly, and hurried below. He flopped into his chair and buried his face in his hands.

A bare minute later there was a casual knock and Cuzens entered. Kydd pulled himself together. 'Mrs Giles,' Cuzens said, as though this was all Kydd had to know.

'Who?'

'Ma Giles. Come t' see the women.'

Kydd made his way up. On the quayside a lady of mature years was angrily waving a book at him. Her shrill cries were overborne by the Bedlam between decks. Kydd went down the gangway to see her. 'Sir, are you the captain of this ark of misery?'

Something about her fierce determination made him hesitate. 'I am that, madam.'

'Then is there no spark of godliness in you, sir, to deny

those unfortunates the solace of their faith?' The book, he saw, was a well-worn Bible. 'They are condemned to a life of—' Kydd gave her permission to board and, accompanied by a guard, she primly mounted the gangway to perform her ministry.

Kydd hesitated before he followed her – above the clamour he could hear tearing sobs nearby. It was a woman prostrate with grief, far beyond the tears and cries of the others, her face distorted into a rictus of inconsolable tragedy. The man who held her was himself nearly overcome and admitted to Kydd, through gulps of emotion, that their daughter was one of the female convicts aboard.

A daughter: betrayed and abandoned, now about to be torn from their lives for ever. Was it a mercy to allow them aboard to a tender farewell in the hell and chaos that was the 'tween decks? What kind of last memory of their child would they take away?

'Mr Cuzens,' Kydd croaked loudly, 'two t' come aboard.' Instantly he was besieged by other tear-streaked faces shouting and weeping.

Kydd glared venomously at the gawpers taking in the spectacle and mounted the gangway again. Pitiful bundles in piles on the foredeck were, no doubt, personal possessions. It was within his power to refuse them but Kydd knew he could not. Time pressed; he tried to persuade himself that once under way at sea things would settle down.

'Everyone off th' ship b' two bells, Mr Cuzens. I'll have the crew mustered forrard afore we single up,' he ordered, grasping for sanity. There was no mercy in delaying; there were now but three hours left for goodbyes. 'An' send word t' the Shippe that the free settlers c'n board when convenient.'

The hard-faced leader of the guards reported all secure: he could be relied upon for the final roll-call and, with luck, there would be no need to go below before sailing. Leaving the deck for Cuzens to attend to the terrified, bellowing cow that was being pushed into its pen forward, Kydd took refuge in his cabin once more.

He closed his eyes. It was a hideous nightmare and it was only just beginning.

Roused by the announced arrival of the first free settlers, a disdainful family from Staffordshire whom he welcomed and showed to their cabin, he returned and closed his eyes once more. Again a knock and Cuzens waddled in. 'Trouble,' he said with just a hint of satisfaction. 'Y' other settler kickin' up a noise. Came wi' a chest bigger 'n the longboat an' won't board wi'out it.'

Kydd held in his temper. 'Where?'

Cuzens pointed to the wharf. A thin man in plain brown sat obstinately facing away on a vast case, a good six feet long. Next to it was neat, seamanlike baggage that, on its own, would stow perfectly well. Kydd clattered down the gangway and approached him. 'Now then, sir, ye can't—'

The man jerked to his feet in consternation and spun round. It was Renzi.

'N-Nicholas!' Kydd gasped, shocked and delighted at the same time. Renzi was thin, sallow and painfully bent, but his sunken eyes burned with a feverish intensity. 'Why, dear friend, what does this mean? Do y' really—'

'Thomas. Mr Kydd, I did not think to see you . . .' He had difficulty continuing and Kydd heard an impatient Cuzens behind him.

'Y'r books, I believe?' he guessed.

'Yes,' Renzi said defiantly.

'Mr Cuzens, take this aboard and – and strike it down in m' cabin f'r now.' The mate ambled off, leaving them with the few remaining onlookers. 'Nicholas, if you—'

Renzi straightened and said carefully, 'This is my decision. I ask you will have the good grace to respect it.

'You may believe I have had time to think long and deeply about my situation and there were aspects of it that were distressing to me. It is now my avowed intention to find a fresh life – and cut myself off from a wasted past. There is a new land waiting, one where hard work and imagination will yield both self-respect and achievement.'

'Nicholas – you?' It was beyond belief that Renzi could—

'It is not a matter open to discussion. I have formally resigned my commission and am now a free agent, and there-fore as a citizen whose passage money has been paid I believe I have a right to my privacy. Do you understand me?'

Kydd was lost for words, then stuttered, 'M' friend—'

'Mr Kydd. Our friendship is of long standing and I trust has been of service to us both, each in his own way. That friendship is now completed. I have . . . warm memories, which I will . . . treasure in my new existence. Yet I will have you know that as our paths have now irrevocably diverged I wish no longer to be reminded of a previous life and as such ask that I be addressed and treated as any other passenger.'

'Then, Nicholas . . . er, Mr Renzi, if there's anything I c'n do for you – is there anything at all?' But Renzi had turned on his heel and was painfully mounting the gangway.

Torn by happiness that his friend lived and anxieties about the ship, Kydd took his place near the wheel and tried to focus on the task in hand. *Totnes Castle* must be under weigh for New South Wales very shortly, but was Renzi in his right mind? Would he finally come to himself too late, far out on the ocean with no turning back? Or was he on a slow decline to madness?

Kydd bit his lip: the first part of his world-spanning voyage was going to be the most difficult, the winding route of the Thames to the open sea through the most crowded waterway on earth. An ignominious collision with a coal barge at the outset would be catastrophic, and although they would carry a pilot, the actual manoeuvring would be by his own orders. They would tide it out, a brisk ebb in theory carrying them the thirty-odd tortuous miles to the Isle of Sheppey and the open sea – but this had its own danger: while being carried forward with the press of water the rudder would find little bite. It did seem, however, that the south-westerly would hold and therefore their way was clear to cast off and put to sea at the top of the tide.

'Hands to y'r stations!' Apart from the huddled, tearful groups watching sadly, no one was interested in yet another vessel warping out to midstream for the age-old journey downriver. No taste of powder-smoke from grand salutes or streaming ensigns and brisk signals, just a nondescript barque flying the red-and-white pennant of a 'Bay ship with yet another cargo of heartbreak and misery.

Totnes Castle pulled slowly to mid-channel, slewing at the increasing effect of the tide. The taciturn pilot stood next to the wheel, arms folded, while Cuzens stood back, watching Kydd with a lazy smile. He must have done the trip dozens of times, thought Kydd, resentfully. On impulse he said quietly, 'Mr Cuzens, take her out, if y' please.'

The mate jerked in astonishment. 'You mean—'

'Aye, Mr Mate. Let's see what ye're made of.' Kydd stepped back. He was quite within his rights, for among the terms of his articles was an injunction to see that the first mate was 'instructed in his duties' as what amounted to deputy master.

Cuzens hesitated, then cupped his hands. 'Lay aloft, y' bastards.'

They made the depressing flat marshes of the estuary late in the afternoon and by nightfall had dropped the pilot and were making sail for open sea – and a land unimaginably remote.

The same south-westerly that had helped them to sea was now foul for the Channel. Kydd decided prudence was called for in the darkness and felt his way into the crowded anchorage of the Downs and let go anchor for the morning.

Now he had to face his human freight: they had been battened down for the run to the sea, but the nocturnal hours were not the time to be letting them roam the decks: they must remain under lock and key below.

With the guard leader, he went down the hatchway, rehearsing words of admonishment and encouragement. At the bottom of the ladder he turned – and the sight that met his eyes was closer to that of a medieval dungeon than a ship's 'tween decks. The fitful gleam of the lanthorn into the darkness forward revealed scores of bodies draped listlessly over every part of the hold, some on the shelf-bunks clutching thin blankets over four and even six, and still more wedged upright against the ship's side as if afraid to seek release in lying asleep. Moans, coughs, occasional mumbling and muttering mingled with the deep creaking from invisible waves passing beneath the hull in an endless counterpoint. A miasma rose to Kydd's nostrils of more than two hundred bodies

and the unmistakable rankness of vomit. Even the movement of the slight seas round the Foreland had brought on
spasms in some, which in the closeness of the prison hold
had set others to retching. Along with the sour stink of the
night-buckets, it was all Kydd could do to stop himself fleeing
back on deck.

A few raised their heads at the light and disturbance. Kydd's
words died in his throat: for the inmates, darkness was for
sleep and enduring until morning. He turned to the guard
who stolidly returned his gaze. What might be going through
these poor wretches' minds was beyond imagining – half a
year confined to *this?*

Shaken, Kydd clambered back to the blessed night air and
stared out at the calm sea scene denied to those hidden under
his feet: dozens of vessels placidly at rest with golden light
dappling the sea under their stern windows, a half-hidden
moon playing hide-and-seek in the clouds.

He took a deep, ragged breath and turned to go below.
Mowlett stood before him as though to bar his way. 'An
agreeable enough scene, Mr Kydd,' he said softly.

Kydd could not find pleasantries in reply.

'Surely you are not discommoded by what you have seen
below. You may view its like at any time in any gaol in the
land. It is of no consequence.'

'It was not as I . . . Damn it, they're human beings, same
as we,' Kydd said raggedly.

'Of course not,' Mowlett responded, as though to a child.
'They're not human at all, old fellow – they stopped being
human when sentenced in the dock. Now they are government property, exported for the term specified, and form
the freight you are being paid for. When you deliver them
to the colonials in New South Wales they will go into a

257

storehouse and be handed out to whoever lays claim to a free government issue of labour. They have no other purpose or existence.'

The Isle of Wight lay close to larboard in all its dense verdancy but Kydd's gaze was to starboard, to the tight scatter of houses and grey-white fortifications that was Portsmouth Point and the entrance to the biggest naval harbour in the land.

Totnes Castle's anchor took the ground at the Mother Bank, well clear of Spithead, the famed anchorage of the Channel Fleet. Before, there had been fleets of stately ships-of-the-line riding at anchor, but now in these piping days of peace, there was emptiness: only ghosts remained of the great ships that had fought to victory at St Vincent and the Glorious First of June. And his own *Duke William* in which he had learned of the sea.

Eleven more convicts were embarked by hoy and Kydd's orders were complete. Sail was loosed, and in a workmanlike southerly he shaped course for Plymouth, their final port-of-call in England for last-minute provisions and water.

They sailed past the triangular mass of the Great Mew Stone and into the Sound, then across to Cawsand Bay. Leaving the mate to take men to Drake's Leat to fill casks with clear Dartmoor water, Kydd made ready to go ashore, his the unenviable task of cozening down the costs of fresh greens, fish and potatoes that would allow his ship to face the months of voyaging that lay ahead.

Far off he made out *Teazer*, one among many in the Hamoaze, mastless and high in the water, still and unmoving in a line of small ships. It was a sight of infinite melancholy.

It was a hard, crisp January morning when *Totnes Castle* finally left English shores, the winter beauty of the country never so poignant. The ship's bows were headed purposefully out-ward bound and even those fortunates who could look for-ward to returning in due course would not see it again in much less than a year.

As soon as Rame Head was safely astern and the ship irrevocably committed to the ocean, the first convicts appeared on the foredeck. Pale, unsteady and shivering at the sudden change in air, they stumbled about, manacles clinking dolefully. Some went to the side where they hung unmoving, others stared back at the receding land for a long time. Still more shuffled about endlessly with not a glance at the country that had given them birth.

Kydd tried to read their faces: there were case-hardened men, some of whom would have been reprieved at the gal-lows, along with a scatter of sensitive faces distorted by misery, but the majority looked blank and wary, muttering to each other as they moved slowly about their defined area of deck.

At the main-hatch a barrier stretched across: forward the convicts shuffled and clinked, aft was a broad expanse of deck for the passengers. The only ones embarked were the free set-tlers; Kydd had entertained the family from Staffordshire at the captain's table for dinner; the man was going out with plans to establish an industrial pottery but had little else in conversation. He and his insipid wife were huddled in deck-chairs to leeward while the daughter sat at their feet and worked demurely at her sewing.

Alone in a deck-chair on the other side was the *Castle*'s other settler and passenger. Kydd had been repelled at every approach: at the very time he so needed a friend, his closest had withdrawn from his company. He knew better than to try to press his attention, even though the book Renzi held had not advanced a single page.

The crew seemed to know what was expected of them and, for the most part, kept out of his way. They were few compared to the manning of a warship where the serving of guns required so many more – and had a different relationship with a ship's master: they had signed articles for a single voyage with specified duties and wages.

In the afternoon the female convicts took the deck. Prison-pale and ragged they blinked in the sunlight, tried to comb their hair and make themselves presentable.

Kydd called all the officers to his cabin. When they were assembled he opened forcefully: 'Now we're at sea I want th' people to be out on the upper decks as much as possible. How do we do this?' He looked at Cuzens, then at the others, but saw only incomprehension and veiled irritation. Not waiting for a reply he went on, 'An' why do they need t' be in Newgate irons the whole time? Strike 'em off, if y' please.'

There was a confused murmuring and Cuzens said darkly, 'Guard commander makes them kind o' decisions, Mr Kydd.'

'An' I'm in charge o' the guards. If they needs fetters we use leg-cuffs an' a chain – what th' Army calls a bazzel.'

'You ain't seen a mutiny, then?' the young third mate said, with a sneer.

Kydd held a retort in check: *he* would certainly never forget the bloody Nore mutiny. 'With guns on th' afterdeck charged with grape and ball, each o' you with pistols an' swords and the crew with muskets – an' you're still a-feared?' He let his contempt show and the murmuring faded. 'Now, I mean to—'

'Ven we get th' vimmin?' the close-faced Dane spat. At first Kydd thought he had misheard.

'He means, when d' we get our rights an' all?' Cuzens came in forcefully.

He was quickly supported by the third mate. 'No sense in makin' the cuntkins wait!' he chortled.

Kydd exploded. 'The women? Ye're asking me f'r—' He could not continue. That the law required degradation and misery he could not question; that he was the agent of it was wounding to a degree, but where was the humanity and natural kindliness that any soul, however taken in sin, might expect from a fellow-creature? What right did these men think they had to prey on any more helpless than they?

All his frustrations and pent-up feeling boiled up. 'Get out! All o' you!' he shouted hoarsely. 'Now! G' damn ye!' He stood up suddenly, sending his chair crashing to the floor.

Then he slumped, trembling with anger but trying for composure. It was not only the base demands they were making but the whole sordid business of penal servitude that was sapping his humanity. Yet if he was to return to claim a proper master's berth his only chance was to deal with it and make a success of the voyage. If *only* Renzi would—

A soft tap at the door broke through his bleak thoughts. Mowlett entered carrying a large phial. 'As doctor, Mr Kydd, I prescribe a medicinal draught, to be taken at once,' he said firmly.

The sharp tang of neat whisky enveloped Kydd. He took a stiff pull and felt its fire – it steadied him and he looked sharply at Mowlett. 'Thank 'ee, Doctor.'

'Would you object if I speak my mind?' Mowlett said quietly.

'If ye must,' Kydd said, bristling. 'But I'll have y' know I won't have any seaman aboard the *Castle* makin' play f'r a female convict.'

'Please understand, I know your position and honour you for it.' Mowlett had dropped all trace of banter and spoke with sincerity. 'However, for all our sakes a small piece of advice I would offer.

'These 'Bay ships have been plying the route now for above a dozen years and I dare to say are proficient in the art. They have necessarily developed practices to deal with conditions that many might find . . . remarkable. For instance, in the matter of females mixing promiscuous with the crew.' He held up an admonishing finger. 'No doubt you have not given it overmuch thought, dismissing it as a moral scandal, but there are elements of practicality that you should perhaps consider.'

Kydd glowered but allowed Mowlett to continue. 'Putting aside the obvious fact that, it being the custom in the past, you will be setting the entire crew to defiance should you stand in their way, you will not be amazed to learn that most of your felonious ladies are no strangers to the arts of Venus and will in fact warm to the opportunities on offer to take up with a protector.'

At Kydd's expression Mowlett hastened to add, 'Yes, a protector. Has it crossed your mind how much common theft, sneaking, bullying, lonely hardship must be suffered out of your sight below? In any case, Mr Captain, whether you like it or not the consorting will happen.'

Kydd could think of no immediate response and he fell back on the larger issue: 'Y'r transportation is a vile thing, Doctor. The suffering, the misery!'

'Perhaps, but reflect – they have now a chance. If you ask

it of them they must inevitably reply that what you provide is infinitely better than the hangman would serve.

'But to return to your women. I would venture to say that, whatever you are able to do, the consorting will take place privily. Animal spirits will ensure this – is it not better to regulate than condemn?'

Kydd stared down moodily.

'Those more uncharitable than I would perhaps be tempted to point out a certain degree of what might be considered hypocrisy in you, Mr Kydd,' he added meaningfully.

'Hypocrisy?'

'Why, of course! Or has the Navy changed its spots so completely that the sight of women flocking aboard a wooden wall of old England coming into port is no longer to be seen? Or that these same have put out for some harmless recreation with the honest tars?'

'They have a choice!' Kydd snapped.

'Quite so – therefore do you allow *your* ladies their choice, should they desire, Mr Kydd.'

'I shall think on it.' Kydd fidgeted with his sleeve. 'No one t' take up with any without they agree,' he said finally, 'and they shall tell me so 'emselves in private.'

'An eminently practical solution.'

'An' we'll get windsails rigged, a bit o' fresh air in that stink-pit. Yes, an' have 'em up in the sun – without irons, except they deserve it. At least we can do something f'r the poor brutes.'

He looked Mowlett directly in the eyes. 'You mentioned th' Navy. We might take some lesson from there. Let's see. We'll have two watches of convicts to take the deck b' turns, an' each morning we'll have a fine scrub-down.

'Each mess o' six will have a senior hand who'll take charge an' see all's squared away. An' a petty officer o' the deck who'll take charge o' them. We'll give 'em something useful t' do in the day – men to seaming canvas with the sailmaker, females to . . . Well, a parcel o' women can always find things t' do.'

Chapter 12

Renzi stood by the weather main-shrouds, now so worn with use, and gazed forward to where the cry of the lookout indicated land would soon be in sight. New South Wales. The other side of the globe, as far as it was possible to be from England – any further and they would be on their way back again. Four and a half months of wearisome sailing – it seemed like a lifetime. The banality of the other settler family, the ever-present sight of the shuffling condemned, the absence of anyone with any pretence at education . . . Without the solace of his books he would not have survived this far.

'I see it!' squealed the settlers' vapid daughter, rushing to the barrier. Convicts soon crowded forward anxious to catch their first glimpse of an unguessable fate, but Renzi stood back, a half-smile marking his detachment from the excitement of landfall as he contemplated the events that had led to this moment.

The fever that had carried him ashore to the Lazaretto had nearly killed him: he had little recollection of the twilight of existence there, only the later swirling chaos and screeching nightmares as he had struggled to lay hold on life.

Then Cecilia.

It had been she who had watched over him as his consciousness emerged from its horrors, had been there when every token of life itself was so precious, her voice of compelling tranquillity, soft, comforting, his assurance of life.

He had begun to mend: still Cecilia sat by him, reading softly, responding to his feverish babbling, her dear image now coming into focus with a smile so indescribably sweet – and for him alone. For her sake he had concentrated on getting better – until the melancholia had come.

Black and dour, the spreading hopelessness bore down on him, at times with such weight that he had found it necessary to turn to the wall so she would not see the tears coursing. Long days of trying to draw on his pitiful resources of strength, scrabbling for the will to live, to go on.

And after the endless hours of depression came realism, his past life stripped of its vanities and dalliances, foolish notions, pretences; he could see himself as he had never done before and despised the revelation – one born with the immense advantages of privilege, including an education of the first order and opportunities of travel, and what had he done with it?

His sea experience on the lower deck had been a self imposed exile for the expiation of what he considered a family sin.

As a result of his father's enforcement of enclosure of common lands, a young tenant farmer had committed suicide in despair. Renzi should not have gone on to the quarterdeck – that had been an indulgence. Could he return to his ancestral home to resume as eldest son? He had dealt with that question at the walls of Acre when he decided to disavow his father. There was nothing more to be said. And what of his King's commission? This was avoiding the issue. He had none of the fire and ambition of sea officers like Kydd; for Renzi the sea was an agreeable diversion – and therefore a waste.

What was left? There was nothing he could point to as his own achievement. For the world, it was as if he had never been.

It had been a cruel insight to be thrust on him at his lowest ebb but if he was to live with himself it had to be faced. Most importantly, he recognised that his feelings for Cecilia had deepened and flowered and there was now little doubt that he would never love another as he did her. But his detachment, logic, which before had served so well to control and divert the power of his emotions, now turned on him and exacted a price. *If* he cared for Cecilia to such a degree, was it honourable to expect her to join herself to one with neither achievements to his name nor any prospects?

It was not. Obedience to logic was the only course for a rational man and therefore he would act upon it. He would remove himself from Cecilia's life for her sake. But logic also said that, should he, in the fullness of time, find himself able to point to a notable achievement wrought by himself alone, then he might approach her – if she was still in a position to hear him.

In the long hours that he had lain awake he had made his plans. As soon as his strength allowed he would silently withdraw from her kindnesses and make his own way as a settler in the raw new world of Terra Australis. By his own wits and hard labours he would carve out a farming estate from the untouched wilderness, create an Arcadia where none had been before, truly an achievement to be proud of. And then . . . Cecilia.

The colonial government was generous to the free settler. It seemed that not only would the land be provided for nothing but that convict labour would be assigned to him, indeed tools, grain and other necessaries to any who was sincere in their wish to settle on the land. Admittedly he knew little of tillage but had seen much of the way the tenant farmers of Eskdale Hall had gone about their seasonal round. As a precaution, however, he had invested heavily in books on the art of farming, including the latest from Coke of Holkham whose methods were fast becoming legendary. Even the passage out was provided for; and thus he had carefully severed all connections with his old life and committed wholeheartedly to the new, boarding *Totnes Castle* in Deptford – to be confronted by, of all those from his past, Thomas Kydd.

He had resolved to cut all ties to his previous existence until he was in a position to return with his noble mission accomplished: Kydd was of that past and both logically and practically he should withdraw from his company as part of his resolve.

It had been hard, especially when he had seen what the voyage was costing his friend, but then he had witnessed Kydd lever himself above the sordid details and, by force of will, impose his own order on the situation. Now they must go their separate ways, find their own destinies at the opposite ends of the earth.

The coast firmed out of blue-grey anonymity: dark woods, stern headlands – not a single sign that man was present on the unknown continent. Conversations stilled as they neared; the land dipped lower until it revealed a widening inlet.

'Botany Bay, lads,' one of the seamen called. It was a

name to conjure with, but no ship had called there with prisoners since the early days. Their final destination was a dozen miles north. *Totnes Castle* lay to the south-easterly and within hours had made landfall at the majestic entrance to a harbour, Port Jackson.

A tiny piece of colour fluttered from the southern headland; as they watched, it dipped and rose again. They shortened sail, then hove to safely offshore. The pilot was not long in slashing out to sea in his cutter.

Renzi watched as he climbed aboard; thin and rangy and with a well-worn coat, he looked around with interest as he talked with Kydd, and soon *Totnes Castle* was under way again for the last miles of her immense voyage.

They passed between the spectacular headlands into a huge expanse of water stretching away miles into the distance. The first captain to see it had sworn that it could take a thousand ships-of-the-line with ease.

Helm over, they continued to pass bays and promontories, beaches and rearing bluffs. Densely forested, there was no indication of civilisation – this was a raw, new land indeed and Renzi watched their progress sombrely.

Quite suddenly there were signs: an island with plots of greenery, a clearing ashore, smoke spiralling up beyond a point – and scattered houses, a road, and then, where the sound narrowed, a township. Substantial buildings, one or two small vessels at anchor, a bridge across a small muddy river and evidence of shipbuilding. And, after long months at sea, the reek of land. Powerful, distinctive and utterly alien, there were scents of livestock and turned earth overlain by a bitter, resinous fragrance carried on the smoke of innumerable fires.

After a journey of fourteen thousand miles, the torrid heat

of the doldrums and the heaving cold wastes of the Southern Ocean, across three oceans and far into the other half of the world, *Totnes Castle*'s anchors plunged down and at last she came to her rest.

'Please y'self then – an' remember we don't change after, like.'

'No, no – I understand,' Renzi replied. The boorish Land Registry clerk sat back and waited.

It was unfair. Renzi was being asked to make a decision on the spot affecting the rest of his life: which of the government blocks of land on offer would he accept as his grant? But then he realised that more time to choose would probably not help, because many of the names were meaningless. Illawarra? Prospect Hill? Toongabbie? He had turned down land along the Hawkesbury river in Broken Bay – it was apparently isolated and miles away up the coast – but he had read that expansion was taking place into the interior beyond the Parramatta river.

'Where might I select that takes me beyond the headwaters of the Parramatta?' he asked.

The clerk sighed. 'There's a hunnered-acre block goin' past Marayong,' he said, pushing a surveyor's plan across.

It was a cadastral outline of ownership without any clue as to the nature of the terrain but, then, what judgement could he bring to bear in any event? The land was adopted on either side so it could be assumed that it was of farming quality. 'That seems adequate,' Renzi said smoothly. 'I'll take it up, I believe.'

Within the hour, and for the sum of two shillings and six-pence stamp duty, Renzi found himself owner and settler of one hundred acres of land in His Majesty's Colony of New

South Wales, and thereby entitled to support from the government stores for one year and the exclusive services of two convicts to be assigned to him. The great enterprise was beginning . . .

Naturally it was prudent to view his holdings at the outset, and as soon as he was able he boarded Mr Kable's coach for the trip to Parramatta. This was his country now and he absorbed every sight with considerable interest.

Sydney Town was growing fast: from the water frontage of Sydney Cove continuous building extended for nearly a mile inland. And not only rickety wooden structures, but substantial stone public buildings. Neat white dwellings with paling fences, gardens and outhouses clustered about and several windmills were prominent on the skyline.

The coach lurched and jolted over the unmade roads, but Renzi had eyes only for the country and the curious sights it was reputed to offer. He heard the harsh cawing of some antipodean magpie and the musical, bell-like fluting of invisible birds in the eucalypts. He was disappointed not to catch sight of at least one of Mr Banks's kangaroos – perhaps they only came out at certain times of the day.

Parramatta was drab and utilitarian. His books had informed him that this was the second oldest town in the colony, but with his land awaiting ahead he could not give it his full attention and hurriedly descended from the coach to look for a horse to hire.

Avoiding curious questions he swung up into the saddle of a sulky Arab cross and, after one more peep at his map, thudded off to the west. The houses dwindled in number as did cultivated fields and then the road became a track, straight as a die into the bush.

Gently undulating cleared land gave way to sporadic paddocks that seemed vast to Renzi's English eye. Then the pathway petered out into an ill-kept cart-track through untouched wilderness. He knew what he was looking for and after another hour in the same direction he found it, a small board nailed to a tree, its lettering now indecipherable.

He took out his pocket compass, his heart beating fast. This was the finality and consummation of his plans and desires over the thousands of miles: this spot was the southeast corner of his property – his very own land into which he would pour his capital and labour until at last it became the grand Renzi estate.

He beat down the ground foliage, then found a surveyor's peg and, on a line of bearing nearly a half-mile away through light woods, another. One hundred acres! In a haze of feeling he tramped about; in one place he found a bare stretch on which, to his great joy, a family of big grey kangaroos grazed. They looked up in astonishment at him, then turned and hopped effortlessly away.

Bending down he picked curiously about the ground litter. Coke had stressed the importance of tilth; this earth appeared coarse and hard-packed under the peculiar scatter of the pungent leaves of eucalypts. Renzi was not sure what this meant but the first ploughing would give an idea of which crop would be best suited. He wandered about happily.

As the sun began to set he had the essence of his holding. There was no water, but the lie of the land told him there must be some not far to the north. For the rest it was light woods of the ubiquitous piebald eucalypt trees and a pretty patch of open grassland, if such was the right description for the harsh bluish-green clumps. With a lifting of his spirits he decided the Renzi residence would be on the slight rise to the south.

Back in Sydney, he tendered his indent at the government stores: tools, grain, tents, provisions, even rough clothing. The obliging storeman seemed to know well the usual supplies asked for and the stack of goods grew. Fortunately he was able to secure the immediate services of a drover with a small team of oxen – for a ruinous price – and set them on their creaking way amid the sound of the ferocious cracking of bull-hide whips and sulphurous curses, his year's supplies piled high in the lurching wagon.

Finally he attended at the office of the principal superintendent of convicts. There was no difficulty with his labour quota: he had but to apply to the convict barracks at Baulkham Hills with his paper.

In a fever of anticipation Renzi arrived at Parramatta with all his worldly possessions, rounded up a cart and horse, and very soon found himself with two blank-faced convicts standing ready; one Patrick Flannery, obtaining goods by deception to the value of seven shillings, respited at the gallows and now two years into his seven-year exile, and Neb Tranter, aggravated common assault and well into his fourteen-year term.

'My name is Renzi, and I am to be your master.' There was little reaction and he was uncomfortably aware that they were staring glassily over his shoulder with heavy patience. 'Should you perform your tasks to satisfaction there is nothing to fear from me.'

Flannery swivelled his gaze to him and raised his eyebrows. 'An' nothin' to fear from us, sorr!' he said slowly, in an Irish brogue.

'Very well. We shall be started. This very day we shall be on our way to break the earth near Marayong for a new farming estate.'

'This is t' be yourn, sorr?' Flannery asked innocently.

He nodded proudly.

'Ah, well, then, Mr Rancid, we'll break our backs f'r ye, so we will.'

With his convicts aboard in the back of the cart, Renzi whipped the horse into motion and swung it in the direction of his land. Neither the sniggering of bystanders nor the childish waving of his convicts at them was going to affect his enjoyment of the moment.

As the miles passed and they neared their destination Renzi allowed his thoughts to wander agreeably. Perhaps it was time now to bestow a name on the estate: in this new land so completely free of historical encumbrances he was able to choose anything he liked – *Arcadia intra Australis* suggested itself, or possibly something with a more subtle classical ring that would impress by its depths and cunning allusion to a hero in an Elysium of his own creation.

Surprised, he saw they had arrived at the board on the tree. 'Er, here is, er, my land,' he said.

The two convicts dropped to the ground. 'Thank 'ee kindly, sorr,' Flannery said, with an exaggerated tug on his forelock and a sly smile at Tranter.

'Do we unload, Mr Rancy?' Tranter asked, his eye roving disapprovingly over the virgin bush. He was older, his large frame now largely desiccated but for a respectable grog belly.

'Of course we—' snapped Renzi, then stopped. At the very least the undergrowth had to be cleared first. The tools were all in the ox-wagon, which had set out well before them but they had not passed it on the way. 'No – not yet,' he muttered, and tried to think.

The two grunted and stood back, arms folded, eyes to a glassy stare again.

'We wait for the wagon – it should be here soon,' he said, with as much conviction as he could muster.

A flurry of subdued pattering on leaves began, then dripped and took strength from the cold southerly that now blustered about, soaking the ground and their clothes.

'What now?' said Flannery, in a surly tone.

Renzi could think of no easy answer. In the ox-wagon there were tents and tarpaulins; here there were books by the caseload and attire suitable for a gentleman of the land. How long would that pox-ridden wagon take to heave itself into sight?

'I know whut I'm a-goin' to do,' said Flannery. 'Hafter you, Mr Tranter.'

'No, Mr Flannery, 'pon m' honour! After y'self.' Then the two dived as one to the only dry spot for miles – underneath the cart, which was still yoked to its patient, dripping horse.

Obstinately Renzi held out for as long as he could, until the heavy wet cold reached his skin. Then he crawled under with the two convicts, avoiding their eyes.

'Mr Flannery?' grunted Tranter. 'Yez knows what Marayong is famous fer?'

'What's that, then, Mr Tranter?'

'Why, snakes, o' course! This weather they firkles about, lookin' for the heat o' bodies t' ease the cold. Shouldn't wonder if'n there's some roun' here,' he said, looking about doubtfully.

'Have a care, then, Mr Tranter – they's deathly in New South Wales, one nip an' it's all over wi' ye!'

275

Renzi ground his teeth – nothing could be done until the ox-wagon came up and the delay would cost him another day's extortionate hire of the cart and horse. At least, he thought wryly, he had the last word: if he was to lay a complaint of conduct against the convicts they would be incarcerated in cells instead of having the relative freedom of the outside world.

Later the next morning, with the wagon arrived and the tents finally pitched, tarpaulins over his stores, Renzi felt better. In fact, much better: he had Flannery and Tranter down range hacking trees to form an initial clearing with instructions to preserve the boles for use in constructing living-huts. It was time to step out his floor plan. It was to be a modest three rooms, with perhaps out-houses later – the details could wait.

With a light heart he went to see how the two labourers were progressing. 'What are you fellows up to?' he demanded, seeing one lying at his ease on his back chewing a twig and the other picking morosely at the ground. 'You can see how much work we have to do.'

'Aye, don't we have a lot o' work indeed?' Flannery said. 'An' all with this'n.' He held out his mattock. The flat part was a curl of bright steel where it had bent hopelessly.

Renzi took it: cheap, gimcrack metal. Either the government stores had been cheated or he had. He rounded on the other. 'On your feet, sir! If your duties are not to your liking you may certainly take it up with Superintendent Beasley.'

Tranter did not stir. 'I'm wore out,' he said sullenly, flicking away his twig.

Renzi held his temper. 'Get a fire going, then, if you please. You shall be mess skinker for tonight, and we both desire you will have something hot for us at sundown.' Irritably, he brushed away the flies that followed him without rest.

It was hard, disheartening work, felling the gums and man-handling the trunks up the slope to Renzi's clearing. By sundown there was nothing but a derisory pile of thin logs and a large, untidy heap of brushwood scraps. But a fire spread an acrid smoke that deterred the flies and in the gathering blue dusk Renzi pulled out his collapsible card table with a chair and collapsed wearily.

It seemed churlish to sit while others must stand, so he found other 'chairs' and the three laid out their meal – flour and water pancakes with boiled pulses. 'Lillie-pie an' pease,' Tranter grunted defensively. Renzi thought longingly of his precious few bottles of Old World claret hidden away – this was the most special of occasions but to sacrifice . . . Later, perhaps, he decided, and helped himself to another scoop of half-cooked pottage.

That night in his tent, distracted by the wavering drone of a mosquito seeking his flesh and the menace in the unknown scuffles and squeals in the dark bush outside, Renzi never-theless felt exalted by the experience of finally setting foot in his future. But, he wondered apprehensively, what would the next day bring?

An hour or so after midnight, as he lay sleepless, it started to rain again.

It took a week just to clear the lower part of his land. Renzi had decided, with a little advice from Mr Coke, to turn this over to grain as being the more apposite to the soil type as best as he could recognise it.

The hardest had been the grubbing up of tree-stumps,

which fought back with a fiendish tenacity; every single one cost sweat and labour out of all proportion to the tiny area of bare ground won. Aching in every bone, Renzi slaved on, day by back-breaking day.

His hut was finally built, with not three rooms but one – purely for convenience of time, of course, but even so it could be accounted home. The sides were chinked with mud and the roof of interleaved saplings was spread with the canvas of the tents as a temporary measure. An experiment with a fire at the centre was a disaster: the hut filled immediately with billowing smoke. The related domestics, therefore, would be placed firmly outside.

Against all the odds a landmark was reached. Renzi had not only constructed his first residence but was now ready to begin crop production. Eagerly he checked Coke again. First he had to plough: he intended to borrow an implement for the first year. Then it would be hoeing or harrowing – or did that come after seeding?

With rising excitement Renzi reviewed his dispositions: the convicts would continue to advance the clearing up to the land boundary ready for whatever crop he decided should be there. So, meanwhile – first things first: a plough.

His nearest neighbour would be somewhere over to the east. He tidied himself up and, taking his pocket compass, set out from the known position of the board on the tree. There were no tracks but a confusing jumble of simple paths led through the grassy undergrowth. He tried to follow them – but merely flushed out a couple of kangaroos who made off rapidly.

Striking out by compass was the only reliable method and he set course for the north-east corner of the block. Over a slight rise he could see thin smoke spiralling above the trees. He hurried towards it and a small hut came into view, with a woman in a coarse dress working at a vegetable garden.

She looked up in dismay and ran inside. A man emerged, cradling a musket. 'Stan' y'r ground, y' villain!' he roared.

'Renzi, Nicholas Renzi, and it would appear we are to be neighbours,' he called, in what he hoped was an encouraging tone.

'Come near, then, an' let's see summat of yer,' the man said, still fingering his gun.

Some little time later Renzi was sitting at a rough table with a mug of tea. 'Don't see nobody one end o' the month to t'other,' the man said, after admitting to the name of Caley. 'So, yer've got the north selection,' he ruminated, rubbing his chin.

Renzi took in the hut; it was well lived-in but Spartan, of wattle daubed with clay and finished with a thin white lime-wash. The floors consisted of bare, hard-packed earth. There were only two rooms, the other patently a bedroom. 'That's right, Mr Caley. It is my avowed intention to establish a farming estate in these parts and reside here myself.'

Caley looked archly at his wife. Both were deeply touched by the sun, but she had aged beyond her years. 'Ye'd be better throwing y'r money into th' sea – gets rid of it quicker,' she said bitterly.

'Now, now, Ethel darlin', don't take on so.' He turned to Renzi and explained: 'We bin here three year come Michaelmas, an' things ain't improvin' for us. A hard life, Mr Renzi.'

'What do you grow?'

'Thought t' be in turnips – everyone needs 'em if they has horses. But look.' He gestured down the cleared space in front of the hut. The rows were populated only by sorry-looking stringy plants. 'Supposed t' lift 'em in February, but no chance o' that with 'em lookin' so mean, like.'

Should he offer his extensive library on horticulture and agricultural husbandry? Renzi pondered. Coke of Holkham would be sure to have a sturdy view on turnip production. Sensing that possibly they might not welcome advice from a newcomer, he changed tack. 'I must say, your convict is not the most obliging of creatures. I've seen labourers on my – er, that is to say, some estates in England, who would quite put them to the blush in the article of diligence.'

Mrs Caley snorted. 'As you must expect! These're felons an' criminals, Mr Renzi, an' has no love f'r society. They're wastrels an' condemned by their nature, sir.' She smoothed her hair primly. 'Not a'tall like we free settlers, who try t' make something of the land.'

Caley smiled sadly. 'That's why we got rid o' ourn – cost thirty shillin' a month in rum afore they'd pick up a hoe.'

'Sir, I'd be considerably obliged should you lend me your plough. If any hire is required I would be glad to—'

'Mr Renzi.' Caley drew in his breath and let it out slowly. 'We don't have ploughs. We uses only th' harrow an' a deal o' sweat,' he said emphatically.

Renzi hastened to make his little hut before dark. Unseen animals scuttled away at his approach and a sudden clatter in the trees above startled him. When he reached the clearing, he saw that the convicts had allowed the fire in front of the hut to die to embers, and he cast about in the gloom for leaves and kindling, annoyed that they had neglected such an obvious duty before supper. The fire caught sullenly, with much dank smoke and spitting.

In the gathering dark he trudged down to their tent but as he approached, tripping on jagged stumps and loose branches, he heard loud snoring. He did not have the heart to wake them: clearly they had turned in early, weary after their day. He made his way back to the hut to scrape together some kind of repast.

Throwing aside the canvas entrance flap he went inside. By the fitful glare of the flames he could see that one neat stack of his possessions had been put to disorder. With a sinking heart he knew what he would find. He was right – every one of his precious half-dozen claret was gone.

Chapter 13

Kydd watched Renzi depart *Totnes Castle*, then turned back to his ship. The last convicts filed down the gangway to the wharf and away to their final fate. The shouts of overseers and the clinking of fetters faded into the distance, and Kydd was glad. He had done his best: they were unquestionably in better shape than when they had been disgorged by their gaols in England, but their presence had made him feel tainted by the reek of penalty and hopeless misery.

He looked out over Sydney Cove. A thief-colony, there was no escape from its origins. On the muddy foreshore was a whipping post and beyond the point was Pinchgut Island, a hundred yards or so long with a gibbet in view at one end, the white of a skeleton visible through flapping rags.

Ironically, the ship now seemed empty and depressing without her human cargo; the stores had been landed and the officers' ventures spirited away. Now there was little for him to do but complete the paperwork that would mark a successful conclusion to the voyage.

With what crew were still sober tomorrow, the *Totnes Castle* would be warped out to lie at anchor. She would remain there until the little shipyard on the west side of the cove could take her in hand to remedy the hundred and one defects that needed attention before her return to England. With only a small number of skilled shipwrights and caulkers, and other vessels ahead of Kydd's, a time of weeks was being talked of. It was a depressing prospect.

It had wounded Kydd to see Renzi step over the side to his destiny without so much as a backward glance: they had shared so much. He wondered how his friend was relishing his new life wherever he was in the interior of this strange land. But this was what Renzi had chosen as a course in life, and Kydd would respect it.

After the long voyage, however, he was curious to experience the untrammelled space and new sights of land. In any case, when the *Castle* was careened across the harbour she would be uninhabitable: sooner or later he would have to find quarters ashore.

There was a bridge over the little rivulet at the head of the cove that led into the settlement proper. He stepped out along the wide street past the ship's chandlers and warehouses, standing back to allow the passage of two carts pulled by yoked convicts, thin and sunburned, their heads down.

Only one road of significance was evident, leading inland along the banks of the watercourse: in one direction the rocky foreshore of the western side, with its crazy jumble of hovels, more substantial structures and shipyards; in the other, a scatter of cottages, stone buildings, and in the distance over the low hills, a puzzling mass of regularly spaced dwellings.

Turning up the slope towards them he lost his footing and

stumbled; reddish mud-holes were everywhere. Strangely haunting birdsong came from outlandish trees, and here and there a garden with alien plants caught his eye.

Closer, the dwellings turned out to be a convict barracks, complete with flogging triangle and chapel. Beyond, there were empty fields and the ever-present dark-green woodlands. It was time to return – Sydney had little to offer the weary traveller.

Trudging back, Kydd passed a neat cottage. His mind was bleak with depressing images and at first he thought he had misheard the greeting. Then a low voice behind him called again, this time more confidently: '*Tom Kydd!*'

He swung round to find a young man staring at him from the paling fence of the house. 'Sir, ye have the advantage of me,' Kydd said, trying to place him.

'It has been some years,' admitted the man, with a secret smile. There was something familiar about him; the intensity of his gaze, the slight forward lean as he spoke. 'William Redfern,' he said at last, but it did not bring enlightenment. 'A convict I am, on ticket-of-leave,' he went on, then added, with a quizzical uplift of his eyebrows, 'and for the nonce, sir, assistant surgeon at His Majesty's Penal Settlement of Norfolk Island.'

Kydd looked intently at him. The man continued softly, 'And, Tom, your shipmate as was in *Sandwich* . . .'

It all came crashing back – the ferocious days of the mutiny at the Nore when Kydd had stood by his shipmates through a whirlpool of terrible events but, for reasons he still did not fully understand, he had escaped the rope at the last minute.

'You were surgeon of . . .' He found it difficult to go on. Until now he had believed that the sentence of death on the idealistic young Redfern had been carried out – yet here he was. 'Aye, I never thought t' see ye again, William,' he said slowly. Ticket-of-leave implied that, while trusted, Redfern was still a convict under sentence – he must have been spared the noose and instead transported to serve out the remainder of his time. Kydd had gone on to quite a different life.

'And do I see you still topping it the sailor?' Redfern said lightly.

Not sure how to respond, Kydd muttered a few words of agreement.

'Do come inside, old fellow,' Redfern suggested. 'I'm sure we'll have a yarn or two to spin.'

They entered the homely dwelling and Redfern found a comfortable chair for Kydd near the window. He excused himself, then returned with a bottle of rum. 'I do sincerely welcome the chance to raise a glass to an old shipmate!' He grinned broadly. 'And drink as well to the luck that sees us both here instead of dancing at a yardarm!'

Kydd found it hard to treat these baneful ghosts from his past lightly but managed a smile.

Redfern then asked, 'How did you . . . ?'

'I was pardoned,' Kydd said quietly.

'Then I give you joy of your fortune.' He swilled the rum in his glass then went on, in a different tone, 'You're master of the *Totnes Castle*.'

'Aye, f'r my sins.'

'Then you've done well in the sea profession. Did you leave the Navy . . . afterwards?'

'No.' Kydd saw through the look of polite enquiry and knew he could not lie. 'I was a lucky wight, an' that's the truth of it. Not more'n six months after, at Camperdown, I took th' eye of the admiral an' went t' the quarterdeck.'

'I stand amazed! And, by God, I take the hand of a man

who has had the backbone to seize Dame Luck by the tail and give it a hearty pull.'

Kydd blushed and took refuge in his rum.

'So, while we've been taking our rest at His Majesty's expense you've been cresting the briny, as it were. Did you smell powder after that at all?'

'Nothing t' speak of – that is, apart fr'm our meeting at the Nile.'

'The Nile? You were with *Nelson* at the Nile?'

Kydd nodded, embarrassed to see Redfern regard him with something suspiciously like awe.

'And now, for your own good reasons, here at the other end of the earth in New South Wales. Is the land to your liking and expectations, Mr Kydd?'

Redfern would obviously have no feeling for the place, Kydd reasoned, and said wryly, 'It smells too much o' the prison – an' I've never seen a country like this. T' me it's like young flesh on old bones, if ye take m' meaning.'

Redfern leaned over and spoke with a quiet intensity: 'Appearances can deceive. This country is like no other – there are some who call it a thief-colony but they mistake its destiny. Here, those who have fallen afoul of society's expectations are offered a second beginning, a new life. If they seize their chance there is a future for them here, free of encrusted prejudices and attitudes of old, somewhere they might reclaim their dignity and freedom.'

He stopped then said slowly, 'Mr Kydd, here we can have hope.'

'But y'r lashes, barracks . . .'

'Yes – for those who cannot put aside their selfish antagonism to the social order. Now, think on it. If a convicted felon has a mind to it, he can ask for and be granted a

286

ticket-of-leave. Freedom. He may then take up a trade, marry, live in his own dwelling – in fine, he will be once more a credit to society. Now where in England may he do this, I ask?'

'You are still . . . ?'

'Yes, Mr Kydd. I am a convicted prisoner serving out his time – but equally I am assistant surgeon to the Crown on Norfolk Island, of not inconsequential status I may add. And there are more like myself who have taken advantage of this enlightened position and have thus advanced in the social order. You should think also of the free settlers who arrive on these shores with the sole purpose of wresting a living from the soil. Together we are creating nothing less than a new nation.'

He hesitated, then slumped back and considered Kydd with hooded eyes. 'But this is not of any interest to one who will shortly depart for more civilised climes.'

Kydd smiled. Perhaps there was something in what Redfern had said. 'I've stepped ashore in Canada, m' friend. They're making a new nation there an' it's just as hard a country. If 'n they can raise a nation by guts an' spirit, then so will you.' He emptied his glass, then added, 'But I'm not t' shortly depart – the *Totnes Castle* is t' be careened an' repaired afore I'll be on m' way.'

Redfern returned the smile. 'So you'll need lodgings. I'd not recommend the usual seafarers' rests – they're to be found at what we term the Rocks. No, if you wish, you may stay here, if sleeping on my examination couch does not discommode. I have the use of this cottage during my regular visits back from Norfolk Island. Now there's a hard place – *peine et dure* indeed . . .'

'That's kind in ye, sir. It's been a long voyage,' Kydd said. Redfern would be agreeable company and he had no real wish at present to be among the rowdy jollity and lusty vigour of sailors ashore. 'Tell me,' he asked, 'what are th' two Frenchmen lying across the harbour?' It had been niggling: in a time of peace they had every right to be there but he had not seen any sign of working cargo.

'Why, have you not heard? It caused not a little stir when they came. This is the celebrated French expedition of Commodore Baudin! Given special status as a neutral by the Admiralty in a voyage of survey and exploration in the south of New Holland and Van Diemen's Land.

'Nearly prostrated with scurvy when they arrived, and you would not conceive the commotion when a little later our own *Investigator* puts in!' He chuckled. 'Commander Flinders, sent by the Admiralty to do a like task. Both believe they are alone in this uncharted realm, making discoveries and naming names, until each meets the other at the same enterprise.'

'Where is Mr Flinders now?'

'You haven't noticed? The rather grubby little North Sea collier the other side of what we call Garden Island. Why don't you pay him a visit? He'd be sure to welcome a man of events.'

Kydd completed his letter, a formal request from a fellow officer to come aboard HMS *Investigator* if convenient to visit. As he was about to sign his name he hesitated – they were of equal rank – then he dashed off Lieutenant Thomas Kydd at the foot. There was no way as a convict-ship master he wanted it known that he was an ex-commander, Royal Navy.

A courteous reply arrived almost immediately and Kydd lost no time in making his way out to the little ship. Only a hundred feet long and about three hundred tons, Kydd estimated – not much more than dear *Teazer*, but she was a very different vessel. Stout and roomy with a beam that spoke of a broad bottom and shallow draught, she was a workaday collier disguised as a ship-of-war and undertaking explorations on a scale not seen since Captain Cook.

There was not a scrap of gold leaf or other naval ornamentation but Kydd felt a growing respect, even awe, for this humble ship so newly emerged from the unknown regions.

He was met at the side by her commander. 'My ship is all ahoo, sir – it's my intention to sail just as soon as these scallywag shipwrights can set her to rights.' Flinders was of slight build and about his own age; Kydd was struck by his eyes, soulful against dark hair. 'Shall we take refuge below?'

In *Investigator*'s great cabin, smaller even than Kydd's quarters in *Totnes Castle*, every conceivable surface was set out with papers and charts. On one, a large black cat with white figuring looked balefully at Kydd, then leaped straight at Flinders, who caught him neatly.

'This is the noble Trim,' Flinders said, as he affectionately stroked the jet-black fur. 'The butler in *Tristram Shandy*, of course. He's been aboard since the first, and must be accounted the most nearly travelled of all his tribe.'

Flinders found a chair for Kydd and sat at his desk with the cat curling fussily into his lap.

'Sir, y'r fame is assured fr'm what I've been told about y'r exploring,' Kydd began.

Flinders inclined his head civilly. 'Should the Good Lord and the rotten timbers of this ship allow, I shall complete a circumnavigation of this vast land, Mr Kydd.'

Kydd leaned back in admiration. What it must be to swing a bowsprit between two headlands where no man had been before! Was there to be a bay opening beyond, deep and broad, or was this to be a mysterious passage separating two great lands?

He knew that the man before him, within this present voyage, had finally established that New Holland was one immense continent, there was no navigable channel leading from a vast inland sea or any other. Flinders had achieved this and therefore solved the last great geographical question remaining. There was no doubt that his name would be known to history.

'Ah, Mr Flinders, I'm curious – for th' fixing of the longitude, should ye sight something of interest.'

'A hard question! If it be convenient to come to an anchor, then I find the method of eclipses of Jupiter's keepers answers when taken with a worked lunar distance. The chronometers are there to verify. Under way, of course, it is a task for the compass and a carefully measured log-line to fix the position relative to the last known.'

'A compass is a fickle enough thing t' use in strange waters.'

Flinders looked at Kydd sharply. 'Indeed. Yet on this voyage I have observations that may persuade you. I am to communicate these to Sir Joseph Banks but the essence of them is that there is a fixed error attributable not to polar magnetic orientation but magnetism induced in the ship's own upright iron fittings by the earth's vertical magnetic component. A deviation, sir, not a variation.'

At Kydd's serious expression he intoned gravely to a properly respectful cat:

> 'Then through the chiliad's triple maze they trace
> Th' analogy that proves the magnet's place,
> The wayward steel, to truth thus reconcil'd
> No more th' attentive pilot's eye beguiled . . .'

Flinders stood and selected one of his charts. 'See here,' he said, outlining the continent. 'Terra Australis, or "Australia" as I've come to call it.' His voice dropped as he continued: 'From a hundred and twelve degrees east to a hundred and fifty-three – over forty degrees in width, the same distance as from Africa to the Caribbean, London to Muscovy. What must lie hidden within its inland immensity, awaiting a bold man's discovery?'

He laid down the chart carefully. 'You have not seen the half of its wonders here. There are penguins, giant crocodiles, nameless creatures of fantastical appearance whose only home is this land, and snakes of a size and deadliness that would match any. And territory of a wild beauty that speaks to the heart – and of all nations we are called to grow and populate it.'

Careening could not begin until another vessel had been completed, and the shipwrights resolutely refused to work on the lower strakes of *Totnes Castle* until then. It was a very different pace of life in the colony from England, for hurry had no place in a society where events were so few and far between.

Redfern was an agreeable companion but had medical duties, and would soon return to Norfolk Island, and society, even in this remoteness, made a distinction that placed the idle redcoats of the New South Wales Corps ahead of a mere merchant-vessel captain, especially of a convict ship.

In two weeks Commander Flinders in HMS *Investigator* had departed for the north; Kydd watched their progress out to sea from the lonely signal station atop the southern head of the harbour entrance, seeing her last communication with the colony and her sails bright against the steel-grey of the empty ocean diminishing in size as she stood well out to make her offing.

Back at the cottage he decided to write to Cecilia. There

was possibly a chance that a returning ship would sail soon and take it to England; otherwise he would find himself carrying back his own letter to her. Still, it would occupy the time.

He stared out of the window to gather his thoughts, nibbling the end of his quill.

He supposed Renzi would have written to her before they left and explained his departure, but if he was in the same mood of disengagement from his old world then it was likely she would have had no word of his decision.

But what could he say when he himself had no idea of where Renzi was or how far along his path to attainment of whatever it was he yearned for? No doubt he could find Renzi but respect and reluctance to intrude prevented it. He would omit anything about him therefore.

What would seize Cecilia's interest and imagination, then, here in this wild and remote corner of the world? The wildlife, certainly: the curious whip bird, wonga pigeons and smaller folk like the white-footed rabbit rat. He had seen black swans, calm and serene – fine-tasting they were, too – as well as the big, bounding kangaroos and the unknown tribes of nocturnal creatures that could turn the night into a riot of unearthly sounds.

She would want to know about society: it would amuse her to see the earnest striving after fashion by the ladies when their only resources were six-month-old newspapers and the odd articles of dress brought in as ventures by visiting ships. And it was not so easy to explain how difficult it was to maintain a distance from the convicts when so many walked free about the town with a ticket-of-leave that enabled them to pursue a trade or even engage in business.

In fact, how could he convey the whole feel of a settlement

established for the purpose of the removal of criminal elements far from society at a time when it was so clearly being altered and improved with permanent building and an inflow of free settlers?

There were other things: there was not a drop of beer – it did not last the voyage and there were no hops here for a brewery. Rum was the universal tipple, with wine only for the well-off.

Then there were the black people. Around Sydney Town, the Eora loitered on street corners with lobster claws in their bushy dark curls, their bodies smelling of rancid fat; some sprawled hopelessly drunk. Dark tales were still told about occasional spearings and the kidnap of white women, and one runaway convict had recently come staggering back with stories of bodies roasting on a fire.

There would certainly be many things to tell of when he returned – when he returned. For him there would be his promised ship, but for Cecilia . . . What could he say? Cecilia must now face her own future.

He dipped his pen and began to write.

The invitation came one morning as a blustering southerly rain squall eased. Kydd disliked the rain: it caused runnels of reddish water to cascade into the harbour from a thousand bare surfaces, making roads a squelching trial, and today he was due another wearisome argument with the shipyard.

It was an odd invitation; personally written, it was addressed to a Lieutenant Kydd and signed by a Philip Gidley King. Then it dawned on him. This was a letter from the august person of no less than the governor. Puzzled, he read on. With every amiable solicitude it apologised for the remissness in not earlier inviting a fellow sea officer to his table and hoped to remedy the omission that Friday evening at an informal affair with friends.

'M' dear William, what am I t' make of this?'

Redfern looked up from his journal and took the letter. 'Well, now. It does seem as if you have been recognised, old chap. This is Himself, of course, and you must know that, since the First Fleet, every governor has been a naval officer. He must be curious about you, my boy.'

'What sort o' man is he, then, as you'd hear it?'

'Sociable and affable – been here right from the start in 'eighty-eight at Botany Bay – and while you've been quilting the French he has done a service for New South Wales, in my opinion. It was in sad dilapidation before. The lobster-backs held the whole place to ransom by trading in rum and the colony was going to rack and ruin. Now we have brick-built houses and roads, quite an achievement with no resources at hand.'

'Aye,' murmured Kydd. A useless penal colony at the ends of the earth would be all but forgotten by a country fighting for its life against a despotic revolution.

'And don't forget that as a naval officer he is a rare enough creature, and he faces not a few enemies. The traders are few in number but they want to run the port for their own ends and are wealthy and powerful. And he has the military: the marines were all sent back to the war and we're left with the sottish rogues in the New South Wales Corps. When you add in the big landowners, like MacArthur, who have their own conceiving of how they should be governed, you will know his task is no light one.'

'Has he th' bottom f'r a fight?'

Redfern grinned without humour. 'I think so, friend. He's the son of a draper born in the wilds of Launceston and knows what it is to stand before gentlemen and prevail.' His face clouded. 'I honour him most for his fearless support of those who have paid their penalty and want to contribute to their society. There are many – your MacArthur is chief among them – who would deny us the right and take the odious view that, once a criminal, the blood is tainted and we must be deprived for ever of any chance to aspire to higher things.'

'Do have some more silver bream, Mr Kydd. You'll find then why it's famed for its succulence,' Mrs King said brightly, easing a morsel of fish on to his plate, then motioning to the servant to offer it to the other guests.

It was indeed a fine dish and Kydd did justice to it. 'Tell me, Mrs King,' he mumbled, 'what is th' name o' the sauce? It has a rare taste.'

'Ah, that is our Monsieur Mingois having one of his better days. It is his Quin's fish sauce.'

King beamed at Kydd. 'Rather better than we find on our plate after a week or two at sea, hey?'

'Aye, sir – an' you'll be remembering th' midshipman's burgoo an' hard tack, not t' say other delicacies an enterprising young gentleman c'n find!'

Laughing gustily, King looked fondly at his wife. 'L'tenant, not so free, if you please, with your sea tales in front of Anna.' She dimpled and stifled a giggle.

Picking up his glass, Kydd enquired politely, 'The French still in harbour, sir, is it resolved as t' who may name th' new-found territories? Commander Flinders or . . . ?'

'Why, we, of course,' King answered smugly, 'Flinders was there before them. For all their "Napoleon Strait", "Josephine Bight" and such, they were pipped. We have sea charts of our south such as would make you stare, sir.'

295

'Mr Kydd,' broke in Mrs King, 'were you indeed an officer at the glorious Nile with Admiral Nelson? I've only just heard.'

'Why, er, yes, Mrs King,' Kydd said. Now he understood: it had only just been discovered that he was a hero of the Nile, which placed him at a social pinnacle in this faraway outpost and had earned him the good-natured envy and curiosity of the governor, himself a naval officer and far from the excitement and honours of active service.

'Goodness, how exciting! We shall have a *soirée* and all my friends will come to hear Lieutenant Kydd speak of his adventures. Such an honour to have you, Mr Kydd, believe me.'

'I'd be interested m'self, if I'm to be invited,' the governor said stiffly, but with a friendly gesture leaned over to top up Kydd's glass. 'Should you have been received by the first governor, your invitation to Government House would say, at the close, "Guests will be expected to bring their own bread."'

He waited for the dutiful merriment to subside and went on, 'But as you might remark it, we have advanced a trifle since then. We are all but self-sufficient in basic foodstuffs and I have my hopes for a form of staple that may be exported. Coal, sir. We have made substantial finds on the banks of the Hunter river, and by this we may at last be able to expect a net inflow of specie and thus pay for our imports. And put a stop to this barbarous practice of payments in rum.'

The obvious sincerity in his enthusiasm for the enterprise touched Kydd. 'Sir, th' fine stone buildings I see on every hand are a great credit t' your colony. Y' have faith in its future, an' I hope t' make my return one day to see it.'

'Thank you, Mr Kydd. I have my faith also – but it shall be so only because the inhabitants themselves will it so. Sir, to be frank, there are those who would see a land with two peoples, the free settlers and the emancipated. They see the one in permanent subjugation to the other. I am not of that kind. I believe that if a convict is offered hope and rehabilitation and accepts, then he is redeemed and may take his place in our society. I will not have it that there are two races apart in the same land.'

'Hear, hear!' A strong-featured man further down the table raised his glass to the governor. Others murmured approbation.

'I dream that this settlement shall mightily increase, shall prosper by the labours and blood of both bound and free and, with our staple now secured and a mighty port at our feet, within a lifetime we shall be a great and wonderous people upon the land.'

A burst of applause broke out. Kydd watched the faces: hard, sun-touched and lean. Some of these were probably the 'emancipated' of whom King had spoken, and each had a sturdy, unaffected air of resolution that made the governor's dream seem so very possible.

'Do tip us the poem of Sydney Cove, Jonathan, if you will,' King directed at the strong-featured man. Then he turned to Kydd and said, 'Penned by Erasmus Darwin at our establishing and only now proving true – except for the bit about the fantastical bridge across the harbour, that is.'

> 'There, rayed from cities o'er the cultured land,
> Shall bright canals and solid roads expand.
> There the proud arch, Colossus-like, bestride
> Yon glittering streams, and bound the chafing tide;
> Embellished villas crown the landscape scene
> Farms wave with gold, and orchards blush between.'

It was met with proud cries and hearty table thumps. A realisation dawned on Kydd: beyond the tawdry and makeshift of the raw settlement, beyond the flogging triangles and penal apparatus, there were those who were going to bring a new country to life by their own efforts and vision.

For the first time he understood what was impelling Renzi. What he had seen was beyond the dross of the everyday. He had known that New South Wales had a future, a splendid future, and the country would owe it to Renzi and his kind. Such sacrifice – and so typical of his high-born friend.

His eyes stung as he wondered where Renzi was at that moment.

Chapter 14

The bad blood between the convicts and the new men was getting worse. Willis, whom Renzi had hired to act as wrangler, was big and swaggering, with a foul mouth. The other was a laconic Portuguese seaman who, for some reason, had put himself out for hire as a farm labourer. Probably it was the money, Renzi mused wryly – it was costing four shillings a day for him and five for Willis, a shocking sum compared to rates in England but it was the only way he could see to get the work done.

Still, they were making progress of a kind. The land to the north had been cleared and hoed a good half-way back. Renzi had watched as the men sowed the seed, scattering the corn grains with wide, sweeping gestures just as he had seen done on the ancient fields of Wiltshire. It was the obvious crop: whatever else, the colony would always need bread.

That had been over a month ago, and now to his intense delight tiny needles of green were emerging. He threw himself into the work with renewed energy: half of the land for corn, half for root vegetables – out of consideration for his neighbour, not turnips.

. He laboured on, happy in the knowledge that while he worked his crop was steadily growing, maturing. In effect, this was his future wealth buried until he saw fit to draw upon his account. The metaphor pleased him and he went back to his hut for a mattock to help the others with the clearing.

Angry shouts and barking carried up from the working party. It would be Willis, setting off Tranter again. Flannery would then cleverly needle the big man and the cycle would go on and on. Renzi stumped back down to the group, who continued squabbling as if he was not there.

The dog's witless barking made him see red: he had been forced to buy the cur when their attempts to fence in the growing shoots against the nightly raids of hungry kangaroos had failed – the animals had simply bounded over the barrier. Now if he wanted to preserve anything of his precious green shoots he had to put up with the dog's din during the night.

'Shut your cursed noise!' he bawled at the men.

'It's Flannery agen,' spat Willis, rolling up his sleeves theatrically. 'He don't do as he's bin told!'

Flannery threw down his hoe in front of Willis. 'Orl right, me ol' bully-cock, what's it t' be then?'

Renzi ground his teeth. 'If I see you two rogues brawling once more I'll – I'll . . .' But what *was* there to do? He calmed himself. 'Now, Flannery, you and Tranter go—'

'Ye're bein' robbed,' Flannery interjected, his eyes fixed on Willis.

'What do you mean?' Renzi asked uneasily.

'Willis 'n' the dago, they're takin' y'r silver.'

'Explain!'

Flannery's cynical smile had the chill of truth about it and Renzi braced himself. 'They knows that ain't corn!' He kicked at the painfully weeded dirt, then yanked out a green tuft. 'See? It's some kinda grass, is all! You've been gulled. They knew it weren't corn all along, jus' played along t' take y'r coin!'

Renzi took the straggly tussock; he had no real idea what sprouting corn looked like. 'And you knew of this?' he challenged Flannery, as he let it drop to the ground.

'You're th' chief, roight enough, Mr Renzi. We does what ye say, an' wi' no opinions,' the man said.

Straightening, Renzi stared at the untidy acres of thin green. He had been living in a fool's paradise but what should he do now? He had to think.

His first reaction of hot anger was overcome with a sharp dose of cold logic. In this situation the obvious course was to bring the malefactors to justice. But would this not expose him to scorn and laughter in the colony where he was seeking acceptance and advance in society?

He got rid of the two hired men but retained the convicts – they were not costing him anything except the inevitable rum. However, his means were being eroded at a startling rate; it was time to take stock. The one thing that he would never contemplate was tamely submitting to fate and quitting. He was still master of his land, he had living quarters, wide acres of cultivated land and, for what it was worth, the two convicts. He would find more corn, and seed it himself, then see this difficult time through to a successful conclusion.

And had it not been the doughty sea hero Sir Francis Drake who had said, so long ago, 'There must be a beginning of any great matter but it is the continuing of the same to the end until it be thoroughly finished that yieldeth the true glory'?

Renzi took heart at the strong words and sat down to plan. The first thing was to secure the corn. This was only obtainable in Sydney Town so there was no alternative but to make the journey.

For several months now he had not seen any fellow human being beyond his rough-mouthed workers and the plebeian couple on the next selection, and he found himself looking forward to the trip. He would dress decently, his chest of gentlemanly wear unopened since arrival, and there was a growing list of articles to buy that were trifling in themselves but which would go far in easing life on his farm estate.

The Parramatta coach jolted and ground grittily to a stop and Renzi descended thankfully. Stretching after the journey, he surveyed the scene. Merely seeing other people in the road buoyed his spirits and the feel of the fine clothes next to his skin was sensual and uplifting. He strode off down the road.

Renzi slowed his pace as he came to the bridge over the stream: he had been told that there were shopping establishments along the foreshore and he reviewed the list in his mind. Besides the corn, only one thing could be considered necessary – indeed, vital – but he had no idea where he might go for it.

Ahead, he saw a gentlewoman, a handsome female followed by a maid. She glanced his way, her strong features appraising. Renzi lifted his hat and swept down in a bow. 'Dear madam, I would be infinitely obliged should you assist me in one particular dear to my heart. Do you know of a library at all, a subscription library, perhaps, for the gentlefolk of this town?'

She paused, her glance flashing to his elegant morning coat that had left a London tailor's not nine months before. 'A library? I fear there is no such in New South Wales. The people are generally of quite another sort.' Looking at him directly, she said, 'Sir, you must be a stranger to these parts, but I do confess, I cannot recollect the news of the arrival of someone of quality . . .'

Renzi smiled and bowed again. 'Madame, Mr Nicholas Renzi of – of Wiltshire.'

Offering her gloved hand the lady responded, 'And I, sir, am Mrs Elizabeth MacArthur. My husband is of the military and we have interests on the land. Pray walk with me for a space, sir, we seldom see interesting strangers. The sun is so obliging today, don't you think?'

'By all means, Mrs MacArthur,' Renzi replied with feeling. The last time he had held intelligent converse seemed an impossible age ago.

'A strange and beautiful land, Mr Renzi. And so distant from all else in this world. Would it be so impertinent of me to enquire what brought you all this way?'

Renzi hesitated. 'I believe I am to establish an estate, of an agrarian nature of some size.'

There was an immediate guardedness in her manner as she shot him a keen look. 'Oh, then I find I must pray for your success, Mr Renzi. I do hope you are not constrained in the matter of capital,' she continued carefully, watching him. 'This is such an odious country at times.'

'That is of no matter,' Renzi said airily. 'It is only by unremitting diligence in agricultural husbandry of the first order that will bring forth the fruit of the soil, as the celebrated Coke of Holkham does so truly inform us,' he added.

'Oh,' Mrs MacArthur said faintly, as they moved on. 'Tell me, Mr Renzi, how do you mean to conduct the affairs of your estate? There are so few skilled stewards of the land to be had at this remove. Will your holdings be . . . extensive, do you think?' she added lightly.

'Not at the first, I shouldn't imagine.'

'Um, a substantial portion, perhaps . . . ten thousand acres?'

'Oh, not quite as much to begin with, I believe,' he answered uncomfortably.

'Then?'

'Perhaps – a hundred acres or so,' he said lamely.

'A hundred! Mr Renzi, what will you do with a hundred acres?'

'I'm seeding corn at the moment, and I thought later swedes or wurzels would answer.'

'S-swedes and . . .' She stopped and stared at him in amazement. 'I thought – dear Mr Renzi, forgive me. Do I understand that you have come all the way from England for a hundred acres of . . . ?' Her look softened and she touched his arm. 'I can only admire your faith in our country – but the land here is harsh and barren, the vegetation strange and noxious, the soil thin and parched and the seasons quite topsy-turvy. Men have tried to grow your corn and with so little success, and – and I fear your swedes will not find so ready a market.'

They walked on in a taut silence until she resumed sadly, 'One day this will be a fine land – but not for an age. It will be tamed by men of vision such as yourself, but not in grain or any other cropping. Our future will not be in whaling, trading or even coal. We need a commodity that can be shipped for long months without decay, that is difficult for the world to produce. In short we must have sheep, Mr Renzi.

Merino sheep with the finest wool there is, but which demands so much open range. That will be our future.'

Slowly Renzi stripped off his finery and laid it in the chest, fighting the depression that had clamped down on him. He pulled on the threadbare workaday jacket and trousers, their stink of sweat almost unbearable. The canvas roof of the hut was now mildewed and in places hung in rotten strips; his treasured books were starting to fox and fade.

He went outside to speak to the convicts. At least within the hut was stored three bags of good seed-corn and he would have it in the ground as soon as he could get the lazy swabs to stir themselves.

Tranter was hacking morosely at the earth with his hoe while Flannery, in neat, economical and perfectly useless movements, tickled it. Renzi snapped at the pair with foul sea oaths and was rewarded with dull smiles and a marginal increase in energy.

Damn it, but he was going to win or die for Cecilia. For her sake he would see past the present setbacks, dreariness and hard labour into the time to come when his achievement was secure and he could proudly lay before her—

'Wha–?' There was a tremor of fear in Flannery's voice as he pointed down to the edge of the land. Renzi followed his direction. An Aborigine had suddenly appeared noiselessly out of the trees, and now stood still as a statue, watching them.

This was not one of the tame black men who hung about the town in rags but a quite different species. Naked, he was daubed with white clay in patterns and adorned with animal's teeth and a bone through his nose. He clutched a barbed spear near twice as long as himself.

'What's he want?' Tranter asked loudly, nervously lifting his hoe.

Two more Aborigines appeared silently and stood behind the first. 'They's coming f'r us!' yelled Flannery. 'I'm away, begob!' He dropped his hoe and ran back down the track. Tranter scrambled after him, leaving Renzi to face them alone.

The first Aborigine lifted his spear and shook it, uttering hoarse cries. The others joined in, noisy and menacing, stamping on the ground. Then they dropped to a crouch and began to advance over the clearing in short zig-zag dashes.

Renzi hurried to the hut and rummaged frantically until he found his cheap musket. They were closing with no doubt of their intentions: one threw his spear and it whistled past Renzi's ear, piercing the side of the hut. He raised the gun in an exaggerated flourish but they came on undeterred.

Renzi tried to think. The musket was supposedly loaded but the priming might have been damped by the rain. And even if it was ready with a live charge what should he do? Fire off his only shot to try to frighten them – or shoot into their bodies?

The first Aborigine was now yards away and snarling with the effort of bringing back his spear for a throw. Renzi took aim and fired. The heavy ball flung the man backwards; he flopped several times on the ground, mewling, then lay still. The others vanished as noiselessly as they had come.

Renzi hesitated, but only for a second: it was probable that they would be back. There was no time to be lost. Taking only his musket he ran down the track to the Caley cottage and explained breathlessly what had happened. A makeshift defence was mounted and they waited for an attack.

The hours passed and eventually Caley looked at Renzi

and said pointedly, 'Don't hang about after a spearin', usually.'

'I'll go back,' Renzi replied. 'If they're still about I'll fire a shot.'

He tramped along the track to his property – and stopped rigid at the sight that met him. Where the hut had stood was now a ruin. His possessions were strewn about, the chest robbed of the clothing and, most heartbreaking of all, his books were torn and scattered in every direction.

Trembling with emotion, he tried to take in the pitiful scene. A lump in his throat grew until it threatened to choke him.

Chapter 15

'So kind of you to come at this notice, Mr Kydd,' Governor King said importantly, 'Do sit – I have a matter of some gravity to discuss with you, touching as it does on the security of our colony.'

Kydd was mystified. There had been wild rumours about the French, at the moment lying peacefully across the harbour and about to sail soon, but this would scarcely concern him.

'Do I understand it to be the case that you will be returning to England shortly?' King asked.

'Aye, sir – just one or two matters still in hand that should not delay me long.'

'Then we can count ourselves fortunate, Mr Kydd, for there is a service of some urgency that you, sir, are uniquely suited to perform for us.' King steepled his fingers and held Kydd's eyes. 'The French and we are now at peace. Yet this does not mean there is no danger to be apprehended from that quarter – they are in need of an overseas empire for their trade concerns, and are active in that object.

'And now, sir, that which I expressly warned their lord-ships about is come to pass. Colonel Paterson informs me that he overheard Commodore Baudin's officers speaking in warm terms over dinner of their intention to effect a plan-tation of their people in the island of Van Diemen's Land, 500 miles to our south, now it is proven to be a separate land mass from New Holland.' He paused. 'I need not trouble to detail to an officer of the Royal Navy the severe stra-tegical consequences of the French maintaining a species of fortress there!'

Kydd nodded gravely. Van Diemen's Land had no settle-ments of any kind by any nation, and therefore stood as an empty wilderness awaiting the first to claim it. To lose the territory would be a catastrophic blow and its consequences could not be greater for this distant outpost of England. 'Sir, does not th' government know of this as a possibility?'

'They have been informed,' King said heavily, 'and will, no doubt, respond in time. However, to wait for most of a year for a reply is not a course open to me. I would be judged harshly by the future, sir, were I to sit passively by while the territory is expropriated by others. Therefore my duty is clear: I intend to plant a colony of our own in Van Diemen's Land, with or without instructions and support from England.'

'Sir.' Surely he was not being asked—

'It is essential that we act as speedily as we are able, but even so, to prepare in depth for a descent that is permanent will take time. The French are sailing: we need to act now to forestall them, not wait cravenly. It has always been my conviction that M'sieur Baudin, being a principled gentleman given right of free passage as a scientifical, would not think to violate its terms, but he has a master in Paris who would not hesitate.

'This is at the least a serious reconnaissance for the most propitious place for a first French colony, and at the worst . . .' King paused significantly. 'I do believe they intend to move very soon on Van Diemen's Land and by landing a small party thereby establish a claim.'

With a growing apprehension Kydd heard King out. His sympathy was all with the man who was making positive, vital decisions in total isolation. The stakes were clear: this was the reality of the clash of empires at first hand, the striving of nations that would end in this vast land speaking one language or quite another, an allegiance to Crown or to revolution. It was a situation in which a false move by either could result in misunderstanding, even war.

'Mr Kydd, I have no vessels of force I can send to persuade the French from their course, not even one King's ship. Therefore I must proceed by other means.'

He went to his desk and pulled out several large sheets of paper. 'These are Commander Flinders's notes of his recent explorations. You see they are not yet made up into a sea chart but they will be adequate for our purposes.'

'Sir, ye haven't said—'

'My plan is to dispatch two vessels south – one to the west of Van Diemen's Land and the other to the east. They are to find the French and by any means dissuade them from their intentions.'

'Er, dissuade, sir?'

King's eyes went opaque. 'You will understand now how pleased I am that at these times there is an officer of renown and discernment at present here in New South Wales. Mr Kydd, it is not within my powers to appoint you to a naval command but as governor I may make you master into a colonial government vessel. Should you accept, you will have my full support in any action you deem necessary upon a meeting with the French. Will you consider serving your country thus?'

'Of course, sir,' Kydd said instantly. How else could he respond?

'Thank you, sir. You have no idea how this eases my mind in these very unusual times. Shall we get down to detail?

'Lieutenant Robbins will take the westerly search in *Cumberland* and yourself the easterly in *Suffolk*. I apprehend that the most likely places for the French will be Port Dalrymple in the north or somewhere in the Derwent to the south. This is not to discount the possibility that they will consider an initial landing on the large northward islands, therefore I am requiring that Lieutenant Robbins will go to the west, including King Island, while you will take the easterly half. Is this clear?'

'Sir. Th' *Suffolk* – what sort o' vessel is she?'

King looked apologetic. 'The same as *Cumberland*, an armed schooner, country-built here in Sydney Town. Very handy craft, we use 'em for every task. Forty tons, square sail on fore and main, I should think well suited for your use.'

Forty tons! A sixth the size of little *Teazer* – but then he recalled that Flinders's famous circumnavigation of Van Diemen's Land had been in a like-sized vessel.

'Well, Mr Boyd, let's be about th' storing,' Kydd said briskly to the mate. *Suffolk* was indeed tiny – and so was her crew: just eight seamen and Boyd. Six of the eight were convicts on ticket-of-leave, but to Kydd's eye they seemed diligent and competent enough.

There was little more to be done than store for a three-week voyage; clearly the schooner was to be employed because she was available. Bobbing to a single buoy off the jumble of structures that was the shipyard, she was heaved in to the little jetty and a chain of men set to loading.

It was a commonplace sight, yet this plain-looking craft was shortly to leave the colony for regions of the south that had been unknown to man just six months previously, and on a mission contending for dominance with a foreign power.

Kydd's written orders had just arrived, with what could be gleaned from the maps and observations of explorers down the years: from the Cook of thirty years ago through to the recent discoveries of Flinders. And it would be Thomas Kydd, former wigmaker of Guildford, who would navigate in those same nameless waters.

Lost in reverie he did not notice at first the familiar figure on the jetty. 'Nicholas! Ahoy there – step aboard. Ye're very welcome!' Remembering his friend's vow of separation Kydd wondered what Renzi was doing there, then noticed, with concern, the sun-darkened complexion, the worn clothing, the deep lines in his face.

Renzi made his way up the gangplank. 'Mr Kydd – Thomas,' he said, but did not offer to shake hands. Kydd's heart tightened. Something was wrong. He remembered the doctor's words in Guildford about a tendency to depression after the fever, leading some to suicide.

'Why, Mr Renzi – Nicholas. Is there aught I c'n do for ye?' He kept his tone as neutral as he could.

'There is, sir. I have a request of you,' Renzi said awkwardly.

'Name it!'

Renzi looked away quickly, and when he turned back, his face was unnaturally set. He fumbled for words. 'Er, you will know that the colonial government sets great store by the securing of a staple, a sure source of income for the colony as would allow it to stand alone.'

'Aye, but you would know more o' this, Nicholas,' Kydd said warmly, trying to encourage his friend to relax a little.

As if following a set speech Renzi continued, in the same tone, 'And being consonant with my diversifying of agrarian interests it occurred to me that an opportunity exists to combine the two with advantage. In fine, it would oblige me exceedingly should I be able to investigate the seal fisheries of Bass Strait at the first hand with a view to an investment.'

Kydd was taken by surprise. 'Er, is it—'

'I will be plain. Do you see your way clear to providing me passage south to learn of the fisheries? You may be assured of any payments involved,' he added, with a trace of pathetic defiance.

There was no room in *Suffolk* for any passenger – and in any case, as far as Kydd knew, he would not be touching at any lawless seal-catching islands. 'Dear friend, d' ye understand that there's nothing I'd like more, but m' hands are tied. This is t' be a government voyage o' grave importance an' these concerns must come first.'

'I – have heard. All New South Wales knows of what is being planned. It so happens that yours is the only vessel this six weeks that is venturing south,' Renzie said coldly, then added, 'It might be said, however, that my mission falls not far short of it in importance for the longer term of this colony.'

'Nicholas. If it's known as I've taken advantage o' my position as master to offer passage to a friend . . .' He stopped. For some reason of his own Renzi needed desperately to reach the sealers; he had to help and he racked his brain for a solution. 'Mr Renzi, it gives me th' greatest pleasure t' offer

313

ye th' post of official interpreter to the *Suffolk* mission. The wages are, er, a penny a day an' all found.' Faultless French would be indispensable when it came to the delicacies of a confrontation – and, damn it, they had to water the vessel, why not at a sealers' island?

'That will not be necessary,' Renzi said stiffly. 'You may rely upon my duty, should it come to a meeting with the French.'

'Ye shall berth in my cabin,' Kydd said. It was all of eight feet long and five broad but they could take turns in dossing down. 'Shall we have y' baggage?'

Suffolk left Sydney Cove in a fine north-westerly, the schooner leaning to the wind before rounding Pinchgut island for the run down to the harbour entrance, careful to leave the ugly boiling of white water that was the Sow and Pigs reef well to starboard.

The first deep-sea swell lifted their deck as they shaped course to pass between the Heads, the open ocean spreading in a vast expanse ahead, the vivid blue of the sea and the vaulting white of the cheerful clouds washing away the memory of the dross and dirt of the land.

Safely out to sea the tiller went down and *Suffolk* headed southward. She was plain but sturdily crafted, and took the seas on her bow with a willingness that resulted in a lively pitch and roll. Kydd let Boyd con the vessel; he guessed that the other man was the usual master of *Suffolk*.

He had last crossed these seas in *Totnes Castle* but shortly they would reach Bass Strait. Its very existence had been unknown to him then: he had brought his ship south about Van Diemen's Land, through the high seas and gales of the Southern Ocean. Now he was to enter largely uncharted waters; if they were shipwrecked they might lie undiscovered for years – it would be prudent to consult again the notes and charts he had brought.

The tiny cabin was not occupied: Renzi was standing by the foremast looking shoreward. On impulse Kydd came up to him but his light words died before they were spoken: Renzi had shown no sign that he was recognised. Kydd left quietly.

They reached thirty-nine degrees south in a streaming north-easterly and it was time: instead of continuing south past the mass of Van Diemen's Land *Suffolk* angled south-westerly directly into the strait, heading as fast as she could for a point just half-way along the remote north coast, Port Dalrymple, so recently surveyed by Flinders.

If the French were to be anywhere this was the most likely place. Reputed to be the finest sea sanctuary for five hundred miles, with a capacious river longer and wider by far than the Thames at London, it would make an excellent place for a settlement.

However, a hundred and fifty miles of rock-and-island-strewn sea lay ahead and all that Kydd had was a chart of generalities compounded from those who had hazarded their ships there, and the tracks of the few explorers who had been this way. Anything out of sight of their line of advance would not appear on a chart. Only the most strict vigilance of the lookouts would preserve *Suffolk*.

The north-easterly, however, veered into the east and freshened; the schooner plunged and bucketed in seas that had turned gun-metal grey and Kydd's anxieties increased. If the winds veered much further towards the south they would be headed, and he had no wish to be tacking about in the darkness of these waters.

Late in the afternoon an irregular stretch of land was sighted: it had to be Van Diemen's Land. Kydd's reckoning placed it close to their goal but caution made him order a seaman forward with a lead line. When soundings were fifteen fathoms he let go anchor and waited out the night.

In the morning it was simply a matter of deciding whether their destination was up coast or down but Kydd quickly spotted the bluff and the sandy beach leading along to a low finger of land that Flinders's notes indicated was the entrance to Port Dalrymple. They passed by slowly offshore and confirmed the broad opening before turning to make their approach.

Baudin's *Geographe* or *Naturaliste*, was probably snugly at anchor inside, her company busily occupied in building a fort, perhaps laying out the settlement ready for the settlers to come. A confrontation would be worse than useless, vastly outnumbered as they would be, and he would be lucky to avoid an international embarrassment.

He was in possession of letters from the governor of the colony of New South Wales indicating that His Majesty considered that the Act of Possession of the First Fleet at Botany Bay in 1788 was binding in the case of Van Diemen's Land, and that he would regard any infringement of sovereignty as an unfriendly act.

It was a thin pretence: the separation of Van Diemen's Land into a distinct land mass invalidated any claim that included it. What Kydd planned was a bluff: he would sail in innocently and display much surprise at the French landing. Had they not heard of the British settlement at the other end of the island in the south? That their claim had been preceded by an act of colonisation some time before? With luck, this would buy time.

With the biggest ensign aboard fluttering at the main the Colonial Armed Schooner *Suffolk* bore down on the low rocky point, marked 'Low Head' on the chart, the entry point for Port Dalrymple. A sweeping curve of sandy beach came into view but Kydd had eyes only for the wicked reefs that Flinders had been so at pains to fix, especially the dreaded Yellow Rock.

The water was visibly shallowing and the dark writhing of bull kelp below the surface was a menacing token of the undersea crags to which it clung; the betraying blackness fringed with white of a half-tide jumble of stones was another reef towards mid-channel but the notes sturdily promised safe passage if they kept to the Low Head side of Yellow Rock.

They passed beyond the low finger of land and a vista of the upper reaches of the river opened up – a remarkable view of a broad channel with deep-sea access, flanked by land so different from New South Wales. Kydd's glass was up instantly, searching for tall masts, sweeping the banks for any sign of habitation, flag poles, huts.

There was nothing, but this was only the start of miles of navigation into the interior at any point of which the French might have decided to make their settlement. Inside Low Head, a shallow but perfectly formed semi-circular beach beckoned and Kydd anchored both bow and stern, then had the boat readied. 'Mr Boyd! I'm steppin' ashore t' see what I can. Give me a gun should ye sight anything.' He went over to Renzi, who was sombrely watching the shoreline. 'Nicholas, should y' desire t' stretch y'r legs . . .'

'Thank you, I do not,' Renzi said distantly, and resumed his vigil.

Kydd took hold of his feelings. If the next few hours

ended in grief it would be his name attached to the failure, his the blame for the consequences. Someone to share this, even just by sympathetic understanding . . .

'Shove off,' he growled. There were two seamen at the oars, another in the bows. The boat stroked inshore until it crunched into pale sand in the centre of the beach. Kydd clambered over the thwarts and dropped over the bows. There was a musket in the boat but he was unarmed: he had no plans to stray far.

Bare dunes fringed the beach, behind them the dark green of vegetation. Leaving the men to stay by the boat he puffed to the top of one dune and looked down on a tangle of gnarled, papery-barked white trees and feathery casuarinas around the still, brown depths of an inland lagoon. There was no indication that man had set foot there before, no road, no track or anything other than the whispery quiet of a land as old as time.

He shivered and turned back to face the broad reaches of the river, and from his higher elevation raised his telescope and carefully quartered the scene. The far bank seemed flat and swampy with the blue of distant hills, and everywhere the dark green of continuous verdure right to the water's edge, so unlike the parched soils and stark landscapes of Port Jackson.

He wandered down and around the lagoon, tramping noisily through the undergrowth as he looked for signs. There might well be black people living near, Kydd reasoned, who could tell him if other Europeans were about. Or be fiercely hostile to any who trespassed on their land.

Nothing. And all around strange eucalypts, harsh grasses with the occasional ghostly pale dead gum tree and the haunting fragrance of oils released from crushed leaves.

He scrambled back; the tide water had receded but the seamen had kept the boat afloat. Kydd squelched out to it. There was nothing for it but to set out upstream.

In the beguiling peace of the placid waterway *Suffolk* spread topsails and left the entrance astern. There was an ageless somnolence to the river. From the time of creation until just a year or two ago this land had never seen a white man; now Kydd's own track would be added to the few on the chart.

A near conical misty blue peak rose above the distant trees. Mount Direction. It was over twenty miles further on and had been recorded by Flinders as of more value than a compass, given the several local magnetic anomalies that had distracted him. Kydd seized on the sight for its human connection in the unknown wilderness.

The schooner sailed on. For a dozen miles they were able to steer a straight course. Then they followed a lazy bend to bring Mount Direction ahead once more for another eight or nine miles of easy sailing through country that, but for its untouched verdancy, might have been in Oxfordshire.

It was peaceful yet eerie, sailing in such a picturesque landscape – an unseen river shoal might bring their voyage to a lurching end, or the sight of a stockade and fort would herald the presence of the French. For nearly thirty miles they made their way until they reached the limits of Flinder's exploration: it was far enough. Kydd was not equipped as an explorer and the river had contracted considerably. Wherever else the French had gone, there was no sign of them in Port Dalrymple.

His orders were clear: the next most probable site for a French settlement was in the far south, at the other end of the island. Yet could they possibly be anywhere else in the north? Somewhere in the fifty-mile sprawl of the Furneaux islands at the north-east tip of Van Diemen's Land? Robbins in the *Cumberland* was convinced that they would be found at King Island in the corresponding north-western tip.

Should he not at least take a look first before committing to the voyage south? The Furneaux group, however, made a perilous maze of islets and shoals, and any kind of inspection would take days. There had to be a quicker way of finding Baudin and his ships.

He had it. He would go to Renzi's sealers and ask them if they had seen the French. And there was a prime place to go – islands that lay directly athwart the passage through Bass Strait, between the continental mainland and the Furneaux group – Kent's group.

'Mr Renzi, I believe it t' be time to make visit to y'r sealers.'

A tiny smile appeared. 'Thank you, Mr Kydd.'

Kydd laid course for the islands. According to the hand-drawn chart, there was clear water all the way. With time fleeting by he would chance a night passage. However, it would be cloudy and dark and their first warning of danger would be the gleam of white breakers in the murk. *Suffolk* turned her bowsprit north-east and sheeted in for a long beat.

Morning dawned on a tumbling waste of grey-green water and the irregular rounded summits of what appeared to be a double island. 'Cap'n Kent's group,' Kydd said definitively. It was not hard to recognise from the description: as they drew nearer, a deep-cleft channel became evident that completely separated a steep, hummocky island to the east from a smaller to the west.

The islands had been explored only the previous year and Kydd had just the pencilled remarks by the explorer, Murray of the *Lady Nelson*, on an earlier rudimentary map. He approached cautiously. Granite pillars tinged with the yellows and reds of lichens soared out of the sea at the entrance – a bare few hundred yards across and leading into the cleft passage.

A landing place was marked not far inside. They entered – and in one dizzying motion were gyrated broadside to their track, then round and back again in the grip of a current so fierce that miniature whirlpools formed and re-formed as they were swept along.

About to roar orders to hand sail, Kydd felt the wind die. The sails hung limp, an extraordinary thing with the sea wind's bluster only yards away out of the passage. Helpless, they whirled along as fast as a man could run. Kydd's order changed hastily to an anchoring, but as the readied bower splashed down, a blast of wind from the other direction bullied and blustered at them for long minutes until the lee gunwale was awash. The williwaw eased, and *Suffolk* swung to her anchor into the current while she snugged down to bare masts.

'A tide rip,' Kydd said to Boyd. 'I should have known it, th' passage running at such a parallel t' Bass Strait. Would've been helpful t' make mention o' this on the chart.'

The boat was prepared, a mast stepped for the run in to the little cove. 'Nicholas?' Kydd was cheered at the first sign of animation he had seen in his friend. Renzi looked about with interest as they curved towards the sandy beach at the head of the cove. A dark-timbered boat lay upside down in the dune grass.

Avoiding rounded red-stained rocks they hissed to a stop at the water's edge and clambered out. Immediately, the back of Kydd's throat was caught by the thick reek of a waft of blubber-oil smoke. A track beaten through the tussocky grass led past the upturned boat. Renzi took the lead energetically and they hurried forward.

Over the rise the track threaded through more dramatic granite pinnacles and suddenly opened into a rough clearing with half a dozen crude huts, constructed of driftwood and bark. In front of one a short man in a leather apron stiff with gore was stuffing chunks of seal flesh into a vast try-works over a fire.

'Wha' do ye want?' he shrilled nervously. His appearance was the most squalid and dirty that Kydd had ever seen, his grey beard and whiskers sprouting unchecked, his eyes beady and suspicious. An Aboriginal woman emerged from the hut and stood goggling at the intruders.

Renzi seemed taken aback but stepped forward and offered a wicker bottle, which the man snatched greedily. 'I'm here to enquire about the sealing trade, with a view to, er, invest-ment,' he said doubtfully.

The man hefted the bottle and shook it next to his ear before he answered. 'You gov'ment?' he squeaked.

'No,' Renzi said. 'Nor Navy. I want to know directly about you sealers – what's the cost, what's the profit, what you have to do.'

The man cocked his head to one side and cackled harshly. 'Has ye got any vittles? Man gets tired o' seal an' penguin meat b'times.'

'I'm sure I can find you something if my business is con-cluded satisfactorily,' Renzi offered.

The man nodded. 'What d'ye want t' know, then?' He took a long swig from the bottle, and then began. It was a bru-tally hard life: men were left alone with provisions on the impossibly remote islands of Bass Strait to hunt seals. A ship would return months or even years later to retrieve them, with their accumulated pelts and oil. Some were entirely on their own while others were joined by runaway convicts and drifters to become sealing gangs.

It was clearly extremely profitable: from nothing to hundreds of sealers, possibly more, in just the few years since discovery implied that an insatiable demand was driving a massive expansion of the industry.

Renzi lightened visibly at this but Kydd broke in impatiently: 'M' friend – we need t' know – have ye b' chance heard anything o' the French? Two fair-size ships bound west'd? We think they want t' claim an' settle somewhere in Van Diemen's Land. Have ye heard tell at all?'

The man screwed up his face in concentration and replied, 'Did see ships, but three on 'em.'

'Three!'

'Two big an' a pawky sloop a week ago. Could be y' French, but me eyes ain't as they was.'

It was doubtful but Kydd persevered: 'Was they t' the north or south o' this island?' If they had taken the north side they were probably on their way through the strait – Robbins and *Cumberland* would find them. To the south would imply that they were somewhere along the northern coast where *Suffolk* had been. And if the wretched man was mistaken or lying . . . the French might even now be dropping down the east coast of Van Diemen's Land to make their landings in the far south – in the Derwent.

'Ah, now, I can't rightly remember. North, was it?'

'Thank ye,' Kydd said. The man could tell them little more. 'Now, Nicholas, if you've hoisted aboard enough o' the sealing profession . . .'

Renzi hesitated. 'Dear fellow, if it were at all possible to remain an hour or two more, it would gratify my curiosity infinitely to observe the procedures to be followed in . . . acquiring the pelts.'

'Y' wants t' see?' The man's gap-toothed smile widened as he looked pointedly at the bottle. At Renzi's understanding nod, he chortled. 'Come wi' me.'

The trail led to a ridged summit overlooking a wide slab of rock, slimed with droppings and inclined down to the sea. The area was nearly covered with seals, pale fur seals and their darker-skinned pups lying in the weak sun, suckling, flopping up from the water's edge or squabbling with each other. Seabirds wheeled above, their cries piercing the din of squealing and barking.

'We waits f'r low tide – more room ter move.' They watched as other sealers hefting clubs and lances appeared and crouched out of sight of the seals.

A sudden hoarse animal cry was quickly taken up by others. The gang of sealers had got to their feet and were racing in from both sides along the edge of the water, cutting off the seals from their escape. When the two lines of men met they turned in and set to the slaughter.

The ungainly animals had no chance: wildly swinging clubs smashed skulls in a gleeful orgy of killing. Terrified beasts squealed and tried to flounder away, but were overtaken and mercilessly dispatched. In a very short time the foreshore was aswim with blood from a hundred corpses.

The last of the seals herded far up from the sanctuary of the sea suffered a similar fate. In a pathetic gesture of defiance one male seal turned on his killers to defend the females but it only served to make his attacker miss his stroke and the creature screamed in the pain of splintered bones. In disgust the sealer moved on from a damaged pelt, leaving the animal to thrash about in its final agony.

It had taken just minutes. Now the frantic pace slowed as the butchery began. Each piteous body was deprived of its skin, leaving an unrecognisable bloody mass; blubber was peeled away and carried off to the tryworks while an occasional long-drawn-out shriek came from an animal incompletely killed, whose skin was torn from it while still alive.

A charnel house of blood, bones and viscera on the rock slab waited to be washed off by the next tide but of the life that was there before there was nothing left.

The silence on the summit above was broken by the sealer. 'We takes th' skins an' salts 'em down. Wan' t' see 'em? We got more'n two thousan' skins an' three hunnerd barrels of oil ready,' he said proudly. 'China market takes all we c'n get.'

Before nightfall *Suffolk* was stretching south past the bleak fastness of Furneaux Island with the intention of reaching Banks Strait by dawn; on board there was little conversation and Renzi slipped below, his face pale and stricken.

In the morning a backing north-easterly met the strong east-going tidal stream and an unpleasant toppling sea kept the decks wet, the motion uncomfortable. However, the same conditions meant that the many half-tide rocks and islets were betrayed by sullen breaking seas in flurries of white round a jagged dark menace.

Black Reef was laid well to starboard by noon and, easing away southward in accordance with orders, the little vessel began the run to the opposite end of Van Diemen's Land. Now clear of the rock-strewn Bass Strait and into open water it was plain sailing with no fear of peril. All square sail was set with the favourable northerly and the schooner seethed along; Kydd sent the men to their meals and Boyd went below for a rest.

It was pleasurable sailing; the northerly still had the warmth of the continent and the seas were moderate, the ship well found and willing. Kydd missed the precision and bluff certainties of the Navy but that was now in the fast-receding past. In a short while he would be on his way back to England and his promised merchant ship – and who knew? His naval service in command might be attractive to the prestigious East India Company in the grand routes to India and beyond, and with his experience in the commercial sphere mounting, he might well be offered . , .

His thoughts turned to Renzi. He had changed, now so unlike his previous elegant self. Gone was the noble poise and sureness of touch, the quiet logic informing a character of calm self-possession. In its place was a brittle defensiveness, a pathetic pretence at what should have been a natural instinct – the station of well-born gentleman. Whatever had happened since he put down roots in New South Wales had affected him severely, and now this business with the sealers. Just what did it all mean?

Automatically Kydd glanced up at the rigging; the sails were all drawing well and trimmed to satisfaction, but his eyes were caught by the sight ahead of clouds in a peculiar regular formation. He had seen precursors to foul weather around the world – the Mediterranean *tramontana*, electrical storms off Africa and, indeed, howling gales in the North Atlantic; this seemed of no account, though, and he dismissed it from his mind.

He breathed deep of the clean sea air and found himself drawn to his family so far away, especially his sister Cecilia. Was there anything he could do for her? It would have been a sad blow to lose the position that had elevated her beyond expectation. Ironically, he mused, she had suffered from the same declaration of peace that had brought to an end his own treasured career.

Boyd came on deck, paused, sniffing the wind and reorienting to current conditions. He looked forward and stiffened in alarm, then hurried aft.

'Sir, we must get th' sail off her.' The cloud had consolidated into a remarkable elongated roll that lay curiously suspended above the sea for miles across their track, not at all suggestive of danger.

'How so, Mr Boyd?' said Kydd, looking at the oddity. There had been nothing like this before the onset of any bad weather in his experience, but Boyd seemed disturbed by the sight.

'This is y'r Southerly Buster, Mr Kydd. 'Twill be a rare moil soon, sir. Wind c'n swing a whole sixteen points in a minute or so and catch ye flat aback.'

Kydd was learning more about this strange southern world with its different stars in the heavens, and seasons turned on their head, but it would not do to defy the elements. 'Very well, Mr Boyd, do what ye will t' get the barky in shape f'r it.'

All square sail vanished, followed by the foresail, leaving *Suffolk* languidly rolling to a jib and close-reefed main. The line of cloud advanced and distant hanging curtains of white on the grey told Kydd that this was a species of line squall – but it was closing at a disturbing rate.

'We'll rig hand lines,' he ordered. These were secured along the deck for safety; *Suffolk* was not so big that she could withstand a sudden roll when the squall hit.

The quality of light altered as the cloud threw a dull pall over the seascape – and then it was upon them. The warm, reliable northerly transformed in an instant to a chill, streaming bluster and, as promised, it shifted around in bursts of spite until, in gusts of cold, driving rain, it stayed steady in the south.

Things had changed radically. No longer bowling along before a soldier's wind *Suffolk* could no longer think of voyaging south; the savagery of the southerly blasts had rotated the vessel round and she scudded before the wind, headed for who knew where.

Over to larboard was the empty wilderness of Van Diemen's Land, and to starboard, the open sea leading to New Zealand and the South Seas. Kydd had neither the charts nor provisions and water for such a protracted deviation.

If, on the other hand, he sheeted in and made for the coast to larboard there was all the danger to be met on a rock-bound seaboard. But if he could find shelter to ride it out the situation would be saved. 'Down y'r helm an' we're running f'r the coast,' he yelled, and without waiting went to his cabin and pulled out his precious chart, bracing at the wild motion that had his tiny lamp swinging jerkily. It would be touch and go – there were but two possible havens: south of the Bay of Fires in the far north and the Freycinet peninsula somewhere to his north-west.

The only alternative was being lost in the wastes of the South Pacific. But being at last reckoning only some twenty miles off the land there was still time and daylight to coast south until they found shelter.

On deck Kydd was grateful for the thick coat he had snatched before coming up: the temperature had plummeted since the squall hit. The rain came and went in miserable drifting curtains as they barrelled along through the seas rolling in abeam. In a short time they sighted the dark, uneven coastline of Van Diemen's Land. Cautiously Kydd eased *Suffolk* round and began to search.

He knew what he was looking for and by mid-afternoon had sighted it. A spine of serrated uplands, light-grey and naked above dark green woodlands on the lower slopes, a single large island at its finality. Again they leaned to the winds and thrashed past the island, seeing its tip enveloped in explosions of white from the surging waves until they had reached the great bay beyond.

They were still not safe: from early maps Kydd knew that he would need to sail deep into the south-facing bay, per-haps to its end before he could be sure of shelter from the malevolent southerly.

Suffolk rounded the island and raced up the bay before the wind once more, passing craggy ridges and squat headlands until a long glimmer of sand ahead warned of the head of the bay – but, praise be, the final rearing of dappled pink granite peaks provided a lee of a good two miles of calmer waters and, with infinite relief, Kydd gave orders that saw *Suffolk*'s anchor plunge down and all motion come to a halt.

Renzi was sitting morosely in the cabin when Kydd went below to strip off his streaming oilskins. Worn and tired by the battering of the weather, Kydd threw his foul-weather gear outside and slumped on the edge of the bunk.

'Be obliged if ye'd shift out o' there, Nicholas, an' let me get t' my charts,' he mumbled, against the rattle of rain on the little skylight. Renzi seemed not to have heard. 'If ye would be s' good—' Kydd began heavily.

'I heard you the first time,' Renzi snapped, rising and squeezing past Kydd, who bent under his chair, fumbling for the tied bundle of charts and sailing directions.

'Why, *thank* 'ee,' Kydd said sarcastically, slapping the folio on to the bunk and spreading out the contents.

'My pleasure,' retorted Renzi venomously.

'Be buggered!' Kydd exploded. He saw the dark-circled eyes and sunken cheeks but he had no patience left for the strange petulance in Renzi. 'What ails ye, for God's sake, Nicholas? Have y' not a civil tongue for y' friends? What's wrong with ye?'

'Nothing! Nothing that can possibly be of concern to you.'

'Nothing t' concern me? What about Cecilia? Do y' write t' her the same as ye serve me?' Something about Renzi's manner caught his suspicion. 'Y' haven't written to her, have ye?' With rising anger he said, 'She knows y' here at th' end o' God's earth setting up t' be a – a gentleman o' the land, an' after all she's done f'r you y' won't even tell her how ye're faring?'

Suspicion sharpened at Renzi's stubborn silence. 'Ye never told her, did you?' he said in disgust, 'You jus' walked away leaving her t' wonder what's become o' you. That old soldier's yarn about needing t' cut y'self off fr'm the past! Why, ye're nothing better than—'

'Enough! Hold your tongue!' Renzi turned white. 'You don't know the half of it. This is my business and mine alone. You will not tax me with my faults and still less my decisions, which are answerable to me only.' He continued thickly, his chest heaving, 'We are constrained to this vessel for the present time but I wish you to know that any conversation between us I consider to be unnecessary until we reach Port Jackson. Good day to you, sir!'

A cold dawn revealed a more settled sea state, the forceful wind still in the south. Time, however, was pressing: hard work at the diminutive windlass in flurries of rain brought in the anchor, and under fore and aft sail they left the steep and barren Freycinet peninsula astern, bucketing along uncomfortably in steep seas coming in on the bow.

There was little Kydd could do to plan for eventualities. It now seemed so obvious that any French settlement would be in the south: it would be easy to defend, furthest from the existing British colony and in a climate closest to Europe. But to dissuade them if this was the case . . . It was difficult to conceive of a more hopeless objective.

The ceaseless southerly now beat in; soaked by rain and spray from romping grey seas thumping and bursting on the larboard side, Kydd slitted his eyes and tried to make out their course ahead. He had allowed two points of the helm a-weather for leeway in the run down to Cape Pillar and prayed it would be enough – the note on the chart had promised an iron-bound coast and if they were to be embayed between two capes . . .

Then slightly off the bow to starboard a vision slowly appeared from out of the misty, drifting curtains of rain squalls. High and majestic, a mighty rampart of basalt, an uncountable number of vertical columns like devilish organ pipes nearly eight hundred feet high. It could only be Cape Raoul.

Thankful beyond measure, Kydd waited until they were past. Now all they had to do was turn north-west, enter Storm Bay and the Derwent. *Suffolk* made fine sailing, her schooner rig well suited to the close coastal task of a maid-of-all-work around the colony, but as they sailed on in the gathering murk of evening they were faced with a new danger. According to the chart Storm Bay forked into two inner leads, both to the north-west. One led to the sheltered calm of the Derwent, the other to the ever-shallowing snare of Frederick Henry Bay. But if in the gloom he erred too far to the westward he would come up against the other shore of Storm Bay.

He set a strict compass course according to the chart and stood by it as they plunged on, his uneasiness increasing as the stern coastlines faded into the twilight. 'Another light!' he snapped – he could barely see the binnacle – but before the lanthorn arrived he saw something that touched his being with the eerie chill of the supernatural. Attuned to the angle of the waves and the steady pressure of wind on his cheek, his seaman's senses told him that they were on the same course but the compass was calmly stepping away to the west. Five – ten – fifteen degrees away: should he put up the helm to counteract? Or hold whatever course the compass told?

'Ease t' starboard,' Kydd muttered at last. It ruined his dead reckoning but he had to compromise between the two. The white of the helmsman's eyes flashed in the dimness as he looked anxiously between the compass and Kydd.

Unbelievably, it happened again – this time in the opposite direction. Five, ten degrees and more; frantic, Kydd tried mentally to compensate but, with a seaman's sixth sense, he knew that land was looming near. To shorten sail would be to lose the ability to react quickly, but to keep on a press of sail could end in shipwreck.

'Send a hand wi' a lead line forrard,' he threw at Boyd.

A man stumbled to the bow and began the swing. He had just sung out the first sounding – eleven fathoms – when he stood rigid, his voice rising to a falsetto. 'Breakers, f'r Chrissakes!' He pointed to larboard and a roiling white in the sea that, in the heightened atmosphere of the half-light, was cold with menace.

They could no longer bear for the Derwent. Kydd's

thoughts skipped chaotically in his tiredness, clinging to scraps of reality. He became aware of a long dark mass in the night, precipitous and bold, lying parallel to their course. Flogging his memory to bring the outline of the chart to mind, he could have sworn there was no headland facing them – an island? They were close enough to hear the sullen roar and thud of the seas that ended their onrush at its rocky foot. If an island, there had to be a lee at the end, before the coastline proper.

'Get that swab forrard t' work,' he roared, in his anxiety, and to Boyd he snarled, 'Stand by t' anchor – yes, to anchor, damn you!'

He glanced at the helm. 'Steady, lad,' he said to the frightened youngster. The island seemed to go on for ever until, quite suddenly, the dark bulk fell away. 'Down y'r helm, now!' he barked, and cupped his hand to bawl, 'Stan' by, forrard!'

As he had suspected the wind fell away to a confused gusting and the seas quieted. 'Let go, forrard!' he shouted, and felt rather than heard the rush of cable over the deck. 'Douse y'r fore 'n' main,' he ordered the men at the brails, then sensed the schooner feel her anchor. He stared into the darkness for any clue as to where they were but saw nothing and simply thanked Providence that they were now snugly at anchor where but for a few yards they could have been yet another wreck on this desolate shore.

In the wan light of morning Kydd strained to see where they were. *Suffolk* was snubbing contentedly to her anchor on the northern end of a steep island, but not half a mile distant was a long, low beach that extended for miles in both directions. If they had continued past the island in the night they would have ended shattered and broken on a sandy shore.

The chart told the rest of the story. He had been right: apart from a small wedge-shaped island past Cape Raoul there was no other in Storm Bay. Therefore this had to be Betsey's Island, just at the mid-point between the two leads of Frederick Henry Bay and the Derwent.

'Let's be having ye,' Kydd briskly told Boyd. 'Hands t' unmoor ship.'

It was a matter of less than an hour to win the three miles to the west, which placed them past the sloping face of Cape Direction and squarely in the spacious channel of the Derwent for the final leg. As with Port Dalrymple, Flinders had named a peak Mount Direction. Now ahead, it would show the eventual navigable head of the river, but what dominated all was the flat-topped bulk of a four-thousand-feet high mountain: Mount Table, the chart said.

If there was to be a settlement then, sensibly, it would be at the foot of the great mountain. But the open bay before it was hidden from view round a point. They sailed on in trepidation: what would be the form of the French occupation? Huts, the streets laid out already, a *tricolore* floating out above soldiers drilling on a square?

There were no boats criss-crossing the calm waters but the ships had probably left some time before. They passed a smaller mountain, every man of *Suffolk*'s crew on deck, staring forward. Then, suddenly, they were beyond the point and into the wide final bay beyond.

For a split second Kydd's mind was filled with dread in anticipation of what he would see but a hasty swing about by eye showed nothing to interrupt the smooth carpet of dark green vegetation spread out in every direction. His telescope went up rapidly to inspect every part of the shore-line.

And then it hit him. The French were not there! He had been to the two finest locations for a settlement in Van Diemen's Land and found them both unoccupied. It was beyond belief that any Frenchman in possession of the same geographic knowledge as himself would pass up the chance to plant his colony in the best setting available in favour of a lesser. The only reasonable conclusion was that they had made it in time. King's plan to forestall the French with a sub-colony could proceed. This new land would speak English and be a little piece of England at the far end of the earth, and generations to come would mark this year as the birth of their land.

Filled with awe and wonder at the implications, Kydd ordered *Suffolk* to the head of the cove where the Derwent entered, but it was not really necessary: the river narrowed quickly and could no longer take deep-sea vessels. Any settlement would be nestled under the great mountain. Their business in the south was now concluded and they could return to the civilisation of Port Jackson.

The voyage of return would be five hundred miles and more – it would be prudent to water before they set out. The nearest watering, however, was a complete unknown in this wilderness, but then Kydd remembered Adventure Bay at the far end of Van Diemen's Land. There, Captain Cook himself had stopped to water, as had Bligh and others.

Suffolk went about and left the fertile green coves of the Derwent astern, making her southing in several broad reaches. As they dropped down the river Renzi appeared from below and sat on the foredeck staring into nothing, a bent and lonely figure.

Storm Bay opened up; away over on the larboard bow would be Cape Raoul and the open sea but they kept in with the land to starboard until they reached the long island that had so figured in the logs and journals of famous explorers. Half-way along, a demi-lune bay all of seven miles across opened up – Adventure Bay.

Kydd could have reached for his chart and seen precisely where both Cook and Furneaux had watered, but he had no need: the position was clear in his mind. Bligh was then serving as master under Cook and had remembered the location when he needed to water *Bounty* on his way to Tahiti. He had last cast anchor in this pretty bay as recently as 1792. The French were known to have followed Bligh, and Flinders had called here on his epic circumnavigation.

Kydd gazed at the sweep of land, then out to sea: at this point they were at the furthest extremity of Terra Australis. Any further would lead directly into the Great Southern Ocean; the long, heaving waves he saw now had last met land at Cape Horn and, touching New Zealand on the way, were bound there once again. In truth, this place was the uttermost finality of the world.

If he stepped ashore now, he would be the only civilised being alive in the whole of the remote wilderness of Van Diemen's Land. The thought grew sharper but instead of wonder it led to an overwhelming sense of loneliness, of a degree of isolation from humanity that beat in on his senses and made urgent the need to set course back to the world of men.

Kydd gave an involuntary shiver and then became aware of Renzi. The man was visibly near breaking. 'T-Thomas,' he said, in a hollow voice, 'if you would, might we – walk together?'

There was no need to explain: Renzi was asking for privacy to talk to his friend at last. 'O' course, Nicholas,' Kydd replied, with as much warmth as he could, and set the schooner to anchor as Captain Cook had, in the shelter of Fluted Cape, where a placid freshwater creek could be seen issuing down to the beach.

'Clear away th' boat,' Kydd told Boyd, and they were rowed to the broad beach. 'Carry on wi' the watering, if y' please,' Kydd said, and he and Renzi were left alone to trudge along the beach. Nothing was said. As they paced, Renzi kept his eyes fixed on the hard-packed, discoloured sand, the hissing of their footsteps and harsh cries of unknown birds the only sounds. The dense, dark-green forest came right down to the water's edge but a broad clearing began to open up, the result of some long-ago wild-fire.

'Shall we . . . ?' Sensing Renzi's unspoken need to be out of sight of the others Kydd steered them off the beach and into the desolate place.

Away from the sea a sighing silence settled about them, the occasional snapping of undergrowth and their laboured breathing seeming curiously overloud. The terrain was coarse and undulating with blackened and fallen tree boles and they were soon out of sight of the ship; then, over a small rise, the woodland began again, even more densely than before.

Renzi came to a stop. His face had the pallor of death and his eyes were wells of misery. Kydd waited apprehensively. 'Dear fellow,' Renzi began, in a dreadful caricature of his usual way of opening a philosophical discussion, 'you – will know I am a man of reason,' he coughed twice and continued hoarsely, 'and I have to tell you now, my friend, that

I am – betrayed by my own logic.' His voice broke on the last words, tears brimming.

'Why? How c'n this be?' Kydd said softly. Renzi looked directly at him and Kydd was appalled by what he saw in his face.

'As I lay on my fever bed things were made plain to me. I shall not bore you with details – but I became aware that, for all the advantages of birth and intellect, my life is a waste. I can point to not a single achievement. Not one! Nothing!'

He covered his face and his shoulders began shaking. Kydd was shocked: this was worse than he had supposed and made little sense. 'Why, Nicholas, t' win the quarterdeck is an achievement that any might think—'

'No! There are coxcombs strutting the deck who owe it all to the accident of good breeding. This is no matter for pride. But you are a naval officer so above your station in life by right of striving and courage. You are now the captain of a ship! That is what any might call an achievement.'

Renzi's chest heaved with emotion. 'We will be at war with the French in months – with their arrogant posturing, there is nothing surer. You will be given a King's ship and go on to win renown and honour. That is equally sure.' Irritably he waved aside Kydd's protestations. 'This is your nature and your achieving, and you must glory in it. But I – I do not have the fire in my blood that you have. I am contemplative and take my joy in the fruits of the intellect, in the purity of creation, in – in—' He broke off with muffled sobs. Then, with an effort, he rallied. 'It seemed the logical course, to leave the old world and enter the new where I might wrest from nature – *ab initio* – a kingdom of the soil, a fine achievement to – to . . .'

'To what, Nicholas?' Kydd asked quietly.

'To lay before Cecilia.'

338

Defiantly Renzi looked up at Kydd, his hands working. 'Cecilia . . . who, I own before you this day, is dearer to me than I can possibly say to you. One whom I would dishonour were I to press my suit without I have achieved something worthy of her attention. And – and – I have failed! I have failed *her*.' His face distorted into a paroxysm of grief. He dropped hopelessly to his knees and broke into choking, tearing sobbing.

It was as if the world had turned upside down for Kydd to see Renzi, who had been so calm and staunch by his side through perils and adventures beyond counting, brought so low. Kydd's heart went out to the tortured soul who was his friend but what could he do? Tentatively, his hand reached out – then his arm went to the shoulder until he was holding Renzi's shaking body as the racking sobs took him. Renzi did not resist and Kydd held him until the storm had passed.

'All – all is t-to hell and ruin in Marayong, and so I w-wanted to see if the sealing industry would answer instead, b-but when I saw the slaughter I thought that if Cecilia knew of it how she would d-despise any fortune won from the blood and lives of i-innocent animals and – and therefore I have n-nothing left to me!'

Cruel sobs shook his gaunt frame again and Kydd knew that the last months must have been a living hell for his friend. What Renzi needed now was the will to live, a future, hope that things could be different.

'Then you are free, brother,' Kydd tried brightly.

Renzi raised his head. 'Wh-what did you say?'

'Forgive me talkin' wry, I was never a taut hand wi' words, but do ye not think that fate is a-calling you t' tack about, make an offing fr'm what was?'

'Thomas, p-please—'

'Nicholas, you've tasted life t' the full, been t' places others c'n only dream on. You have a rare enough headpiece as can tangle with any – is it not th' time to give a steer to the rest of us? Can ye not bring order t' the cosmos and tell we mortals how it will be with us?'

He lowered his voice. 'Dear friend, can ye not remember those night watches? I can, an' now I admit before ye that those yarns on the fo'c'sle I hold precious in m' memory. Your destiny is never to be a slave o' the soil – can ye not see it in you that a pen suits afore a plough?'

Renzi held still.

'I put it t' ye, if you set to it heart and hand, you'd make a better fist of explaining this ragabash existence than all th' philosophic gentlemen who've never passed beyond their own front door. Nicholas, this is y'r future. You shall write a book o' sorts that settles it f'r good an' all. This, dear chap,' Kydd brought out all the feeling he could muster, 'is an achievement as no one of the ordinary sort can lay claim to, and therefore must be worthy o' Cecilia's notice.'

As with any brother, it was hard to conceive that his sister might be the one to evoke passion and turmoil in an otherwise admirable character but it had to be accepted. He waited apprehensively for a response.

Renzi drew himself up with a long, shuddering sigh. 'Just so.' He pulled a handkerchief from his sleeve and trumpeted into it. 'But it would be more apposite – in view of my fortune in the matter of travel – to consider, perhaps, a more ethnical approach. Possibly a study of sorts, a comparing of the human experience – of a response if you will, of the multitude of the tribes of man to the onrush of civilisation, a Rousseau of our time if I were to be so bold. It would have to be in volumes and—'

340

'As I thought as well,' Kydd said, in huge relief. 'A great work. Worthy of a great mind.' Then, as furtive as a thief in the night, an idea sprang into being, a wonderful, incredible idea. 'Nicholas,' he began innocently, 'o' course you shall have passage back t' England in the *Castle* but what happens then? Shall ye not have y'r voyages an' adventures that will give you grist for y'r mill? It does cross m' mind – that is, if'n you're right about Gen'ral Buonaparte – that I'll get m' ship.' He paused significantly. 'Now, if that happens as ye say, then there'll be a need f'r the captain t' have one by him whom he might confide in, one as knows how th' world turns, c'n tell me why things are – an' can be a true friend.'

Kydd hesitated, then went on, 'So I'm offering – that whatever ship I'm in the post of captain's secretary will always be there for y'r convenience, y'r guarantee that you'll be able t' hoist in y'r ethical experiences wherever we might cast anchor th' world over. Just a convenience, o' course, y'r right t' be aboard, we say.'

The words tailed off. Renzi looked seaward, then slowly turned to Kydd with a half-smile. 'It does seem that the conceit has some degree of merit. I'll think on it.'

Author's Note

In many ways *Command* is a watershed book in the Thomas Kydd series. My hero has actually achieved the majesty of his own quarterdeck, and his life will never be the same again. It may seem an improbable transformation of a young perruquier of Guildford, press-ganged into His Majesty's Navy less than ten years before, but the historical record tells us that there *were* Thomas Kydds, not many admittedly, but enough to be tantalising to a writer's imagination. Yet we have so few records of their odysseys – how they must have felt, what impelled them to the top.

What actually triggered this series were some statistics that I came across. It seems that in the bitter French wars at the end of the eighteenth century, there were, out of the hundreds of thousands of seamen in the Navy over that time, 120, who by their own courage, resolution and brute tenacity made the awe-inspiring journey from common seaman at the fo'c'sle to King's officer on the quarterdeck. And of those 120, a total of 22 became captains of their own ship – and a miraculous three, possibly five, became admirals!

Some readers have asked if there was one of these men on whom I modelled Tom Kydd. The short answer is no, he is a composite of them all and a result of my author's imagination. But in him there are certainly elements of those like William Mitchell, a seaman who survived being flogged around the fleet for deserting his ship over a woman – 500 lashes – and later became an admiral; Bowen of the Glorious First of June, and still others – in *Victory* at Trafalgar her famous signal lieutenant, Pascoe, hailed from before the mast and the first lieutenant, Quilliam, was a pressed man, who like Kydd was promoted from the lower deck at the Battle of Camperdown.

The great age of fighting sail was a time of huge contrasts and often very hard conditions, admittedly, but at least in the Royal Navy then it was conceivable for a young man of talent and ambition to rise far above his station. I do remember my feelings when I became an officer, having begun my sea career on the lower deck. And sometimes I idly wonder, had I lived back then, *could I have been a Tom Kydd?*

I owe a debt of gratitude to the many people I consulted in the process of writing this book. Space precludes mentioning them all but I would like to convey special thanks to Joseph Muscat of Malta, whose encyclopaedic knowledge of Mediterranean craft was invaluable when I was doing location research, and Captain Reuben Lanfranco, director of the Maritime Institute of Malta for his insights into his nation's sea heritage; also to my Australian researcher Josef Hextall, half-way across the planet, who provided me with engrossing and detailed material on the early days of Australia. As always, my appreciation of their efforts must go to literary agent Carole Blake, marine artist Geoff Hunt RSMA, editorial director Carolyn Mays and assistant editor Alex Bonham.

Carolyn heads up a superb literary and creative team at Hodder & Stoughton; my thanks to them all.

Last, I salute the contribution of my wife and literary partner, Kathy. Kydd and Renzi now seem so real to us both, and we look forward to bringing their adventures to you for many more books to come.